WINTER
IN THE
CITY

Winter in the City

Edited by

R.B. Wood & Anna Koon

RUADÁN BOOKS

BOSTON, MA

Winter in the City: A Collection of Dark Speculative Fiction

Anthology Copyright © 2024 by Ruadán Books, Inc.
Individual Works Copyright © 2024 by their respective authors.

Paperback ISBN: 979-8-9912587-0-8
Library of Congress Control Number: 2024945733

Anthology edited by R.B. Wood & Anna Koon
Cover Art & Title Design by Kip Ayers
Cover & Interior Design / Formatting by Todd Keisling

First Edition

RUADÁN
BOOKS
www.ruadanbooks.com

For Jim

TABLE OF CONTENTS

FOREWORD: WHERE YOU ARE IS WHO YOU ARE
MERCEDES M. YARDLEY...9

DHAKA
ANJUM NOOR CHOUDHURY....................................15

PARIS
SARAH READ 37

LONDON
LILY CHILDS 61

SALT LAKE CITY
BRIAN EVENSON 85

AMSTERDAM
TIM LEES 97

JERUSALEM
JONATHAN PAPERNICK 121

ATHENS
NICK MAMATAS...149

PRAGUE
KATHERINE TRAYLOR..165

Brooklyn

    Richard Kadrey...189

Montréal / Tiohtià:ke

    Rich Larson 211

Dublin

    Christian Fiachra Stevens....................................229

Lewisburg

    Mike Allen 251

Helsinki

    Xan van Rooyen 285

Queens

    Sam Rebelein 301

Cleveland

    Gwendolyn Kiste 327

Manila

    Mars Abian..341

Zagreb

    Matt Hollingsworth..355

Cambridge

    Bracken MacLeod 377

Acknowledgments..405

About the Editors..407

WHERE YOU ARE IS WHO YOU ARE

Mercedes M. Yardley

There's something inherently magical about place. The setting grounds a story and infuses it with unique magic. Say I'm telling you about a woman with a terrible secret. That gives you the general idea, doesn't it? It leaves you with a certain feeling. Now imagine that story takes place in Germany, 1942. Why, darling, that simply changes everything. Or it takes place in modern New Orleans. Perhaps China in the 1400s. Laos. Nigeria. Puerto Rico.

During the snowfall in Estonia.

The harvest in San Jose.

Winter in Yekaterinburg.

Each destination brings its own charm, its own ambiance. Suddenly the simple story of "a woman with a terrible secret" has context, has texture, and is dripping in rich detail purely because the background is more tangible. The reader can imagine warbling birds or marching soldiers or the mysticism of the area. The tale is infused with distinct colors and scents of night markets, or the cold dust of the moon, or the sunlight filtering through the sea. They experience cultures both familiar and new.

I love the quote "Where you are is who you are," by Frances Mayes. It suggests that our identify is intertwined with place. Our setting changes us fundamentally, and it does the same with our art and literature.

R.B. Wood and Anna Koon took this concept and put together an extraordinary anthology celebrating this theme. It is *Winter in the City*, this anthology that you, dear reader, now hold in your hands. And what an exquisite collection it is! It is full of some of the cleverest, most otherworldly, joyful, and heartbreaking tales I've had the pleasure of reading in quite some time. Each story takes place in a different city during wintertime and the authors do a fantastic job bringing each location to life. We meet gods-that-aren't-gods, tricksters, and killers. We follow young men deeply passionate about their causes, women called to new covens, and the bittersweet solace found in engraving bones. There are liminal spaces that want to devour you, parties of horror, ghosts, specters, and the wrongly resurrected. These stories are masterfully told, carved out in place and time like portraits in the snow itself. Breathe the frigid air. Feel your cheeks go rosy in the cold.

I hope you enjoy this beautiful, well-crafted anthology. It was curated with the utmost care. The stories are breathtaking and the interior itself, done by Todd Keisling, is rife with wintry darkness. You're in for a treat, so please enjoy *Winter in the City.*

Yours in wonder,
Mercedes M. Yardley
Las Vegas, August 2024

Winter in the City

DHAKA

Anjum Noor Choudhury

Darkness does not die.
Darkness has no foe.
Friends of Darkness—
They're who reign here.

- Open Secret, Kaaktaal

The night air reeked of paint thinner and kerosene.

Aziz trembled all over, not so much from the slight nip in the air but from the adrenaline rush that followed blocking traffic with his fellow party workers, emptying a bus of its driver and passengers, then smashing and dousing it.

Across the bend in the road ahead, law enforcement manning the gates of a high-security compound alongside five white elephant statues discretely abandoned their posts, leaving only the elephants and stalled commuters to bear witness as Aziz lit a Molotov cocktail and hurled it at the bus.

The flames spilled everywhere in a fluid sweep, out the

windows, and up the walls, shrouding and shriveling the metal frame, challenging one another to touch the stars, unfurling sticky tongues in want of more, preferably live kindling.

Hulking motorcycle helmets protected Aziz and his companions from the blaze. And identification. The opposition party's slogans they bellowed would pin this on the other guys. Enveloped in black smoke and burnt rubber stench, their chants took on an air of drunken revelry. Aziz still trembled, vibrating with power. Power to instill fear. Power to bring the world to a standstill. Power to shape the nation's future.

Power to command fire.

He basked in his accomplishment's flickering glow. If only his parents could get it through their simple, small-town heads that *this* was what real success looked like. Not some flimsy degree that may or may not culminate in a dead-end job that wouldn't pay much, and would most certainly deprive him of any respect and chance of escaping the cesspit his forefathers languished in all their lives.

His head swam, and balance faltered at how bright his future promised to be. He watched the flames, teary-eyed and throbbing. Watched a single undulating flame split in two, the offshoot oddly still, almost confused about its part in the dance around it. An odd feeling gripped Aziz. Like he was being watched. The rigid flame tilted its flickering head sideways as though in appraisal of him. It looked one way, then the other, bobbed sideways to peer out the next window and the next, backtracked unsteadily. Then ducked, becoming one with the blaze.

Aziz brushed it off as a side-effect of all the fumes and chanted with greater gusto.

Beyond the fire's tarnished gold glow, in the shadow of the trees encircling the lake, he spotted a figure, short and slight, its manner ill at ease. A pair of thin, piercing lights flashed across its face with its every move.

Fucking journalists. Always sticking their noses where they don't belong.

A fresh surge of indignation and power propelled Aziz in its direction, bamboo baton in hand. Over the sidewalk's guardrails and up the lakeside promenade as it scurried away. He'd beaten the last one within an inch of its life. Maybe this time, he'd finish the job.

Rounding the bend, he lost sight of it as it crossed into the tentacular shade of a banyan tree. A dense congregation of rickshaws and their drivers was gathered before it. The rat had likely taken refuge among them, knowing no one would dare rattle a horde of sinewy-calved men who lived off navigating the city's lawless streets.

No matter. He'd get the next one.

The chanting was winding down when he returned to the charred bus. He and his companions mounted their motorcycles. Across the road, law enforcement resumed their posts by the elephants.

The helmet army drove off into the night, leaving the air ringing with the shrill and protracted honks of their horns.

It was winter in an election year. Dhaka was suffocating in an unrelenting particulate haze, its blood flow cut off by a tangle of laminated campaign posters and banners and skein upon skein of low hanging, often live, wires. The streets were ceded to boisterous campaign rallies assured to turn violent, but the formally employed could carry on as usual, courtesy of a newly opened metro rail.

Kubuddhi couldn't find a way back home. The rot in this city was irreversibly ingrained, its stench many times more potent than any corpse. There was nothing left to entice his kind to visit, and, over the decades, knowledge about the doorways between this world and his had faded from collective memory. The only way one crossed over now was by accident, as Kubuddhi had done.

There were others like him. Stuck. Searching the city's neglected, congested, filth-ridden streets for a way back. Retreating to graveyards and stalled construction projects when the cadarvine fumes from human tongues became too much. Haunting putrefied election camps, government offices, banks, and tuition centers when frustrations became hard to contain.

There were also those who accepted they were stuck. Those who chose to revisit the ancient tradition of adopting humans, protecting them from the world and their follies, molding these fallible creatures in their image. It wasn't as preposterous as it seemed, they told Kubuddhi. Because the humans weren't all that bad. Some of them—like the little girls who taught their cats to read, or the elderly couples making the most of their pensions and each other's company, or the booksellers and stationers in New Market—smelled very clean indeed and were hardly any work at all. In exchange for their guardianship, they got a home away from home, not completely cocooned from the putrescence, but just enough to make their indefinite stay bearable.

Kubuddhi didn't see the harm in it. It couldn't be worse than the stink that risked knocking him unconscious anywhere, anytime, or an unlicensed, sleep-deprived bus driver running him over with impunity or sharing a graveyard with five others stranded here like him. Besides, he was a prince of princes. A glittering comet in a field of asteroids. Surely, he had more to impart to these humans than the others. Surely, as a superior being, he had some philanthropic duty to the underprivileged and uncivilized.

He preferred to uphold this noblest calling somewhere insulated from the noise, haze, and falling temperatures. Somewhere nice and spacious and pleasing to the eyes. Somewhere upscale. Like the luxury apartments in Baridhara or Gulshan 2, though the occupants of these spaces tended to have poorer morals than most. Still, as the others said, they weren't all that bad. Kubuddhi searched high and higher, and as the dry winter air became more poisonous and the never-ending campaign rallies reached a fever pitch, he halfheartedly settled on a relatively innocuous household of six.

Father had the worst breath of them all but rarely stayed

home. Mother narrated and recorded everything she did in a day on a mobile device. The two children often featured in the scenes she staged, and two maids and countless screens looked after them when they weren't needed. They acted out often—for attention, out of entitlement, and bewilderment over their actions occasionally having consequences. At the same time, they read the Quran with a hujur every afternoon, and Mother and Father never missed a prayer. Kubuddhi saw this as a good sign because fear of God meant there was scope to mend their ways. Scope to teach them a valuable lesson.

Kubuddhi soured their milk, burst their pipes, crashed appliances and devices, misplaced their belongings, and infested their walls with mold. All to no avail. Such trivial occurrences, he realized, weren't enough to inspire them to change. Real, radical change necessitated dismantling the illusion of invincibility.

So he sparked a fire with a faulty space heater cable, let the flames consume the heater, and then spill out onto its surroundings. It seemed to have worked at first. Mother's first reflex was to save her children. Covering their mouths and her own, she rushed them downstairs to safety. But as the wait for fire services drew out, and the fire swallowed more and more valuable property, she ordered the building manager to go back inside and put it out with the decorative extinguishers hanging in the lobby. The manager, resistant at first, obeyed under threat of losing his job.

The fire raged for another five hours. The manager didn't

make it out alive, and Kubuddhi didn't watch over the family another night.

He searched the city for another home, far and wide this time, rather than up high. The threat of fire loomed everywhere he looked. In restaurants that stowed their gas tanks outdoors and in emergency stairways. In residential buildings doubling as chemical godowns. In slums where stoves ran all night to dry clothes and keep warm. In every building, caught in a cat's cradle of electrical wires. He found a few good promising places—good people who smelled nice and didn't require anything of him—but he questioned how much help he'd be when the inevitable fire broke out. Worried his good intentions might end up harming someone like they had the building manager.

Aimless and miserable, he wandered, always circling back to the spot by Dhanmondi Lake, where he'd stumbled into Dhaka. He didn't expect any answers—the vandalized bus had been cleared minutes after the helmet army fled, eliminating any chance of learning what happened or returning the way he came—and he didn't care to cross paths with the delinquent who chased after him—the fellow's breath was so rancid, it could have burned a hole through his helmet. The locality just had an inexplicable pull that kept bringing him back.

A few blocks away from the five white elephants, through a break in the sidewalk's guardrail next to Yusuf's Grand Shop, a flight of wide-treaded stairs led down to an open-air eatery that overlooked the lake. Moping about, Kubuddhi often spent hours staring at the dark, green-tinged waters and the ten-story luxury apartment building that rose from its bank at an awkward angle.

"Whereabouts are you from, my friend?" a voice asked early one morning, pulling him out of his stupor.

An old man was settling into one of the eatery's red plastic chairs. Bald at the crown with a shock of white hair that fell over his thick muffler and tweed jacket's collar and a thick mustache, just as white. He bore an uncanny resemblance to a human physicist, long dead, whose work on space and time came precariously close to unlocking the laws governing ties between this world and Kubuddhi's.

Kubuddhi frowned as he looked himself over. He was in a human form he'd modeled on the stunted, jelly-bellied, noodle-limbed, and rooster-haired fellows who overran the city. "What makes you think I'm not from here?"

"It's usually outsiders who're transfixed by Chisty's Yacht."

Kubuddhi looked over his shoulder at the apartment building diagonal to the lake. "Yacht, huh?" he snorted. "Looks the same as every other monstrosity around here."

"Which only confirms you're not from here. If you were, you'd know there used to be a yacht-shaped palace in its place not long ago. Jahaj Bari, it used to be called. A great boat of red brick with over forty palatial rooms, great vaulted windows, and towers whose spires climbed up to eight stories."

How odd. Vessels of that description were not native to this world, not even among the power-hungry and affluent. They were, however, known to roam the farthest reaches of Kubuddhi's world.

The old man invited him to pull up a plastic chair and ordered two teas and a plate of shingaras. "It used to belong to a holy man. A spiritual leader and a dear friend of mine who went by the title Sher-e-Khwaja. He used to offer every prayer at Eidgah Mosque, and in the evenings, he'd go to the field to meditate under the stars and commune with the divine."

Kubuddhi knew the field. Enclosed by a damp-stained pink Mughal-era wall, it was on the next block, across a street currently being excavated to transfer overhead wires underground. The atrocious modern six-story mosque and nine-story minaret behind the field were still under construction. He imagined there must have been a smaller, more harmonized structure in its place at some point.

"His line of business is still shrouded in mystery, but by the 80s, he'd come into considerable wealth and begun to move in very powerful circles. But his devotion never wavered. He continued offering every prayer at Eidgah and spent every night ruminating in the field. Then, in late 1991, he started construction on Jahaj Bari.

"As you can imagine, the building's design set many tongues wagging. I was no exception. I told him it was a waste of space. That a property so large could easily accommodate twelve apartments he could rent out. As if a man of his means needed passive income, ha!. But instead of mocking my pauper's mindset, he recounted to me a most peculiar story.

"Of how, some nights, when he sat meditating in Eidgah Field, his solitude would be disturbed by an influx of beggars.

Only they did not come seeking shelter or alms. They came for something among the wall's arches. And when they found it, fiery skirmishes would ensue at great peril to the old walls.

"I asked him what they sought, and he said he couldn't tell the first few times it happened. Then one day, he saw it—the wall past one of the arches vanishing to reveal a palatial red vessel, coasting among stars of colors his eyes couldn't comprehend. It was only there, a blink. Long enough for one, maybe two of the gathered to step through, leaving the rest, well, stranded."

A doorway home. Kubuddhi couldn't believe his ears.

"I said I had to see this for myself," said the old man. "That I was going to accompany him to Eidgah that evening. But he told me I wouldn't see anything. For it was still warm, and by his observation, the vessel only appeared on wintry nights when the moon was at half-phase."

"And?" Kubuddhi asked breathless. "Did you eventually see it?"

"I did. The following winter. Through the fourth arch left of the prayer niche in the southwestern wall. It was a brief glimpse, but its majesty shook me to my core. I would've probably built a replica of it, too, if I had the resources." He sighed. "But if I've learned one thing in all my years, the world does not care for such splendor. For the longest time, the city corporation disposed of garbage right in front of the mosque grounds. Then, after my dear friend passed, his children tore Jahaj Bari down in favor of that," he said with a dismissive wave at the lakeside apartment building.

"But the boat…it still appears at Eidgah?"

"Why, yes. And getting to it is a lot less chaotic, too."

"How?"

"Oh, there's a gatekeeper now. Yes, yes, he passes around a bucket for everyone to put in an identifying trinket. Then, as the time nears, he draws them one by one and gets everyone to line up in that order. And after that, whoever manages to get through gets through."

Kubuddhi scrutinized the old man. He didn't stink of rot, but his astute eyes and forthcoming nature felt suspect. "If there's such a crowd every time, how come no one's ever mentioned it to me?"

"Maybe they don't know," the man shrugged. "Jahaj Bari used to be a beacon of sorts—a clue that there's a way home close by—and now it's gone. But far more likely is that they do know and won't tell. You know, to improve their chances of getting through."

So the others he'd met—the ones who'd encouraged him to keep himself occupied by caring for humans—might have known about the Eidgah passage and willfully deceived him. Incensed, Kubuddhi came away from his encounter with the old man determined to beat each one of them to it.

The only question was, how?

The answer came a few days later when he recognized a foul odor over that of the secondary garbage transfer station he was passing. He'd only encountered it once before, but there was no mistaking who it was.

Still, early in the afternoon, children and their minders had yet to begin trickling into the playground beside the secondary garbage transfer station. The rare stretch of open space was walled in by hoardings of Mojo Cola and housed playground staples like a slide and a jungle gym, a host of creaky rides, and a bouncy castle. Aziz sat at the Mojo Cola-sponsored canteen beside the bouncy castle with a cold and over-fried chicken burger, a packet of Mr. Twist, and, of course, a Mojo Cola, too bitter to notice the garbage stench in the air.

Someone had removed the banner he'd had printed. The banner he'd paid for out of his pocket and spent hours compiling and doctoring images for: of corpses of the opposition's alleged victims, of the opposition leader bearing a pair of long fangs dripping with blood, of her minions' heads transplanted on monitor lizards' bodies. He'd risked his life to string it up between electrical poles on a busy commercial road, and now some fucker had removed it before ruling party authorities could take note and reward him for his dedication.

He didn't have enough for another banner. He'd spent whatever money his parents sent paying off his motorcycle and his party stipend on petrol. His diet mainly consisted of biryani from the packets distributed at rallies and more biryani from weddings he crashed. He was three months behind on hostel fees and wasn't sure if he still had a seat at university.

He'd done everything to prove he was a loyal and

hardworking party worker, yet he had nothing to show for it. He commanded respect, but only among the inconsequential and when wearing his helmet. Power was elusive as it was tangible. He could barely grab a fistful before it slipped through his fingers like sand.

A flash of light caught his eye. A short, scrawny, shabbily clad fellow with a protruding upper jaw, not quite boy nor man, dawdled from one playground amusement to the next, uncertain about how any of it worked. He caught Aziz staring and dragged his bare feet to the canteen table. "Helmet uncle, o helmet uncle, I'm so hungry. Spare me some money for food."

"Ei, don't bother me now. Go, get lost."

"O helmet uncle, I haven't eaten anything all day." His irises were brown, bordering on red, and the glassy whites of his eyes caught the light when he turned towards the sun.

Aziz was gripped by an odd feeling that he'd met this fellow before.

Stepping closer, he said, "Open your heart and spare me your chips."

"Hey, hands off my stuff!" Aziz shoved him away. "Are you deaf? I said get lost!"

"O helmet uncle, don't be like this. You should be fighting for the likes of me. But here you are, treating us like the folks in the AC cars do."

Bristling at the comparison, Aziz barked at the canteen's vendor to give the fellow a vegetable roll on his tab.

"May Allah take you far and make you a great man," the fellow said, wolfing down mouthfuls of shredded vegetables wrapped in soggy breaded skin. "I knew you weren't like them, like the folks whizzing over everyone on that elevated expressway or the folks in that Gulshan fire—did you hear what happened? The wealthy sirs and madams got out and then sent the manager to his death. But that's how it is, right? Everything's forgiven if you've got the money."

"And you're no one if you don't."

"Mm. I've heard there used to be a man who lived around here, a holy man so rich he built himself a boat-shaped castle on the lake just because he could. They say politicians from both parties came to him for his blessings before every election, but you tell me, would they care about these blessings if he was poor?"

Of course not. The blessings likely came with handsome donations or agreements to siphon and launder public funds. Faith was a performance—something to be leveraged for advantage. Sway public opinion. Aziz witnessed it firsthand every day.

He held his tongue, though. Anything that could be misconstrued as criticism of the ruling party would land him in jail. For all he knew, this fellow was an informant for a rival trying to get him ousted from the party. "Hey, stop talking my ears raw with your nonsense. Just take your roll and leave."

"May Allah take you far and make you a great man," the fellow said again, deferentially raising the flaccid remnants of his roll to his forehead. His eyes flashed bright as he turned on his heels and left.

Aziz dwelled on the elevated expressway as he finished his burger, chips, and cola. How he could never use it because motorcycles weren't allowed entry, and he didn't have a car.

Cars, boat-shaped castles, a politician's ear—that's what real power looked like, the kind that stayed in your grasp. Real power didn't come from burning buses or printing banners. Real power just needed money. Money by the truckload.

He donned his helmet to go on the prowl, thankful nights set in earlier in winter. The roads burst at the seams with traffic, reverberating with a swelling cacophony of honks that knew no peak. Aziz set his sights on an unsuspecting office employee leaving his place of work. His bamboo baton went unnoticed, maybe even ignored, in the bustle. He cornered the man and demanded he cough up three lakhs in three days if he wanted to keep his legs intact.

They both knew going to the police was futile. Three days later, Aziz was three lakh takas richer.

The helmeted delinquent targeted office workers, tea vendors, vegetable sellers, internet and cable service providers, and small businesses across Mohammadpur, Mirpur, Pallabi, Darussalam, Kafrul, Shyampur, and Old Dhaka. Careful not to hit too many in one neighborhood. Smashing property, merchandise, and bones when dues were late.

Kubuddhi's kind had adopted many among the extorted. They did little besides watch, because all of them were wary their meddling might make things worse.

They never saw this delinquent's face. His reek was distinctly unforgettable, though, and it grew more potent by the day.

Aziz printed more banners and posters smearing the opposition and praising the ruling party. His motorcycle's fuel tank was always full. He ate every meal at a table in an indoor restaurant. Bought a cotton quilt for his bed, a winter jacket for the road and brocaded vests and imported cologne to wear to weddings. He couldn't rent an apartment he could have to himself—landlords weren't keen on bachelors—so he paid off his hostel arrears. He even hired an Uber to take the elevated expressway to the airport and back.

Soon, he'd buy a degree from some private university, maybe even a foreign one, to placate his parents. Buy a car, then an apartment.

Things were looking up.

Yet everything seemed to be going wrong. His motorcycle stopped working mid-rally. His banners were pulled down, posters plastered over. Curdled borhani at a wedding gave him food poisoning. The election camps he helped erect either collapsed or caught fire. A forked fishbone got caught in his throat. His cell phone went missing. A brick tossed from a construction site missed his head by a hair.

And always, there was a nagging feeling he was being watched. He supposed that it was a natural response to having wealth, not that it would stop him from going after more. As the days grew colder, the haze thicker, and the sun disinclined to shine its light on the city, his paranoia assumed the form of the fellow from the playground, his short, wispy form always lurking in his peripheral vision, his eyes glowing in the dark shadows of his hostel room, watching him, even in his dreams.

He drifted awake late one night, curled in a ball and shivering despite being wrapped in his new quilt. There was a draught in the room, and the shadows cast by the bars on his windows appeared to move. Willing his eyes to focus, they slowly converged into one long, skinny arm.

The fellow whipped his head over his shoulder, his iridescent eyes boring into Aziz. He'd squeezed his head and torso through the bars, drawing himself beyond the body's natural elastic limit to pluck his motorcycle keys from the clothes stand.

"Hey!"

Dangling the key before Aziz with a taunting smile, the fellow snapped back out the window through its bars like he had no bones. Aziz leaped out of bed to go after him.

The half-moon fell in step with Kubuddhi on his way to Eidgah Field. He didn't know if he'd make it in time. Only that he couldn't arrive too early or a second too late.

He let himself in through a side gate opposite a KFC and dropped the motorcycle key into the gatekeeper's bucket. He recognized many of the faces gathered before the southwestern wall and could tell none of them regretted not telling him about the passage, just like he wouldn't regret what became of this night.

The gatekeeper began to draw trinkets from the bucket. Kubuddhi's didn't come first, second, or even fifth. The sixth was about to be called when an unpleasant stench pervaded the mist. Confusion rustled through those assembled the more potent it became. Its source scampered outside the wall, drawing attention from the gatekeeper to the floral grill gate behind him.

The delinquent stumbled in. He stopped in his tracks upon seeing everyone. He'd left his helmet at home, but his odor left no doubt as to who he was.

The swell of indignation among Kubuddhi's fellow visitors was palpable. To many, perhaps most, his unexpected arrival was serendipitous—one last shot at proving they were superior like they'd always believed. At fulfilling their philanthropic duty to the less fortunate. At delivering justice.

The delinquent's murderous eyes found Kubuddhi in the crowd. But they didn't remain on him long, for all around him, his fellow visitors shed their beggars' rags and human skin.

The hostile glow radiating from them stung Aziz's eyes. Filled him with a sinking dread that this wasn't something he was meant to see. What had, at first glance, appeared to be a couple of street rats had, in an instant, morphed into a brawn of creatures neither human nor animal, standing on hinds and all fours, with twisted horns of scaly bark, blue fire for skin, and swirling sandstorms raging through their veins. Lightning slashed the dark depths of their maws, their claps sounding in his head, fraying his eardrums raw with bellows of, "Where's the money? Return it to its rightful owner."

"I have here a magenta bangle," he heard a faint voice call. "Owner of the magenta bangle, come on up."

The demons didn't budge.

Backing away, Aziz tried the gate he'd entered by. It was locked.

The gate to the northeast was still open. Bolting across the damp grass, he threw his weight at it before it, too, locked shut. A series of resounding *snaps* stopped him from crossing the unpaved path separating the field and mosque. Choking in surprise, struggling to stand, he willed himself to look down.

His legs were dislocated and broken.

His arms followed suit.

He fell to the ground, face-first, eyes shedding agonized tears, mouth ajar in a silent wail. Great talons flipped him onto his back. Pressed down on his neck. Lightning-tongued jaws lowered to force black exhaust fumes down his throat, their thunderclaps repeatedly saying, "Where's the money? Return it to its rightful owner."

These abominations had taken his motorcycle key. His phone before that. Now they wanted to take his money? His outrage outweighed his pain. Nostrils and mouth dribbling blood, he rasped, "Fuck you! It's mine. Only mine. All mine."

They sank their talons into his flesh. Hoisted him up the minaret by his feet and thrashed him hard against metal and concrete. And when he still refused to reply, they flung him into a nest of poster and wire.

Bound him and squeezed him.

Stuck live tips in him.

Drove him to the brink.

Then reeled him back in.

"Where's the money?" they asked again and again.

"I'll take it all, you'll see. Till this city kneels to me."

A gush of blinding white stars was the last thing he remembered. Then falling.

In the pitch dark that ensued, the excavated street next to Eidgah Field stank worse than if a sewage pipe had burst.

Only the gatekeeper and one other of Kubuddhi's kind waited for the boat with him.

"What do you suppose is happening there?" the gatekeeper asked of the others.

Kubuddhi had been too anxious to register the human's presence. He was surprised to find it was the old man he'd met by the lake.

There was no time to acknowledge their reunion, though. Without any ado, a great castle-shaped red boat moored at some star sea appeared in the fourth arch to the left of the prayer niche in the southwestern wall.

The two visitors in attendance dashed across the threshold.

"Fi amanillah, my friends," the old gatekeeper called after them.

Catching one last glimpse of him over his shoulder, Kubuddhi felt a pang of guilt for gaming this rare, goodhearted human's efforts.

But there was nothing to be done now. The path to Dhaka winked shut.

Aziz was pulled from a ditch eight feet deep, mangled, pulped, critically burned, and somehow still alive. He was cognizant that the truth would make him a laughing stock. So, lying in the ICU, fighting for his life, he lied, telling the authorities he'd been kidnapped and tortured by opposition party workers.

State-run media pounced on the opportunity to make him the ruling party's poster boy. Many would anoint him the deciding factor in the party's victory a few days later.

With each election cycle to come, his influence would grow. He would have his car and castle, and he would have politicians from every side seeking his 'blessings.' He would take it all until the city kneeled to him, just as he'd promised to some stranded outsiders one strange winter night.

Anjum Noor Choudhury is a speculative fiction author and climate policy researcher from Dhaka, Bangladesh. She is the author of *The Divining Thread* (HarperCollins India,

2022), and her short stories can be found in *Escalators to Hell: Shopping Mall Horrors* (From Beyond Press, 2024), *Tangle & Fen* (Crone Girls Press, 2023), and *Selene Quarterly Magazine: The Complete Series* (Aurelia Leo, 2022).

PARIS

Sarah Read

Henri kept his markers in a pouch hung from his neck, beneath his shirt, so the warmth of his body would keep the ink from freezing. It was not convenient to rifle frozen fingers past the collar of his jacket, trying to divine each color by touch alone. But he didn't have to do it often. There were few people walking the Place du Tertre. The holiday tourists had long gone, and those that remained were not stopping, but hurrying past to get out of the wind or to get to the river where, for the first time since Le Grand Hiver in 1709, the Seine had frozen.

It was a spectacle, and the city had made the most of it. Skating, sleigh rides, sculptures. It drew the meagre crowd from the square as cold stone draws heat from a body.

Henri did not want to sit in the square today either, but it was Saturday, and that meant Paul would come for a portrait with his date, and that meant tonight Henri would have hot food.

Paul brought his dates to Henri, every Saturday, to have their picture drawn. Henri could draw Paul with his eyes closed, but the woman's face was different every week. Never the same features twice, and hardly any resemblance among them, except that they all smiled sweetly, sat patiently, while Henri traced their features in pigment.

Henri tucked his hands beneath his arms to warm them, to keep his fingers from becoming stiff and clumsy. Paul finally came, a slight figure trailing him. He sat on the narrow folding stool to the left of Henri's easel. The woman stood beside him, a shy, awkward hand on Paul's shoulder.

She did not smile as much as the others. It was as if the cold had frozen her face, but Henri drew her smile bigger than it appeared. He could see how it would look in the lines writ on her ruddy cheeks.

He worked quickly, swift lines unrolling their likeness. He pulled the paper from the clips and handed it to Paul, who paid and tipped the same as he did every week. Then he handed Henri an extra bill—twenty Euros. Henri stared at him in surprise.

"For waiting out in the cold," he said. "Get yourself something at the ice market tonight. That's where we're going."

Henri nodded his thanks and began to pack his easel as Paul and his date disappeared down the road toward the frozen river.

The ice market—he'd forgotten that was happening. A special faire with stalls right on the river's ice. There would be hot food there for cold tourists—and there would be tourists. It would make better sense for him to set up his easel there, on the frozen Seine, than to freeze himself here in a deserted Montmartre. He strapped his stool and easel to his back and set off.

The ice market was miserably festive—the cold too much to bear, the lights and spectacle making the best of things. The worst would come later, when the city lights went out, when infants and elderly would freeze in their beds. In the meantime, music and strings of glowing bulbs reflected off the captured river, light laughing off the ice like cut crystal. Every shade of blue reflected underfoot.

Henri tried to draw it all, sketching the rows of tables and lines of bundled visitors. No one sat for a portrait—no one wanted to unwrap a scarf or bare their faces for longer than it took to sip a steaming coffee.

Henri had a coffee and wandered the market stalls. His feet halted in front of one as if the ice had seized him. It was a stationer, an art supplier—one he didn't recognize. An old woman sat behind a table laid with paper and notebooks, paints and pencils. The woman was as pale as the snowbank behind her, her cataract-glazed eyes the color of hoarfrost, silver hair hanging like icicles from beneath her scarf.

Henri gestured to a pack of pencils in a vibrant mix of shades. He wouldn't have to thaw those to draw with them.

The woman moved like a glacier wrapping the pencils in

brown paper and passing the parcel to him under the string of lights that flickered overhead. As soon as his hand touched the paper, the lights went out.

Henri blinked away the light traces that dotted his vision in the sudden darkness. The dark felt so much colder, though the lights had given no heat, and Henri felt suddenly, uncomfortably aware of the crust of ice underfoot—how much trust they'd all put in its brittle impermanence. How long could a skin of ice stop a river?

There were muffled cries all around him as the market stirred in panic, and then all went silent.

Henri's stomach cramped with anxiety. There was no more music, no murmur of tourists, no more hum of espresso machines. As if life itself had frozen.

He spun on the slick surface, scanning the dark for the shoreline, for a way up to solid streets and familiar alleys. The edges of his vision clouded as he breathed too quickly, too shallow, panting as he clawed his way to ground.

He made it to a park bench and pulled his stool and easel from his back so he could sit and catch his breath. He gripped the bench's armrest so tightly his hand shook from fatigue. In his other hand, gripped just as tightly, was the parcel of pencils.

The paper wrapping had become disheveled in his panicked retreat from the ice market. He hoped the pencils inside had not broken, that the soft clay cores had not shattered inside their thin wooden housing. It had been years since he had drawn with pencils. He had curated his own contemporary style in ink and left the more classical compositions to his colleagues in the Place du Tertre. He did not know why he had purchased them, except he wanted to. An impulse. They had called to him. And he realized with a jolt of guilt that he had not paid for them. The dark and silence had fallen before he could pull Paul's tip from his pocket.

Henri stood and turned back toward the river. He should go back and pay the ice woman. But his legs shook at the thought of braving that frozen flow again. He could see no lights, hear no music. The market was likely still in chaos, and he doubted he could even find the woman again, not in the panicked crowd, not in the dark.

He pulled the torn paper away from the parcel and let the glow from the streetlamp fall across the line of pencils that stood like soldiers in regiment in their cardboard sleeve. They were tinted graphite with enough clay pigment to lend his sketches a whisper of life.

Henri made his way back to his apartment, a one-room shambles teetering behind a fashionable Montmartre storefront. It was near midnight by the time he crossed his threshold. He set his stool and easel by the door, his satchel beside them, and fell into bed, where he would stew for days in a fever, a heat fit to melt the river and summon an early spring. He burned till all fear of the ice was a clouded memory.

Saturday came, as it always did, and Paul came, as he always did, a new woman on his arm.

It was still cold, the city locked in ice, the death toll rising every dawn as bodies were discovered like statues in their beds.

Paul sat frozen still as his date fidgeted at his shoulder and Henri sketched them, slowly, his hands unpracticed with the pencils clutched in his numb, curled fingers. He drew in a fugue state, eyes clouded and unseeing, drawing from memory and instinct, the lines appearing as if called from nothing. It was only when his hands fell into his lap that Henri realized the drawing was done. He shook his head clear and stared at his work, eyes darting from the page to the couple beyond the easel, Paul's face tinted with confusion and impatience.

The drawing was good, Henri was relieved to see, Paul's features true to life, familiar. But the woman… She did not smile in the drawing, as she did in the flesh. Her sketched face was creased with pain, eyes flat and lifeless, a ring of purple bruises shaded around her throat. A ruby bead of red graphite dribbled from the corner of her pale mouth.

Henri ripped the paper from the easel clips and crushed it in his hands.

"Hey!" Paul called out, standing, his date stumbling back from him. "Why did you do that?" He reached for the paper, but Henri pulled it back, close to his chest.

"It's no good," Henri said. "I thought I could try with pencils, but I can't. I'm sorry." He shoved the pencils into his bag and threw the strap over his shoulder. His heart hammered beneath the rumpled paper he clutched there.

Paul's hand shot out again as Henri straightened and the paper tore away in his grip. "I'll decide if I want it or not," Paul said, unfolding the picture.

"No…" Henri whispered, but it was too late. Paul's eyes grew wide as he skimmed the portrait, his gaze rising slowly to meet Henri's.

Henri backed away.

"What's wrong with it? Let me see," the woman said, reaching for the paper Paul still held stretched before him. He crushed it again before she could see it, his glare still leveled at Henri.

"What is this supposed to mean?" Paul said, but Henri was backing away.

"I'm sorry, I'm sorry. I've been ill…" Henri mumbled.

Paul took a long stride toward him, rage refiguring that familiar face into a mask Henri could have never imagined for it, an anger that etched new lines into a visage he'd only ever seen frozen in a smile.

"I'm sorry," Henri said again, and he turned and ran. His satchel bounced at his hip, but he'd left his stool and easel behind. And he'd left the drawing behind.

He needed practice, that was all. It was an unfamiliar medium, and he was still fevered, and it was still nightmarishly cold. Henri listed the reasons to explain what had happened. He shivered in his bed, Le Grand Hiver raging outside with another wave of frigid wind that drove the crust of river ice into heaping peaks that ground against the stone banks like glacial ploughs. The river's surface was no longer a glassy lane for skaters, but a razor field tinted with the city's pollutants.

Henri rolled a pencil between his fingers, a blank page taped to the wall of his apartment. Practice.

There was only one face he knew well enough to draw from memory. He set the pencil tip to the page, and the curtain fell in front of his vision again. His hand moved and his breathing slowed as a state like sleep overcame him. He did not know how long he sat drawing, but when his vision returned, the picture was done.

It was Paul, but not as Henri knew him. His face twisted in rage, his foreshortened hand reaching out, so real it looked as if he might curl his fingers around Henri's throat.

The bruises on that woman's neck, her blank expression, that drop of blood the brightest spot in the picture, drawing the eye.

Henri's eyes avoided Paul's in the picture, drifting to the background. Dread gripped his stomach. The building behind Paul's shoulder was the bank across the street from Henri's apartment. The pink-tinged plaster, the slightly hanging shutter… It was the view from Henri's own window. He'd drawn Paul in his street, angry and threatening.

It's only anxiety, Henri thought. He'd upset Paul, and that had upset him in turn. The cold was getting to him, the stress, his fever.

Shouts sounded from the street, a bang and clatter, more raised voices.

Henri steadied himself against the wall, his heartbeat thudding at the base of his throat. Fear froze his joints. Trembling, he shook as he moved to grab his satchel, not daring to look at the window, and he ran from his room down the hall to the stairs that would deposit him in the back alleys of Montmartre.

Henri's coffee steamed as he let it warm his frozen fingers until a skin of ice formed on the surface. He pressed it with a fingertip and watched it fracture, the thin sheets drifting on the coffee's dark surface. It was how he'd imagined the ice market ending, stalls and visitors clinging to drifting rafts above the dark river.

He needed to go back. He needed to return the pencils, or pay for them, or ask the old woman why… If it was the pencils or madness. Or the cold.

He hadn't returned to his apartment. There were artist safe houses, which were neither safe nor houses, scattered through the city, and he drifted between them, shivering on warehouse pallets while his fellow vagrant painters burned their own canvases for warmth.

He'd have added his stool and easel to the fire if he had them, but he'd left them behind when he'd fled the square, fled Paul, on Saturday. It was Saturday again.

He would go back for them, see if they were still there, and find a spot to hide and wait. If Paul came, he would draw him, secretly, from a distance. A nice picture this time, and he would give it to Paul as a gift, an apology. He hoped it would be enough to assuage the man's rage.

The ice market's success had brought tourists back to the city, which had brought artists back to the Place du Tertre. Artists lined the street, places set, portraits blooming on their easels.

Henri's place sat empty, his stool and easel still there. A chunk of limestone sat atop the stool, a paper stiff with frost pressed beneath it.

Henri pulled the paper free and unfolded it. It was part of his own drawing, the one he'd done for Paul the previous week. It was only the eyes torn in a strip, the intensity of Paul's gaze captured in Henri's pencils. Henri let the rock fall to the ground where it shattered in a rain of ice. He put the paper in his pocket, grabbed his stool and easel, and disappeared into the crowd.

There was an embankment behind the square with hedges that lined the space, and from there he could see his empty spot through a veil of frosted Ivy.

Paul came at his usual time, in his usual way, a young woman on his arm. Different, again, from the woman he'd drawn last week. Paul stared at Henri's empty spot, then turned to the artist next to it, spoke, nodded, smiled, and took his seat.

Henri moved quickly, pulling his pencils and paper from his satchel, setting up his easel.

The fog threatened to close in on his thoughts again as he drew, but he fought it, pulling himself by force back to a presence of mind, straining his eyes along the lines he scratched over the paper. He needed to work quickly, to finish before the other artist did, before Paul would take his date and vanish into the city.

Henri struggled to keep his eyes clear and his mind focused. His vision narrowed to a circle, then a tunnel, then only a coin of light, as if he were falling down a deep well.

Light returned when the drawing was finished. Paul's familiar face smiled from the paper, eyes glittering, teeth bared, a sheet of running red cascading down his cheek. To his left, his date, her face in ravaged tatters. Skin hung in ribbons from shredded bone, torn eyelids like wet curtains over empty sockets. Her hair had been roughly shorn and strands of it clung to the blood on Paul's face.

Henri moaned and leapt back from his easel, sending his stool rolling away into the garden. Sweat sprung from his forehead and froze there. He scraped at the ice on his face and as he raised his eyes, his gaze met Paul's over the rim of the hedge.

They stared at one another, peered into one another. Again, Henri ran.

He left his stool and easel behind. He left the drawing behind. He ran toward the river, to the twinkling strings of market lights. His satchel bumped against his hip as he ran, the pencils rattling inside, their cores no doubt shattered to powder. They'd probably disintegrate if he sharpened them.

His breath fogged ahead of him, an icy cloud that dulled his sight. He pushed through it, breath after breath, block after block, till he saw the market lights. Crates lined the river's edge behind rows of empty tables. The ice had melted on the surface and refrozen into rippled drifts of razor glass.

Henri tried to trace his way to where the stationer's stall had been, near the Pont des Arts. He had seen the light glowing from the Louvre's pyramid over the rooftops of the palace. He must be close. He crawled into the shadows beneath the bridge's support pillars and pulled his coat close. He waited for the old ice woman, for the market to open. He no longer had any money to pay for the pencils, nor did he think she would take them back after their hard use, but he had questions, and he hoped he might somehow make things right or undo this trouble he had found himself in.

His stressed body craved sleep, but this winter, sleep meant death. He pulled the pencils and paper from his bag, the only thing he could think to do to keep himself awake. The pencils had scattered into the deep seams of the bag, their tips worn blunt. A few more sketches and he would have to sharpen them, and the battered cores would break and fall away. A wave of grief surprised him. He wanted no part of this magic, but the thought of losing it made his throat tighten.

He let the fugue tunnel take him this time, oblivion warmer than reality, and the pencil guided itself to whatever end it desired. He was vaguely aware of the cold biting at his nose, the sound of distant voices sliding across the ice, and the gentle scrape of lead on paper, but he felt no passage of time.

When the fog released him, it took his eyes a moment to adjust to the dark. Evening had fallen, and fallen harder under the bridge's shadow. Only the fizzing glow of fairy lights lit the paper before him. The paper itself was nearly black, a shaded field of shadow but for a core of light cutting through the grey to illuminate a grainy row of crumbled skulls. Among them, his own face, still holding to its flesh, or most of it, and the rest of his body nowhere in the picture.

Henri choked on the cry that rose in his throat. The dark pencil was still clutched in his fist, the tip worn almost flat with all the shadow it had conjured. He dropped the pencil and watched it slide down the embankment to catch on a ridge of ice.

He stretched his cramped legs to go after it and grazed his head on the rough stone of the underside of the bridge. He pressed his hand to his tangled hair.

He'd seen skulls like that plenty of times. Artists haunted the catacombs of Paris as often as they haunted its abandoned warehouses. Millions of skulls lined the walls of those tunnels, the bodies removed from Les Innocents and the overflowing parochial cemeteries of Paris.

He retrieved his lost pencil and crawled out from below the bridge. He scanned the rows of tables lining the river. The market was as busy as before, though now the tourists spilled their coffee as they tripped over uneven ice. He spotted the table by its colors, rows of rainbow in bright circles of paint, squares of white paper like windows to winter. And the wrinkled woman behind them, bundled in layers of rags stained with paint.

The table was not far. Past a baker selling pastries, a stand of frozen fruits, and a newsstand.

Tourists had gathered not around the confectioners, but around the news. Henri peered past their shoulders as he passed and saw the sprawling headline.

Another tourist found dead in Montparnasse.

Beneath that, a photo, a young woman, a face he knew too well, that his hand had traced intimately, broadening her smile.

Henri pushed his way to the front of the crowd and pulled a paper from the rack.

Coffee spilled around him to the sound of angry murmurs and sharp swearing. He unfolded the paper to see the whole article. At the bottom was a parade of portraits, small faces, all in grey, all so familiar that the paper shook in his hands.

He let the crowd swallow him, let them push forward and make him invisible as he folded the paper under his arm and backed away, digging his heels in to keep him from falling. He didn't pay for the paper. Just as he hadn't paid for the pencils.

As he stumbled out of the crowd surrounding the newsstand, his hip hit the corner of the stationer's table, sending the string of lights swaying, their reflections in ice spraying prism refractions. Henri pressed his hands to his eyes as he righted himself and found his footing on the slick river.

His bleary eyes focused on the old woman who smiled at him from behind the wraps of her threadbare scarf. Henri's question caught in his throat. He stared at her, tracing the lines of her face as if he meant to draw her. He reached wordlessly into his bag and pulled out the pencils, points worn blunt, bodies notched and dented.

"I didn't pay," Henri whispered passed the tightness in his throat.

The old woman laughed, carving the lines deeper into her face. Her teeth were as brown as the liver spots that covered her hands.

"You have," she said.

Henri was relieved. He hadn't remembered paying, but perhaps he'd left something on the table in all the chaos.

"And you will continue to pay," the woman said. "Forever."

The air of the market seemed to grow colder, the lights dimmer.

Despite the cold, Henri's shirt dampened with sweat, which froze and chilled him even more.

He backed away from the table, pencils clutched in one hand, the newspaper in the other. His own heartbeat rushed in his ears, loud as a thawed river, and the only thing that cut through the sound was a familiar voice.

Henri spun and slipped on the ice, landing hard, his knee ground into the sharp crest of a frozen wave. His pained shout drew glances from the crowd, eyes tracking him just as he needed most to hide. People reached for him, hoping to help, but he evaded them, slipping along the razor ice, leaving his clothes in tatters, pencils and newspaper still clutched in his hands till he made his way past the people to the shore.

He stood and realized his satchel was missing, left behind when he fell. He dared not go back for it. Paul was milling through the crowd, the woman he'd sketched still at his side, her face not yet the ruin Henri had drawn. He unfolded the newspaper again. Six women, all tourists, their bodies all found at landmarks. A blonde named Lisa at the Eiffel Tower. A dark-haired beauty at Notre Dame. They'd all been murdered, found on Sunday mornings. And Henri had drawn them all on Saturdays. But Henri's Saturdays with Paul went back much farther than six weeks. Paul had been Henri's customer for nearly a year.

Henri's stomach felt as cold as his hands. He raised his gaze again to Paul and the young woman who followed him. That woman would die tonight. Henri was the only one who knew it. And Paul knew that Henri knew. But as Paul rushed the woman away from the newsstand and the crowd, Henri realized that he also knew where they were going.

Tourists would flock to the catacomb's entrance in Place Denfert-Rochereau, line up at the tour stand at the top of the steps for the grim exhibit. The guides act as if that is the only way in, as if the exit through the gift shop is the only way out. And no one gets in at night.

But you can get into the catacombs from almost any part of the city. Out can be harder.

Henri slipped his pencils and newspaper into his pockets before prying free a manhole cover in the street. The cold metal burned his fingers, the rim of ice cutting into his skin. Slick metal rungs set into the stone vanished into the dark of the passage below. Henri had no light, not even a book of matches to guide him through the tunnels. He knew Les UX would have left some at intervals along the route, but he'd have to find them in the dark. Henri lowered himself into the passage and pulled the cover back into place above him, sealing the dark in.

It was warmer below ground. Out of the wind, insulated by meters of limestone, the catacombs maintained their temperature year-round. As Henri's eyes adjusted, he realized he was not in total darkness. Dim light spread from far down the passage. Low voices seemed to carry on the light.

Henri approached with slow caution, not wanting to startle whatever cataphiles had set up camp out of the cold. It made sense that the tunnels would be busy with those seeking shelter. Henri wondered why he hadn't thought of it himself. But he didn't like the tunnels. In the tourist stretch, at least the human remains were artfully displayed in patterned memorials. But that was only one-and-a-half of the three-hundred and twenty kilometers of tunnels that threaded the stone beneath the entire city of Paris. Beyond the beaten path, bones were tossed casually in piles, haystacks of splintered limbs coated in lime and lichen. A reminder that hierarchy persists even in death.

Henri's thoughts flashed to his last drawing, to his own severed head lined up with the rows of skulls. He had walked right into his fate.

The glow and low voices came, as Henri had suspected, from a gathering of vagrants keeping warm. They offered him one of their glowsticks, and he took it gratefully before heading off into the tunnels in the direction of the Ossuaries.

Henri's feet ached against the hard stone floor of the old mine tunnel. He'd fled Paul's rage for miles across the city, and now he ran toward it, toward the anonymous tourist, latest of many, who sat for his drawing and then vanished, disappearing into the violence of the winter city. Where the cold kills the weak and Paul kills the unwary.

He didn't know what he would do if he found them. He was no fighter. And all he had on him were the cursed pencils and the newspaper.

The pencils, he was sure now, drew the future. Or at least the intent of the subject. Could it be intent only—that some of those Saturday women had lived? But some had not, and the paper in his pocket proved it.

Henri held the fading glowstick aloft and saw the ceiling painted with a black stripe of soot. He was getting closer. The torches of centuries had blazed the trail that would lead him to the well-walked paths of l'empire de la Mort.

He passed graffiti murals and wax-coated altars, stacked cairns and black, bottomless wells. The city underground was as vibrant and enigmatic as the one above. And just as dangerous. Both had Paul.

As Henri entered the Ossuary through a back tunnel behind a wall of stacked bones, he heard voices. Moaning. The sharp, retorted impact of flesh on flesh. But it wasn't distress he heard. It was amorous.

Henri kept himself concealed behind the wall of bones and peered through the empty sockets of a skull. The ancient face granted him a narrow window into the room, a death mask from which to view the source of the sounds which filled the low-ceilinged chamber.

It was Paul and his Saturday woman, naked, driving at each other atop Gilbert's tomb. Lit candles were stuck into pools of wax on the floor, their light glowing off the dust-caked perspiration of their bodies.

Henri flinched back. He tucked his nearly extinguished glowstick into his pocket, and his fingers closed around the cluster of pencils. He pulled them out and pressed them to his lips, squeezing his eyes shut, trying not to hear the wet smack of the couple not ten feet away. No one was dying, or at least, only metaphorically, as the Saturday woman screamed en la petite mort.

Her scream cut short. Henri's eyes flew open. He returned his face to the skull, seeing with its eyes.

Paul's hands were wrapped around the woman's throat, her fingers raking at his as he squeezed. Her body shook atop him as his face contorted in a mix of rapture and rage.

"No," Henry whispered through the skull's mouth.

He pulled the newspaper from his other pocket and spread it across the bone-strewn stone floor. Heedless of the print already there, he began to draw. This time, the dark did not take him—he was already in it. The fog did not cloud his focus, he molded it, breathed it into shape.

He drew Paul, the face he knew best of all faces. He drew him distorted through meters of water, refracted through a thick layer of ice, his face grated on the underside of the thawing river, dragged by currents pulling out to sea.

Paul shouted. The woman gasped in ragged agony. A loud thud sounded, chased by the smell of extinguished candles.

"Who's there?" Paul called through the smoke.

Henri ignored him, scraping his pencils over the print, obscuring the faces of the dead women with an image of Paul's own end. He drew Paul's blood wisping from a thousand wounds into the freezing water. The woman's ragged cough disguised the laugh that boiled out of Henri.

He'd been living on blood money. Paying rent and eating from the money Paul gave him every week to draw his doomed girls. And they were here, he knew—a few more bodies among the millions.

And if these pencils drew the future, Paul would join them.

But the tips of his pencils gave out, lead flattened, before he was finished.

Henri panted, shifting from pencil to pencil, as the crunch of foot on bone circled the edge of the wall. He looked up to see Paul looming, candle in hand, his eyes reflecting the flame as he towered over Henri. In his other hand he held a knife.

Henri moved first. He pulled a thick femur from the pile at his feet and swung. Paul leapt back and the candle winked out, its last light caught in the gleam of the blade arcing toward Henri.

Henri slipped to the side and brought the femur down hard on Paul's arm. The knife clattered to the stone floor and Henri grabbed it before darting into the tunnel concealed behind the stack of bones.

Knife in one hand, pencils in the other, he heard Paul roar behind him.

He hoped the woman had run. Hoped she had coughed her way deeper into the tour tunnels, where she'd find the stairs leading out. Henri ran deeper into the catacombs, sure Paul would be close behind.

He'd left the picture. Left his spell behind, his future unfinished. His pencils shook flat and useless in his hand as he traced his path back into the maze.

But he had a knife.

Henri paused and listened. Paul's footsteps sounded distant behind him.

He pulled the glowstick from his pocket and set the knife to the pencil tips, carving away the sheath of wood to expose more lead. Just as he exposed a length of tip, it crumbled to his feet. The shattered cores would not tolerate sharpening, as he'd feared. They'd been carried too roughly, abused, shattered within their bodies like bones broken in a fall.

Henri stifled a frustrated sob. Pigment was pigment. Art was art. He retrieved the fallen tip from the tunnel floor and popped it past his lips, holding it cradled on his tongue. He cut away more wood, pulling more clay lead from the pencil, adding it to the rest cupped carefully on his tongue.

Paul's thundering feet grew closer. Henri hurried. He splintered the last of the lead free, shoving it into his mouth and taking off running again, chewing, grinding the pigment to a bitter paste.

He reached the iron rail that surrounded the well just as the flickering light of Paul's re-lit candle rounded the corner.

Henri plunged his fingers into his mouth and stirred, scooping the paste onto his fingertips. He turned to the ancient stone wall and dragged a line down its surface. He fingerpainted Paul's face, contorted, bloated, a diminishing line of bubbles receding toward the ceiling as Paul's heavy hands closed down on him.

Henri squirmed, spinning in the man's grip, and lashed out with the knife as he shoved.

Paul's grip released, his arms flailing as his back hit the thin iron rail that surrounded the circular well. His bare feet slid over the granules of bone that peppered the floor like gravel, and his body tilted, hips over shoulders, as he arced over the railing and into the water below.

Henri raced to the edge just as Paul's trailing feet disappeared into the cloudy green water. The water frothed and foamed with the man's struggle. Then it slowed to a gentle rock, waves sloshing at the base of the stones. Then it stilled.

Henri waited till the still silence of the catacombs was

absolute. Then he vomited a rainbow of pigment into the water. The sick sunk in swirling ribbons, the signature on his masterpiece.

The Saturday woman was not in the tomb chamber. She must have fled, as Henri had hoped. She would find help, he was sure—the cataphiles would guide her to safety, or she would find the surface and save herself. He would draw it, but there was no art left in him. The barest grains of pigment stuck between his teeth were not enough to conjure futures, so he swallowed them, and prayed for the strength to get himself out.

His clothes were in tatters from the river ice, his body aching from the running and fighting. He shook with fatigue, for lack of food, and want of shelter. Le Grand Hiver doesn't take only the weak. She takes the unlucky.

Henri made as much of the trip belowground as he could, out of the wind, before he dared breach the surface. It was past midnight, but he knew the city was still awake, too cold to risk sleep.

He ascended in the Jardin du Luxembourg and made his way to the river, to the Pont des Arts, and the fairy lights glinting in the eyes of the old woman.

They stared at one another, him in ruins, her in amusement, until Henri peeled his bitter tongue from the roof of his mouth.

"Have I paid enough, now?"

The woman smiled, her liver teeth and carven face like a statue left to rust. She nodded.

"That took less time than I thought," she said.

Henri frowned and, on instinct, reached for the parcel she handed him. His hand closed on the paper wrapping before he could think better of it.

As anxiety fought its way from his mind to his heart to his hand, it was interrupted by the ear-splitting crack of the river breaking free.

The pencils were all he had to hold onto as he fought his way off the ice again, across Paris again, to the Place du Tertre, where he'd left his easel, and where the Spring and thaw would bring new faces, new futures.

Sarah Read's stories can be found in various places, including Ellen Datlow's Best Horror of the Year vols 10 and 12. Her first collection *Out Of Water* is available from Trepidatio Publishing, as is her debut novel *The Bone Weaver's Orchard*, both nominated for the Bram Stoker, *This is Horror*, and Ladies of Horror Fiction Awards. *Orchard* won the Stoker and the *This Is Horror* Award, and is available in Spanish as *El Jardin Del Tallador De Huesos*, published by Dilatando Mentes, where it was nominated for the Guillermo de Baskerville Award. Her second collection, *Root Rot & Other Grim Tales* is available through Bad Hand Books. Her second novel, *The Atropine Tree*, will be released from Bad Hand Books in 2024.

LONDON

Lily Childs

Someone read me some Burroughs yesterday; it was that girl – the one in the yellow girdle over on Clancy. What a mind. What vision. Reminds me of me. *Burroughs*, that is – not the Clancy girl. Some folks say people can't live in a constant dream state like that. I don't believe them – they should just read the man; he's got it all going on. I can see it in his words, smell it, taste it. It feels like I knew him in a previous life or some such shit, except I'd have skipped the insecticide habit – not my thing – don't need it. There's enough going on in this freak-out fucking world without yesterday's drugs. Gotta keep it pure, Suzannah, gotta keep it pure.

Now Suzannah – she's got a banjo on her knee and that weird costume going on. She told me it's Alabama barmaid retro chic, but that girl? She's never dipped lower than Philly and is as English as they come. Gonna find me a way into that corset o' hers, flap out those scrawny tits, and head on down to her private London, see what I can find there.

S he's hanging out in other places today with those boys. *"They're not bad, Zillah,"* she always says to me, her accent all clipped and posh. *"They're just angels in the wrong skin."* The trouble is, Suzannah don't see their wings like I do. Ain't no feathers on those motherfuckers' backs, just scales and tatters. I can't tell her, though. She clings too hard – it took me days to unravel her from my own skin when I first met her a few years back when the weather was too hot, and the city steamed. All I wanted was a dip, a looky-see, to peak into her places; her head, her soul, her past. I don't *touch*. She thought I was in love with her – whatever that is. I let her down gently enough, and she drifted on. Drifted downtown.

I get this thing where I can stand next to someone and catch a piece of whatever they're zoned out on. Sometimes, I see it lingering around them like some nuclear aura, all yellow and filthy. I avoid that shit; walked right into a haze of it once and puked my guts up. But a violet breeze? That's a different story; it mellows me out until I'd swear God made America and Republicans shit in their own backyards. A little taste of that will keep me peachy throughout the day. So, I'm hanging at my window, watching the snow, and thinking I might go for a promenade in the park to steal something sweet when along comes Suzannah, aglow with rainbows. She sparkles as her bare feet tiptoe on the frosted path. She feels no pain.

Come here, pretty one. Let me share.

She doesn't hear; she's too stoned, but then she turns and staggers straight into the traffic. Her eyes are all over the place, and that smile? It's a slit, a slice. They've cut her from ear to ear. She's a walking, dripping scab. The ribbons of that fucking corset hang down from one side where they've been ripped from the bodice, leaving her almost naked while she trips into the path of speeding cars.

"Hey!"

I'm off that windowsill and skidding on ice down the path, waving hands like some evangelist. She makes it, tires screeching in her wake, mouths screaming at her back. Her rainbow darkens to a shimmering, purple bruise – a storm on the street. She hits the sidewalk, the life almost gone from her. I get there just in time to catch a cupful of thunder and tuck it away for later.

They call my home a shelter. It serves its purpose, and I've got pretty things all over the walls. Don't matter if I get moved on and someone takes them away 'cause they're nature's gifts, and I can always grow or pick me some more. Besides, I always make my way back here from wherever I've been, somehow.

Suzannah freaks at the ivy trailing over the magnolia paper like I've got spiders coming out of the cracks, but I shut her in, hold her down – and wait until the calm comes.

It does, eventually. It's given me time to examine her wounds, and they're more superficial than I first feared. Her wide mouth – well, that had to sting, but it's cut rather than ripped right open. She'll be scarred for sure, like me, if she lives. But it's her colors; they scare me. They've turned to sludge, the worst kind – I want no taste of them. I learned long ago to imagine myself up an armour of mirrors if I need it; it keeps me safe and reflects it back.

Suzie's barely breathing so I crawl off her bones and call for Carl – he's always somewhere.

"Who is she, Zillah?"

He's all kind of serious with a permanent look of wonder.

"A friend."

"You know you're not allowed drugs in here…"

"I didn't pump them into her. She's got friends of her own. HA!"

Carl jumps back like I just bit his ass. "What the fuck?"

"Sorry, Carl. Friends? What kinda friends do filth like this?"

'Course I know the answer to my own question – plenty do, tripping and sharing junk 'til they're shitting in the streets with rotten holes in their groins, losing legs, losing life. I don't know what Suzannah's taken – but I don't want her to die.

The paramedics get here just in time to rip that corset off her so they can ram a needle into her chest, but she's too far gone, and she *does* die. She dies right here on my bed.

They ask who she is, and I tell them the little I've gleaned from her whispering lies these last six months or so.

Nothing will happen. All I know is I can't stay here anymore, not with the shape of her etched on the sheets. Carl knows it. He tells me to wait, then returns with a list of other shelters in the area and further out, past the black borders of this state. I know some, never heard of others. But I don't know where I'm going this time. I slip the list into my ruck with the few bits and pieces I own and a new treasure.

Think I'll go north for once.

I can see a ferry from the shore. It tosses and roils on the cold waves. Can't afford the fare, even if I was tempted. Anyway, I've found me a better way to travel. These glory millionaires with plastic mansions along the East Coast ought to spend more of that money on security. I'm holed up in a hut; the owners probably call it a *Summer House,* but here in the depths of a New York winter, I'm grateful for its fake fire and black-out shades. I stay here at night to avoid the gardeners and the pool boy keeping the place sweet should the owners decide to drop in on their way home from Paris or Dubai, or London.

London's where I'm going. Had a glimpse of it already.

The tassels tremble beneath my slow caress. It's just like that first time. Shaking, shuddering little visions that fade in and out. I'd brushed against Suzannah in the street back then and thought I'd forgotten to wake up; the dreams of drifting through dark, misty alleys were clearer to me than the hoards of commuters that crowd out the dustbowl sidewalk, the corporate slaves. Then – gone. I was back in the bright and cold reality of a worthless life in a place I don't belong.

The corset's not yellow anymore. I've been trying to study it without flipping over to London – I'm not quite ready yet

– so I've been poking it with a jacaranda stick which seems to dissipate the energy. Fuck knows how I knew how to do that. Anyway, seems like the fabric was gold once, or at least had gold stitched into it. There's still a few threads poking through, wiry and scratchy, where the inner lining's worn away. It must have been such a beautiful thing once upon a time in some damned fairytale girl's wardrobe. Or maybe Suzie was telling a little bit of truth. I can imagine a showgirl strapped into it, serving up dances between drinks and fucks.

A sound, a ripple in the air, distracts me.

Shadows penetrate clouds of burnt umber.

Fingers lick my spine.

Cold breath chills my neck.

Oh, but I love me those shivers when the temperature outside plummets, and for a moment, your insides are hotter than your outsides. There's a storm brewing so hard it's squeezing my brain to a walnut, but I don't care. I'm waiting for the explosion, for hailstones the size of golf balls. Gonna dance me to London in a New York storm, wrapped in old gold and a tentacle of ribbons.

Didn't expect it to happen so fast.

Didn't expect to drop feet-first in front of a horse-drawn cab, neither.

"Get outta the way, ya stupid…"

No time to worry about where I'll wake up, but wake up I do. There's so much fabric hanging off me, it weighs a ton and it's tight, *really* tight. My eyes flutter open, all ladylike, and I'm still in this fucking great gown. It's so golden it hurts to look at it, and I can see how the pale corset I stole from Suzannah's corpse was all that remained of this radiant robe.

Whispers filter in from the corner of the room. I watch from my bed until, eventually, a smart gentleman emerges from behind a screen, followed by a mousy thing in a maid's outfit. They do some old-fashioned bowing and curtseying, and I wonder if I'm on stage in a *cor blimey* musical. But there's no theatre curtain; no audience apart from the costumed clowns that stand either side of the enormous bed I'm lying on.

I can see the man is desperate to speak, but I get in first.

"Where's the pea?"

He opens and closes his mouth several times, unable – presumably – to understand what the hell I'm talking about.

"Must be a hundred fucking mattresses on this bed. But I ain't no princess 'cos I can't feel no pea."

The pair blush. Guess they don't curse in this part of the world. Then the old goat sniggers.

"I believe, Maude, that her Ladyship is referring to the Andersen children's tale, The Princess and the Pea. Would I be correct, Madam?"

"That you would, erm...?"

"Larrocks, Madam. Your butler here at Meads House."

I stare at him. He stares at me. Maude stares at the floor.

"Forgive me," I say after a long awkward silence, trying to suck a posh English plum. "I think I must have had a bump on the head. I don't seem to remember arriving here." *Or who the fuck I'm supposed to be.*

Larrocks has caught on to that.

"Madam, Meads House is your new winter residence in Berkeley Square. As you know…"

Did he just wink at me?

"His Lordship has taken your son to Quebec until March to show him the business ropes."

My son?

"I'm sure you recall that young Clive is keen to become involved in the family's enterprises as soon as possible, university not being his, ah, *preferred* method of progression."

How quaint. My son's a money-whore, too stupid to get an education. Talking of money, well – thinking about it, I'm gonna need some stuff while I'm here, wherever this is. *When*ever this is.

"Larrocks," I say, playing with that accent again. "Fetch me today's newspaper, would you?"

Larrocks nods at Maude who scurries off, her little nose twitching, vole-like. Guess these servants all play different roles and I just insulted the butler, the top dog.

"Would her Ladyship like some tea to ease her nerves? Or an iced tonic, perhaps?"

"Depends what's it in it. Bring me the bottle, and I'll judge for myself."

He winces at my poor command of the language. I'm gonna have to play on this bump on the head business, or I'll end up in another psych ward.

"Wait!" I catch him before he backs out of the room, shutting the double doors as he goes.

"Madam?"

"I wonder if you ought to call the doctor, Larrocks. I don't feel too well."

"Please don't concern yourself, your Ladyship. Doctor Ryeslip is on his way."

I close my eyes, and it all goes dark. Dark like I've never seen in my life.

"**W**hat happened? Did she fall?"

"Not exactly. The cab driver said he was on his way back to the stables at the end of his shift when she just appeared in front of the carriage. Scared the horses witless, she did. No idea where she came from."

"Surely she must have run out in front of them from the pavement?"

They deliberate my sudden fall to earth for a while, and then it gets interesting.

"What in the blazes was she doing out alone on the streets? It's freezing out there."

The doc's clearly appalled by the apparent neglect.

"Well," Larrocks's voice drops to a soft low. "They did warn us before she came up to town that she was somewhat wild-hearted. She's an American, you know."

Really? Dammit, if I don't make my tongue bleed, biting down on it to stop the giggles. I choke instead and Ryeslip comes bumbling over, a Dickensian stereotype, bursting out of his ornate waistcoat, little round specs embedded into a nose that glows redder than his cheeks.

"Give me something for the pain, Doc" I plead.

Larrocks has these great slug-like eyebrows that rise at my request. I hadn't mentioned the pain before now. Ryeslip is all over me, pulling my eyelids up, down, sideways. He feels my head and shakes his own, tutting all the while.

"Where does it hurt, your Ladyship?"

"Oh come on, enough of this ladyship crap. Just call me by my name."

Ryeslip looks like I've stabbed him in the gut. Larrocks sighs audibly. I know it's not the done thing, but fuck this, I don't know how long I've got here, and whatever time's left, I want to spend my way.

"Lady Lucillah," the doctor continues. "If I could simply ascertain the area of concern then I shall be able to determine the required prescription for a tonic."

"Look," I say. "I heard you guys talking, and you're right. I am kinda wild." (*How wrong that sounds.*) "But I ain't Calamity Jane or Pocahontas. I'm just a woman that likes to do her own thing, where and when she feels like it."

I'm almost tempted to bring up the Suffragettes coming their way in a couple-a-decades' time with their clout and their causes, but this pair of middle-aged toffs are already completely confused by my outburst. It's not worth it. Ryeslip, I notice, has developed a purple sheen around his feet – gout, inevitably. I want no influence from that port he must swill. It's a headache in a bottle. Larrocks, on the other hand, is a sly one. I see traces of Chinese poppy glimmering with gold, and when little Maude comes-a-knocking with an enormous newspaper, I can see she's one for the gin. Well, well, well.

I pull at Ryeslip's sleeve.

"Fetch me something, Doc. Go on. None of that laudanum shit. Something to make me happy. Nothing too strong."

Ryeslip has diplomatically backed into the corner of the room, head bowed. Maude is unfolding that fucking newspaper, making a racket beyond belief, but it serves to muffle my conversation with the good doctor.

"I have just the thing, Lady Lucillah. A tonic blend made from a natural curative from the South Americas, the coca leaf."

I snort like I never snorted charlie. This is ridiculous.

"You're too kind, Doc," I say.

I won't use the stuff. Like the tainted shadows I see shimmering around imbibers and addicts, I only need to be in the presence of poisons to be able to scratch the itch. It'll do. Ryeslip nods to himself and bids me goodbye with a promise to return within the hour. Larrocks lets him out but remains in the room. I want him gone; there's something about him that gives me the creeps. I wouldn't even be surprised if he knows. About me. About Suzannah. About the corset of gold.

"Maude."

She recoils as though I've slapped her, from all the way over here, from my bed.

"Would you help me out of this dress into something more comfortable?"

I'm getting the hang of this English parlay.

Once Ryeslip's returned and handed over his little gift, I'm going to party for an hour then escape onto the streets of London.

It's 1898. Victoria's still on the throne, all empirical, but it don't stop her being as big an opium sucker as 21st century junkies. Worse, she's the pusher, too, by default. Her fault. Everyone's dealer. They say I might meet her at some ball next month. I'm supposed to be impressed. Fuck that.

"Decline," I say. "I've got better things to do."

Maude can't take it.

"But… it's Her Majesty. The invitation is, well, an *honour* your Ladyship."

"Not where I come from, Maude. C'mon. Help me get out of this monster and into something loose."

"Loose?"

"Sure. This corset's fucking killing me."

I think Maude's going to cry.

"Listen, sweet little mouse. I say it how it is. I'm sorry if it offends. You're just gonna have to man up and deal with it."

She tries, then starts to sob, funny little snuffles and nose bubbling with snot. When I reach out to give her a hug, she stiffens. Yet again, it's not the done thing. She stands, and as she begins to unlace the corset, I *shift* like I've shot fifty storeys down the world's fastest elevator. I grab Maude's hand; it's trembling.

"No. Leave it."

She must think I'm a psychopath. Mixed messages and all that.

"Sorry," I say. "What I mean is, can we get the rest of it off? Leave the corset 'til last?"

She undresses me like she's supposed to until I'm standing there looking mighty fine in just the golden corset, which has pinched even my scrawny waist into the width of a fat boy's wrist. Maude's totally embarrassed by my removal of the balloonish knickerbockers, looking everywhere but at what's between my naked thighs.

"Okay." I finger her fingers. "Let's do this – slowly."

We attack the knotted ribbon together. With her helping it seems to stop the shift. I guide her, indicating that we can relace it, but looser, so that I can breathe. Or at least that's what I tell her.

There's a mumble of voices outside the door, and I know Ryeslip is back with my little pick-me-up.

"Tell me," I whisper at Maude. "Where do you go at night?"

The maid steps back, her lips suddenly tight.

"I'm sure I don't know what you mean, my Lady."

A knock at the door.

"Come on, Maude. Give it up. We both know you like a tot of mother's milk of an evening."

She shudders and backs away. She thinks I'm going to fire her ass.

"Wait. I mean it. Where do you go? Will you take me later? I just want some fun. No one needs to know."

The door's opening.

"I'll make it worth your while."

I sound like some old Film Noir starlet. I like it. Ryeslip enters the room looking not only pleased with himself but also somewhat under the influence of the soon-to-be proffered tonic, judging by the umber hue at his throat.

"I finish at eight," Maude whispers, wrapping a cloak around me to protect my dignity from the doctor, who should know better than to enter a lady's boudoir without permission, *don't ya know*. I give her the biggest wink and she blushes. It's sweet.

"I'll be waiting."

Lady and the Tramp, out on the town. Except she's the lady.

How was I to know what they'd do? Suzannah's angels are here. Same guys. Same skin. This time, I can see their filthy wings; bones full of malevolent marrow, feather shafts fat with venom when they should be hollow. They'll never fly, high though they might be. What I want to know is how they got here. Why they killed Suzannah. And why they've just killed Maude.

Her head's in my lap. Just the head. The snot that had bubbled from her nose back in my bedroom now coats her entire face. Her neck is a turbulent scarf of frothing red, which soaks through the cloak she'd covered me with. It streams, steams in the chill of the city night onto my bare legs. Sticky.

I heard her call them 'The Gin Seekers'. I thought she was just a girl who liked a good drink, but from the pushing and the shoving and the scream still carved onto her face, she must have owed them big time. No more, though. Whatever her debt, it's lost. They tossed her body away like some useless rag. They didn't see me. But I saw them. I fucking saw *them*. Gin seekers? Skin seekers is what they are.

I can't go back to Berkeley Square, not with Maude's skull-mess all over me. I need to get away from here, but those angels? They're lingering, their feet hovering inches above the ground, above the ice. I'll never get past them. There's one, slightly shorter than the others – squat with muscles like someone's hammered him with a compressor; he's their leader or master or whatever macabre moniker these freaks use. He stands in the middle of a clumsy circle, surrounded and protected by them as they posture and preen. He's mean. Meaner than the rest of them put together. And as much as I can see the crud seeping from his soul in waves, I realise he's sniffed me out.

The fat, broken nose trembles like a dog's, his mouth a downturned grimace as he sucks in my scent. He breaks the circle, striding on air faster than is possible until he's right in front of me, where I'm hiding behind a pile of crates, backed up against a wall wet with moss.

What can I do? He's got me.

I stand up.

"I'm not afraid of you."

Maude's head flies from my fingers and slaps hard into his jaw, spraying him with fluids. It's enough. I'm scooting around that corner, invoking some New Age white-light defence shit, and I run, not looking back until my bare feet slip in something faecal and wet, and I come crashing to my knees.

I'm gonna get killed.

I wait.

I'm still waiting.

Take a look over my shoulder.

They're not there.

No chase.

No angels.

A clip and a clop and a clatter of hooves and wheels, and before I have time to wonder what the hell to do next, a fancy carriage pulls up beside me, its door squeaking slowly open. Now, I've seen me those Ripper movies, so when a voice says "Get in" I'm ready to take off the other way, but there's something familiar about the voice.

"Zillah, quick."

It makes me shiver. Who the fuck knows I'm here?

It's Larrocks, of course, it is. I do as I'm told – a first. He's still dressed as a butler, but there's a steely look in his eye that wasn't there back in Berkeley Square.

"You stink," he says, and throws me a very modern towel. I wipe the crap out of my toes, staring at him, trying to recall if I've met him before London, before 1898.

"Who are you? I mean, really?"

"It's not important. We just need to get you out of this place. They'll know where to find you, you idiot."

He's raging at me like I'm a kid. I get caught up in the energy behind that anger; it's invigorating. My head pops with it.

"Hey," I grin. "Have one of Zillah's best smiles before you burst something."

I bloom at him, lips kinking in a twist. I've been told it's adorable. I keep it for special occasions. Larrocks sighs; throws himself back on the padded leather seat.

"You don't remember again, do you? I thought when you showed up you knew what you were doing this time. Where've you been? Everyone's been looking for you."

I shrug. No clues then.

"Stumbling," I say. "Dragging myself from town to town for thirty-odd years, sucking up trouble and spitting it out." Larrocks remains stiff. He's waiting. I give him nothing. "Look. I don't know you, And who's 'everyone'? I don't do the *friends* thing so who the hell are you talking about?"

"Zillah, just how big are these pockets of yours? These holes with no memories?"

Put like that, I understand what he's getting at. I've been drifting my entire life seems to me, though I always end up back with Carl in Manhattan. The thought shakes me, and I realise I'm fingering the scar on my face, the crease that defines me. As what though? As who?

"I don't know."

Suddenly, I'm small as a kitten and nothing like as cute. I'm scrunched into a ball, wrapped in terror. Larrocks reaches out to me.

"It's alright. You're in one of your phases. We need to get you back to New York, safely."

"Back to the 21st century?"

He takes my hand.

"This *is* the 21st century Zillah."

I'm supposed to believe him. It's true I climbed into a London carriage and fell out of a black sedan, but I know where I've been – and it wasn't this fucked-up backwater American town that's still creaming off the 60s.

I've made him tell me his name, at least. And it *does* ring bells, great churning church bells that splice into the scars on my flesh, making them sting, permeating them with songs of sadness.

"Johnny Reeds," I say. "How many times have you saved my life?"

"Enough. And it's John. Just, John."

We're sitting at a bar in this unfamiliar town. The sky outside is nicotine yellow, the cars coated with an invasive frost as pretty as a migraine arc. I hug a neat Jack while Johnny downs a second. He looks exhausted.

"You've got to understand Zillah. The way you see things? It's different, *special*."

That gets a snort from me. It's one of the words they

use just before they section me. That, I remember. But not afterwards. Not until the next time.

"See you ditched the butler's garb."

He shakes his head.

"I was never…"

"I know. But to me that's exactly what you were. You and the doc and poor little Maude. All terribly English in a terribly English house in a terribly English city."

He sighs. He's good at that. He swivels me around on the bar stool, points outside.

"See that place? Just there? It's a florist's and tea rooms. And that woman dressing the window?"

It's Maude. I don't say it.

"You staggered in there just as she was serving up breakfasts, then you passed out."

I can't make any sense of it.

"The doc?"

"A paramedic."

In my head, in my head, in my head, it can't be. "But the angels. Surely…"

"The what?"

"You know. The guys that killed Maude." Even as I say it, I see the English maid, quite alive, arranging hydrangeas in that shop front of hers. Johnny's gonna laugh at that one, get me carted off to a clinic. I look away, resigned to my fucking fate. No point running.

"You mean The Gin Seekers?"

My head snaps back. I stare him out. Those haunted eyes win the game. It's my turn to whisper.

"That's what *she* called them."

"That's what everyone calls them. It's what they call themselves." He drops a nod to the barkeep who carefully measures us another tot each. Johnny's downed his before it even hits the bottom of the glass. He leans forward.

"They killed Suzannah."

It's an explosion in my head, hearing her name again. My flesh starts to crawl and I realise I'm still wearing the remains of the corset over a skinny black vest and shorts so short I forgot they were there. The faded girdle is barely more than a few shredded ribbons that dangle down and tickle my bare legs, yellow and tobacco-stained like the sky outside. I'm wearing Suzannah. I'm trailing her death, dragging it with me.

"How do you know Suzannah?"

He sucks in air. Blows it back out again. There's no cigarette.

"She's… she was my sister."

The room's always there for me, Carl told me again when I walked across the shelter threshold this morning. They'd moved the kid who'd been using it during my absence to a smaller place – he looked a meek one; I won't get a kicking for it. My things are gone from the walls again, but that's cool; I can find new pieces.

I tell Johnny to wait as I hang up the few items of clothing from my bag. There's not much. He sits patiently on my bed, and when I'm done and turn to him, he says, "Are you sure you can do this?" There's a light of hope behind the tears washing his eyes.

"Let's go."

We're outta there, seeking gin, seeking seekers.

They're hanging out where Suzannah told me, about nine or ten of them. Ordinary men, boys. No wings. And there he is – that squat, angry little shit who runs the gang. He's barely eighteen.

"Mysore," Johnny whispers. To himself. I don't recognise the name.

We watch from Johnny's car, windows half down. One of them strips off his T-shirt and struts across the concrete, getting nods and whistles from his audience who wrap themselves up against the blossoming snow. T-shirt boy turns his back to us and there's a huge tattoo, still fresh and raw at the edges. It shows a tilted bottle pouring liquid over a peak-titted nubile. She undulates as he struts, causing the liquid to splash over ornate letters. G. I. N.

"What are they doing, running moonshine as well as meth?"

Johnny shakes his head.

"It means Girls In Need. They seek out vulnerable girls, dope 'em up, put them on the street and slice them when they don't pay."

"Same old, same old," I shrug. "So what about Suzie?"

He doesn't take his eyes off the Seekers when he answers my question.

"You knew her. Always dreaming. Always trusting the wrong people. She came over from London to live with me about five years ago. Worked for a while then she started drifting."

Just like me.

"You let her?"

"She wasn't a kid. I had about as much control over her as I do of you."

I honestly don't know what to make of that remark. But it doesn't matter because The Gin Seekers have seen us, and… Jesus, their wings *are* real.

"Johnny!"

"I know."

He doesn't drive away. He gets out of the car and he's got all these little blades pinging from his knuckles, from his knees, from his shoes. He runs *at* them instead of running away. It stops them in their tracks 'cos he's faster than them, almost flying towards them. I don't know what I thought he was going to do, but I didn't expect him to kill them. I open the car door and without even looking back, Johnny shouts at me over his shoulder.

"Stay in the car. Lock the doors."

He's trampolining; bouncing on the balls of his feet, swinging around in spirals, and slicing his attackers' faces. They're at him like hornets, but Johnny's the sharpest. Their blades might be bigger, but he's got more on him than the rest of them put together. His fingers are scissors, all the better to cut throats. There's blood spraying everywhere and he's doing it – killing them – he must be, but I can no longer tell because the windscreen is dripping with red.

I won't do as I'm told; I won't. I'm out of the car, a little pistol I saw him hide under his seat earlier, shaking in my hands. I don't even know what to do with it, whether it's loaded. But I'll use it if I have to. Or try.

I don't have to.

The gang members are already pulling back, some of them openly sobbing, wounds gaping under their arms, along their spines. And I know what Johnny's done.

"Your turn," he says. Mysore is on the ground, his face pressed into the concrete, Johnny on his back. "Suzannah said you were angels."

The leader of The Gin Seekers tries to reply, but his teeth are smashed, and his tongue's so swollen it's poking from his lips like a slab of pocked meat. He may not be able to speak, but he can scream and fuck me, but he hollers and squeals when Johnny stabs a fat knife under one of his shoulder blades and slits.

"Pigs might fly," Johnny spits into Mysore's face as he labours over the gristle before turning his attention to the other side. "But your flying days are over."

I give in to nausea and puke in the gutter to the sound of my saviour clipping an angel's wings.

I'm on a high tide, flowing in and out. Fast, faster, too fast. Fuck – next thing I know, I'm in the hospital, black and blue. Not my body, my mind. Johnny's gone like he was never here in the first place. I won't forget him this time; at least, I'll try not to. The angels are gone too, cleaned up, cleared out.

I told the white coats what happened, about Suzannah and London, about Johnny and The Gin Seekers. They don't believe me. No evidence, they say, and I should get some rest.

It's probably better that way.

It may not be the truth how some folks see it, but it's my truth. And for now – that's all I have.

LILY CHILDS has an obsession with misunderstood demons and takes unsavoury delight in Victorian underworlds, twisted myths and the necrotic. She writes Gothic horror, psychological crime and ghost stories and has contributed tales to numerous anthologies since 2009. Former Horror Editor at *Thrillers, Killers and Chillers* ezine, Lily has recently completed her first novel, *Sixsmith*, where asylum-wandering wraiths bound to past and present by the supernatural acts of a violent sadist, scream for their voices to be heard. Lily lives by the sea in the south of England with her daughter, husband and black cat, Scarlet.

SALT LAKE CITY

Brian Evenson

I arrived quite late in Salt Lake City, hours after every restaurant had closed and hours before any would open again in the morning. It was bitter cold, a light dusting of snow on the ground, and the air itself felt sparse, like there was too little of it, like no matter how much I breathed in, it would never be enough. I was not used to the altitude anymore, I told myself, since I had not lived in Salt Lake City for a number of years. However, some portion of my oxygen-deprived brain suspected it was more than that.

My flight from Los Angeles had been delayed by an hour, then by two, then finally, five. They told us repeatedly that we must stay in the boarding area because as soon as the plane was ready the flight would leave immediately. I fell for this, so remained, hungry and uncomfortable, at the gate for hours, only getting up when I saw our pilot making his surreptitious escape. I hurried to the restroom only to find said pilot at the urinal adjacent to my own. *Uh-huh*, I heard him say, *uh-huh. Sure.* At first, I thought he was talking to himself, but then I realized there was a piece of plastic clipped over his ear. He told this piece of plastic that the delay was due to a passenger on the previous flight, the flight from Salt Lake City to Los Angeles, having opened the door during descent and leaped out. Or not leaped exactly; he had been sucked out along with several bags, a man's shirt—somehow torn right off his body—a number of shoes and socks, and a carrier containing a small dog. A Maltese, maybe, he thought, though he admitted he was not certain. And then he noticed me listening, stopped talking, zipped up, and left.

I almost didn't board the flight. If I hadn't already waited so long and didn't have a meeting for a potential acquisition in downtown Salt Lake City the next morning, I wouldn't have. It just seemed like a bad omen. I tried to Google what the pilot had said had happened on the flight but found nothing relevant. Was the incident being hushed up? Perhaps this sort of thing happened all the time but was always quickly swept under the rug.

Ideally, I would have liked to have asked the pilot a few questions before boarding. For instance, would we be flying on the same plane? I suspected not. I suspected that once a door was forcibly opened, a whole set of safeguard procedures had to be followed, and the door had to be replaced and the new door certified as airworthy. Was "airworthy" really a word? Probably the delay was due to the airline having to find another plane rather than waiting on a replacement for the door. But it would have been nice to know for certain.

The pilot was now huddled with the crew near the entrance to the jet bridge. Though I could imagine approaching him alone to ask my questions, I could not imagine speaking to him with all those others as my audience.

And I also had questions I wanted to ask about who the person was who had thrown open the door and been sucked out. Male? Female? Tall? Old? Young? Deranged? Was he, if it was a he, like me, from Utah? Why did it feel important to me to know that? Was he, if it was a he, Mormon? Or, like me, an ex-Mormon? How much, in short, like me was he?

I mention all this just to give you some idea of the state of mind I was in when we touched down in Salt Lake City five hours late and in the middle of the night. Perhaps it explains something. There is something fractured about Salt Lake City, to begin with, a sense that it is two cities at once, one religious, the other secular. Most of the time, these two overlapping cities coexist and engage in a kind of awkward insouciant dance, each pretending to be unaware of the other. *Be in the world but not of the world* was the maxim I had been made to memorize as a young Mormon child, which had always made me feel that the culture I had grown up in was engaged in an artificially-induced form of schizophrenia, that the people who were out in the world around me were not always occupying the same world as me. In a word, I found myself ill at ease being back in Salt Lake City, and the flight delay amplified this. Being here made me feel as if I were not myself. But "myself": what, really, if anything, did that mean?

I was starving. I hadn't eaten for what felt like days. I had even missed the small packet of peanuts normally served on the plane because someone on the plane, so the pilot announced at the beginning of the flight, had a peanut allergy apparently so severe that the opening of a single bag of peanuts anywhere on the plane would lead to his demise. When we landed at the Salt Lake City airport, before disembarking, we were told that because of the lateness of our arrival, there were very few remaining taxis and that these would be dismissed soon, so I hurried past vending machines and down the escalator to hop into one and then sat there helplessly because the driver refused to budge. In the end, there were four of us, all strangers, crammed into the same cab, each paying the full rate to go into the city, and I was the last to be dropped off at my hotel.

At the front desk, I was asked if I wanted a goldfish for my room. "A what?" I said, certain I had misheard. When it turned out I had not misheard, I was so startled that I said, for lack of anything better to say, "Yes, please." I held out my hands, ready to receive a bowl, but then was told I would find the goldfish waiting in my room. This made me feel that I was being assigned *to* a goldfish rather than a goldfish being assigned to *me*. I was, I felt, being permitted to share a goldfish's room.

"I'm starving," I informed the somewhat disheveled clerk at the desk. He just nodded. "Where can I find an all-night diner?" I asked.

There wasn't one nearby, I was told. There was apparently one about twenty minutes away, but the clerk said that by the time I called a cab, and it arrived and drove me there, it would almost be time for the diners within walking distance to open. It would, he claimed, be better to wait until morning.

I wasn't so sure it would be. I was starving, but I was exhausted, too. Still uncertain, I went up to the goldfish's room. It seemed to be circus-themed, replete with elaborate and nauseating draperies, as if I were lost in the petticoats of a giant and garish clown. The goldfish was in a bowl on the nightstand, exactly where I would typically set my wallet and phone. I dropped my bag on the floor and then collapsed, sprawling onto the bed, fully clothed.

I lay there for some minutes. I couldn't sleep. I was too hungry to sleep. Plus, I felt something was watching me. I looked over. The goldfish was staring right at me, its tail lazily swishing to hold it in place. I closed my eyes and turned my head away, but I could still feel the creature staring at me. *Perhaps*, I thought, *it wants me to get the hell out of its fucking room.*

I got up, telling myself that if I fell asleep now, I would sleep through my meeting, fail to make a successful acquisition and be fired. I put on my coat and left the room.

Before I knew it, I was outside and walking. The streets were deserted at this hour. I could see the mountains looming just beyond the city, visible against the night because of the snow that covered them. The air seemed even colder than before, so cold that my footsteps sounded like bones snapping. Not human bones: small bones, like the bones of deceased and long desiccated birds. I was freezing. I told myself I would warm up if I walked quickly enough. But no matter how fast I walked, I did not seem to be warming up. Maybe there was a convenience store nearby where I could find something to eat, but as I kept walking, the street seemed to grow more and more residential. *I should,* I told myself, *go back.*

I did not go back.

And then, suddenly, almost without my knowing how it happened, someone was walking beside me. I did not feel threatened, though I cannot say why. His manner, perhaps. He was tall, a little paunchy, and walked with a slight limp. He was about my size, or, rather, exactly my size. Indeed, he looked very much like me—so much so that I found myself disconcerted. I had a hard time looking at him any way but sidelong, and from furtiveness of the glances he kept casting over at me, I suspected he felt the same. Unlike me, he had no beard and was clean-cut, hair trimmed short. For just a moment, it felt like Salt Lake City had split me in two, that here I was, someone who was both in the world and of the world, walking beside the me that was *not* of the world, the self that had remained trapped here when I had left.

But then I remembered the moment when, in 1984, living in Salt Lake City and attending East High, I had gone to an all-ages punk show at the Indian Center to see a band called the Potato Heads. For days prior, people had asked me if I was the bassist for the Potato Heads, and when I finally saw them play, I understood why. He not only looked like me, he even played his bass guitar exactly how I imagined I would play a bass if I knew how to play it. He saw it, too: after the set, he walked toward me and then saw me and stopped dead. And then, very carefully, he walked a wide semi-circle around me to avoid me.

And here, years later, here he was, walking beside me. If it was him. It was hard to make him out clearly in the dark. But it was at least possible.

"Hey," he said. It was as if when he said it, he was using my voice.

"Hello," I responded. "Have we met before?"

"Going to Gilgal?" he asked, ignoring my question.

"Gilgal?" I didn't know what he was talking about. I had never heard of a Gilgal. "Is it far?"

He shrugged. "Another block or so. You're walking straight toward it."

"Can I get something to eat there?"

He stopped abruptly and turned to face me, staring straight at me for the first time. My steps stuttered, and I stopped as well. His eyes were so steady and unblinking that it took all I had not to look away. And then he shook his head, turned away, and began moving again.

Gilgal. There was, on the street we were on, nothing but ordinary buildings, a few businesses. An ivy-smothered 19th-century brick building that had been repurposed as an office interiors store. A smallish house set back from the road. An aging apartment complex that had been updated by having panels of pre-rusted metal attached to it, as if Richard Serra had had a brief but unsuccessful stint in architecture in the Beehive State. Another house, decaying brick. And then, beyond that, a long driveway.

"After you," said the bassist, if that's who or what he was, and made a sweeping motion with his hands.

I followed the drive back until the road behind me was lost from view. It ended in a gate. *Gilgal Gardens*, a sign on it read, followed by the hours of operation.

"It's closed," I said. "It won't open for hours."

"That's not meant for you," he said. "You're hungry. Clamber over." When I made no move to do so, he reached over and pushed me toward the gate.

In a moment I was up and swinging my leg over the top and dropping to the ground on the other side. The bassist was suddenly there beside me, though I had not seen him go over. He tugged me forward.

An asphalt path led back to stone paths and through a series of sculptures. A large piece of flattened quartzite with the body of a man holding a sword etched into it: "Captain of the Lord's Host," it was titled. The head of the statue remained unworked: a strange, lumped swelling of rock, as if the head had swollen to enormous proportions. An arch of balanced stones and a keystone, with four large stone books to one side and a smoothed spire to the other. A small, artificially constructed cave. A bible verse carved into stone, a man's decapitated head nestled beside it, its gaze stunned as if unable to believe it had been parted from its body.

"Why is all this here?" I asked.

"Gilgal," the bassist said.

Two hearts made of stone, one pale red, the other dirty white. They were nestled in a small cave that seemed as if it could be a split-open chest, two hands reaching down from the cave's ceiling as if to push the hearts together. A dismembered and overly large stone body: a huge foot, bits of half-buried arms, a leprous head with closed eyes.

And then, finally, around a corner, a sphinx—but even from a distance, I could see the face was wrong. Not a woman's face, but a man's and familiar too: the face of the prophet Joseph Smith, founder of the Mormon church. I came closer and closer still until I found myself standing between the sphinx's legs, touching the face.

"Go ahead," said a voice behind me, and when I turned I saw the bassist had pursed his lips into a kiss. "Feed."

I looked back at the sphinx and saw now a slick line of darkness gathered between the statue's lips. As I stared, the stone lips groaned slightly and opened a little further, a black bubble slowly congealing. I brought my head forward and opened my mouth, and began to suck, drawing out the viscous substance until it started to ooze down my throat.

Behind me, I felt the weight of another body pressed against my back, the pricking at the base of my neck as something with impossibly fine teeth bit gently in. I paid this no heed, just kept sucking, sucking, feeling at once full, too full, and yet as if something was simultaneously being drained from me.

Back at the hotel, morning now, a message was waiting at the front desk: the meeting was cancelled. When I took out my phone to call to reschedule, I found I had left it in airplane mode. There were a dozen messages on my phone, none of which I had been aware of until just then.

I listened to them. The earliest had come the day before, while I was waiting in LAX for the plane to take off. *Don't come,* the voice of my boss said and then went on to explain that Mahonri, the person in charge of the account I had been scheduled to try to acquire, had apparently been sucked out of a plane. His body had not yet been recovered and might never be. "He was not even supposed to be on a plane," said his boss, the head of the company, in the message, and then mentioned that they were in the process of rectifying certain "financial improprieties" that, with Mahonri's death, had come abruptly to light.

I tried to call him back. He didn't answer.

The goldfish was dead, floating upside down along the surface of the water. I carried the bowl into the hallway and abandoned it there. The room belonged to me now.

I stripped off my clothing and settled into bed, then turned off the lights. I could still taste the darkness thick in my mouth. I could still feel the pricking at the back of my neck. *I will*, I told myself, *sleep for a few hours and then I will once again leave Salt Lake City, this time, I hope, for good.* I drifted off slowly, imagining I could hear the rush of the wind around the plane that later today would carry me away, my hand flexing gently as, in my waking dream, I reached for the chrome handle that would open the airplane door.

BRIAN EVENSON is the author of a dozen books of fiction, most recently the story collection *A Collapse of Horses* (Coffee House Press 2016) and the novella *The Warren* (Tor.com 2016). He has also recently published *Windeye* (Coffee House Press 2012) and *Immobility* (Tor 2012), both of which were finalists for a Shirley Jackson Award. His novel *Last Days* won the American Library Association's award for Best Horror Novel of 2009. His novel *The Open Curtain* (Coffee House Press) was a finalist for an Edgar Award and an International Horror Guild Award. Other books include *The Wavering Knife* (which won the IHG Award for best story collection), *Dark Property,* and *Altmann's Tongue.* He has translated work by Christian Gailly, Jean Frémon, Claro, Jacques Jouet, Eric Chevillard, Antoine Volodine, Manuela Draeger, and David B. He is the recipient of three O. Henry Prizes as well as an NEA fellowship. His work has been translated into Czech, French, Italian, Greek, Hungarian, Japanese, Persian, Russia, Spanish, Slovenian, and Turkish. He lives in Los Angeles and teaches in the Critical Studies Program at CalArts.

AMSTERDAM

Tim Lees

I don't suppose you remember the Ahn. Few people do, these days, though once, they were considered a significant phenomenon – "harbingers of seismic change," as one excited pundit called them. Today, they're just another piece of history, gone the way of bell-bottoms and platform shoes. The world moves on.

They looked like anyone. You couldn't spot them in a crowd. But you'd be hunched over the gas fire in your rented room when one of them would gradually congeal out of the air beside you, whispering some cryptic or uplifting phrase: "The real world is a much, much bigger place," perhaps, or, "Give it a minute. You'll get used to it." Then they were gone. They didn't fade or wink out. It was more as if you'd turned your head a moment (though you hadn't), and they'd vanished while your gaze was elsewhere.

For eight or nine months, maybe a year, they haunted us. We all saw them. Me, my friends – my generation. Raised in the boom, matured in the bust, that was us. We lived in bedsits and shared houses, already in our twenties, and still waiting for our lives to start. It wasn't our fault. Yet into this unhappy scene, the Ahn infused themselves, hailed by some as prophets, angels, messengers of God.

I hated them.

To me, they were wish fulfillment, compensation – phony reassurance that our lives were meaningful, even while every aspect of society said otherwise.

Besides, I'd got my own ideas about the Ahn.

People would talk obsessively about their meetings, analyze each word and gesture, reel off dates, times, locations –

That didn't mean those meetings actually took place. Or not in any real, objective sense.

No witnesses, no onlookers. Ahn encounters were invariably solitary. Even in public, it was always as if everybody else had looked away, right at the crucial moment.

The Ahn were creatures we *remembered* – remembered what they'd said, what they'd looked like, what they'd done. If we saw them at all, we saw them in the rearview mirror.

The Ahn lived in our memories. In memories, and nowhere else.

This, then, was my theory, which I'd expound at length, usually to the annoyance of whoever I was with. Though I kept quiet, staying with Henk and Beth. Somehow, I knew already that they'd not approve.

I just didn't know why.

A msterdam.

Forget Anne Frank, van Gogh, the Rijksmuseum. To anyone my age, back then, the place was Partytown. Pot was legal. There were cafés, clubs and bars. Porn and prostitution. In England, fashions had moved on, but the 'Dam was full of aging hippies, and despite its touted decadence, a quaintly bourgeois air prevailed, a mood the haze of cannabis seemed merely to enhance: "Chill out, man."

And yes, it had its seamy side. You could get hurt there, and hurt badly, if you didn't watch yourself. But Terri was a bright girl, and when she told me that's where she was going to live, I wasn't worried – only saddened I'd see less of her. I was still in England then. She sent me postcards: *Having a great time, you should visit.* Even when the cards stopped, I wasn't much concerned, or not at first. There could have been a dozen reasons: new job, new home, new boy- or girlfriend. Terri's love affairs, whether with men or women, tended to be brief, but she'd a gift for staying friendly with her exes, as I well knew. The postcards were her trademark, her way of saying, *Hi, I'm thinking of you.* A lot of us received them. Sometimes, I'd even send one back.

I missed her postcards.

And perhaps, if things had been a little better in my own life, I might have shrugged it all off, and moved on. But Terri's silence – so unlike her – came to gnaw at me.

I missed her, that's the truth. Missed her far more than I'd thought I would.

I knew the guy that she'd been staying with, Henk Visser.

I'd met him on my own visits. So one night, mildly drunk, I commandeered the hallway phone and called him.

"Terri there?" I said.

Simple question. Only that's where things got weird.

There was a long, long pause.

I heard him take a breath.

No, he said. She wasn't there.

Where was she?

He didn't know.

When had he last seen her?

Oh, a month ago. Two, maybe.

"Two *months?*" I said.

"She is fine, I am sure. You should not be anxious."

Henk's English was good, but his accent was as thick as soup. I couldn't read the nuances, and the more blasé he seemed, the more uneasy I became.

He gave an awkward laugh.

"You know Terri," he said. "Here one minute, then –"

"I'm coming over."

I made some rapid mental calculations: time, money, commitments. I couldn't afford a hostel. Could I stay with Henk? Just for a night or two?

"You are welcome here, of course. We have no guests at the moment. But I think you are worried about nothing. If you wait a few days –"

"See you Tuesday," I said, and put the phone down.

As it was, I got there Wednesday. I'd spent Tuesday on the bus to London, then a train to Harwich for the overnight ferry. We see-sawed, lurching through the waves. I slept patchily, and once, I dreamed of Terri, something I hadn't done in years. We were in some kind of dispute, I don't know what about, and she was stubborn – more so than I'd ever seen her. She said, "I want to do it, and I'm going to do it." None of this had ever happened in real life. I struggled to come up with counter-arguments, but the best that I could manage was, "For me? Please?"

Then I woke up.

An Ahn was standing over me. His face was half in shadow, and I could see right through it to the wall beyond. He was only visible where the light hit him full-on.

"You don't have to explain yourself," he said.

It was nonsense, of course – one of those pithy sayings they'd come out with, so vague that it was easy to take personally. But I got up quickly, went down to the bar, ordered a beer and a whiskey. Halfway through the beer, I bought another whiskey.

I didn't sleep again.

Henk Visser lived near Oosterpark. There was a healthy street life here, even in the winter chill; tall, handsome Somali women haggling with the local street vendors, breath like smoke in the morning air. Henk was home. Lean, slightly stooped, and looking studious in his horn-rimmed glasses – he'd been working on his doctorate for years – his long brown hair was streaked with gray, and the brackets around his mouth were more pronounced than I remembered them. He met me with a formal handshake, then took me for breakfast at a local café.

"You look tired," he said.

"You've heard from her…?"

"From Terri? No."

The café was loud. Crowded. We ate Uitsmijters and drank big, rustic-style mugs of hot, black coffee. We did some catching up, just for politeness' sake. Then I lit a cigarette and said, "Terri."

He moved his hands, searching for words.

"She comes and goes," he told me. "That is Terri, yes? Always moving, always something new." He took a drink, hiding his mouth. "She has many friends," he said.

"Friends? You mean relationships?"

"You know. For a drink, a meal. That sort of thing."

"No one special?"

Henk smiled and touched my arm. "Relax, my friend. She spoke about you often, and always kindly. She was not seeing anyone, I think."

"She sent me postcards."

"Yes…?"

"Street scenes. Van Gogh pics. Oh – and a raunchy one from a sex shop. But she put that in an envelope, thank God."

"The postcards. Yes."

"Then nothing. Nothing at all. Two months now. And that's not like her, is it?"

The coffee machine gave a hiss, drowning conversation. After which, Henk said, "She will turn up. Have faith. People come and go. This is natural, I think."

"Natural."

"Of course! Now you are here, you can ask questions, you can see if anyone knows. But don't forget: you must enjoy yourself. This is vacation, yes?"

I hadn't thought of it like that.

And I didn't now, either.

Henk's girlfriend, Beth, had the ground floor flat, while Henk's was right above. I could sleep at Henk's place, he said. He'd stay at hers.

"I hope you will be comfortable here. This is our temple."

I laughed, then realized he was serious.

He put a mattress on the floor for me.

"You would like to smoke a joint? It will help you sleep."

I watched him skinning up, and we passed the spliff between us without saying much. Then he rose, slapped his thighs, and made to exit.

"I will be downstairs. Come see me when you wake, yes?"

The joint didn't help me sleep. But for the first time, it made me wonder what it was that I was doing there, as if my obvious motive – searching for a missing friend – were somehow spurious or insincere, and my unconscious mind was planning something much more devious.

England could be brutal, and I didn't blame Terri in the least for leaving, seeking out a kinder, more benign regime. We'd been close once, and even now I saw her as a big part of my life. But her exile, then her disappearance, hit me in a way that I could not define, as if my own identity were somehow compromised, some crucial element cut out of me. I'd felt the same after my father died, or when I'd split up with my first serious girlfriend. In my current stoned and dream-like state, it seemed that finding Terri would return a vanished aspect of myself – my youth, perhaps – my hope.

And more: it was the right thing to do. Chivalrous, even a little bit heroic. Yet when I thought about it, this, too, looked suspect. Did I really see myself as some kind of knight errant, a Philip Marlowe, out to find a damsel in distress?

If so, I'd no idea where to begin.

I woke late in the afternoon, rested but edgy, and still stoned. I took a look around the room. A temple, yes. But to whom?

A Dali print on one wall. Opposite, a picture of the Buddha and the wheel of life. On the mantelpiece, a retort filled with a bright green liquid (candle wax, maybe?), and next to that, the wedge-shaped skull of a bird; a pair of ram's horns, two silver chalices, a sheaf of joss sticks in a brass holder. Elsewhere, mortars and pestles and a homemade dagger with runes and other symbols scratched into the blade, like something from a horror film.

Then, tucked away under a dust sheet at the far end of the room, I found a backpack and a pair of cardboard boxes, stuffed with somebody's possessions. And I felt my heart jump.

These were Terri's, obviously. I saw clothes, sketchbooks, cosmetics, and other personal items, things I doubted that she'd just abandon. For the moment, I didn't feel entitled to go through them, piece by piece, but I did a quick, cursory search in the hope that something might leap out at me.

What I wanted was a diary. *Tomorrow, I leave for...* But there was no diary. I flicked through her sketchbooks. I'd forgotten what an artist she was. She worked mainly in pencil, or with colored crayons. Copies of van Gogh – details, not the full picture – then some scenes from life, faces at a bar, sunset over a canal, and portraits. I recognized Henk and one or two other people I'd met during a previous visit.

At last, in what I took to be her most recent book – half-full, and with some chilly winter scenes – I found pictures of a young, good-looking guy, more punk than hippie, with his short, spiked hair, earring, and pierced lip. These were her final drawings. Under one, she'd written, "Nik." Nik, with no C. Typical, I thought. A new boyfriend? She'd certainly put work into the studies, no question there.

I went downstairs and showed the book to Henk.

"You know this guy?"

He frowned, shook his head.

We smoked another joint.

"I will take you to talk with her friends," he offered. "Perhaps you will… discover something." He rose and took his coat from the hanger. "Who knows? Perhaps we will find this mysterious Nik, eh?"

He was far too casual about it. But never mind – at least I'd got a start.

The canals were frozen. Crows and seagulls rummaged in the debris scattered on the ice, strutting like little gauleiters, or pecking irritably at each other. A row of barges had been moored along the bank, then trapped by the freeze. We stopped at one, and Henk called, "Mike? Mike? You are home?"

Mike was Irish. He'd known Terri from the bar where they'd both worked, and the way he spoke, I guessed that they'd been lovers. We huddled in his tiny cabin, smoking cigarettes and drinking black tea with cinnamon. "She was fun," he told me. "Always positive. She cheered me up."

I asked him if he thought anything bad had happened to her.

"She knows what she's about," he said, and smiled. "Magic lady…"

He suggested other people I might contact.

"Anyone named Nik?" I said. "Spells it N-I-K."

"Ah. She's got lots of friends. I don't know all of 'em."

As we were leaving, he drew me aside. "Careful who you trust," he said. "People love to visit here, but none of it's real, y'know? Remember that."

I asked him what he meant.

"Word of advice," he said. "Just in general, eh?"

The next few days were full of meetings like that. Everybody knew her, nobody knew where she was. One afternoon, I sat in Vondelpark, watching the skaters on the frozen lake, fascinated by their grace as they circled one another, back and forth, wishing that my own life had a little of that style, that sense of fluency and order, like the movements of a smooth, well-oiled machine.

I lit a cigarette.

The Ahn beside me said, "You want a goat, go to the goatherd."

"Shut up," I said.

"You want –"

"*Shut up!*"

But I was sitting alone, yelling at nobody.

Perhaps I should have made connections earlier. With its wealth of New Age posturing, the 'Dam had quickly taken to the Ahn, even more so than at home. In England,

I knew a songwriter who claimed the Ahn gave him his lyrics. I had friends who carried notebooks to record their Ahn encounters, tried to photograph them (no luck there), or begged them for some item as a keepsake (scarf, coat, wristwatch – and again, no go). The Ahn were oracles to these people, or at very least, the equivalent of horoscopes in a daily newspaper. There were books of Ahn sayings, divided into subjects: *When you lose your job, When your partner leaves,* and so on. I found them slick and trivial, more like something out of greeting cards or fortune cookies than any practical advice. Stripped of context, they meant nothing – random sentences, vague enough you might imagine they were personal. The human mind is built to look for patterns, after all, and we find meanings, even where none exist.

That's what I saw with Beth.

Henk's girlfriend, the woman in the downstairs flat, was English: small, dark-haired, and brittle-looking. Our first encounter wasn't promising, though maybe she was tired; I'd asked her where she'd lived in Britain, and got back a chilly, hip, "All over, really." (What was I meant to say? "I've been there, too"?) The next night, though, was very different.

A colleague at work, she said, had had a meeting with the Ahn so profound it changed her life. As usual, the details were a little vague, but Beth's excitement was just bubbling over.

"The *energy* she's giving out! It's *amazing!* She says it's like she's *high* all the time!"

Henk's response struck me as curious. He smiled, and told her, "Soon now. It will not be long."

"No," she agreed. "Not long."

She spun on her heels, almost pirouetting with the thrill of it.

After that, Henk and I went to a bar and met more of Terri's old companions.

But not Nik. And no one knew who Nik might be.

Nik. It had to be him.

The more I thought of it, the more convinced I was: if I could find him, or somebody who knew him, then maybe I could find where Terri was, too.

The portraits gave the game away. There was so much detail, so much expression. These weren't quick cartoons. They were labors of love.

Was it all that simple, then? A new romance? If so, no wonder she'd lost contact with her old friends. What's more distracting than a love affair, when all's been said and done?

Yet something didn't sit right. Was I jealous? She'd always seemed to dance through life, and if I'd sometimes called her frivolous, I wondered now if I weren't simply trying to bolster up my own sense of myself – as if my meager little life were somehow more authentic, more grittily "real" than hers.

I took that final sketchpad. There were street scenes, just before the page with Nik. Some had dates and locations. If he lived or worked near any of these, then maybe I could find him. It was a long shot, but the best I had.

I explained all this to Henk. He nodded solemnly, then clapped me on the shoulder.

"Do not forget to enjoy yourself, my friend. This is a vacation, yes?"

He looked at me as if I were a patient in need of therapy.

Enjoy myself? I thought.

That wasn't why I'd come.

So, book in hand, I headed into town. I found the first place easily enough, a little streetside café where I bought a drink and sat, watching the staff, the patrons and the passers-by. No Nik. He'd have stuck out a mile among the locals, with their thick mustaches and receding hairlines. But no matter. I'd a trail to follow. Two more "respectable" locations, and then –

There's a part of the city everyone knows. The guidebook calls it "the sailors' district," but nowadays it swarms with tourists, and I doubt you'd find an actual mariner in half a mile or more. It's got clubs, and sex shops, but its real fame rests with the women in the windows. Terri's rapid sketches caught them, and the looks on the faces of the passers-by, some recoiling, some eager, some clearly disbelieving. In one, she'd drawn a troupe of Japanese tourists, in identical black suits, marching like a Sunday school parade between these half-dressed, living mannequins. The reality, though, was pretty dull. The windows were curtained, giving them a comfortable, domestic look, and the women inside could have been middle-aged housewives, bored almost beyond endurance; they sat, smoking, or staring blank-eyed, oblivious to onlookers. Touts called from the club doors, faintly thuggish in their anoraks and boots. It was all profoundly unerotic. I was just about to turn around, give up, go home – and then I saw him.

Lounging in a doorway, watching me.

Nik.

He wore a short black leather jacket, and the flash of neon caught the piercing in his lip so that it seemed to blink in rhythm with the light.

For a moment, we just stared at one another.

"Nik…?"

He cocked his head.

"You know Terri, right?"

He raised a small joint to his lips, took a drag, and said nothing.

"English woman. *Terri*, yeah?"

I held the sketchbook up. Showed him his portrait. He nodded, approving.

"I know her."

He had an accent. Eastern European, maybe. He tipped his head for me to follow, and together, we walked, the noise and bustle of the red light district soon falling away behind.

He handed me the joint.

Now, I knew this was a bad idea. I needed a clear head. But from habit or whatever else, I took a drag, and then another, feeling the smoke ease through my veins, and my steps grow light, till I was floating, drifting down the street with no volition of my own.

He said, "I think this is a hard time for you, yes?"

"Eh…?"

"Everyone is moving on. But you are… left out, I think."

I shook my head. "No, not a bit."

He smiled, disbelieving.

"You must relax," he said. "Enjoy your time here. Terri is quite safe."

I remembered Henk saying the same. It brought me back to myself, and broke the spell. I was following a stranger, in a city that I scarcely knew –

"Where are we going?"

"I am taking you to her."

"Yeah, well," I said. "Don't try any funny stuff, OK?"

"'Funny stuff'?"

"Yeah." I made my voice sound hard and menacing.

He laughed.

"You have my picture in your book. You know that we are friends. And both of us, we are friends of Terri. All is good, yes?"

"You were waiting for me."

"I was."

And that was it: I'd got him.

"You're lying," I said.

I stopped walking. He stopped, too.

"You weren't waiting. You can't have been. 'Cause I didn't know where I was going myself. Or when I'd get there. See?"

I looked at him in triumph.

"Yet there I was." He shrugged. "My friend," he said. "It

is a simple thing. I can take you to her if you wish. If not, you walk away. Uh-hm?"

He took a few steps, then looked back at me.

And like a faithful dog, I followed.

It was a modern, brick-built house. Its very ordinariness was somehow reassuring, and I felt myself relax a little. Nik took out a key, opened the door, and gestured me inside.

I told him, "After you."

It wasn't Nik's place. That was obvious. It looked like a family home, very bourgeois, very straight: armchairs, coffee table, sofa, TV. Small, painted street scenes on the walls, and in the rear, a dining table with a set of high-backed, wooden chairs.

I raised my head, and at the top of my lungs, called, "*Terri?*"

Nik smiled.

"Sit, my friend, sit."

"You said she'd be here."

"Sit. Please."

I took the armchair nearest the door. He took the sofa.

I lit a cigarette.

I felt weightless, giddy, like a balloon full of air.

Neither of us spoke.

There was a problem with the lights. Or with my eyes. A kind of flickering I couldn't blink away. Then something moved across my vision, left to right, a shadow, but pale, like a sheet of gauze, wafting through the air.

Nik sat and watched me.

And slowly, bit by bit, it dawned on me that there were others in the room. I couldn't see them, but I could feel their movements, hear their laughter.

For some reason, this didn't worry me. Much the opposite – it explained the trouble with my eyes; they were trying to adjust, that's all.

And someone said my name.

I jumped up.

"Terri?" I said.

Her voice! And with that, the shadows seemed to spin around me. The light surged. I could see her. Yes! Talking, laughing – talking to somebody I still couldn't quite register, but Terri – she looked young, the way she had when we'd first met, the Terri I'd known four, five years ago –

"Where's the party?" she said, and then, answering herself, "Well, it's *here*, isn't it? I mean, *obviously*."

Other figures shimmered into view, though they were vague, like ghosts or fragments of a person: the hem of a dress, swaying to some half-heard tune, the gleam of light on a cocktail glass, or a sudden shadow, skittering across the floor.

I rubbed my eyes.

"Terri," I said again, but my throat was dry, and the name came like a frog's croak.

Yet Terri, too, looked fragile, as if only partly there. I could see through her – see the room beyond, wherever she failed to catch the light. Her left arm, the orbits of her eyes – I felt a sudden panic, afraid she'd vanish before I'd even had a chance to talk to her.

"You could go round the world like that," she said.

To somebody. Not me.

I took a step, collided with the coffee table, and when I looked again, she'd gone.

Nik, likewise, seemed to shiver and grow indistinct.

And that's the moment when I understood.

"You're Ahn," I said.

"Uh-hm. And Terri, too."

"That's ridiculous. She's not –"

"True, though."

He trembled, like a lightbulb ready to burn out.

"I know her. I – Christ. I slept with her, for God's sake! And the postcards. And the sketchbook –"

"You remember it all."

"Yes! I –"

And I stopped, dead. I *remembered* her. Remembered all our conversations, and the way she'd talked to me when I'd been down, or cheered me up when I'd been lonely.

Compensation. Wish-fulfillment.

Creatures of memory.

But no. I had the sketchbook – actual, physical proof. "Look," I said, holding up her pencil work. "Look, look –"

But Nik, like Terri, was already gone.

I could have stayed. I could have searched the place from top to bottom, hunting for clues. What stopped me was a weird sense of propriety. This wasn't Nik's house, or mine.

Suppose the owners came home? What would I tell them? What would I say?

I left, and later, sat on a bench by a canal, trying to make sense of what I'd seen.

I couldn't do it. And in many ways, I still can't.

They were messengers from God. They were guardian angels. They were products of our own inherent need for validation – an urban legend come to life.

They were fakes, delusions, fairy tales, a comfort for the damned, for the losers and the might-have-beens, and I begrudged my own place in that number, regardless how appropriate it may have been.

They were the Ahn.

They slipped into our world from somewhere else, a higher plane, a different state of being. They came to us as ghosts, as seedlings that would grow and grow the more we needed them.

So many stories. So many different explanations. Take your pick.

The truth was simpler.

They'd come to us to breed.

They didn't reproduce as we do. Instead, they recruited. Not everybody was acceptable to them. I don't know the criteria. But a spate of disappearances around the globe, mostly in major cities, marked the last phase of their presence here.

And me? I sat on the bench till I was stiff with cold, dizzy with a kind of vertigo, as if the whole world had been stood on end. All angles changed, all perspectives lost.

Then I went back to Oosterpark. Confronted Henk. He owned up that he'd lied to me. He'd been worried, he said, that my attitude would make things difficult for Beth and himself.

"My *attitude?*" I said.

"You are not open. You do not believe."

"*Believe?*" I said.

I couldn't think straight. All I could do was echo him.

"We are hoping to ascend. Beth and me. To be one with them. We were sure we would be taken. But they took Terri, not us. It was… hard, you know? I can't explain. When you phoned, asking for her, I could not tell the truth."

"You might have tried," I said. But my anger was already fading. I saw the disappointment in his face.

"And the authorities. You understand? If we admit someone has disappeared – it is not so easy. They are suspicious. They are clamping down."

He handed me a cigarette – a peace offering.

"We did not think," he said, "that you would actually come visit."

"I said I would."

"When we met before… you did not look like a searcher. Like someone who digs deeply into things. We thought…"

He shuffled his feet.

"We thought that you were… shallow. Materialistic. I

confess – we were baffled by what Terri saw in you." He managed an uncomfortable laugh. "Forgive us," he said. "Now we must start again. It is still possible for us, I think. For Beth and me. There may be time."

I blew smoke in his face.

"You knew Nik, too, didn't you?"

"I met him once. He was already marked. Chosen. His ascent had begun, I think. Now we are stuck here. I told you to enjoy yourself. It would be better, perhaps, if you had not found out."

Better if you had not found out.

I thought about that on the ferry home. Is it better to be ignorant? I don't think so.

I have her postcards still. I always kept them. Once, I thought the Ahn were creatures formed in memory, and today, that's all I have of her: the memory. Though sometimes, I imagine I can hear her voice, always at unexpected moments – waiting for a train, or pushing through a crowded store, or simply sitting, looking out over the city, and she whispers in my ear. I seldom understand the things she says, but they're warm, and kindly, and encouraging; and once, she said, I think to me, although I can't be sure, "Wasn't it fun?" and I answered her out loud.

"Yes," I told her. "Yes, it was."

TIM LEES is from Manchester, England, but now lives in Chicago. He is the author of the much-praised historical fantasy *Frankenstein's Prescription* (Brooligan Press), and the "*Field Ops*" books for HarperVoyager (*The God Hunter, Devil in the Wires, Steal the Lightning*). His latest story collection, *The Ice Plague and Other Inconveniences*, is available from Incunabula Media https://incunabulamedia.com/, as is *The Other Country*, his account of working in a psychiatric hospital. Besides health care work, he has held a variety of jobs, including film extra, conference organiser, warehouse worker, teacher, and lizard-bottler in a museum.

JERUSALEM

Jonathan Papernick

Even before they climbed aboard the train at Savidor Central Station, Geffen knew they were being followed.

As the oldest of the three, just a few months past his bar mitzvah, Geffen considered himself the commander of this operation. He was the *mefa-ked,* and it was his responsibility to keep his friends safe.

Tal, with his long, girlish eyelashes, was two years Geffen's junior, and Romi, just eight years old, had never ridden a train before. They each wore ill-fitting coats, hooded sweatshirts pulled low over their faces. Tal, who needed braces to correct a gap-toothed overbite, wore his father's Hapoel Be'er Sheva football scarf wrapped loosely over his mouth for good measure.

Since their return, they spoke only in hushed tones and the subtle telepathy found in certain twins.

"Will I really see Abba?" Romi said, as she settled into a seat by the window, her big blue eyes wide with yearning.

"I hope so," Geffen said, his voice barely above a whisper.

Romi's fingers and knuckles were raw from where she had chewed at the skin, and Geffen took Romi's clammy little hand in his. She crushed Geffen's fingers with relief as the doors closed and the train pulled out of the station and headed up towards Jerusalem.

Geffen heard there were mystics in the ancient city who could bring their parents back to them if they produced an object belonging to their loved one for the rabbis to bless. The passing of the recent Hanukkah holiday reminded Geffen that a "Great Miracle Happened Here," but he was too old to believe such nonsense. He had seen things with his own eyes he never imagined possible, and now he knew there really were monsters in the world.

But he still had hope, because there was nothing else.

Geffen's father's dive watch no longer told time, and Geffen wore it fastened loosely on his wrist, reminded of the magical stories his handsome father told about scuba diving in the Red Sea, visiting shipwrecks named the Satil and the Yatush, corals and octopus and bright schools of fish close enough to touch.

Tal's father's scarf still held the pungent scent of his father's sweat. A tube of his mother's red lipstick, a reminder of her soft kisses.

Romi insisted on bringing her father's pure white Persian Longhair, Klooma, who had waited patiently for Romi and her family to return. Geffen told Romi to take something else instead, and Romi agreed on her father's purple Crocs which were mostly melted and Romi wouldn't mind if a wise rabbi took them away forever. They were almost at the train station when Geffen heard Klooma mewling from the depths of Romi's backpack.

The train burst onto the lush coastal plain, leaving Tel Aviv and its glass towers and billboards behind. Fat raindrops poured from a grey sky, spattering against the windows as fields and orchards rolled past. Geffen's desolate mother would be frantically looking for him and his friends now. They had to be careful not to put their mission at risk, so they kept their heads down and spoke to no one.

Someone was behind Geffen, an unmistakable presence raising the hairs on Geffen's neck. He swung his head around but saw only an old woman with a damp gray snood matted to her head, sleeping with her parched mouth open. Someone had been there seconds before, the familiar scent of cheap tobacco and bitter coffee lingering, the air charged and glittering where some dark presence had been. Geffen's heart lurched, and he craned his neck to look down the train car. He saw nothing aside from a young couple arguing animatedly about the disappointments of love.

"I'm hungry," Tal said, poking Geffen in the ribs.

"Did you bring something?"

"I forgot."

Geffen, who had gotten used to hunger, told Tal to deal with it.

"I'm hungry too," Romi murmured.

Afraid she'd start crying, Geffen dug a bag of sunflower

seeds out of his jacket and handed them to Tal and Romi to share.

"I want to go home," Romi said.

Geffen reached out to stroke Romi's cheek. She flinched and turned her face away, her reflection in the window blurring against the slashing rain.

They rode in silence, and Geffen tried to imagine the sturdy presence of his father, his best friend in the whole world, sitting beside him, reciting his favorite poet: *Jerusalem is a port city on the shore of eternity.* He closed his eyes and tried to piece his father together like a jigsaw puzzle, the low timbre of his voice calmly intoning the wisdom of Yehuda Amichai: *Behind all this, some great happiness is hiding.* Geffen pictured the pale scar beneath his father's left eye shaped like a shooting star, the coarse, curly hairs that always poked out the top of his shirt, his lean, muscular arms burnished like copper from working in the desert sun, that one yellow tooth. Geffen couldn't fit them all together as one image, but rather a collection of jumbled parts that conjured only sadness.

"Is there really snow there?" Tal said.

"More than you can imagine," Geffen replied.

The train entered a tunnel as it began its ascent. Geffen's ears pounded with the pressure change, and he told Tal and Romi to yawn or swallow to clear their ears. The cat squirmed in Romi's backpack, and she had to shush it to calm it down.

When they emerged from the tunnel, the flat plains had transformed into rocky hilltops and valleys blanketed in white as far as the eye could see, the red-roofed houses perched precariously on the rounded peaks practically obscured. Jerusalem Pines dotted the landscape dressed in their winter finery. Romi smiled a familiar smile Geffen had not seen in a long time and it warmed him to see it.

They rode up the long escalators at Yitzhak Navon Station, clinging to each other — one escalator and then another — Geffen cautioning Tal and Romi not to look back. He'd learned the word vertigo once but could not remember it now. The third escalator seemed to be the longest of all. Geffen, sensing something behind him, turned to see someone moving quickly up the steps, pushing past a Haredi couple, knocking into a loaded granny cart, angry voices growing louder as the figure got closer and closer.

Tal must have felt the vein jumping in Geffen's wrist because he ran with a primal surge of energy before Geffen could say a word. They raced the rest of the way up the escalator, Klooma screaming behind them in Romi's backpack, until breathless, they found themselves in a large arrival hall intended to welcome visitors to Jerusalem. There were few visitors these days, and the hall was full of posters and signs demanding "BRING THEM HOME NOW." Geffen hurried through the hall without so much as glancing at the familiar faces on the posters.

He found himself in front of the station with Tal at his side, snow falling silently around them. The air was clean and bracing, a cloud of steamy breath issuing from Geffen's mouth like a dragon loaded for bear. Tal unwound the scarf from his face, sticking out his tongue to catch the tumbling flakes.

He looked almost happy, his gaunt face glistening with the melting snow, one perfect flake settling on his eyelash for the briefest instant, shot through with light like a precious jewel. Romi had been right behind Geffen but wasn't with them now. Her little legs were shorter, and she was the slowest of the three. Geffen ran back inside the station, his heart exploding in his chest. He couldn't lose Romi; he couldn't lose Romi too.

Geffen found her right away, standing before a poster, cradling Klooma in her arms.

"She knows. She knows that's Abba."

"Come on," Geffen said. "We have to go."

He helped Romi zip a squirming Klooma back into the backpack, scanning the hall for some sign of pursuit. Whoever had been behind them on the escalator was gone.

"Hold my hand," he whispered. "And don't let go."

A sudden squall of wind blasted the three of them as spectral figures appeared and disappeared through the slanted veil of falling snow, their black outlines indistinct, misshapen by the burdens they carried. A Hasidic man shrouded in a prayer shawl passed so close to them with his knobby cane that Geffen could hear the rattling breath in his throat. Then he was gone as quickly as he appeared, like being erased from a whiteboard in school.

"What now?" Tal said.

"I'm cold," Romi said.

Geffen could make out the flashing blue light atop an army vehicle and made his way there, careful not to slip and fall, and pull Tal and Romi down with him. He had always been sure-footed and quick, but the thick snow slowed their progress, and for an eternal moment, it seemed they would never get closer to the beacon atop the jeep.

A dark-skinned soldier with a mustache blew cigarette smoke out the window.

"Where is the ancient city?"

"Has it gone missing?" the soldier quipped.

"I'm looking for a rabbi."

"Jerusalem has plenty of those."

"How do I get to the Western Wall?"

The soldier pointed the burning tip of his cigarette toward the glass shelter of a light rail stop Geffen hadn't noticed, where the red letters of a scrawling LED announcement signaled when the next tram would arrive. A clutch of figures huddled close under the overhanging roof, piled so high with snow that Geffen wondered if it might collapse on their heads. The three trudged towards the shelter, the ceaseless storm swirling around them like mute apparitions, an indeterminate hum roiling on the wind.

A woman bundled in a shapeless wool coat held a string bag of bright green apples in her arms. She noticed Romi shivering beside Geffen and Tal, and reached a wizened hand into the bag and produced a perfect apple. She handed it to Romi as if she were gifting her a prized possession. Romi snatched it up and slipped it into a pocket of her backpack.

Geffen thought he could hear a distant digging sound somewhere beneath them, deep underground. He'd heard the furtive banging and scraping before, but it was louder now, bolder and more persistent than ever, getting closer all the time. Even in Tel Aviv, on the eighth floor of the unfinished apartment tower where he and his mother were staying, he heard it, always expecting someone to pop out of a hole in the floor and snatch him away.

The tram pulled up a moment later with a large plow attached to the nose of the sleek silver car to ensure the tracks were clear of obstruction. They boarded and took their seats, grateful to be out of the cold. The tram glided through the frozen city, passing squat limestone apartments and shops along Jaffa Street. Sharp icicles hung from arches and windowsills and the undersides of the small iron balconies that adorned the low structures. A limp flag hung listlessly from a building, its frigid blue star contorted into something resembling a winking eye. They passed the empty *shuk* at Mahane Yehuda, the monument at Davidka Square. The few open shops at Jaffa Center sat darkened like rotted teeth in a milk-white mouth. A recording announced each stop in a voice meant to soothe, but Geffen's stomach quivered with nerves. He hoped he was doing the right thing, bringing Tal and Romi along with him on this journey. They were so young, and they needed their parents. The way Tal perked up at every noise, expecting this time his parents had returned, told Geffen he had to do something more than sit around and worry and wait.

Who knew if they were alive or dead?

But what else could he do?

A stone statue of a winged lion stood on a rooftop, projecting eternal indifference as they approached their stop. They alighted from the tram at City Hall before it made its sharp leftward turn into the eastern part of the city. The snow was piled as high as Geffen's shoulders in some places, well above Romi's head, but the footfalls of countless moving feet had carved out a narrow path. A group of Hasidic men returning from prayer shoved past Geffen, knocking Tal into a snowbank. They wore clear plastic bags fastened over their large-brimmed hats and spoke in a rapid guttural Yiddish Geffen did not understand. The men moved on like a noisy murder of crows, stark black against pure whiteness, becoming two-dimensional sketches on the landscape before disappearing quickly into the storm.

The children crossed the street at an intersection where a small passenger car spun its tires uselessly through a slushy mess. Tall date palms swayed in the wind, their flanks and ragged leaves frosted white, standing sentry before the crenelated ramparts of the Old City, rebuilt for the last time 500 years earlier by Suleiman the Magnificent.

Not long ago, Geffen, Tal, and Romi's faces stared back from the sad gallery of the sand-colored walls, their pictures projected in mute appeal along with all the others taken from their homes. Now, the walls were bare, dusted here and there in intricate lattice patterns and arabesques, sharp drifts climbing the wall like a siege ramp. The hum on the howling wind became more distinct as if trying to articulate something of great import.

Jaffa Gate, one of the seven gates leading into the walled city, appeared in the distance, its arched portal promising respite from the frigid wind. Geffen squeezed Romi's hand, signaling they had arrived at the Old City, when a projectile struck him in the stomach, knocking the breath out of him. A snowball whizzed past his head; another thwacked Tal in the back. They heard laughter all around them and the cruel taunts of *Yahud! Yahud! Yahud!*

Half a dozen shouting teenage boys surrounded them and pelted them with snowballs packed with bits of ice and rock. One caught Tal in the mouth, and he began to bleed, his red blood dappling the snow before them. Romi's eyes were wide with terror, and Geffen sandwiched Romi between he and Tal. She was crying, and Geffen snatched up a handful of snow to counterattack, but the group of boys was closing in fast. One had packed something into the cuff of a makeshift slingshot, whirling it above his head with deadly intention as he chanted "*Allahu Akbar!*" Geffen was about to say, "Take me and let them go." He had been through worse than whatever this noisy gang of kids could offer, and he was sure he could escape in the mayhem of the storm. But he couldn't leave Tal and Romi alone.

An enormous boom filled the sky like a warplane breaking the sound barrier or an incoming barrage of rockets. Geffen knew to rush to the nearest shelter when the sky filled with streaks of light, but he had seen the jagged veins of lightning threading the sky just before the unlikely thunder. The feral boys surrounding them had been focused on their targets and had missed the crackling light show above. Another boom echoed across the sky, the very heavens shaking with the wrath of millennia. The attackers dashed towards the nearby wall, pressed themselves against the packed snowbanks, and curled up in defensive positions. The thought of incoming rockets had never made Geffen happy before, but now his heart raced with joy as he pulled Romi behind him and sprinted towards Jaffa Gate, with Tal quick on his heels. Yet another crash of thunder exploded above them, and Geffen, for perhaps the first time in his life, believed some higher force had intervened to save he and his friends.

They crossed into the Old City through Jaffa Gate and faced a small plaza normally bustling with vendors, tourists, and taxis. Romi asked if those boys had really meant to hurt them, and Geffen lied and said, of course not, they were just playing rough the way boys do. Tal scooped up a handful of snow and held it to his bleeding lip. Buried cars squatted like sleeping sheep against the ancient bulwarks of the Citadel, where the Tower of David rose into the sky like an exclamation. Romi had stopped crying, and she unzipped her bag to stroke Klooma and whisper soft words in her ears.

"Where do we go now?" Tal said. His lips were bright red, as if from blood, but Geffen realized Tal had applied his mother's cherry red lipstick as a healing kiss to soothe his wounded mouth.

The children skirted a shuttered tourist center advertising walks on the ramparts, a money changer with an ATM inside, and a desolate hole-in-the-wall hostel called the Petra

Guest House. They entered the narrow alley of a partially covered bazaar, sloping down and down towards the heart of the walled city. The corrugated metal awnings designed to keep out the heat of the blazing Jerusalem sun left a gap wide enough for high piles of snow to fill the entire middle of the street. Most of the shops were closed, but a man in a souvenir shop artlessly plucking an oud out of boredom insisted they look at his carpets, which could be had for a special price. The low stone stairs leading down were slick and slippery, iced over here and there like a death warrant, and Geffen considered snatching a walking stick from the man's display. They heard footsteps behind them echoing off the locked iron gates of the shops, and Geffen swiveled his head in fear. But the broad smiling face coming their way was beaming and beatific. The man wore a large backpack humped on his shoulders over a puffy orange ski jacket, his eyes wide with awe.

"Is this really where Jesus walked?"

Geffen kept moving, urging Tal and Romi forward.

"Did Jesus Christ walk these streets?"

"My friend," a man in a heavy knit sweater called out from a shop that was little more than a cramped cutout in the stone walls. He sat on a plastic chair beside a three-coil space heater surrounded by olive wood knickknacks: camels, crosses, nativity scenes, praying hands. In heavily accented English, he asked, "Where are you from? Texas? Alabama? Here we have pieces of the True Cross, just for you."

The street was entirely covered from the elements now,

and brownish runoff meandered down the center of the street in slow trickles. Mangy cats picked through piles of garbage all around them. Klooma meowed from Romi's backpack, clawing to get out.

"Don't let her out," Geffen said.

"But she wants to play."

The half-starved cats, one missing an eye, another hissing furiously at Tal with bared fangs, didn't look like they wanted to play.

They came to a claustrophobic, low-ceilinged junction where a pair of *Magavnikim* dressed in their green uniforms and tactical vests and berets stood, M-16s slung casually across their chests. A fierce-looking Ethiopian in mirrored sunglasses asked them where they were going. Before Geffen had a chance to respond, the other border guard, pointing to his right and the twisting alleys of the Arab *souk*, said, "Not that way." Without asking where Geffen, Tal and Romi were heading, he pointed in the other direction and said, "You take the Street of the Jews.

They passed above a sunken street and the remaining columns of an ancient market dating back to the time of the Roman conquest, then the massive domed edifice of the rebuilt Hurva synagogue, its small stained-glass windows ablaze. They were getting closer, and Geffen was starting to believe he really was going to see his father at the end of this journey.

"I'm tired," Romi said. "And I'm cold."

"We're almost there," Geffen said.

They descended a steep set of stairs, leaving behind the narrow streets and empty courtyards of the Jewish Quarter, and slipped through a dormant metal detector to see the enormous stones that made up the Western Wall glowing at the far end of a snow-filled square. Even at this distance, its majesty knocked the breath out of Geffen. The golden Dome of the Rock was still visible on the Temple Mount above despite the churning static of the storm. Geffen had been to the wall just once, on a school trip that included the Holocaust Museum, the biblical zoo, and a picnic beside a windmill offering stunning views of the city below. He remembered his teacher telling him it was the last remnant of the Jewish Temple, destroyed by Titus and his army 2,000 years ago, and that it was the holiest site in all of Judaism.

The municipality had worked hard to clear the square of snow, but tall mountains of the stuff piled here and there threatened to topple over in an avalanche of futility. Even so, the newly fallen snow reached halfway up their shins, so they had to labor to cross the icy plaza in frustrating fits and starts. A few visitors took pictures and called out across the barren square, and their plaintive calls pierced Geffen with their melancholy.

Geffen told Tal and Romi to wait by the public bathrooms; they could even go inside to warm themselves up, but he had to go by himself since girls were not allowed to approach the wall where Geffen was heading, and Tal had to keep her company.

Ordinarily, hundreds of men would be praying at the

wall, chanting and swaying in their devotion to God. Only a solitary man in a black gabardine overcoat shoved a push-broom back and forth across the stone floor before the massive wall. Geffen's heart sank. Had he come all this way for nothing? It was a foolish idea to think his plan could work. He was such a child. Hot tears formed in the corners of his eyes when he suddenly heard the sound of voices chanting, countless voices, one on top of the other, coming from a discreet entryway adjacent to the wall. He looked inside, and beneath the curve of the stone ceiling, lit up in golden light, there were hundreds of men with beards and bouncing side curls, dressed in black, bobbing back and forth in prayer. Geffen had found the place! His rabbi was sure to be here. It smelled of wet wool and bodies in motion, and Geffen waded into the mass of praying men, proud he had found his way here on his own.

A skinny Litvak, not much older than Geffen, with a sparse beard and acne, asked Geffen if he was Jewish. Geffen nodded yes. "Did you have your bar mitzvah yet?" Geffen nodded yes again. The Litvak wore the traditional black suit and white shirt that made him look like a penguin and a huge black hat that gave the impression he was playing dress-up. He asked Geffen if he would lay tefillin and say a few short prayers. Geffen said he was in a hurry, and the pimply-faced kid had to lean close to make out Geffen's words.

"What's the rush?" His sweet breath stank of decay, and Geffen had to swallow down his gag reflex.

"I'm looking for a rabbi who can bring my father back."

"Back?" the Litvak said. "From where?" And then a look of recognition passed across his pale face, a maddening combination of pity and true belief. "He'll return when the Messiah comes."

"No," Geffen said, squeezing the kid's skinny arm. "There are rabbis who can bring back…"

The Litvak pulled his arm out of Geffen's grip. "For that, you have to go to the City of Air. There, you'll find mystics and, magicians and kabbalists. But not here."

"Where is that?"

"Go home, little boy. Unless you'd like to stay and study Torah."

Geffen made his way back to his friends with a leaden heart, afraid to tell them he had failed. They weren't going to see their parents today and might never see them again. He could just make out Tal and Romi through the falling snow, and then he saw Romi open her backpack so Klooma could jump out and play in the snow. He had told her specifically not to bring the cat, and now there it was, almost invisible against the pure white backdrop, little paws testing the frigid surface with tentative feline suspicion. Geffen saw it happening in his mind the instant before Romi screamed a blood-curdling shout, "Kloooooooooommmmaaaaa!"

The cat bolted in the direction of an adjacent tunnel leading back into the winding streets of the *souk*, opposite from the direction they came, flying so swiftly it barely left its prints in the snow. Romi followed, continuing to scream, "Klooma, Klooma, Klooma!"

Geffen caught up to Romi and Tal, but the cat was way ahead of them, stopping every time they got close as if to taunt her pursuers. They found themselves breathless in a narrow alley, far from where they had entered the *souk*, the shuttered shops giving way to humble homes hemmed in by the accumulation of the snow. Someone was grilling meat, and the mouthwatering aromas of cumin, sumac, and finely chopped parsley made Geffen's stomach grumble.

The cat was gone, and Geffen said it wasn't safe to be here, that they had to head back before it got dark, and that Klooma would be fine with all the other cats who ceaselessly wandered the city.

Now that Romi had found her voice again, she roared. "Shut up! Don't say a word, or I'll kill you!"

Geffen and Tal both paled in shock at Romi's words, and then they realized it wasn't her voice coming from inside her but that of one of their captors, right down to the way he rolled his r's when he spoke. "They've all forgotten about you," the voice roared. "Nobody is coming to save you."

Geffen threw his arms around Romi, pulling her close, but the hideous voice continued shouting, "You are worse than a dog, a pig, a monkey."

Romi had a distant, far-away look in her eyes as she continued to shout invective at Geffen and Tal. A window above them opened and a woman said something in Arabic they couldn't understand.

"We have to go," Geffen said. "Now."

He and Tal tried to lead a catatonic Romi out of the

alleyway, but she wouldn't budge, so Tal helped lift her onto Geffen's back. She wasn't very heavy, but it was hard to make progress through the slippery maze-like network of streets and alleys, which all seemed to lead farther and farther from where they wanted to be. Sometimes, Geffen could swear he felt angry hands grabbing at him, pulling him down, and he hid his face from passersby. A battered Bobcat snowplow edged its way past a donkey tethered to a lonely wooden coffin who brayed and snorted with displeasure, clouds of gamey steam issuing from its flaring nostrils. Church bells clanged urgently from the nearby Christian Quarter. A Cathedral's roof had fallen in beneath the weight of the snow, and a distant screaming filled the air as first responders hurried past. Romi clung silently to Geffen, breathing her soft breath in his ear as they navigated their way out of the *souk*.

They found Klooma grooming herself atop an overflowing garbage bin, her white fur matted from the snow. She eyed the trio cautiously as they approached, licking one forepaw with its barbed tongue, then the other. Romi didn't acknowledge the cat. This time, they were too exhausted to run to catch Klooma, and the cat simply hopped off the bin and swished its lean body back and forth as it led the way forward.

"Do you think she knows how to get out of here?" Tal asked. His voice was raspy from disuse.

"I don't know," Geffen said. "But we're really lost."

Klooma looked back at regular intervals to ensure they were still with her, her feather-light steps barely registering on the ground below. Again, Geffen sensed they were being followed, something or someone just beyond their reach in the darkness sparkling, a voice or a thousand voices, whispering like a breath on the wind. Klooma led them down a narrow passage dripping with black streaks of ice melt and stopped before a blue double door made of sturdy wood ornamented with a simple Shield of David. Klooma began to meow and paw at the door, and it opened after a moment to reveal an old man with a long white beard and glimmering eyes shining from the deep folds of his wrinkled face. He wore a black silken kippa on his head and beckoned for them to enter.

"You found me," he said. "Come inside."

Geffen considered turning around and walking away, but his bones ached from the cold; Romi was getting heavy, and he had no clue how to find his way out of the maddening labyrinth of the Old City.

"Quick, it's not safe," the old man said.

Tal was the first to step inside, stamping scales of snow off his feet as he entered. Geffen followed, easing Romi from his back. She slunk to the floor, back against the wall, with her legs flopped out in front of her like a rag doll.

The small, high-ceilinged room was warm like a bath, and a sweet, earthy scent of old books filled the room. Loaded shelves lined the walls with countless volumes, their leather bindings bearing the names of holy texts. Aside from the expected sets of The Tanakh, The Mishnah and the Jerusalem and Babylonian Talmuds, there was also *The Zohar, The Bahir, Sefer Yitzirah, The Book of Secrets,* and a strange book called *The Book of Raziel the Angel,* which glowed slightly from its spot on the bookshelf. The room was brightly lit but there seemed to be no source of light, no lamps or fixtures, no candlesticks or windows leading to the outside.

The old man beckoned the children to join him at a kitchen table in the center of the room. More books and scrolls were piled there, and he lifted them off with a grand sweep of his arm and placed them atop another tottering pile of books. He brought them each a glass of cloudy tap water and insisted they drink after he muttered a prayer of thanks. Geffen drank the water down in one gulp, realizing he hadn't had a thing to drink since Tel Aviv. The water reinvigorated him, and Romi, too, seemed to come back to them. Klooma jumped into her lap, and she stroked the cat's fur absently.

"You're the first ones to come to me," the old man said with laughing eyes.

"You know why we're here?" Geffen said.

"Of course."

"You're a rabbi?"

"You can call me Gaon."

"And you can bring our parents back to us?"

The Gaon paused for a long moment, his papery skin almost translucent. The high blue veins running through the tops of his hands looked to Geffen like a network of rivers and their tributaries.

"Moses, our great rabbi of rabbis, with the helping hand of Hashem, blessed be His name, brought forth our ancestors from bondage in Egypt. I cannot do that."

A tiny squeak issued from Tal's throat, and Geffen,

overcome by the sorrow of everything he had endured, was about to berate the old man who had somehow bewitched them to travel all this way full of hope in the midst of a storm for nothing.

"But," the Gaon said, raising a long, bony finger, "I can bring them back to you if the *Malach HaMavet* has taken them to the next world."

A sour taste filled Geffen's mouth, and his hands began to shake.

"Do you have something belonging to your dear ones?"

Geffen slipped his father's watch off his wrist and placed it on the table before the Gaon. The time had stopped just after 6:30 AM. Tal unwound his father's football scarf from his neck and placed his mother's lipstick on the table. Klooma batted a paw at Romi, and she fished into her bag, producing her father's Crocs. She found the green apple in the side pocket and was about to take a bite when the Gaon snatched it out of her hand and tossed it to the far side of the room. "Don't eat that apple."

The Gaon asked Geffen his father's name and his father's father's name. Then, taking up the dive watch in his hands, he closed his eyes and rocked back and forth, back and forth, silently reciting some esoteric prayer Geffen could not imagine. The Gaon's eyes rolled back in his leonine head showing only the jaundiced whites, his lips moving rapidly, a spray of spittle issuing forth like a fountain. When he was done, he opened his eyes and intoned, "I believe with complete faith that there will occur on this evening a resurrection of

Shai, son of Yitzhak as it is willed by the Creator, may his name be blessed, to bring forth this soul from the dust so that it may return to this world and walk among its loved ones until called again by Hashem to the next world."

The Gaon did the same for Tal and Romi.

They sat in an expectant silence not knowing what would happen next. Finally, the Gaon spoke. "Now you must take these objects I have blessed with the power of the Almighty and bring them to the highest point on the Mount of Olives. Among the sacred tombs there, you will build men and women of snow and in their bellies..." Here the Gaon pounded his belly with his fists. "You will bury this watch, this scarf, this pair of shoes, this trifle and you will recite the words I recited over these objects. And when you have done that, you will press your lips to the mouth you have created and blow your living breath into its mouth."

Geffen had heard the legends about men being created from clay, never from snow, but the Gaon spoke with such certainty he began to believe. "And then?" Geffen prodded.

"If they have passed to the next world their souls will fuse with their bodies and they will be yours again."

Tal asked where on the Mount of Olives they were supposed to do this.

The Gaon's voice boomed. "As close to the heavens as you can get."

"I don't want to go," Romi said.

"Do you want to see your Abba again?" Tal snapped. "Because I need my *Imoosh* and *Aboosh.*"

"I'll carry you and you can wear my sweater," Geffen said.

"Look, Klooma wants to go." Tal prodded the indifferent cat with his toe.

"I don't like the snow."

"After today, you'll never have to see snow again," Geffen said.

"Promise?"

"Promise."

The Gaon led them to the door with a warning to be careful. "You know you are being pursued."

"I know," Geffen said.

"Now that you've met him face-to-face, you will be pursued for all your days."

"By who?" Tal said.

"Amalek!" the Gaon warned. "Amalek has mastered the art of sin and will never rest until he is destroyed."

The Gaon slipped a small silver amulet into Geffen's hand and said it would keep him safe as long as he kept moving.

Outside a bakery, Geffen snatched a wooden tray used to carry bread and pitas on one's head and fashioned it into a makeshift sled for Romi. He looped a piece of rope through an opening in the tray and dragged Romi behind him. She sat bundled up with Klooma in her lap. The Gaon told them to exit through the Dung Gate, and they found their way there a little after nightfall. The snow was coming down harder than ever, and a vicious wind had picked up, making their faces sting. The Muslims were being called to evening prayer, countless muezzins chanting from their minarets and mosques in a kaleidoscopic overlay echoing throughout the eastern part of the city. Geffen had once found these haunting melodies beautiful. He could hear them from his bedroom at home carried on the wind from the other side of the fence, so close, but a world away.

"*Hayya ala-s-Salah, hayya ala-s-Salah.*"

"I want to go home," Romi said.

Tal turned to Romi, eyes ablaze and said, "You have no home!"

The muezzins continued, calling the faithful to prayer, "*Allahu Akbar, Allahu Akbar.*"

Amalek was so close now that Geffen could feel his cold breath on his neck, but he pressed onward, figures materializing and disappearing in swirling gusts. Before them he saw a man on horseback raise his sword high before rising into the sky and vanishing. They sloped down into a steep valley, passing close to the black tips of cypress trees swaying in the wind. Geffen's muscles burned but he refused to hand off the sled to Tal who tried sliding down the slope on his back but only ended up sinking into the cold grip of the snow. The Mount of Olives was at the other side of the valley, and they made their way past the huge rock-cut tombs of Absalom and Zechariah standing in eternal silence beneath the angry sky.

A thousand times Geffen wished to quit and turn back as he struggled up the wintery slope through the ancient necropolis, the wicked winds whipping around them spitting curses and threats. The Old City was well behind them now, the Golden Dome of the Rock barely visible in the distance through the wall of snow. They were walking over the stone graves of the dead now, buried deep beneath them under layers of packed snow. These dead would be the first to rise when the Messiah finally comes, but now all they could do was lie in the frozen darkness waiting.

"How much farther?" Tal said. His face was raw and red, eyes watering.

"We haven't gone high enough. We have to keep going."

"But I'm freezing," Tal cried.

Romi loosened her grip on Klooma who skittered across a flattened plateau of snow and began to meow purposefully.

"There, right there," Tal said.

Geffen was afraid if they didn't manage to get high enough on the slope, they would be too far from whatever power the Gaon had conjured for them. It must have been nearing midnight and his legs ached and throbbed. His numb hands were cramping terribly. He agreed they had found their spot and Romi climbed off the sled and began gathering snow with her little hands, rolling it into a ball around her father's Crocs. She did so with a grim determination, her pink bow of a mouth a tight bloodless line in an expressionless face. Tal quickly joined, forming two rough spheres around his parents' belongings, urging Geffen on.

Geffen recalled the Gaon's words that they would be safe from Amalek as long as they kept moving, but now they had stopped. The whipping winds swirled closer around Geffen, threatening shapes forming amid the sparking snow, dark ropy flames braided among the intricate flakes. He could see Amalek's sneering smile in the flickering light, hear his laughter roaring on the wind. Geffen waved the amulet all around him, hoping to create a protective square from within which they could work. He removed his father's watch from his wrist and got to work rolling out the snow with his wretched hands. Before long the three children stood facing four figures made of snow, three men and one woman. Then they dug through the snow to find pebbles and rocks to form the eyes and mouths, placing them just so on the faces of the snowmen.

Geffen said the words the Gaon told him to say. Tal and Romi followed. They each stepped forward and placed a kiss of life on the stone mouths of the snowmen.

For an instant everything was silent, before a blaze of lightning flashed across the sky, the deep boom of thunder cannonading off the walls of the Old City, filling the valley below with its decree. Then the snowmen began to melt away, sinew and bone weaving together before their eyes, organs forming, a beating heart, a pair of lungs, skin and teeth and hair. And now Geffen's father stepped forward, the familiar scar visible beneath his eye. Tal's parents, and Romi's Abba too, stretched out their arms and took a long breath. They wept with joy to be reunited with their children as they embraced beneath the falling snow.

Geffen threw his arms around his father, took a deep draught of his familiar scent, felt his heart beating through his shirt. His father held Geffen tightly as if he would never let go and he said, "I love you, I love you, I love you."

Now Amalek towered above them, laughing, icy fingers scoring Geffen's back, pulling at him, but Geffen refused to let go. He clung to his father even as the winds began to take him, even as Amalek pried at their embrace.

And then, Klooma, Romi's father's Persian Longhair, stood alone among the frozen tombs of the Mount of Olives, receding laughter high on the wind as the roaring storm erased any evidence that Geffen and Tal and Romi had ever been there.

JONATHAN PAPERNICK is the author of six books, including *The Ascent of Eli Israel, The Book of Stone,* and *I am my Beloveds.* He is an Assistant Professor in the department of Writing, Literature and Publishing at Emerson College where he has taught since 2007.

ATHENS

Nick Mamatas

Who on Earth would visit Athens in winter? The city, its sidewalks a shambles as if a Titan had picked the whole thing up and then dropped it, is rainy and cold. Nothing's built with insulation, and utilities are so expensive that the locals would take their baths in their tiny coffee cups if they could.

People with no money for tickets or hotels in the spring or early summer, my mother had said. *Depressed crazy people, that's who goes to Athens in winter,* she said. *You should go. Buy two seats.* And now here I was.

"Smart people come," said Theos Antónis, my uncle. My father's brother, mind you. "It's a good time to come. Don't let the gloom make you melancholy. It's a festival!" He's a little guy with a wide smile and I'm a great big one with no smile, and he's under an umbrella and I am not, and he is wearing a hat and also sporting a sensible houndstooth suit jacket. The man is practically disguised as a expatriate pensioner from Leeds. We're walking down Ioannou Chrisostomou in cramped Nea Smyrni, and every so often some Greek kid walked by, hooted, and said, "Oh, a man with an umbrella! Greetings, Your Highness!" or just started pointing and laughing. The Pakistani or Nigerian street peddlers smiled and tried to wave him over to buy some damp trinkets—masks or beads or hollow plastic clubs to whack people with later.

Antónis looked over at me. I'm soaked by the mizzle, like everyone else, and some heavy drops of water from a nearby building had just splashed onto my hoodie. "You're blending in already," he said. "Ah, here's my car." It's a Nissan Micra in orange and looks okay from the outside because the rain had cleared off most of the soot, dust, and bird shit. Inside is 100 percent food wrappers and academic-looking books the titles of which would take me several moments to slowly sound out and decipher. "Okay, let's go." We're walking, and might jump on a bus if we can, to Plaka. My uncle just wanted to show me that he'd actually found street parking last week and he'll be damned if he ever gives it up.

"Walking is better, levendi mou," he said. *My handsome.* He means me. "Take a whiff." He's right! The whole neighborhood smells of roasted meat and sugar—much better than the diesel fumes and armpit stench, and admittedly wonderful baking bread smells, of summer in the city. It's no Mardi Gras or Carnivale, but Greece celebrates the pre-Lenten feast pretty well. It's *Kreatini*, meat week, and the city is hoppin' with old-timey cultural stuff despite the dreary weather and the lack of tourist dollars. There are pop-up souvlaki and sausage stands on almost every corner, and the restaurants are grilling as well, doors wide open despite the chill. God died for this, thank God.

That's part of why I'm here. My uncle is a leading expert, or at least a leading superfan and weirdo, on the Karagozois shadow plays, and I'm interested too. Karagozois is a trickster figure with one loooong arm, and he's constantly hustling the pasha of the Ottoman Empire, who through the magic of puppet theater, lives across the street but never seems to recognize that Karagozois has variously claimed to be a chef, a doctor, a professor, the world's great musician, a dragonslayer et cetera while being raggedly poor with three starving children. Karagozois was about as *au courant* as a Three Stooges film festival would be, but during holidays the old shadow play set-ups get hauled out again and the old puppeteers warm up their singing voices for the shows. Call me Curly, boy howdy.

Here's what's been going on these past few months. Very early one morning, because I am a midnight snacker, I opened the fridge at my parents' house, caught a glimpse of the Acropolis on a container of feta, and whole city came flooding out of the refrigerator. Venetian cannons manned by soldiers in brilliant gold and green and red roared and singed my eyebrows straight off. Then I *was* one of their cannonballs, flying and spiraling and blazing hot, slamming into one of the rocky walls at the base of the Acropolis. I landed in the dirt, a human body with limbs and a face and a mouthful of street mud and lifted my head to see the tanks of the junta, the ones my parents had thrown Molotovs at before running all the way to Boston in 1973, bearing down on me.

Who picked me up and brought me straight up into the warm twilight but Panagitsa, the bearer and Mother of God, glowing like one bright star on a black night full of stars, warming me and healing me and then dropping me back down onto the city, through the roof of the Parthenon, which was a church for her for much longer than it had ever been a pagan temple. And then came Giannis Antetokounmpo, snatching me up and I was a ball again, but a basketball, and he soared high and swish it was nothing but net the hoop somehow bolted to the forehead of one of the caryatides and a million cell phone cameras flashed, but I didn't land in Milwaukee or even on the floor of the museum where the original statues are kept but on a hillside and the sun was blazing and I was naked and oiled up and surrounded by well-muscled naked and oiled up men and somehow it was my turn to wrestle and I knew how but not well and I was grabbed and hurled and slammed onto my back by a man a third my size and there I was on the Metro, and three college girls yelped and howled that I was looking up their skirts and started smacking me with their *tsantákia* and I stumbled away and out of the coach and out of the train station and onto the beach. I swam for it, sure as one is sure in dreams that one can just swim for it all the way across the ocean into the Harbor and across the Charles and up the driveway of my building and even up the steps to my little apartment and slide under the door like water and slip under the blankets without even having to lift them but then *stabbed!* and I knew it wasn't dreaming because I could feel the center tine of the trident of Poseidon rip through me and something snapped in my back and I couldn't feel my legs at all, like they were gone like they'd been bitten off like I was a shrimp on a fork and I was a mile high and Poseidon bursting forth from the sea was huge the way the horizon is huge and his teeth were enormous like the great marble slab walls of a skyscraper's lobby and then I was bleeding and trying to fold my guts back into my stomach in the worst alleyway in Exarcheia and standing over me was a man with a knife and a big coat hanging over one shoulder and he wore a sash around his waist and smiled under his thick mustache and this was it for me I knew except then out of the dark night snaked this loooong segmented arm and I was plucked away again and the arm retracted and twisted onto itself and held me up before a great dark eye and then I woke up for real in the hospital and there were Greek people there but they were just my parents and my brother Tommy and my cousin Sophia who happened to work in the hospital as a janitor and my doctor was half-Greek they assured me even though I don't care about that sort of thing and my mother kept asking me *why I'd tried to kill myself* and *why at **her** house* and I turned to my father for mercy and for once he granted it and instead of yelling at me or even her he just quietly asked my mother to let me rest.

But I hadn't tried to kill myself. My eyebrows were gone, burned right off, for real. I couldn't move my legs for a week.

"...and it's entirely unfair." My uncle had been talking.

Were he my age and had he been born and raised in America, Theos Antónis definitely would have been diagnosed with attention spectrum something syndrome and drugged to the gills, but here he was just an aged bachelor who only drank brown liquids. "Karagozois is a hero. His name should be like Odysseus; what you call someone clever, wily, even strong and brave, a man who stands up to bullies. Instead," he continued, "it's like malaka. You know why?"

I knew why he thought so, but he was my uncle so I said, "No, why?" I'm glad the rain was sufficiently heavy that Antónis kept his umbrella over his head. Otherwise I thought he might put it to crotch and start stroking. "The long arm; in the ancient days, it was a phallus."

"Are we almost there yet?"

"*Apokries* too," Antónis said, meaning the whole carnival season, "wasn't always like this." He waved at the street, which wasn't even all the celebratory, as we were still a ways from the city center. "It wasn't about Christ, but Dionysus! You know this thing…" He waved his free hand, pantomiming the plastic clubs people smacked each other wish. "Also a phallus! And the confetti we all throw at one another, right in one another's faces, that's—"

"Okay, okay!" I said.

"We're almost there," he said. "Another ten minutes." And then it was back to more Karagozois trivia, but nothing about why that long arm might have reached out to me.

It was another fucking *hour* before we were in Plaka, and I wondered if my uncle was making me walk in circles to lose some weight, but we got there and winter chill aside the area was fairly busy with tourists. Restaurant servers and cashiers wore various "funny" hats and masks and cheap plastic sunglasses now and again, and a few kids ran by in more complete, if thrown-together costumes. Here, nobody jeered at Theos Antónis; they didn't realize he always dressed like the British owner of an unsuccessful racehorse. But there was some jeering, some shouting, coming from elsewhere.

"Look, fascists," said Theos Antónis, gesturing toward a knot of mostly priests and monks on a raised platform, manning an impressive set of barrel barbeque sets they must have imported from the States. He was right though; mixed in with the robed and bearded figures were a handful of young athletic-looking men with the sharp look of people uninterested in fun, even as they handed out free souvlakia and drinks from some gas-powered refrigerators, the sight of which made me cringe. They wore navy and white T-shirts emblazoned with a shape that somehow looked both like a swastika and a Greek meander. They tried handing those out as well to the fair-sized crowd around them. A few of the bigger dudes stationed themselves on the curb, glaring at anyone who looked less than Greek, whether tourist or local and impassively accepted the occasional shouted insults from other revelers. My uncle closed then lowered his umbrella, shook some of the rain from it and took up on odd bladed stance, right foot in front of left, the grip on the umbrella handle like he was shaking hands with it, its tip pointed at the tallest of the priests. I half-expected him to salute with the damned thing, then shout *en garde!* and lunge into the first. He hated fascists. Me too.

My family were all creatures of the left, though you wouldn't know it from talking to them. Back in America, my father complained about taxes constantly. If the preoccupation of Antónis was Karagozois, my father's was calculating how many days a year, how many hours a day, how many minutes per hour he, or whoever sat across from him for more than five minutes, were *slaves* to the government. As for my mother, no politician or celebrity could die without her announcing that they'd obviously faked it for some secret reason, even when Queen Elizabeth died at the age of 96. Tommy was the kind of guy who plastered his Pontiac with a million Bernie stickers, and who paid his back of the house staff off the books, hired teen girls to wait tables based on cup size, and when COVID hit just set the restaurant on fire. *Greek lightning* he called it. None of us had any money and Tommy and I still lived with our parents even though we're both in our thirties, so on that level I guess we did all qualify as Communists. Plus my grandfather was one during the Civil War. He spent most of the time in a cave and when night fell, he'd crawl on his belly down the hill, a knife between his teeth and the glint of the moon in its blade his only light, and then he'd slit Nazi throats and slice collaborator balls right off as they slept.

The next morning, the Nazis left alive would wake up, gather twice as many villagers as those soldiers who died in the town's own small plaka, and gun them down.

We were both hungry but would rather starve than eat

fascist meat, and I was broke and Theos Antónis had forgotten his billfold, so we walked past the fascists and their free food, our faces as twisted as our stomachs. "The line is too long anyway," said my uncle before spitting. The puppet theater was just a few meters away, in the back of an alleyway. Antónis led me to the front row of cinder-block and wood-plank benches, where a bunch of kids were sitting. I pulled on his sleeve, but he waved me off, and everyone greeted him as we passed. The kids even wiggled and laughed as they made room for him and even for me. A couple of them just ran for the back rows when they saw me making to sit.

"Ha ha, reserved seating," Theos Antónis said. Then he fell silent, like a child, and the introductory music struck up—one third polka, one third circus music, one third that snaky zingy styling typical of Greek music. In shadow theater the lights don't go down, they come up. And then out hopped Karagoizis, his long thieving arm waving, his back hunched thanks to carrying the weight of the world. He said hello to several of the kids, even ones who didn't have Greek names—Sumejja and Maxim and Lan—and then said hello to Antónis like they were old pals...and then by name he greeted me. "We will eat!" he declared, "We will drink!" he cried, "And then, hungry again, we will sleep!" My stomach growled.

The first play was more or less traditional: Karagoizis pretends to be a baker with a large oven, and villagers bring him food to cook. Before he and his three starving children can eat, the Turkish commander shows up and demands that Karagoizis send the food across the street to the pasha's castle—but not to worry, the pasha will lie to the townsfolk about the missing food. Karagoizis agrees, but then eats the food anyway, especially a delicious goose with a clarinet-honk and a noisemaker death rattle. The customers, from the Italianate dandy to the Jewish landlord…

"Is this anti-Semitic?" I whispered to my uncle.

"No no," he whispered back. "Everyone loves him." He said something else then, but I couldn't hear it over the boos rising up from the back rows. Boos from grown-ups.

…return for their meals, and even with his long whip arm he can't fight them all off. The pasha arrives with great musical accompaniment, and declares solemnly that the goose has come back to life and flown up to heaven and to leave the poor baker alone.

And when he is alone with Karagoizis, the pasha demands his goose.

And Karagoizis says, "What goose?" Then he snakes his arm up to the top of the backlit screen, pointing toward heaven and says, "Check upstairs."

It's hard to describe a puppet show that it sounds funny rather than creepy, or pathetic. Everyone laughed, though.

"See? Life's not so bad," said Antónis. My uncle liked to think of himself as a philosopher. "You should live it as long as possible."

For the sake of saving face, or family honor, or whatever you want to call dysfunction, my family had all agreed that I would admit that I'd tried to commit suicide, and in a way so comically stupid that Karagoziois would have helped me do it had refrigerators existed during the time of the Ottomans. My parents had a big gas-powered fridge, and lots of debt, medical and otherwise. The house was underwater, mostly figuratively, but since New England snow is mostly freezing rain these days, often literally. Tommy's idea was a simple one: put a few bends in the line where the gas meets the compressor, stuff a little steel wool in the cracks, and then just wait. It was a total coincidence that I'd opened the door to the fridge at the exact moment a bit of wool sparked, and almost a total coincidence that opening the door set the compressor going. It wasn't much of a blast; even my mother could have survived it, though ever since her MS started asserting itself, I did most of the walking and the getting and doing around the house so of course it was me at the fridge.

To keep my brother out of jail and my parents out of court, I confessed that I was so depressed that I wanted to kill myself. I blamed "food addiction." Even Massachusetts doctors and insurance investigators were only stunned for a moment, but that was enough time for me to take off for fucking Athens in February.

Karagoizis plays come in two flavors: the comedic, in which he lies and blusters his way through some job, and the historical, in which he is more of a monologist who describes some important episode in Greek history or mythology. The histories are rarely ever shown because they are boring and unfunny; even Theos Antónis only sits through them out the sense of duty particular to completionists with neurological *differences*. And yet, the next play was announced as a historical, a brand-new one. *Karagoizis and the Little Dictator.*

Karagoizis and his family are starving. What else is new? The pasha is displaced and over his home flies a Nazi flag, one that had obviously just been hand-drawn during the break. That's new. Barba Yiorgos, a giant uncle of Karagoizis in a pleated white fustanella is half his usual size, his entrance music is playing in a minor key. The countryside is facing famine. Karagozois searches for food but instead finds nothing but the top hat of the jailed Sir Dionysios, a Westernized snob. Next to me, my uncle gasps. Can Karagozois boil and eat the hat? Veliggekas, the pasha's henchman appears, and now everyone gasps. He has a Magic Marker swastika freshly drawn over his face and tells Karagozois that boiling water is now illegal under order of the Occupation.

Karagozois does some quick patter about other ways to prepare a hat—broiled with lemon, baked in paper, chopped finely into a salad, covered in honey and filled with nuts for dessert—while his long arm reaches behind him, searching for some help. And he finds something, another long arm! There's only one other puppet in the cast with the long arm, Stavrakas, the flashy tough guy, a *manga* with a big coat and a sash where he keeps a knife. I shiver, and my gut clenches from the food talk and from my memories of the phantasmal man who slashed at me. It gets worse; Stavrakas is already dead. The children in the audience scream and cry and Veliggekas laughs. "Maybe you should eat *him* if you're so hungry!"

Karagozois is lost for words. He stammers *Fa- fa- fa-...* Will he say *Fau?!* or *Eat?!* in disgust, or will he finish another word when he finally spits the whole thing out? *Fasístas!*

And then everyone started screaming. The fascists at the end of the alley shouted that they hand out food to *real Greeks* and it was the Jews who starved people, parents yelled that their howling children were frightened, two right-wing priests bellowed something about Communist propaganda, a couple of cackling teen-agers rose and practically swam through the crowd to face the fascists. American and European tourists cried out "Police! Police!" in English. Theos Antónis screeched in his Athenian nasal voice that everyone was ruining the play. Taking hold of his umbrella, he was ready to start stabbing.

And I felt a hand on my shoulder. I was about to turn around to see who it was when the first Molotov cocktail came spiraling my way. Antónis opened his umbrella, uselessly. Fire splashed about the front rows. A flaming woman near me started howling from a place so deep inside her I thought I'd fall in. The crowd pressed and rushed toward the end of the alley. The fascists had colorful clubs in their hands, but when the first teenager fell after one blow to the head we all knew the clubs were metal ones painted to look like the plastic toys. The adults grabbed their kids and parted like the sea to let the fascists at the puppet show. My uncle countercharged, his flaming umbrella glowing like a cartoon sun, but everything else around me was black as ink. The hand on my shoulder plucked at the nap of my hoodie and lifted me up up up.

I was out of alley. I was smiling at the old couple looking out the window of their fifth floor apartment. Past my belly, between my feet and far below, the streets locked together like a jigsaw puzzle, all weird curves and angles. And then I am up even higher, over Lykabettos Hill and its ampitheatre, higher higher where the sky turns dark and the big old waning gibbous moon is looking at me like an eye and then it blinks oh so slowly like you would imagine an eye the size of the moon would and it is so joyous to be weightless so joyous to be flying free so utterly orgasmic that I know what comes up must go down and I know I have a mission and I find myself out of the alley covered in mostly my own blood that familiar stink of burning hair filling my nostrils and I am cowering behind the refrigerators of the fascist souvlaki station with definitely one broken arm I can't help but hold to my side like a chicken's wing.

Here is what you should know. I was pretty desperate back in Massachusetts. There is no big backstory, no intense trauma, no parents any more abusive than any other Old World assholes who refuse to understand the New. I'm not sad because I am fat, I bop my head to music, I can do a handstand on a bet, Tinder works just fine for me. I just wanted to be dead, so I checked Tommy's work over and over and midnight snacked and got out the *mezedakia* whenever there was call for it and sometimes I was sure I heard some kind of leak or other problem so I would put my ear to the fridge and knock on the door and say *Geia, eímai egó, to arní*, "Hello, it's me, the lamb," in a squeaky little voice as a joke and nobody would laugh because my whole family is a melancholy bunch nothing like your cliché fantasies and of course I was lying when I said I was trying to kill myself it was just to protect the family but really I wasn't *not* trying to kill myself.

Another thing to know is that there are riots in Athens all the time. We're all very used to this, even diaspora boys with American passports like me.

And what you should also know is that in the crush of people running from the riot I saw some little guy wrapped in tin foil—was he supposed to be a robot, a potato in an oven, who knows?— running by and tripped him and grabbed some of the costume with my good hand and he started smacking at me and he hit me in my broken arm I said "Okay, you can go!" and he looked at his bloody hands all red and silvery and I guess believed me, as he got up, gave me the *moutza*—made like he was shoving a palmful of shit in my face, you know— then took off and I got to work on making little kinks in the compressor tubes and wrapping them up in the tinfoil, which was a challenge with one working arm.

But how to get the fascists to come back to their barbeque? Theos Antónis was always saying I have good lungs and a voice for the theatre. I clambered up onto the raised platform and called out for them to come and get me, come and get the man whose pappou took the balls of their pappous and turned *that* into a story for kids, c'mon muscleheads, show the fat American in tennis shoes more expensive than your little scooters what you got! And, well well, a few turned my way so I waved my long good arm at them and whistled and stomped on the platform hoping to trigger the gas-powered fridges as yet more of them broke off from the riot they had started and to come my way and I bet that right before the whole mess exploded and took me, and all of them, out, the glowing red skeleton of an umbrella, its fabric falling from its bones like red leaves on the wind, would float right by and I would reach overhead, grab it, and fly away.

Nick Mamatas is the author of several novels, including *I Am Providence* and *The Second Shooter*. His short crime fiction has appeared in McSweeney's: The Monstrous and the Terrible, *Best American Mystery Stories*, *Ellery Queen's Mystery Magazine*, Tor.com, *Weird Tales*, and many other venues. s. With Ellen Datlow, Nick co-edited the Bram Stoker award-winning anthology *Haunted Legends*, and with Masumi Washington he co-edited the Locus Award nominees The Future is Japanese and Hanzai Japan. His fiction and is editorial work has been nominated for the Stoker, World Fantasy, and Shirley Jackson Awards.

PRAGUE

Katherine Traylor

Waiting on the tram platform at Motol, I can see the full moon through a row of bare winter trees. It's barely six, but the sun is long gone. It never gets dark this soon at home, even in February. Rush hour is mostly over, and the few people waiting with me have a brisk, chilly energy, as if they'd like to leave this island of nowhere as soon as possible. For a while I watch a man in headphones pace the platform, lost in his own music.

My breath streams around me like a dragon's. I take another deep breath and release it slowly, watching the steam rise to veil the golden moon. Concentrating on that beauty helps take my mind off how lonely I am, how almost no one in this country knows or cares who I am.

A flock of birds appears around the edges of the moon, silhouetted against the deepening sky. I can't tell what kind they are from here: pigeons, jackdaws, magpies, swifts? They seem strangely proportioned, either much larger or much closer than you'd expect them to be. They spiral, converging just above the platform before they separate and disappear. I think I see one land at the end of the platform, but it might just be a pigeon. They're ubiquitous in Prague, common as caryatids.

Across the tracks, a little beyond the road, a young woman stands under the moonlit trees. She's all in black, shoulders hunched, even though it isn't that cold today. She's staring at me intently.

I watch her surreptitiously from the corner of my eye. She's in her late twenties or early thirties. Skinny. Gothy. Black feathers ruffle on the hood of her coat.

Hearing a tram, I turn and look for the number. Not mine; I'm waiting for the 9. A few people get on. The tram leaves again in a brief storm of lights and bells.

The woman across the road is still there when it passes. For some reason, I expected her to be gone.

She's still staring. It makes me uncomfortable. I wonder if she's on drugs or somehow mentally unwell. I don't want to get involved, so I look away, scanning the dusk-veiled scenery.

There aren't any trams in sight, only the raven-black silhouettes of pedestrians passing on the street, none straying from their appointed paths. Above them, the sky deepens through turquoise into azure. Stars are picked out in silver-white like gems around the moon, an ornamental piece to gaze at. For a while, I do. The sky here is always beautiful.

Then I remember another gem-studded sky: above a

lakeside house in summer, on the night I said goodbye to my home and family. I thought I was leaving them for something bright and new—that my life was finally beginning. That was before I knew that wherever you go, your loneliness goes with you.

Homesickness pinches at my gut. I cast my eyes down to the gravel bed of the tram tracks.

Someone has arranged a number of flat gray stones across some of the ties. They're of varying shades, all slightly different from the surrounding gravel. Each is marked with scratches too regular to be accidental: not quite pictures, but almost.

Was someone playing on the tracks? It wouldn't be that dangerous here. There aren't many trams, and you can see them a long way off. I feel strangely tempted to pick up one of the stones for a closer look, but I'm not quite brave enough to jump down onto the tracks with everyone watching.

I look across the tracks again at the woman under the trees. I feel she could give me a hint, if she wanted to, about what the stones are. But she's looking at the sky. I follow her gaze but see only the moon. The air is so clear here that I can see individual craters limned in gray across its golden face.

A rush of air, a howling of bells. Another tram pulls to a stop. It's not the 9. A few people get off, and others get on. The doors close. The tram leaves.

When it's gone, the stones on the track ties are exactly where they were before. My fingers twitch with the urge to pick up the largest one, so scarred with scratches it looks like the surface of the moon.

I look down the track. Another tram is coming, but it's still a reasonable distance away. Without thinking, I hop onto the gravel bed, stooping to pick up the stone.

Someone is shouting in Czech, but I don't bother turning. The stone is heavier than I expected and surprisingly warm in my hand, the scratches black on its glittering gray surface. They seem to shift as I turn the stone. I imagine they are about to show me a story.

A hammering of bells reminds me I'm still standing on the tracks. The tram is almost on me. I jump back onto the platform, stone in hand. The older woman harangues me for my recklessness as the doors open and passengers disembark.

Most of the people still on the platform get onto this tram. I can't see from here if it's the 9. The woman who's been scolding me slaps my arm before jumping on as well. When the tram leaves, there's only me, the stone, and a circle of approaching women.

They come from everywhere, all black-clad, all around my age. I'm sure they weren't on the platform before. Maybe they came while I was on the tracks, but they seem to have appeared out of nowhere.

A crunch of gravel makes me turn to see the woman from across the road jumping onto the platform. "Hello," she says, in accented English. "I see you picked it up."

I close my fingers around the rock, feeling strangely breathless. "Did you put it there?"

Her head tilts, birdlike, against her feathered hood. She studies the stone as if she can read it. "What do you see?"

The others cluster closer as I turn the stone around. As I do, the lines resolve into a picture. "A house. A sun."

"Where?" she asks intently. Her eyes are very blue. "Is it rising or setting?"

"Setting." I'm not sure how I know, but it's clear. "I think… For some reason, it reminds me of my house in the US. Like the sun setting there." The image of a fading sky above that lakeside house flashes through my mind, making me shiver. I'd better call home soon.

She glances at the others. "Ah, well," she says, as if sharing a joke. "At least you've found a home here."

"What—"

Another tram whirs towards us, this one with a blazing "9" in the front window. She hooks her arm in mine. "Come on," she says. "This is your tram."

The doors open. We climb the stairs. The other women stream after us onto the tram, until the car is peppered with them. Even among the mostly black-clad commuters, they stand out.

Not knowing what to do, I allow the woman who's holding my arm to pull me with her into a pair of seats. The stone in my hands is still warm. I cradle it against my body like an egg as the tram departs.

The presence of the women creates a strange atmosphere. I can tell all the other passengers feel it: they keep glancing at us sideways as if wary of looking at us directly. I'm one of *us*, I realize suddenly, part of the flock. I'm even wearing black, except for a blue scarf my best friend gave me before

I came here. I touch it absently with the hand that's not cradling the rock.

I start to stand at my stop, but my escort pulls me back down into my seat. "No," she says. "We're going to Bertramka."

I blink, surprised: it's a poorly lit stop, and there's nothing to do there at night. However, it's not far past my house, and I can easily walk back. I shrug and nod in agreement.

Collectively, the passengers seem to breathe a sigh of relief as we get off. We cluster on the platform like black-feathered birds. My guide-slash-kidnapper looks both ways as the tram leaves. Then she runs across the street, pulling me behind her. The rest of them follow. We all fetch up against the gates of Malostranský Cemetery, peering through the wrought-iron bars at the ivy-grown mystery within.

"They close at five in the winter," I comment, gesturing at the sign.

I suspect that they already know that. One slim woman with long brown hair sidles to a smaller gate several feet away. She plants a black-booted foot between the bars, scales the gate like a cat, and flings herself over the wall.

I gasp.

The others laugh as I look up and down the street. There's no one nearby. As I look for security cameras, there's a clank inside the cemetery, and the main gate swings open.

"Come in," intones the brown-haired woman, gesturing theatrically.

My guide has long since let go of my arm. I can leave if I

want to. But I follow them in, shivering with pleasurable fear as the gate clangs shut.

It's pitch black inside. There are no lamps, and the streetlights visible through the gate aren't close enough to penetrate the darkness. I can only make out big shapes: the hulking shadow of the church and the enormous effigy of a man (some prince or priest, or maybe both) kneeling in eternal prayer by the entrance. I come to this cemetery often during the day to walk and admire the atmosphere, but it's different at night: listening, silent, almost waiting.

My guide pulls a handful of jingling change from her pocket and starts towards the statue. "Time to leave the guardian a tip," she says. Stepping over the low wrought-iron fence, she sets a few coins on the statue's base in a little stack, just visible in the faint amber glow of the streetlamps.

The others follow suit. Some of the stacks are taller or shorter or made of different coins. I fish out my change purse and find a jumble of one- and two- and five-crown pieces. Thirteen silver coins: a good number for a cemetery. I clamber over the fence and stack them beneath the statue.

One of the fence's iron spikes rakes my thigh as I climb out again. The others laugh at me as I curse and stumble.

"Why didn't we leave our tips with him?" I gesture at a weathered stone angel standing in the grass between us and the front gate. "There's no fence around him."

My guide puts her arm around my shoulders. "We don't mess with him," she says quietly, drawing me away from the formidable angel. "He's not one to piss off. Count Leopold over there is much more reasonable."

The others are already well ahead of us. They walk in pairs and threes, speaking in Czech and other languages I can't identify. Their silhouettes blend with the tombs until I can't tell who is woman and who is weeping angel. Clouds of their breath float up into the hidden canopies of the cemetery trees: it's colder now that it's fully night. My guide's arm around me is comfortingly warm but thin.

"What's your name?" I ask as we bear deeper into the heart of the graveyard.

She leans closer. "Marta. What's yours?"

"Christine." I laugh. "I'm surprised you don't know. You seem to know everything else about me."

"You think we were watching you?" She sounds amused. "We weren't. Not before tonight."

I start to relax as we press deeper into the graveyard. It's not as dark as I thought. Scattered pools of moonlight stain the ivy that covers most of the graves. The ivy swallows the sound of our footsteps, and I hear nothing from the women ahead except the occasional whisper. There's a stillness here that I've rarely felt outside the walls. With every step, my uncertainties are swallowed by the earth, leaving only quiet.

We go to the section farthest from the church, where few of the ruined graves have been repaired. Some of the women sit on the steps of a mausoleum. Others swing over the fences to the family plots beside it. As they settle, Marta plops herself down on a stone-vaulted grave and gestures for me to join her. I choose the next grave, sitting cross-legged on the cold, fractured vault.

It's not immediately obvious why we've come. The women on the mausoleum steps are leaning on each other's shoulders, chattering in multiple languages at once. I can't understand any of it, but it doesn't matter: the cemetery itself seems to speak to us in a whispering voice older than time—not the voice of the dead, but a voice the dead all know.

I lean back against the icy headstone of my chosen grave. I don't mind the chill, but I'm grateful for the warmth of the runestone in my hand. As the night deepens, we watch the moon pass overhead, framed by the black reaching outlines of the trees. Outside, we hear the trams passing and occasional footsteps on the street.

Nearby is another iron gate. A woman and her daughter pause to peer through it from outside. When they see our shadows move among the gravestones, they gasp and hurry away.

My companions laugh. I find myself laughing, too.

"Do you think they'll call the police?" I ask when we quiet down.

Marta shakes her head. "People mind their own business. If the police do come, we'll hide. They've never caught us."

She calls an instruction in Czech to another woman, who takes a big bottle of wine out of her bag. Someone else produces a loaf of bread. The first woman opens the wine, takes a sip, and pours half the bottle onto one of the graves. She murmurs a few words and passes what's left to her neighbor, who sips and passes, and so forth.

When it's my turn, I drink without hesitation. The merlot has a strange earthy flavor as if it had been strained through dirt.

After the wine comes the bread. It's unremarkable, too, probably from a convenience store, but when I take a bite I can suddenly see more clearly, as if this strange sacrament has invited me into the confidence of the cemetery.

Leaning back against the headstone of my chosen grave, I smile as the woman who brought the bread (pretty and blonde, in a neat hat and a nice wool coat) lays the last of the loaf by her own headstone. She smiles, too, languidly. We're all a little drunk, though we've barely had a mouthful of wine. Conversation slows. But there's more meaning now in the glances we throw each other, communion happening now unspoken.

Marta leans over, nudging me. "Do you still have it?"

"What?" I look down at the stone in my hand. "Oh. Yes."

"Leave it when you go. On a gravestone, maybe."

"Okay." I start to put it down but then wait, not wanting to let it out of my hands yet.

We stay for a long time; well after the day trams stop running and the street goes silent. Sometimes, we get up to walk between the graves, trailing our fingers over fragmented headstones. We sit on the benches, wade through the ivy, and stop to feel out names and inscriptions that have long ceased to mean anything to anyone alive. I feel a connection to some of the graves as if their occupants were reaching back to me across the years, whispering their stories. It must be a privilege to be buried in such a strong community of spirits.

Eventually, the moon sinks out of sight. One by one, the women rise from their places on the graves and file toward the entrance.

I follow, last in line, as reluctant to leave as I was at first to enter. The runestone is heavy in my hand. I find a promising grave (a family plot, its headstone engraved in German and adorned with cherubs) and tuck the stone gently among the ivy. It settles into place like a planted seed.

"Good choice," Marta says. She takes my hand and leads me to the gate, which is standing open once more. Its sentinel lamps flicker as we pass, finding us worthy or unworthy. As the gate clangs shut, I feel I have left something irretrievable behind me.

The others trail across the street like high school girls cutting class, fetching up against the windows of the shops on the other side.

"Who would put a kids' clothing store here?" muses Lera, the woman who scaled the cemetery wall. "When the moon is dark, they come over here to play—those little ghosts, those babies. I've seen them step into the clothing to try it on. Who'd put that on their child?"

"And the gowns," says a blade-thin woman named Ula, who I think is from Slovenia. "How many brides are buried over there? You want to trail their envy down the aisle on your wedding day?" She looks at the gowns, bell-shaped concoctions of sequins and tulle. They're not expensive; this isn't an upscale neighborhood. "Though a couple of these are really pretty. I'd look good in that one." She points to a relatively restrained one that's been marked half-off.

"You'd look good in anything, darling." Marta's voice isn't particularly loud or striking, but when she speaks everyone else falls quiet. "Now, my loves, it's time to go home. We need our beauty rest."

"We could have had that in the cemetery," says Lera, grinning. "We should all sleep there some night. What do you think the caretaker would do if he found us lying on the graves?"

As they all whoop with laughter, I realize I can't tell what languages they're speaking anymore. I understand them all perfectly.

Eventually, they all trail off into the night, and I'm left alone with Marta. She looks up at the face of a nearby building, pointing to an unlit window at the top.

"We'll be there tomorrow night, inside. You can come up any time after sunset. Whenever you're ready."

She doesn't offer clarification but turns and walks up the nearest alley. I watch her till she disappears, melting into shadows. Then, I begin the long, lonely walk up the hill to my street.

My apartment feels emptier than usual tonight. I pace, check my mail, and turn off the computer. Then I go out again, wandering up and down the silent, sloping streets till dawnlight peeks over the hills.

The light makes Prague a different city, a confection of stained gingerbread and drowsing white statues. When I've been walking for a long time, the streets fill slowly with people. Cafes open. I find one and go inside.

When I'm tucked in a booth with coffee and a wedge of cake, I can almost imagine I'm back in college after an all-nighter, dazed and headachy and not quite real. I stir my cappuccino, and a scatter of foam falls across the napkin when I put the spoon down. It looks like a house and a setting sun.

I sit there for a long time. Finally, when the cafe owner starts sending me unfriendly looks, I drag myself from the booth and stagger home. I sleep until nightfall.

That night, I dress in black and walk down to the cemetery. It's black inside beyond the lamps. I hear no voices. Realizing presently that I'm pressed against the iron gate, peering into the graveyard like a ghoul, I sidle out from under the lamps and turn to look at the buildings across the street.

One strange thing about Prague at night is how few of the windows are ever lit. Most of the buildings on this street are dark; perhaps, like my own prewar tenement, they're mostly unoccupied. There's only one light on in the soot-stained building Marta showed me last night: a single window at the very top. It's much too high to see inside, but it must be the place she meant.

It takes me a moment to find the front entrance, which

is hidden behind a wrought-iron gate covered with silver graffiti. I try the handle, but it's firmly locked.

There's a row of buzzers beside the door. Half of them are marked, mostly with Czech surnames. The rest are as blank as the windows. At a loss, I choose one at the top and push.

There's no bell tone, no static. I try the next buzzer and the next, but there is no response. No one is going to let me in.

Whenever you're ready, Marta said. I think I am, but how can I know? I wasn't ready for last night, after all. But I'm glad it happened.

I run my hands absently over the thick stone blocks. They're smeared with smog and acid rain and stains of unknown provenance. The stains form a pattern: a simple house with what might be a setting sun behind it.

Sunset: the end of one time, the beginning of another. A shift between phases. I remember the house by the lake, my family's voices ringing from the windows. I feel a sudden, heartbreaking certainty that I'll never go back there again.

I always thought this sojourn would be temporary, a way to see some of the world while finally figuring out what to do with my life. But there's something in what I've found here that doesn't seem compatible with ordinary existence. If I stay—and I *want* to, more than anything I've ever wanted—there won't be any going back to that house beside the lake.

And I've chosen. I understand that now. This is the place. This is the time.

"I'm ready," I say.

I don't know what I expect to happen. But the house is silent.

I jaywalk across the empty street and look up at the sole lit window. This time I see motion flicker inside.

Maybe it's a test.

The lighted window upstairs is where I need to go. That's simple; there's no need to let myself be held back by fear. Remembering Lera's calm grace as she climbed the cemetery gate, I cross back to the building, wedge my fingers between the bricks, and climb..

For the first few seconds, it's impossible. Then I find handholds and footholds. I shouldn't be able to pull myself up, but my body feels weightless. I scramble up rows of windows, clamber over balconies, steady myself on the decorative molding. Before I think to look down, I'm at the top-floor window.

The room within is dim, lit only by the bluish glow of a television. A dozen women are scattered around it, reclining on bean bags and sofas. My heart warms to see them. They already mean more to me than any friends I ever had.

I tap on the window. Marta's black robe flutters as she rises to let me in. As I clamber over the windowsill, she kisses my cheek and hands me a flute of white wine. "Here, darling. Glad you could make it."

Most of the others are familiar from last night, but there are a few I haven't seen: a powerful-looking woman in huge black boots; a thin, professorial type in glasses. They're all clustered around a TV in the corner, where an obscure art film is playing. Sipping my wine, I return Marta's smile and go to join them.

Time passes. It's companionable. We don't talk to each other, but we don't need to: our bond makes small talk unnecessary. An hour goes by, or maybe three, but I don't feel bored or impatient. We're resting, gathering energy.

As time goes on, my companions' faces change, new features growing and fading in the flickering light: cats' eyes, ram's horns, a vague rippling veil like a sheet of water. I wonder what the light must be doing to me, what features are on my face now that were never there before.

Finally, the movie ends. Marta stands, holding a bottle. In an instant, all our focus is on her.

"Ladies." I don't know if she's speaking Czech, English, or some other language, but I understand her perfectly. "It's time to celebrate our lives, our power, our sisterhood. Come and toast with me." She holds up the bottle.

We all raise our glasses. Into each she pours a splash of sparkling golden wine. At her signal, we drink.

This wine is tart and fresh. It goes to my head immediately. The world pulses around me as I slide into new consciousness. I watch my sisters' souls emerge from the shrouds of their skin: each beautiful and terrible, each far too much for any human body to contain. The shapes I saw by the television's light have grown real now, undeniable. The tall redhead beside me wears a proud set of antlers. Marta's head is crowned by a halo of black feathers.

And as we all look on each other's true faces, I can see their love for each other, how long they've been together: years, decades, even centuries. I've stumbled into something I'm much too small to be a part of.

But they have welcomed me, and I adore them.

Marta goes to the window. "Let's fly." She hands her glass to Lena, climbs over the sill, and leaps.

Part of me is horrified. But mostly I feel pleasantly detached. I watch calmly as the other women set their glasses down and follow her, climbing one by one into the night.

I don't see them fall. Instead, a flock of winged black creatures soars into the night. I stand at the window watching them, wanting to follow but lacking the nerve.

As I stare at the retreating backs of my winged sisters, Marta's voice echoes in my head. "Well?" Her voice is flat but not impatient. "Are you coming?"

"I can't." The words fall out, defeated. "I can't do it."

Her laugh slides down my spine. "You can. Of course you can. But we can't help you. If you get yourself together, come and find us."

As the echoes of her voice fade from my mind, I stare after the flock until I can't see them anymore. Finally, I go back to the TV. The art film has ended, but a menu of others is displayed. I choose one at random and watch it, then another and another, until morning's light begins to thread through the windows. Then I consider leaving. Instead, I curl up on the couch and fall asleep.

I spend the day in the apartment. Time passes in a haze: it's morning for a while, then afternoon, without much difference between them. There's nothing much to do. I sleep, pace, watch movies without remembering them. At one point, feeling hungry, I find some chips in the kitchen and eat them. Later, I spend an hour staring out the window, telling myself that I should leave. But I don't.

I never open the door. Doing that would break a spell I'm not ready to break. But sometimes, I look down the long brick face of the building and wonder if I could climb down again, like a vampire or a cockroach, skittering face-first down to the ground in full view of everyone who's watching.

Or maybe I'd just fall and die. I'm close enough to despair now that I'm not sure it would be such a tragedy.

Eventually, night slides down the street again, overlapping waves of dusk eddying towards the river. The cemetery breathes in shadows and takes on its complete form. Thinking the other women must return soon, I wait for a long time. Then, as the streets quiet once more, I begin to doubt.

It's clear that this apartment isn't usually occupied. The walls are bare, the furniture old and anonymous, and there's a staleness in the air that must have taken more than a day to build. Why would they return when they could go anywhere in Prague or travel to another place entirely? It was only chance that I encountered them when I did. They could choose to move on at any moment, and I would never see them again.

My heart jerks at that thought. This *can't* be the end of my choice, not now that I've crossed so many thresholds. The witches are in my mind, heart, and veins now. They'll be there forever, even if I never see them again. And if I keep going through life as it was, my existence will be a parody of what it was before I met them. I'll be performing those empty motions for the rest of my life, which could be a very long time.

I have to find them. I need to find them *now*. And only boldness and speed will help me.

On the floor near the window stands the wine bottle. I pick it up, hoping there are dregs left, and find nearly a full inch standing in the bottom. I drink it down without a second thought.

My eyes widen as the room grows luminous. All my fear and hesitation drop away replaced by joyful certainty: *this is the way.*

I can see in the dark again. But it's more than that. I'm aware of every sound, every motion. I am an integral part of the city and the night. I know everything about them. Across the street, the cemetery breathes an invitation. The river whispers, hinting at drowned secrets. Shadows thread through the statues on the housefronts, bringing them to life. A magic city, rich with power—the power that now runs through my own veins. There is nothing to be afraid of.

I go back to the window, climb over the sill, and jump.

I don't fall. I float. I'm a feather in an updraft, the shadow of a bird, the lost memory of someone's long-ago dream of flight. I don't know what shape my body has taken, but it doesn't draw any attention from below. I glide across the street, hover above the cemetery trees, and wonder where I should go.

But I'm flying. I can go anywhere.

Petřín Hill is the first place that comes to mind. It's the most visible landform in the city, a vast winter-rusted hill beside the river that overshadows even the nearby castle. I think they even have bonfires there on Walpurgis Night. A perfect place for witches. I fly to the tower-crowned crest of the hill and glide along its night-spelled pathways, looking for my sisters. In the waning moonlight, the park is haunted by flickers of movement that might be ghosts or something else. But there are no witches here.

I go to the river next, sweeping from bridge to bridge. The river island parks are closed, but people linger on the bridges, drinking in the night. None of them look up as I fly by. I search their faces for familiar features, but no mysteries are revealed.

The women could be anywhere: in any dreamscape architecture of the city, hiding behind crenellations, pretending to be statues. Or maybe they're dancing in another graveyard, But they're here somewhere: I feel them. Maybe—

I stop mid-flight as I realize that I know where they are. It only makes sense that they've gone somewhere I can find them.

Laughing—hoping I'm right—I rise and soar towards Motol.

The tram stop is empty, but I know they're here. I turn my attention to the trees along the road. Sleeping birds untuck their heads as I fly from bough to bough, searching for faces in the shadows.

Finally, in a stand of trees behind the tram stop, I see a cluster of silhouettes, much too large to be birds, perched in the branches.

I'm almost afraid for a moment, but I gather myself and glide over to them. Their outlines resolve into the forms of my new companions.

At rest, they look diminished. Maybe it's the approach of dawn that shrinks them, making them women again. The wildness is back beneath their skins now, waiting for the next twilight. I hesitate, reluctant to wake them. Then, seeing Marta drowsing in the crook of an oak tree, I alight beside her.

She smiles, moving slightly to make room. "You found us," she murmurs.

I lean against the trunk, suddenly drowsy myself. "Was I not supposed to?"

Marta shrugs.

Off to the east, sunlight filters up above the city proper. The light gleams dully on the tram tracks below. From here, I can see the makeshift altar where I picked up my runestone a lifetime ago.

"Why did you pick me?" I ask suddenly. "Was I special? Or was I just some random person?"

Marta smiles slightly. In a neighboring tree, one of the other women begins to hum. It's a soft, melancholy sound, a song of leaving things behind. "We didn't choose you," Marta says. "You chose yourself. You could have picked up the stone or left it."

"And I picked it up." I look up at the eastern sky. Sunlight is brightening over the city. Distant flocks of swifts and pigeons wheel over the rooftops. I imagine all of them are witches, flying through a world they no longer truly inhabit. "And I went into the cemetery with you and drank with you. And I climbed the wall and spent the night with you."

She nods. "You took all the invitations. We weren't looking for you, but we were waiting for you. And you were waiting for us, I think."

"Yes." Dawn traces her face in gold. Nearby, the singer hums on.

Far below us, a young woman walks onto the empty platform. Though alone, she doesn't look lonely. She's as bright as the new dawn: powerful and human, ready for whatever life will bring. I wonder if she's alone like I was, or if she has family here.

The woman stops just where I stood two nights ago. She looks around idly for a while, running her hand along the frost-coated railing as she watches the morning traffic.

Finally, her gaze falls to the tracks.

It takes her a second to notice the stones. She stares at them for a long time, maybe wondering how they got there. There are plenty of them left.

And I see it beginning to happen again. She'll jump down in a second and take a stone, and we'll have another sister. I wonder which stone she'll choose, what it might show her. Will her story be like mine? Or is she a different kind of person?

We're *all* watching. As wind gathers the trees into one swelling wave, my sisters tense forward on their boughs. We're all holding our breath, fixing our eyes on the woman below. We are, despite our great sisterhood, a desperately lonely collective. As long as we breathe, we'll draw others to us—always looking for the next one who might complete the circle but will not, adding another glass to our eternal toast.

We wait.

The woman crouches, reaching for the runestones. But they're too far to touch. She has to take that first step off the platform, defying convention and her own fear, and give a passing nod to Death.

In the distance, a clattering sigh: the next tram is coming.

Though she hesitates, I know she'll do it. She looks much braver than me: more confident, more sure. A worthier sister than I am. What might the witches' wine make of her? Maybe she'll grow claws, or golden wings that only we can see. She'll be strong and fearless, a perfect addition to our coven.

But then, just as I'm thinking this, she stands and hurries away, not stopping till she's far down the platform. She takes out her phone and begins to scroll, as if pretending she'd never noticed the runestones in the first place. She doesn't move until the next tram comes. When it does, she gets on immediately and is gone.

After a moment of silence, I look at Marta. "Why didn't she take it?"

Marta shrugs one-shouldered. "Most don't." Her voice is tired. "Maybe she didn't recognize the invitation. Maybe she didn't want it. Not everyone is as courageous as you."

Our sisters settle into place along the boughs, nestling down to sleep. A few peel away from the group, sliding down the trunks of the trees to appear again at the bottom as ordinary women. They melt into the morning crowd that's growing at the tram stop.

Marta leans against me. I rest my head on hers. As another tram departs, we close our eyes and wait for night to come.

KATHERINE TRAYLOR is a US-born writer of fantasy and horror. Her writing is often fairy-tale-inspired, with strong themes of transformation, and can be found in a number of anthologies and other publications. She has spent most of her life working abroad as an English instructor, first in South Korea, and then in the Czech Republic. She currently lives in Prague with her beautiful wife, two cats, a dog, and a growing sea of creative clutter. Follow her online at katherinetraylor.com.

BROOKLYN

Richard Kadrey

In an old Park Slope brownstone, Frost slumped at his desk very close to death.

He'd neglected himself for the last few months, so the nails on his ink-stained fingers had grown long. A chaotic scattering of his writing materials lay on the desk and the floor around him. Disposable pens and cheap legal pads. Expensive linen paper and knife-sharpened pencils. Piles of cyan paper scrawled with perfumed crimson ink—an unopened pack of Egyptian parchment. Lastly was the vellum on which he'd written with a heavy gold Graf von Faber-Castell fountain pen using an absurdly expensive black ink made in a single village on an island just north of Nemuro in Japan. But it was trash. All trash. None of it could contain the depth of feeling required for his story.

Now, in a panicked effort to set down the words properly, he slashed open his left arm with a skinning knife and used an inscribing tool on the exposed bone.

With the help of several clamps and retractors, he managed to hold the wound open. For the first time, the work went well. The words flowed, so he cut himself further, setting down the lines that had been locked inside him for so long. But he was bleeding profusely. It was just before he lost consciousness that he heard a voice he'd waited for all his life. An angel. His guardian. But the voice wasn't pleasant in the way that he'd always imagined an angel's voice would be. This voice buzzed around the inside of his head like a fly bouncing off the sides of his skull. But he knew he would be dead soon, so he answered the angel just to distract himself from the agonizing pain.

"Is this suicide," buzzed the angel softly, "or something more?"

"Does it matter?" said Frost. "I'm going to die."

He took long, shallow breaths and almost toppled over when he tried to sit up. The brocade arm of his office chair was soaked through so that it leaked blood and sweat. A thick crimson pool had congealed on the floor around his bare feet, slumped over as he was, the expanding red was all he could see.

The angel spoke again. "I need you to answer my question because I don't engage with suicides. Suicide is for fools and spiritual cowards. Worse, they have no imagination. So, I'll ask you one more time: Is this suicide?"

The pain and blood loss made it hard for Frost to form coherent thoughts. Still, he managed to whisper, "This is art, goddammit. I'm no suicide."

"Are you a doctor then?" asked his angel.

"No," gasped Frost. "A writer. I just needed…"

But the black closed in, liquid and thick. He felt himself drowning in it, finally losing consciousness and falling to the floor.

The dark and silent place where he next found himself felt vast, like it might go on forever, and that frightened Frost in a way he'd never felt before. After all his searching for the right tools and his experiments in methods, had his life's work led to him this pointless, dismal end? Nothingness? The bottom of an infinite well where he'd crumble to dust with his story unwritten?

Frost tried calling out, but he made no sound. He listened, but there was nothing to hear, and the dead silence of the place weighed down on him. He grew cold while his butchered arm ached as if it was on fire.

Thankfully, after a few minutes, the angel spoke again. "Why did you mutilate yourself like that, writer?"

Frost turned, scanning the dark, hoping to see the angel. The floor felt like damp stone, and he wondered where the water had come from when he realized that he was lying in his own blood.

This time, when Frost tried to speak, he could hear himself. "What I was doing was an experiment in form," he said. "I've written millions of words in pen and pencil, on typewriters and computers. At times, I've written on the backs of envelopes, the margins of other books, and napkins in restaurants. Nothing worked. For this story, nothing worked. I needed something more—radical."

The angel said, "If you simply wanted blood, you wouldn't have opened your entire arm. What were you looking for?"

"The bones. I finally found the right medium. I'll inscribe my greatest story on them."

"Tell me about your story."

"No."

"Come now. What else is there to do here in this nothingness but tell stories? Just give me a hint."

Frost hesitated, then said, "It's a love story."

"Is it a happy story or a tragedy?"

"I don't know yet. That's why I have to finish it."

Frost's body spasmed and went rigid. His skin was glacial. He wondered if this was what going into shock felt like. The weak laugh he mustered turned into a racking cough, and he wondered if this was the last sensation his body could muster before it died.

"In answer to your question, yes," said the angel. "This is what death—your death—feels like. But death isn't always inevitable. I can help you, but I'll need something in return."

"What do you want?" The cold was expanding, like an animal digging into his flesh with frigid claws as it enfolded itself around him. If it subsumed his body, he knew that would be the end. "I don't want to die like this."

The angel said, "Give me shelter. I will live in your flesh and help you with your work."

"How will you do that?"

In the dark, the silence dragged on for what felt like a

century. Then, "If bones are what you need, I'll bring you bones so you won't have to mutilate yourself."

"No," said Frost. "My story is the story of a man's life. It needs to be human bones, not some animal scraps from a butcher shop."

"I can supply whatever you need."

"How?"

"Do we have an agreement? Answer quickly. I can't hold you in this limbo state much longer. Do you want to live or die?"

Frost tried to wrap his arms around himself, but his body had gone completely rigid, and he shook in the deepest, rawest cold he'd ever felt. It seemed like forever, but he finally managed to work his jaw loose enough to croak out, "Live."

"And so, you shall," said the angel.

Frost was exhausted when he opened his eyes—a soul-draining weakness that weighed down on him and made every movement a sluggish effort as if through glycerin. But he was alive. His whole body ached as he turned his head to look at his mutilated arm. The incision was still there, the words still clearly inscribed in the bone, but he was no longer bleeding. He took a deep breath, then another. With each lungful of air, he felt his body reviving. First, he could move—slowly—his hands and arms. Then his legs. He gently twisted his torso left and right, feeling the stretch and contraction of his muscles, along with the bones' subtle realignment in response.

"I feel like I was dead," he said.

"You were. Or practically so. It will take some time before you're yourself again. But no more than a day or two."

"Good. I need to work while the words are in my head. I don't want to lose them."

"Rest now. The words and work will come."

Frost looked at the open gash in his arm. "How can I rest with my arm open like this?"

"Look again," said the angel.

When Frost looked, the wound was closed. There was no blood, just a livid worm-like keloid buried in the shallow flesh of his arm.

"Your arm will remain closed and healthy until you open it again. And when you do, there will be no blood and even less pain. These are the things I can do for you now that you've taken me into your flesh."

Flexing the fingers of his wounded arm, Frost said, "You've saved my life, but more importantly, my work. The only work I'll ever do that will matter. Thank you."

"Rest now and thank me when you've finished."

Frost shakily pushed himself from the desk chair. Each movement was agony. Each breath he took almost collapsed into a gasp. Sweat soaked his clothes when he finally, after several minutes, made it to the bedroom. He stripped off his shirt and pants, letting them fall to the floor. Even settling onto the mattress felt like hot knives boring into each joint.

"You're sure this will pass?" he said to the angel.

"Sleep. And when you awaken, it will be a new day in a new world."

As Frost's eyes closed, he said, "What should I call you?"

"What do you want to call me?"

"My angel? My guardian? My…"

"Salvation? Any of those will do. Creatures such as I aren't concerned about names. Those are for others to invent."

"Angel then. My guardian angel."

"Sleep," said the angel. "There's much to do."

The room was dark when Frost opened his eyes again. They were gummy with sleep, and when he moved to wipe them clean, he was surprised by the lack of pain. He sat up slowly, not fully trusting his body yet. But it was the same when he stood. No pain. In fact, he felt more energized than he had in years. Clearheaded and strong. He checked his left arm to make sure he wasn't dreaming. The lurid scar was still there, running from his wrist all the way to his elbow.

"How do you feel?" said the angel.

"Wonderful. Better than I hoped for. How long have I been asleep?"

"A day and a half. It's night now. Perhaps you should lie down and sleep until morning."

Grabbing clean clothes from his closet, Frost said, "No. I feel great. I want to get back to work."

Once dressed, Frost sat on the edge of the bed and checked

his cellphone. There were two calls, both from his ex, Alli. He sighed and set the phone back on his bed table.

The angel said, "You seem troubled."

"It's nothing. Alli is—was—the love of my life, but things happened."

"Is she the subject of your story?"

Frost nodded minutely. He didn't want to talk about it, but the words came anyway. "What are, what we were, is unfinished. It's why I don't know if my story is a happy one or a tragedy."

"And this is why you won't speak to her?"

"I need to write more to know what happened. And to understand myself. Really, I don't want to talk about it. I just want to work."

"Of course. I'll remain silent until you need me."

Back in his office, the crimson pool of blood under his desk had dried to a brownish stain on the floor. The arms of his chair were also dry, and bore the dark stains of his first attempt at bone scribing. Polished and cleaned, his knife, the clamps, retractors, and inscribing tool lay in a neat row on his desk. Frost pushed up his sleeve and held the blade over the thick keloid on his forearm. His breath became unsteady as he remembered all the pain and fear from his previous writing attempt.

"Is there something wrong?" said the angel.

"I'm afraid. I want to work, but what good will any of it be if I die before I'm finished?"

"But you won't die. Or bleed. Or feel pain as long as I'm with you."

"You said that, but how do I know?"

"There's only one way to be certain. You can write or sit at your desk forever, a coward afraid to finish his greatest work."

"Death isn't what I really fear. It's dying *now*. No one will read the story until I'm dead and they find my bones. I have to live long enough for that."

"As long as you work, your story will be told."

"And no pain?"

"Or blood," said the angel.

When Frost touched the tip of the knife to his forearm, his stomach knotted as if being twisted by an invisible hand reaching through his skin to torment him. But this time, he didn't stop. He plunged the blade into the scar by his elbow and drew it down in a single motion from his forearm to his wrist. It wasn't until he drew air into his lungs again that he realized he'd been holding his breath. To his great surprise, the angel had spoken the truth—there was no pain, just a strangely pleasant warmth along the length of the incision. Nor was there any blood. Somehow, the veins and arteries of his arm had been sealed off so that he was able to see his work without continuously wiping the area clean. Frost applied the bright clamps and retractors to hold the wound open, then picked up the inscribing tool.

He worked the rest of the night, covering both his radius and ulna in neatly formed words. When he was done with one arm, he removed his tools, and the incision sealed itself— skin, muscles, and ligament neatly knitting back together in just a few minutes. With the bones of his left arm fully inscribed, he used the knife to incise his right arm and begin work there. When he finally set down the inscribing tool, a reddish-yellow dawn glowed through his office window. Again, the arm quickly healed itself and Frost rubbed his eyes, drained but satisfied.

"Perhaps it's time to rest again," said the angel.

"I think you're right. I'll start on my legs tonight."

"Good. I can tell your story will be a great one."

Frost flexed his fingers, feeling the muscles of his arms contract and relax normally. He laughed and then, suddenly starving, went into the kitchen and made sausage and eggs, wolfing them both down with glasses of orange juice. When he lay down in bed, his sleep was peaceful and dreamless. At one point, he thought he heard his phone ring, but he ignored it and drifted back into a pleasant oblivion.

Frost worked for a week inscribing at night and sleeping through the day. He'd soon covered the tibia and fibula on both legs, then moved on to the delicate phalanges of his hands. It infuriated him that he couldn't cover his entire skull with words, but it was simply impossible for him to reach the back or the very top of his head and inscribe with any accuracy. Instead, he resigned himself to working on the front of his skull. Removing the flesh there was a trickier procedure than cutting into his arms and legs. The skin, muscles, and connective tissue were more subtle and required more attention than his previous surgeries. But when he finally peeled his face off and revealed the lustrous white bone beneath, he felt a rush of excitement like he'd never felt before. He wept as he worked, not with pain but happiness.

However, his happiness didn't last long.

Days later, as the skin slipped neatly back together again over his ribs, he set down his tools and lay his head on his desk, weary and heartbroken.

"Is there something wrong?" said the angel.

The fly buzzing din in Frost's head startled him. He'd been so consumed by work that he and the angel hadn't spoken in days. Frost sat up, laying his hands on the desk.

"Everything is wrong," he said. "I've used up my bones. There's nothing left for me to write on, and my story isn't nearly over."

"Bones?" buzzed the angel. "If bones are the issue, don't worry. Humans are like mayflies. I can acquire all the bones you need."

"How?"

"Leave that to me. Rest now, and when you awaken, bones will have been provided."

"I can't stand this. I'm so close…"

"Trust me. Your work will be complete. Now sleep."

Frost lay his head back down on the desk and slipped off into a deep sleep where he sat.

When Frost woke, his head throbbed in a dull and confusing way, as if his skull was overstuffed with cotton. His eyes and wrists ached. Scabs—crusted black like an insect's carapace—covered the knuckles of both hands. He had no idea how much time had passed. Hours? Days? He'd given up wearing a watch weeks before, and his cellphone was left face down near his bed. In a moment of despair and frustration, had placed a small strip of electrical tape over the date and time on the upper corner of his computer monitor.

"What the hell happened?"

The angel's voice cut through the pain in his head unpleasantly. "Nothing of consequence. Are you well enough to continue with your work?"

Frost rubbed his eyes with the heel of his hand, feeling the rough keloids from the scars. "I think so, but my bones are done. I have nothing to work with."

"Look behind you."

Frost turned and stared at the cheap blue velvet sofa he'd purchased from a Red Hook junk shop. Seated neatly in a row on the cushions were three human skeletons. The bones were a perfect ivory white. He stared at their perfection for a few minutes, wondering if they were real or part of a grotesque dream. Finally, he rose from his chair and crossed the room on stiff legs to where the skeletons were perched. He touched the top of each skull in turn, running his hands down the ridged vertebrae to the sinuous curves of their clavicles and scapulae, finally touching the delicate connective tissue that kept each one from falling to pieces on the floor.

He said, "Where did they come from?"

The angel buzzed. "As I told you, humans are mayflies."

"What does that mean?"

"Death is always near and usually pointless. Not so with these remains. You will elevate them from useless scraps to art."

Frost touched his fingertips to the mandible of the skeleton at the end of the row. It was strong and smooth, like a pebble washed ashore after being submerged in the sea for millennia. His head was beginning to clear.

"What happened to my hands?" he said.

"I am your flesh now, and I will heal you quickly."

Frost twisted and, with a loud *crack*, wrenched the skull from the skeleton on the end and brought it to his desk. As he picked up his inscribing tool, he said, "I don't entirely understand, but these will do nicely. The work is all that matters. Thank you."

"It's my pleasure," said the angel.

Light streamed into Frost's office, but he worked through the day and into the evening meticulously scratching his story onto the stranger's skull. He covered every inch of it in words of love and longing and for the first time in a long while he was content. "I think my story will have a happy ending after all," he said.

The angel didn't reply. In the silence, Frost enrobed the first skeleton in his story. By the time he was done, his hands were healed, so he quickly set to work on the second skeleton, then the third.

"These aren't enough," he said. "I'm almost finished, but I need more."

"How many more?"

"Perhaps one? I'm getting close."

"Despite the onset of winter, you'll have the one soon. Rest now and when you awaken, you'll continue your work."

"Thank you," Frost said and was asleep almost immediately.

When Frost awoke in his office, his body ached. But the skeleton on the sofa was so elegant and perfect that he forgot the pain and set immediately to work.

The day passed and by the time the sun set, Frost understood with grim certainty that even these bones weren't enough. To finish his story he'd need more. He set down his inscribing tool and, despite the snow falling outside and the chill in his apartment, he was sweating. He removed his shirt, draping it over the back of his office chair and collapsed on the cheap sofa, his mind drifted to the pleasing end he could see coming for his story. He didn't realize that he'd dozed off until he heard a voice. Not the buzzing of the angel, but one belonging to a woman.

"Peter?" she said softly.

Slowly, he opened his eyes and angled his head toward the voice, convinced he was dreaming. Alli was there by the door with her hands tense by her sides, her face grim with sadness and concern.

"Peter?" she said again, and this time Frost knew he wasn't dreaming.

"How did you get in?"

She held out a hand, showing a silver something. "I still have a key. You never asked for it back."

"Oh. It's good to see you," He felt suddenly glad and hopeful. Alli had walked out on him, but now she was back and standing just a few feet away.

Alli looked at him, but her expression turned from one of concern to a deep frown. "No one's heard from you in weeks and you didn't return my calls."

Frost gestured around the room. Alli took a step back when she saw the neat piles of bones surrounding his desk. She turned quickly back to him.

She said, "All those scars... what have you done to yourself?"

Frost looked down, seeing the crisscrossing network of red jagged lines covering his body. Touching his face, he realized how scarred he was there too.

"It's all right," he said. "It's all part of my work. When you read it you'll understand."

"Read what? You're not making sense. What's going on?"

"It's a new story. The best thing I've ever done. If you'll let me, I want to dedicate it to you."

The angel interrupted, "You have no need to justify your work to anyone. The woman is an interference."

"No, it's all right," Frost said. "This is Alli. The one I told you about."

Alli crossed over to the sofa and knelt next to him. "Peter, who are you talking to?"

"The angel. It's what made all this possible."

She shook her head. "There's no one here but us," she said, taking his hand. "You look like hell. Come with me right now. We're getting you to a doctor."

Alli was close enough for Frost to smell the perfume she always wore, a musky combination that reminded him of blood and gunpowder. The feel of her hand in his, warm and soft, was thrilling. He wanted to show Alli all that he'd accomplished. But she pulled him to his feet and got his shirt, slipping it on over his shoulders.

"This is wrong," said the angel.

"And what are you doing with all those bones?" she said. "Is this how you've spent your time? Hurting yourself and collecting—these things?"

The angel said, "No."

Before Frost could answer, Alli pulled him to the office door.

"Never mind. We're leaving right now. Where is your coat? It's snowing outside."

The buzzing in Frost's head rose from an insect annoyance to a chainsaw roar.

"No!" the angel screamed.

When Frost came to on the floor of his office Alli wasn't there. He pulled himself to his feet and called her name. Off balance, he called to her again and stumbled into the sofa. There he found the last skeleton he needed. Alli's clothes were scattered on the floor by the door. Frost dropped down on to the sofa and when he touched the bones, he swore that he could detect a faint trace of blood and gunpowder.

He said, "Is this—? How could you?"

"Mayflies," replied the angel firmly. "All mayflies. Only you, in whom I live, matter."

"I loved her."

"If that's true then show her by finishing your work."

Frost pulled the skeleton to his chest, still unable to process what the angel was saying and refusing to believe that the bones belonged to Alli. When his hand ran down her arm and touched some connective tissue, he felt it to be warm and still a little damp. It was fresh. The flesh couldn't have been flensed from it more than a few minutes before.

After a long silence, the angel said, "You told me that you only needed one more specimen to complete your story. Now you have it. What are you going to do?"

It took Frost a moment to speak.

"I thought I had a happy ending for my story, but I guess not."

"Then you'll continue the work?"

Frost shrugged. "What else is there to do?"

He turned, kissed Alli's cheek one last time and, with all the tenderness he could muster, ripped her skull away from her neck and took it to his desk.

He worked a day and a night on Alli's bones, carefully searching for the exact words to carve into precious remains. Eventually, he finished work on his tragedy with the final phrases on the ribs over what had been her heart. When he was done, Frost threw the inscribing tool to the floor and, with a sweep of his arm, knocked all the papers and pens off his desk. Gently, sorrowfully, he placed Alli's remains with the others, careful that all the bones were in proper story order. Going back to his desk he sat in his chairs simply staring at his collection.

"Alli," he said. "Wherever you are, I hope the story gives you some comfort."

"Congratulations," buzzed the angel. "You've finished your greatest work."

"I guess I have."

"What will you do next?"

"Next? I don't know. Nothing I suppose."

"You're an artist," replied the angel. "You can't live on nothing. You'll go mad."

Frost though about it, stared at Alli and the other bones, both pleased and horrified by his art. He said, "I have nothing left to say. You can leave now."

"What do you mean?" said the angel.

"I mean I'm grateful to you for saving my life and allowing me to finish my story, but it's done. It's time for you to go."

"Why would I do that? You asked for bones and I provided them."

"You killed Alli," screamed Frost.

"You asked for bones."

"Not hers."

"You should have been more specific."

"You sent my body to get all those bones, didn't you? That's why my knuckles bled and my body hurt. They fought back."

"Naturally."

"So, the last thing Alli saw was me murdering her," said Frost. But the angel didn't reply. He brought his hands to his face and wept quietly. "You have to go. I want you gone. Now."

"No."

"Go," Frost shouted.

"Lift your arm," said the angel.

Frost looked at his scarred right arm and attempted to lift it. It didn't budge. When he tried wiggling his scarred fingers they barely twitched.

"What have you done to me?" he asked.

The angel buzzed happily. "You wanted bones. I asked for flesh. We both got what we wanted. I am the body, and you live, as much as you live, in the bones beneath."

"No! I won't exist like this."

"You have no choice."

Frost thought for a moment. "But you still need me, the bones, to move and feed yourself. What if I refuse to cooperate?"

"You would starve yourself to death?"

"I would."

"Starvation is a long and terrible process. I don't believe that you're strong enough for it."

"Try me. You told me that you don't make deals with suicides. Well, that's what I am now. There's nothing left for me to do but to die."

Frost felt his right arm try to lift itself from the chair but his bones went rigid and held him in place. He did the same, again, when the angel tried to move his head and twist his body.

"You're not really my guardian angel, are you?" said Frost.

"I never said I was. Angel was *your* word."

"I'll starve you to gristle. Then, when I stink enough, let the flies and rats finish you off."

"I'll take your flesh with me. You won't live if I leave."

"I know, and I don't care. Just go."

Frost felt something change throughout his body. His skin and muscles felt slack, as if they were melting wax sliding down the side of a candle.

"Very well," said the angel. "But you must allow me the use of your bones to complete the task."

"All right. But no tricks."

"Tricks are for your sort, not mine."

"Use my bones as you need for now."

The angel raised a hand to Frost's chest and dug in with his nails, which had grown long and ragged in the last few weeks. With one terrific tug, it ripped off a mass of skin and pectoral muscle before letting it drop to the floor. Frost screamed.

The angel said, "I won't let the body bleed, but I no longer have any obligation to suppress your pain."

It took long into the night for the angel to peel Frost's torso, legs, and skull of all his flesh. After it roughly ripped the skin from his left arm, it used Frost's teeth to tear off the flesh and muscle, spitting them out onto the floor with the rest of the tissue.

Finally, it was done. Frost barely noticed, delirious with pain and terrified by watching his body torn apart. He wanted to howl in agony, but he lacked the muscles to move his jaw. The scream he was finally able to muster existed only in his mind.

"It's done," said the angel.

"I was hoping that without me, you would die," said Frost in his mind.

"As long as there is flesh, I'll live forever. Goodbye, Frost."

The mass of glistening meat at Frost's feet hauled itself slowly, painfully to the office door, sliding like a grotesque slug of muscles, skin, and organs. It left a trail of blood, bile, and lymph fluid behind as it heaved itself out of Frost's sight.

The thing that wasn't an angel had just enough mass to break through the house's front door, though it ripped itself badly in the process. Now, the not-an-angel bled profusely as it pulled itself through the snow to Prospect Park. Night birds flew from tree to tree like the shadows of ghosts, silent psychopomps waiting to escort souls to whatever came next.

The flesh lay there exposed to them, willing the birds to descend. They did and feasted throughout the night. When the sun rose in the morning, as a hundred crows, Frost's angel took to the sky.

Richard Kadrey is the New York Times bestselling author of the Sandman Slim supernatural noir series. Sandman Slim was included in Amazon's "100 Science Fiction & Fantasy Books to Read in a Lifetime," and is in development as a feature film. Some of Kadrey's other books include *King Bullet, The Grand Dark, Butcher Bird,* and *The Dead Take the A Train* (with Cassandra Khaw). He's written for film and comics, including *Heavy Metal, Lucifer,* and *Hellblazer.* Kadrey also makes music with his band, A Demon in Fun City.

MONTRÉAL / TIOHTIÀ:KE

Rich Larson

Dasha sprawls after sex, stretching her long body along the bed like a sated carnivore, slashing the curtain to one side to look out the window. The city is staticky, veiled by swirling snow. Seven stories down, across an ice-slopped street, the poison-yellow doors of metro Saint Laurent stand slammed open in the wind. The bike racks outside creak and shudder on mute.

"It's just a view," she says. "In a week, you won't even notice it."

I don't know what she means by that. I grip the sawblade edge of her scapula and dig my fingers deep as I dare into muscle. She does the good groan.

"Trapezius," I guess.

Her shoulder bobs a shrug. "I only know bones."

She knows them too well. Her favorite is the hyoid because it set off alone, detached itself from all other skeletal structure to become a horseshoe-shaped house for the tongue. Her second favorite is the sacrum. I can see the shape of hers, the triangular indent, the underskin pinch of it.

"Still snowing," I say, tapping the cold glass of the window.

"Ç'est pas grave," she says, because she's learning French, and that is the phrase she currently likes most.

She rolls over, props herself on one pale elbow, and stares me in the face. She's so beautiful I can hardly stand it: dark eyes cupped by insomnia and smudged makeup, a small pursed mouth that becomes a Cheshire grin for just a moment after orgasm, an oscillation of tousled red hair reverting slowly to brown.

She grazes her palm against my bristly beard. "You're going to be handsome when you're old."

"Krasny," I say, hunting Slavic equivalencies.

She shakes her head. "You sound so stupid when you try to speak Russian."

"Imbetsil," I say.

"Da." She nips my mouth with hers. "You are an imbecile." Her eyes skip down my naked body, then find the black duffel bag at the end of the bed. "Can I carve?"

"Da," I say, but reach over her first to yank the curtain shut.

In the crystalline instant before our view disappears, I see two jumbled shadows emerging from the metro.

A foray back in time to help you understand:

When I first moved here, halfway through a sweat-drenched summer, Quartier des Spectacles was exactly the teeming nightmare I deserved. Crowds. Cacophony. Small children wailing days, drunk uni students shrieking nights, unhoused individuals howling at any hour.

Anxiety and arousal and anguish. All those human noises, backed by the senseless rumble of distant concerts or the ambient thudding techno of midge-lived art installations, kept my head swollen to bursting. I had no room for contemplation. The black duffel bag stayed in the barrel of my unused washing machine.

Then came winter. It felt nuclear; the thronging streets emptied in a matter of days. Tourists vanished, and residents fled underground to the subterranean arcades that stretch like webbing between the metro stations. My walking route along René-Lévesque turned into a vicious polar wind tunnel.

Snow came fast, then thick, deadening all sound. At night, I camped out on my bed, put my guilty trigger finger on the heating vent, and stared down at a deserted city. The washing machine never spun, but I could hear its contents rattling.

When Dasha's done carving, we go to the spa. She is happy with her progress. She bounces down the hallway in her mismatched swimsuit and dances in the elevator, pouting up at the stern black bulb of the security camera. We are the spa's most dedicated regulars: me because I never expected to live in a building with one and have an irrational fear it might suddenly be taken away, Dasha because she developed a taste for sauna when she fled from Ukraine to Finland.

There is a stretch of bare concrete between the elevator and the spa. It sucks the heat from my bare feet and reminds me that winter – briefer than it used to be, often milder, but ever less predictable – would still come inside and kill us if it could. Small scratch marks mar the concrete, maybe the untrimmed claws of a neighbor's dog.

Dasha takes our bundled towels and cradles them in her arms like a baby while I scoop the key from the pocket of my swim shorts. I tap; the lock beeps yes.

Dasha yanks the door open and takes a long, exaggerated sniff, nostrils flared, to inhale the cleaning-chemical smell of the place. We pass three wide windows overlooking Boulevard St. Laurent. Shops are shuttered, and the snow tries to hide them entirely, drifting knee-high against barred entryways.

Dasha impales our towel baby on a hook, steps inside the shower, and twists the knob. Her tousled hair becomes a single slick plane aligned to her spine. I join her under the warm spray, and she grabs me. Kissing in water always feels strange to me, diffuse, like both mouths are part of a vast semi-permeable membrane or are two organisms tethered together by a third.

"Can I stay until the snow stops?" she asks.

"It might never stop," I say.

We go to the jacuzzi, where a soggy Band-Aid lounges poolside, and anonymous clumps of hair ride the foamy jets in circles. The water is gray and deliciously hot. Dasha dunks her head underneath and brings it only halfway up. She glides back and forth. She's always moving, even when she sleeps.

"Krokodil," I say.

She snaps her teeth at me.

We met outside a dive bar in Verdun, where I had been trying to drink my brain quiet. I was on my way out, and she was on her way in, tall but otherwise amorphous in winter gear: knee-length green coat with the hood sphinctered tight, mitted hands gripping backpack straps, baggy beige pants tucked into thick stripy socks tucked into slush-spattered boots.

Seeing even that small slice of her face – cold-flushed cheeks, gleaming dark eyes – stopped me in place. I said 'scuse and held the door for her to enter. I did not think she would respond, but she did, in English.

"Did we meet before?" she asked.

The Slavic accent made her zygomatics seem even harsher, her detached stare more beautiful. I noticed then that her right eyebrow is asymmetric—the inner edge spikes upward.

"Maybe," I said. "Were you here in the summer?"

"No," she said. "I was in Newfoundland carving whalebones." She peered at me, looking more concerned than curious. "You are leaving now? Right now?"

I wasn't anymore.

Nobody else has used the sauna tonight, so it will be a slow climb to ninety degrees. We wait in the steam room, a black-tiled cube that starts out with barely enough room for two but grows exponentially as the antiseptic-smelling cloud billows and thickens around us. The blankness still terrifies me. I try to think of it as exposure therapy.

Dasha rakes one hand along the invisible ceiling so the condensation patters down on my head.

"I had a bad dream last night," she says, conversational. "At first, I thought it was about my brother." Her voice sounds different in the steam cloud, flatter. Her grip on my thigh feels impersonal. "Now, I'm not sure."

Dasha often dreams of her younger brother, who was shelled dead one year ago. When they were children, she terrified him with stories about a monster in the woods, but she always protected him from it, too. She drew circles around their outhouse with magic sap to keep him safe.

"I can give you a sleeping pill tonight," I tell her because that is how I avoid waking up with my hands holding an intangible rifle. "No dreams."

"I like my dreams, asshole. Even bad ones. If you give me a pill, you can give me more molly."

"We can do that, too."

"You're sad again." She drapes herself over me lengthwise, stomach-down on my knees. "Why did you move to the city?" she asks. "It sounds like you were happy in the woods. Now you're here, and you're sad."

"I needed a change," I say, which is what I always say

when people ask why I left a small cabin in Vermont. "More people. More noise."

I hear wet footsteps slap past the steam room as if on cue.

"It's more exciting in the city," Dasha admits. "But I miss the sea. Any sea is good."

I stroke her damp hair. "Dasha. Do you think we met for a reason?"

"To fuck," she says.

Dasha told me about her brother and the monster the first night she slept over, after a half capsule each of MDMA twined our warm electric bodies together. She told me about her village and its bread factory and riding creaky bicycles to the market with her mother and brother. His death to friendly fire came as a footnote, but it was enough to set the duffel bag rattling.

"I was in Finland when I heard about it," she said. "But I couldn't go back, so I went even farther away."

"To Newfoundland," I said because that fact was the first to calcify in my head. "To carve whalebones."

Her eyes glittered. "The family who hosted me, they did whale disentanglement," she said. "So they had these bones, from the ones that die, and they said – *you're artist, you want them?*" She stretched her long arms. "There was a piece of spine this big. But I like to work smaller for scrimshaw, much smaller, and I couldn't bring it with me anyway."

"I have bones," I said.

She found the notches of my vertebrae and pried at them with her fingertips. "You do," she growled. "Give me your spine."

I would have let the possibility die there if not for the high. Instead, I whale-disentangled myself from the sheets, went to the washing machine, and retrieved the duffel bag. I unzipped it with trembling fingers, and when the shiny nylon split open to reveal its jumble of pink-tinged bones, I felt like I was gutting an animal.

"Rabbit," I said, holding up the delicate skull as proof. "A snowshoe hare, actually, is what you'd call it. The rest is mostly fragments."

She took it from me, reverent. "It's beautiful," she says, then sets it on the bed and reaches for the next bone, a sharp splinter of tibia. "You found them where? In the woods?"

"Stumbled across them one day in Vermont," I said. "Don't know why I kept them."

That was a lie and a truth: I knew exactly where the bones would be, but I still don't know why I went back for them.

We're no longer alone when we leave the steam room. A neighbor has wedged himself into the corner of the cold plunge, his tattooed skin turning bright red, gazing out the window. He is Swiss. His name is either Maxime or Sebastien, and he only uses the spa when he's high as a kite.

"Salut, mec," I say, to be neighborly. "Ça va?"

He looks up at us with glassy eyes. "Je viens de voir

quelque chose de vraiment bizarre," he says, jerking his head toward the frost-furred window. "Á l'exterieur."

Dasha follows the motion. "Quoi?" she says, half to me, half to him.

"I saw outside." The neighbor taps his orbital bone. "Some fucking weird person. Some fucking weird person in a costume, I think."

"In the snow?" Dasha asks.

"Yes. Sitting by the garage, beside the entry to the garage, like they are waiting to be let in." He gives a stuttery laugh, teeth chattering. "But they didn't ask to be let in. They didn't say anything."

The cold plunge has a submerged light that reminds me of a deep-sea drone's harsh halogen lamp; it makes his gooseflesh legs look corpse-pale and turns all the little hairs into metal filaments. We were in the steam room for a while. I don't know how long my neighbor has been in the cold plunge, but his hands are turning blue.

"After five minutes, I don't think it's good for you," I say.

"At first, I thought it was two people," he says, unhearing. "Because of the costume."

He raises two shivering fingers and crooks them behind his head.

The second time Dasha came over, she brought her Dremel and needles.

"Better to do it here," she said. "In the hostel, there's no space."

She plugged the tool in below my bedside lamp and arrayed the bones around herself on the floor. In Newfoundland, she'd carved a variety of objects: masquerade masks, nesting dolls, a functioning compass contained in a cortical ring. Here, with just a scattering of delicate rabbit bones, she said she would have to choose very carefully.

"You have any ideas?" I asked.

"Something from a dream. That's how I usually start." She fished three rumpled tea bags out of her pocket and dangled them in front of me. "From the apartment where I clean," she explained. "Since you didn't have any last time." She pressed them into my hand and kissed my nose. "Make me tea. Please."

I watched out the window while the water boiled. Seven stories down, across the ice-slopped street, a crime scene. Throbbing red light from three cruisers and an ambulance. Streets throttled with police tape. Uniforms huddling and dispersing, reconfigured with the passage of time and information.

"Now that it's over, I'll never be sober," Dasha sang, her face squashed between ancient peeling headphones, her eyes hidden by shadow. When she noticed me, she glared. "Don't watch. You can see when it's all finished."

I turned back to the window. Passersby kept pointing their phones at the metro entrance, where a shape that might have been a body rested.

Not all crime scenes look like that. Some are quite lonely.

The sauna is hot, and I can't feel it. My whole body is sweaty ice. Dasha sloshes water across the rocks, cooing to herself in Russian. She sits beside me on the bench and taps the ladle against my kneecap.

"What's wrong?" she asks. "You want me to leave?"

"No. Nyet."

"You're lying about something," she says, tipping her head back against the wooden wall, eyes still fixed to mine. "I know."

I flip the timer and watch the sand begin to shift and trickle. Her knowing became inevitable the moment I showed her the bones. She's familiar with mammalian anatomy. She can separate one animal from another. In some way, I wanted her to know.

"Have you ever gone hunting?" I ask.

"No," she says. "It would make me sad."

Sand trickles slowly through the glass tube. Through the little window in the sauna door, across the foaming surface of the jacuzzi, I can see that Maxime or Sebastien has not left the cold plunge. From this distance, his eyes are horribly soft.

Somewhere, a power line succumbs to its spiked coat of icicles, and the lights go out. Dasha inhales sharply at the sudden dark. Worse is the sudden quiet. I've been in the city long enough to reacclimate to electricity's constant comforting hum; now its absence startles me.

"It'll come back on in a minute," I say, desperate to be right.

We wait in the warm dark.

I went to that small cabin in Vermont because I wanted simplicity. I wanted to hear birdsong. I wanted to chop my own wood and hunt my own food and learn, in solitude, what sort of person I was.

The dark stays. The warm departs. My neighbor does too, slapping away without speaking, which is better than him sinking under the surface of the cold plunge and freezing to death. We step out of the sauna and pad carefully to the window. St. Laurent is pitch black and empty, apart from a single Communauto creeping toward Rue Ontario. The glow of its taillights turns exhaust cloud to blood-billow.

"Let's go back upstairs," Dasha says. "I want blankets."

She wrings out her hair first, leaning her head to one side and choking fistful after fistful of water from the wet strands. Her teeth are chattering.

"Here," I say, giving her my towel to layer over hers.

The elevators are out so we take the stairwell, stamping footprints on the cold concrete. We've done it before, but it's unsettling in the dark. The texture of the rust-flaking handrail is suddenly foreign. When we pass the doors that lead out to the fire escape, tendrils of cold reach through the gaps to stroke my face. There is a strange musky scent in the stairwell, and (this time no sly look from Dasha) it calves glaciers my belly.

On the penultimate landing, Dasha speaks. "The man with the tattoos in the cold bath," she says, "saw the same thing I dreamed about."

We turn the corner, and in the glow of my phone, I see the thing too.

They slump against the wall in such a way that the knobby red sprinkler system must be digging into the flesh of their back – I know because I slumped there once, drunk and grieving.

They are larger than the sum of their parts, with bony legs and arms too long for their child-sized snowsuit. Its fabric is much brighter than I remember, the kind of blue Dasha would call goluboy and not siniy. Wiry white fur sprouts from it in patches.

They have two faces. One is eerie white with beady black eyes: the hare I spotted through a gap in the fog. One is soft and chubby and spattered with blood: the child who appeared in my sights the exact moment I pulled the trigger.

"Come on," Dasha says, and I realize she can't see them. All she sees is that I've stopped moving, stopped breathing. Her cold hand finds mine. "Blankets."

Impossibility yanks the tendons from my legs. I buckle, and have to steady myself with the wall. I am dissolving in dread. When I first gave Dasha the bones, I thought she might alter the ghosts. Reshape them into something benign or whittle them away to nothing. Instead, she's given them flesh.

The smashed-together pair stagger to their feet. It is difficult to say which set of eyes reflects less light.

"You should go home, Dasha," I try to tell her, but my mouth doesn't move, and my hand doesn't unlatch from hers.

The boy looks at me with his black hole eyes. I want to run, to scream, to hide – but I went back for the bones for a reason. I move forward in the same slow trance as when I dug the shallow grave. I open the door to the hallway and usher everyone through.

The musky scent turns more pungent as we walk, clotting in my throat. Dasha's toes whisper along the carpet. The boy and rabbit make no sound at all. It hurts when I turn the doorknob to my apartment. The metal is rough with frost.

"It was cold that morning," I say as if it makes anything different. "My hands were numb. And there was so much fog."

"Which morning?" Dasha asks, pushing past me, past the rustling coat she hung on my open fusebox. She starts changing back into her clothes. I switch on the only battery-powered light, a string of cheap plastic bulbs along the back wall.

The boy and rabbit shamble inside, jaundiced by the yellow light. They look around my apartment, one sniffing the air, the other blinking tear-swollen eyes. Their bifurcated gaze lands on the black duffel bag. Their shared body shudders.

"I want to see the carvings," I say. "Even if they're not quite finished. Please."

Dasha's frown emerges from the neck of her red-and-yellow jigsaw sweater. "Why?"

"I think I had the same dream as you."

She stops short. Stares. Then she unzips the duffel bag and

obliges me, unwrapping her work one tiny figurine at a time. First: a hare. Long-limbed, elegant, for some reason a creature permitted to die. Then: a boy. Small and skinny, swallowed in his snowsuit, six years old according to the police report I read and reread for weeks.

Last: a monster. Towering over its victims, hunting rifle in hand. The head is unfinished, a featureless white bulb, but I already know the face that belongs.

Dasha arranges them on the floor, sliding the boy in front of the hare placing the monster at distance. The smashed-together pair squat down on their haunches to observe. She rotates the monster so its rifle points in the right direction, and I feel the smooth weight of the weapon in my numb hands.

"There," she says. "It was like that."

"It's not a dream," I say. "It's exactly what happened."

Dasha raises her asymmetric brows and flicks her finger. The boy and rabbit effigies go skittering toward the wall. "Pow," she says.

They flinch in their shared body.

"It's true," I say. "The boy had gone missing that morning. He had gone wandering into the woods and wandered too far." I look at the boy and rabbit, who look blankly back. "I killed them both with one shot. And I had been drinking the night before, a little that morning, too. I couldn't think straight. Couldn't do anything but dig."

Dasha looks down at the bones, and the suspicion I know has been building for days finally transmutes into certainty. I watch our brief bond drain out of her eyes. "You buried them in the same hole," she says, in a small, frightened voice I've never heard before.

"I panicked," I say. "I waited to be caught. I waited and panicked and waited. I left as soon as the search parties gave up, I made myself stay away for a year. But, eventually, I had to go back. I had to check. And I thought – maybe I could rebury the boy properly. The boy deserved better."

The rabbit's ears twitch, indignant.

"But something had already dug the grave up," I go on, words burning up my throat like acid. "Maybe bear, maybe coyotes. They'd eaten everything but a few bones. I couldn't tell which were which, so I put them all in my bag, took the border on foot – "

"The idiot who killed my brother, at least he confessed to it," Dasha says, and now her voice is jagged with a fury that overcomes fear. "He didn't hide, run, hide again."

She dumps the duffel bag out, clatter-clatter, and retrieves the lone splinter of tibia. She tested the Dremel on it, deciding on pressure and angle. The tip is needle-sharp now. Maybe this is why we met: not for her to be my savior, but my butcher. To mete out the violence required by violence.

"I'm leaving," she says instead, backing her way to the door and her coat. "And don't you fucking follow."

"It's still snowing, though," I say.

She gives a short, sharp laugh, maybe because she's going only as far as the security desk. "It's snowing forever," she says.

My last view of her is this: jigsaw sweater, pale blue jeans, bare feet stuffed into unlaced boots, pale face half-hidden by red hair, jaw set, eyes dark, one hand clutching her green coat by the nape, one hand clutching the boy or rabbit's carved tibia like a knife. The door drifts nearly shut behind her.

The boy and rabbit clamber onto my bed, shedding wiry white fur. I see a multiplicity of options: I take the fire escape to the top of the building and step off it, or stick Dasha's drill as deep as I can inside my ear before I turn it on, or hide what's left of the bones and ready myself to lie. She won't want to push things in a foreign country.

I leave the bones where they are, only pausing to scoop the figurines from the floor. I climb onto the bed, leaving a respectful space between us, and offer the boy and rabbit my thick plaid blanket. They hesitate for a moment, then pull it over themselves.

"I'm sorry," I say. "Whatever that means, I mean it."

The boy and rabbit don't reply.

We sit in the dark and watch snow swirl past, burying everything the best it knows how.

RICH LARSON was born in Niger, has lived in Spain and Czech Republic, and is currently based in Canada. He is the author of the novels *Annex* and *Ymir*, as well as over 200 short stories, some of the best of which can be found in his collections *Tomorrow Factory* and *The Sky Didn't Load Today and Other Glitches*. His fiction has been translated into over a dozen languages, among them Polish, French, Romanian and Japanese, and adapted into an Emmy-winning episode of *LOVE DEATH + ROBOTS*.

DUBLIN

Christian Fiachra Stevens

I moved into the city centre over a year ago. I'd spent my childhood and young adult life living in the suburbs, standing in the rain waiting for buses that never came and taking long walks home in the middle of the night after failing to flag down a taxi. I was eager to move closer to work, and since I spent the better part of my twenties hoarding cash while living at home out of view from the Irish rental market, I had a nice little nest egg saved up. I thought I'd finally treat myself to some semblance of adult life. So, after eight months of failing to get a single response from any bedroom listing bigger than a walk-in closet, I got lucky. A letting agent had mistakenly forgotten to specify the city when listing an apartment in Smithfield, and I thankfully spotted the mistake and applied. I was baffled and silently ecstatic when I showed up to view the place and found that I was the only one there. I didn't even bother to play it coy, immediately making an offer. The agent didn't care as long as the tenant moved in, as soon as possible.

It was a simple apartment. A one bedroom was just big enough for my needs. It sat awkwardly on top of a trendy cafe that had been modernized and renovated extensively, giving an off-kilter look to the entirety of the structure. I would fall asleep to the sounds of sirens, struggles between rough sleepers, and drunk tourists yelling at nothing. Then awake to the smell of expensive pastries and soft laughter between co-workers starting their day. The building was older than its neighbours; vacant office buildings stood cold in place of what used to sit there, empty derelict housing left to rot. They all surrounded a little cobblestone road just off Smithfield Square and did a surprisingly good job at suppressing the sounds of commotion that often came from there. It turned out that living on the right hidden street in Dublin provided a healthy level of privacy while still having the city at your doorstep.

After moving into the capital, I barely left it most days. There was no need when everything you required was less than ten minutes outside your door. I lived there for three months before I stopped heading into the office altogether. I quickly took for granted the lack of commute when myself and the rest of my colleagues were told we could work remotely. Instead, I rolled out of bed at 8:55 each morning and plopped myself down in front of my computer by nine. People often assumed I found this existence lonely when, in fact, it suited me perfectly. Other than the odd social call, I found that I had little time for strangers or brief acquaintances. I was uncomfortably bad at small talk and described politely by many as "exhausting to be around," so this felt like a fair trade for all involved. Everything else I needed was within arm's reach, whether it was internet access, television, or the space to perform as little exercise as possible to prevent my limbs from falling off. It wasn't long before those visits from family and friends became few and far between. I might have felt hurt if I had noticed this myself, but I didn't. Instead, I just further retreated into my tiny little life and sighed happily at how cosy it felt.

I ordered the cheapest desk I could find and placed it carefully in front of the only window. It looked out the back of the apartment building, away from the hustle and bustle of the cafe entrance on the other side. The ambient noise of the city proved soothing while I worked. The odd time the sun showed itself, it would peak through the flimsy Venetian blinds in front of me and lazily say hello. The view looked out at an alley, small and barely used. Not even the shops and restaurants would avail of it to store their bins either. Probably, they were vandalized too often, or the rubbish truck couldn't fit down the crooked laneway. I wasn't sure. It provided no cover and strangely caught the breeze in an awkward way that turned it into a miniature wind tunnel. Even the homeless didn't seem to sleep down there. The only times I did see anyone walk through it were tourists clearly lost or drunks needing a wall to piss on as an impromptu toilet. The strip of road was grimy and weathered by lack of care, and trash had been stamped into the worn, cracked tarmac so much that it became part of the street's facade permanently. Many side streets in Dublin City looked and smelled like this, and as a result, they were avoided. It didn't bother me at all. I was just happy to have my little abode, with a lovely vista far off to remind myself always that Dublin was most beautiful when one would take a step back, especially as the day wound down. The harsh winter sun would soften as the clamour of the daytime would fade away. For a moment, I'd forget about the homeless hands reaching up to me or the sound of empty needles crushed underfoot on wet pavement. Then I would hear a bottle smash, or a fight occur, or a wanderer yelling at their own echoes and I would be brought back to reality. This was how things went. I would sit, work eight hours, and then wind down in the evening. It took nearly an entire year, as winter came around once more, for me to realize that the alleyway beneath me seemingly didn't exist.

Maybe it was because I rarely left the apartment or because whenever I did, I followed the main road down to the Quays by the River Liffey. But one evening, when a food delivery man got lost on his bike, I had to leave the safety of my nest to find where he had ended up as he refused to budge from his position. The cafe stood on a corner of the main street with a pedestrianized passage flanking its left side that I had never walked down before. It led to a strip of office buildings that were still being built, so there was no reason for me ever to use it. This cyclist had ended up down amongst the litter of cranes that waited for another day to continue adding pristine empty blocks of glass to the skyline. I found him quickly, exchanged garbled pleasantries about poor weather, then hastily took my overpriced pizza off his hands. On the way back through the passage, I noticed something amiss. The alleyway I looked out onto every day should have been somewhere in between. And from what I had always seen from my window, the alley connected to the pedestrian passageway I stood in at that moment. But there was nothing there, no entrance at all. All that was present was a ten-foot-tall red-bricked wall and the empty husks of further unused office buildings leering over me from just behind it. I even stepped back as far as I could and craned my neck in an attempt to peer through the dark glass. I could see deep into the large vacant building, hoping to see something on the other side, but it looked to be only more property under construction. After peeling myself away, I looked up to the back of the apartment and could see that my window was directly facing the back of this building, uncomfortably close. All I should have been able to see this past year was corrugated air vents and large panes of laminated glass. Perplexed, I rushed back up to my apartment, abandoned the pizza on the kitchen counter, and looked back out of my window, expecting to see the office building that had somehow eluded me after all this time. But it wasn't there. Once again, I looked down into this little laneway that stretched through the quiet, cold twilight. I could see the entrance to it as well, where it was supposed to connect to the passageway. I even opened my window and stuck the top half of my body out into the crisp night air to ensure I hadn't been looking at a mural this whole time. But everything felt normal, even the breeze on my skin. I circled the block countless times to make sure I wasn't missing anything. I even checked my carbon monoxide detectors to make sure I wasn't in the middle of some feverish trip. Eventually, I accepted the truth that, somehow, I was living inside an anomaly.

I barely got any work done the rest of that week. I watched the alley intently, hoping for something, anything, to happen. When something did occur, it was mundane. A piece of loose rubbish spiralling down the cobbles, a pigeon, or a seagull briefly landing to inspect a patch of broken gravel. But no person ever appeared. Not once. The strip was so inactive that it made me question all the previous times I had ever seen anyone walk down there, which again was incredibly infrequent. It was like everyone ceased to use it ever since I became aware of the road's peculiar nature. I felt like it was a joke I was purposely excluded from. That weekend, I scoured my limited contact list to find someone to come over for a coffee down by the cafe. I was mostly left on read before a colleague from a previous job said she'd love to catch up.

When she arrived, we sat outside the cafe under the awning, pretending we lived in a warmer climate as we politely sipped away and made small talk. She seemed genuinely interested in how I'd been doing and how my career was progressing, going as far as asking about individual projects and accomplishments I'd achieved. I almost felt bad that I was just waiting an appropriate amount of time before I could bring up the alleyway. I asked her if she had been to the cafe before or knew about the offices being built in the area. She just shook her head and said she didn't know Smithfield very well. It wasn't the answer I was looking for, but it was enough for me. I pushed ahead with the real reason I invited her.

"You want to see something weird?" I finally said.

"Uh, what?"

"Here. Check this out."

I brought her down the passageway first and showed her the building that sat in front of my apartment. She gently mentioned how unfortunate it was that my natural light was blocked, and I responded by excitedly inviting her up. She hesitated and fiddled with her coffee cup, but cautious not to offend, she accepted, and I brought her upstairs a little too quickly. Upon reaching my living room, I eagerly showed her the view of the alley like a game show host revealing a prize. She regarded the scene and myself with puzzled features.

"Uh…"

"Freaky, right?" I asked promptly.

"I mean. I guess?"

"What do you mean 'I guess?' Isn't it wild?"

"Well, it sucks that you can't see anything, but I don't see how it's weird or whatever? That's just what the city centre is like these days." She replied, each word quieter than the last.

Her puzzled features became my own as I looked out the window again. As it had been all week, the office was nowhere in sight, and the mute, empty lane lay below in its stead.

"Do you not see the laneway?" I said matter-of-factly, not turning to face her.

She slowly moved closer and craned her neck over my shoulder, unsure what I was referencing. "The passageway we were just in? No, I can't see it from this angle. It's over to the left; I can almost make it out."

"No, it's not the passageway, I'm talking about the laneway!" I reiterated, losing my patience. "The lane right in front that *connects* to the passageway. "

She looked for a third time, more confused than ever. "I don't, no. Is it like, on the other side of the office?"

"It's right there!" I snapped, spinning around. "How can you not see it?"

She rubbed her shoulders and looked away even though it wasn't cold. I realized I had somewhat raised my voice. I stumbled through an apology, and we returned to the cafe's seating area, where she glided through a few more empty conversation pieces. I gave her little in response and she noticed it was beginning to get late. I asked her one more time to repeat what she saw.

She answered while quickly collecting her things. "Like I said, just the office building. Or at least the part of it that I could make out. It's like right up to your window, and you could probably touch it if you reached out."

"And no laneway?" I returned, still frustrated.

"…No. Sorry."

I leaned back in my seat, silent and annoyed, as she attempted to end the exchange on a softer note.

"Well, it was great to see you. We should really catch up more often!"

"Yeah. I'm just usually busy with work."

"Yeah, I get it." she said, nodding a little too frantically.

"Cool."

"…Okay, well, bye!"

She left quickly towards the square and didn't dare look back, thankful to be swallowed up by the throng of people going about their weekend. I had already forgotten about her as I returned to the passage and stared hard at the office building. How could she not see? Was I the only one who could?

"You shouldn't do that."

The voice came from back towards the cafe. It was a gravelly voice, and although it felt weathered, it also sounded hoarse, like it was rarely used. The city accent added thickness and sharpness to it, which made it easier to pick up on the breeze. I turned to see someone at the mouth of the passage, half hidden by the corner of the cafe, so she peered down at me with one wide eye. Even though I could only see part of her, I recognized her. The old woman was a local. We never spoke, of course, but she always stood out to me as someone who'd been here far longer than most people in the area. Her hair was worn, and she wore a deep lavender cardigan with embroidery-mending along the hem. She often visited the cafe and hung outside making small talk with strangers while her little white and brown Jack Russell greedily lapped up water and cream left out by college kid baristas who were happy to see him. She had been there today while I sat with my old acquaintance. She let the statement hang as we stared at each other.

"I shouldn't do… What, exactly?"

"Shouldn't let it know that you can see it. Very dangerous." Her only visible eye blinked.

"Dangerous?"

She nodded vigorously, her thin, small hand gripping the corner of the brick as she did so. "Don't talk about it, don't look at it, but most importantly, don't engage with it."

Both alarmed and excited, I began walking towards her, only for her to slink away with each step, so I stopped, fearing she might flee altogether. "What do you mean 'it'?"

She ignored the inquiry and hissed in response. "Stop it. No more. Trust me."

And then she was gone. I quickly gave chase only to be stopped by a disgruntled server eager to remind me that I had yet to pay. I complied as quickly as I could, but by the time the card had cleared, the old woman and her dog had disappeared. Frustrated, I returned to the wall and inspected it further. But in the end, all I achieved was counting bricks. I went upstairs defeated.

When Monday came and I sat down to work I immediately noticed that the lane had changed. The wall facing me had been vandalized with graffiti and what was once an unimpressive concrete wall with a dash of carmine diluted by dust was now covered in a caricature of some cartoon man. He had slicked-back chestnut hair, a pale face with a small, sharp nose, and turquoise eyes. The head stood on thin shoulders adorned in a thick black pea coat, which was draped over a matching suit. He looked like something off Wall Street, or a detective from some over-serious police drama. I didn't mind the drawing as much as I minded its dimensions. The purposely placed disproportions unsettled me throughout the day. Its nose was too small and bent, its head too big for its neck, which was too long for its shoulders, and its unrelenting eyes bulged and widened independently of each other, staring in different directions. However, by the time I closed my laptop at the end of the day, the eyes seemed to have made up from whatever argument they were having. Not only were they now a little more in proportion with each other, but they were also looking in the same direction. By the morning of the next day, I was grievously unsettled to find the eyes looking up at me. The cartoon's expression remained emotionless, but the unwavering stare felt hateful, and I often caught myself dissociating in the middle of tasks just to realize that I was staring back down at the mural. I spent the entirety of the following day convincing myself that the man had always looked that way and that I must not have realized at first. That excuse managed to tide me over for another evening, but the proportions continued to shift as the week went on. Its sharp features moulting and bones cracking under its thick skin. By the end of the week, the mural had shifted entirely into some photorealistic version of what once had been a crude Picasso painting of this figure.

I had always been a stubborn person. I was always insisting on logical answers. So even as I stewed there throughout the week, silently terrified, I consistently lied to myself. Nothing was changing. I was just seeing things. It wasn't until Sunday afternoon, while I was washing the dishes, that I realized the obvious truth. The mural was, of course, changing. But not for some supernatural reason. The artist returned each night or early morning to add to their creation. They were probably even creating some time lapse or portfolio. I had never felt so stupid and laughed for a long time upon that realisation. When I went to bed that night, I slept soundly for the first time all week.

That was until I woke up to start yet another week of work, only to find that the graffiti was now gone. The wall was once again the familiar blank slate I had known it to be. Standing a few paces in front of where it had been, the man from the mural itself looked up at me with two turquoise marbles fixated and shining in the grey dawn. His figure now complete, his stare still unbreakable and focused on me as I looked down at him in horror. I stood there for a long time, my brain unable to compute. All my previous justifications and reasoning fell away one by one as time drifted on.

Even as I failed to rack my mind for a logical explanation, my fear gave way to anger, and I shakily opened the window and yelled down to him, as if he would happily explain that this was all some misunderstanding.

"What are you? What do you *want*?"

I didn't really care. I think I just needed to hear him speak. I needed him to act human so I could convince my heart to slow down and that everything would be alright. But he didn't respond, nor did he move. He looked exactly the same as he did in the graffiti, and I would have thought him a statue if it weren't for the fact that once I called down to him, he smiled—a strange smile as unwavering as his stare. I would have missed the change if I had blinked at that moment. But I saw it. And now I was certain he was real. And he was certain that I could see him.

I left my apartment with only my keys and burst out into the freezing air in a T-shirt and jeans. I accepted that I had no idea what this was. But there was one person who may be able to tell me more. So, I scoured the streets and cobbled stones one by one, a shaking wretch from the bite of the cold and the fear in my chest, searching for that strange old woman. I worked my way from Smithfield to Phibsborough and then back down to Stoneybatter. I only found workers on smoke breaks sipping warmth from their cups as they regarded me with suspicion due to my dishevelled demeanour. I gave up on Stoneybatter and continued towards Phoenix Park but to my lucky surprise, I found my mark lounging in Croppies Park: a small patch of green hugging the north side of the Liffey. The woman sat on a bench idly watching the still man-made pond in front of her as her dog snoozed at her side, its head nestled into her lap. It perked up as I approached noisily and alerted its owner. She saw the alarm on my face before I could speak and immediately rose to her feet, dog in hand, as I began to spew words at her.

"You need to tell me what it is. You said it was dangerous? Why am I in danger? You need to tell me how to stop it."

She backed away from my babbling, her mouth agape, unable to find the proper response. Worried that she might bolt again, I grabbed her by the shoulders. The dog became enraged at this and began howling at me in distress. I barely heard it as I gripped her even tighter.

"Please. You need to tell me what to do. You can't leave me like this."

"Get away from me, you idiot!" she yelled.

"Not until you tell me!"

Her eyes darted left and right as if some malignant force would descend upon us at any moment. "Please. You'll make it aware of us both!"

"Why can only we see it? What is IT!" I was roaring at her now. She was in tears.

"I don't know!" she screamed back. "But whatever it is, it chooses people, and then it just… takes them. I don't KNOW."

"Why us? Tell me!"

Her sobs grew louder. "Because no one will notice! It's been happening forever. Haven't you seen them? The missing posters? People just vanishing from the side of the curb?"

I relented somewhat, confused. "No, I… No. I'm not from the city."

She fell to her knees and hugged her dog for comfort. It refused to take its eyes off me even when licking her hands to let the poor woman know that everything was going to be alright. But I needed to know.

"So, can I just leave? If I stay away from the lane, will I be safe?"

She looked up at me with newfound hate. "It's not the street. It's the whole city. It uses these little pockets to find people. And you've just told it that we both can see it." She reverted back into sobs as I straightened and looked around me. The shadow of the skyline now clung to me like a heavy cloak, and I felt the fear she must have felt her whole life.

"And if I leave the city? What then?"

She just cried and shook her head, but I was unsatisfied. I needed to hear it. "What then?" I repeated, my voice rising again.

"Hey!" An exclamation came from outside the park. A man in his forties was rushing across the road towards us, having witnessed a young man berate an old woman. Now acutely aware of my position, I fled. He chased me away briefly before quickly returning to her, where she still sat in a heap, inconsolable. Even as I ran out of sight, I heard her wails and her pet's howls. They blended into one single unforgiving noise as I rushed through the streets, and as I ran, I continued to see him. The man from the mural. It was only in glances here and there. Down laneways in between overflowing rubbish bins. Within the reflection of windows tinted black. Far off in the distance amongst a crowd of people. Each time I saw him and his sickly eyes, accompanied by his strange alien smile.

I ran with no destination in mind, hopelessness clutching my chest and tugging on my arms as I tried to flee. By the time I escaped the mania that fogged my eyes I found myself outside my apartment building as I realized I had nowhere else to go.

It was even colder now as the sun began to sink. For the first time that day, I took a moment to drink in long breaths of air. My panic simmered, and I regained control of my senses long enough to come up with a plan. The old woman had shook her head when I asked if I could escape it by leaving the city. So, I'd go a step further and leave the country.

A part of me tried to reason that this wouldn't help, but I needed to try something. I needed to regain control, or I would become an even bigger wreck than the old woman. All I needed was my passport, my wallet, and my phone. The landlord could take everything else, and my boss could fire me; at this point, I didn't care. I never wanted to see those eyes again. That smile. The only problem was that everything I needed sat neatly in a pile on my cheap little desk right by the window.

I entered the apartment building quietly, ascending to my front door without a sound. I turned the key softly leaving the door open behind me, hoping for a quick escape as I inched towards the living area entrance. I took one final breath for courage and then turned the corner, making sure to stay low so that I couldn't be seen from the street below.

In the end, it didn't matter. The man was right there, on the other side of the window, sprawled out like a spider gripping onto the edges of the frame as his eyes poured in and found me. They were wider and more sunken now, and his smile looked crooked and strained, like his skin might tear from the pain of it. Invisible hooks stretched his features into a monstrous sight as he greedily regarded me as his next victim. Dismay and rage gripped me again as I bellowed,

"Leave me the fuck alone!"

Its smile only grew more twisted as I cursed at it further. I grabbed the nearest object I could find, a speaker I never used, barely larger than a tin of biscuits. I hurled it at the window, hoping for it to crash through and send the figure hurtling towards his demise. It merely cracked the window into broken segments that further fragmented the creature's face. I lunged forward and grabbed my wallet and phone. Realizing my passport was in one of the drawers, I needed to look away for a moment to find it. When I looked back up, the man had shifted again so that his face was level with mine. One of his alabaster hands had peeled away from the side of the window and was pressed up against one of the cracks, its long pale forefinger frozen while scanning the broken line that separated us. I looked at his hand and then back to him. And as he stared at me motionless, I thought I could hear the window begin to shatter. I reeled back and turned, escaping through the doorway, down the stairs, and out of the apartment. I flung the door shut behind as the slam gave an eruption of noise. And then all I could hear was the sound of my own panting as I greedily gulped down air. I never heard the window fully break. I never heard the monster make a sound. But as I stood there in the dark, another cry broke the silence. It was a scream. I knew that scream. The old woman's cries echoed and reverberated off the windows and walls around my head. It was coming from the passageway beside the cafe.

I ignored all my instincts that told me to flee and slowly backed away from the building while moving further to the left so that I could look straight down the passageway. It took me a moment to notice the real change in the fading light. The office building behind the cafe was gone, and the entrance to the secret laneway that up until that moment only existed from the safety of my apartment window now sat in plain view, taunting me to approach. The entrance that I had so fervidly searched for that night was finally open to me, and a new wave of terror washed over my prickled skin. Every fibre of my being told me to run. And I almost did. But a small piece of myself rose above the terror. In a scolding tone, it reminded me what I had done to that old woman, how I had doomed her as much as I had doomed myself. And before I could commiserate on the matter any further, I found myself bounding down the passageway. As the mouth of the lane grew closer, the sound of the scream grew louder and echoed violently off the narrow passage, a booming endless spiral of hate. I stopped just short of the entrance and peered into the lane, which looked just as it had all those days from my living room window. Dirty, neglected, empty. All except for the woman, her dog, and the creature that hunted us. The man was hunched over the woman, sitting on her stomach as he peered down at her hungrily. She flailed at him hopelessly, and he didn't even blink as he went to work on her. He had one hand over her chin and mouth and the other gnarled and grasping the top of her skull. The skin on his fingers seemed to crawl from his hands onto her face and coalesce with her own to cause a tight seal around her mouth as his limbs and her head fused together. Her screams turned into moans, which turned into nothing at all as tears rolled down her cheeks from bulging eyes. They looked deep into his eyes and then past him into mine, pleading for help. He smiled all the while, grey gums and pillars of stone white perfect teeth on show. His head had grown in size to allow for the smile to expand. His mouth was open, holding no tongue, just a black void threatening to consume her like a serpent engulfing its prey. Engrossed with his gruesome work, the man ignored the small dog snapping at one of his legs. The man paid it no heed, nor did he seem to notice my presence. It took everything I had to convince myself to enter that laneway, as every instinct I had screamed at me in protest. I only took a few steps in before the sound stopped altogether.

Not just the rampant growling of the little mutt or the desperate scraping of shoes on pavement as the woman writhed in pain, but every sound. The seagulls squawking down by the Liffey, the far-off buzzing of cars zipping up and down the Quays, the never-ending howling of the wind in my ears. It was all gone. Like I had opened an airlock, and the sound had been sucked out into the nothingness of space. As I felt my ears, thinking for a moment that I had become deaf, I noticed that all movement had ceased as well. The woman, the man, and the dog had all stopped mid-struggle, frozen in time. Finally allowing my fear to exhaust me, I turned once more to flee, only to find my exit blocked by a wall.

A wall that was comically large that it dwarfed the rest of the city. Its facade was caked in what once was colourful graffiti, but now stained from soot and muck. As far up as I could see, there were contorted faces that twisted and moulded around each other in agony, all with sunken eyes, thin lips, and crooked features. In the centre of this tapestry of misery was the man.

His features were no longer disproportionate or overly realistic. He looked almost angelic, without a single blemish or wrinkle or crease to be seen. His expression was kinder. The hue of his skin was warmer. And he looked down at me like a parent welcoming me home after a long trip away. But his eyes still betrayed him. The stare still held his true intentions and regarded me with a flash of delight that could only mean that I was trapped and right where he wanted me to be. I retreated from him and rushed over to the woman, still frozen in fear. I begged her to snap out of it. To tell me how I could escape. I grabbed her shoulders once again in frustration, hoping to shake her from her stupor, only to find her light and hollow. To my continued horror, she fell away from me into pieces, as did the man still drooping over her, and even her little faithful companion still connected to the creature's leg. All three of them collapsed and fell apart like dry sand in the wind. I still held pieces of her, clumped in my hands. They were made of rubbish. Old pieces of newspaper, dirtied and soaked by the elements, their original contents long faded into nothingness. The rest of them were scattered around me in pieces. I looked down at what remained of her face to see that it was never her to begin with. Her dimensions were off, similar, but wrong. She was designed with the express intent of luring me into this creature's lair, and it worked like a charm. Though my senses were dulled from the hopelessness of it all, I could feel the street shift around me. The walls closed in, slower than they needed to, as the creature enjoyed its fresh morsel of food. I didn't bother moving. I didn't even look up. I just sat there staring at the pieces of trash spread out on the ground until the walls reached me, pushing the dirt and the newspaper up onto my skin and stamping it into me until I was nothing but rubbish myself. I screamed a soundless scream as I was crushed, and the last thing I felt before being crumpled between the bricks was a pulse. At first one, then dozens, and then thousands from within the walls. Whether it was the heartbeat of this beast spread out through the city, or the wailing of millions of souls trapped from within it, I couldn't tell. Before I could mull over the question any longer, I was gone.

CHRISTIAN FIACHRA STEVENS is from Dublin, Ireland, where he found his love of fiction from a young age, having written stories both short and long in his spare time. Over the years, he found he had a particular interest in both Horror and Science Fiction which was quickly reflected in the stories he wrote. Now, he often writes tales in either or both genres, usually intertwined with influences from Irish mythology, history, and his own upbringing. He resides in Dublin still, and spends his time between Ireland and the UK, bothering his loved ones with his odd little stories.

LEWISBURG

Mike Allen

ONE

Joel's bad luck began at Carnegie Hall.

His breath blossomed in a cloud that fogged the windshield of his 25-year-old SUV. He wiped away the condensation with a gloved hand and peered at the street sign warning him that he'd be at risk of a parking ticket after two hours on a weekday. A more ominous warning blared from another sign mounted above the first: NO PARKING AFTER 2" SNOWFALL TOW AWAY ZONE!

Leaning forward, he stared up the hill at the performance hall and its humble facade of red brick and white columns. The building was no bigger than a modest-sized church. In fact, the churches directly across the street loomed larger. His gaze flicked to the rearview mirror and the outrageously costumed mannequins stacked in the back seat, partially concealed by a blanket. "How do I get you three into Carnegie Hall?" He smirked. "Practice, practice, practice."

Scanning the empty sidewalks, he added, "And don't get caught."

He stepped out. Clouds filtered the sun's light to a benign gray, their stormy brethren glowering pendulous and dark from the peak-obscured horizon. Icy winds found his skin beneath his scarf and coat, raised goosebumps and reddened his nose and cheeks. How could West Virginia be colder than Philly? *The mountains*, he reminded himself. *It's these awful mountains.*

Talk of the beauty of those mountains always made Joel cringe, hard knots pulling tight between his shoulders and along his jaw. Not that he disagreed — he was counting on spectacular snow-covered vistas to make tomorrow's shoot worth the risk.

A quiver of movement drew his attention, the winds the probable culprit, as past the sprawling Presbyterian church, the graveyard lay barren of visitors. Of the headstones themselves, some slumped half-crumbled, some towered hale and gleaming, both varieties full of specimens predating the Civil War.

Joel laughed despite a stir of unpleasant associations, living and long dead. He addressed the empty street. "I know who's *not* buried there and never will be."

A mocking spring in his step, Joel ascended the walk to the performance hall's portico, passing between an occult-looking armillary sphere and a sculpture of leapfrogging children that possessed in the contortion of their poses an almost demonic wildness. Up the steps to the front doors, which proved unlocked. Joel smiled, already halfway to victory.

Inside, flights of stairs ascended and descended right and left, and beyond the foyer lay a posh lobby desk boldly operating on the honor system, sporting stacks of priced postcards to which he could have helped himself, had he cared enough, leaving the absent staff none the wiser until inventory count. Past the desk, the rows of theater seats, and the quaintly small stage; high school auditoriums boasted wider prosceniums and deeper wings. He hopped onto the stage, loudly proclaimed a dirty limerick to the empty house, and laughed.

His mirth was cut short as darkness carved the silhouette of a man out of the light coming from the entrance. He recovered almost as quickly; might as well lean in. "Hi, there!" he called. "I hope I didn't offend you." He grinned broadly. "I've also got more where that came from, if you want?"

No response. Joel blinked and squinted. No silhouette. "Fine," he said. "Freaking myself out again."

The riskiest part of the venture came next, as Joel wrapped the mannequins in their blanket and secured the bundle in the special harness he'd made out of leather dog leashes specifically for stunts like this. In broad daylight, he carried the awkward bundle up the steps to Carnegie Hall. Once he had them tucked behind the door, he peeked outside.

Behind the gray church across the street, a woman in a thick blue coat bent to inspect a yellowing tombstone. Joel tensed, but she paid him no mind.

With a sigh of relief, he returned to work, assembling the

mannequins, reattaching their arms and legs. He seated them in the center of the front row. One had gruesomely gory clown masks over its breasts and privates. One had crucifix-style spikes through its hands and feet and a crown of barbed wire, its skin covered with marker ink drawn to look like trickling blood. The third had a papier-mâché elephant head sculpted over the right breast, the head of a donkey over the left, and a dildo painted with a red and blue barbershop spiral rising from its crotch. From the stage, he took the first video and snapshots, with and without his conveniently collapsible tripod.

Two social media accounts bore his urban explorer handle, **@baccer_spit**, a term that summed up all his feelings about his childhood in Greenbrier County. The best stills — that is, the most disturbing — would go to Instagram, the edited video to TikTok. But not until he was safely back in Pennsylvania.

Tripod back in his inner coat pocket, disassembled mannequins rewrapped in their blanket and harness, he started up the stage right aisle, only to spy a head darkening a front door window, peaking in. He dashed to a side exit that led into an empty art gallery. His footfalls echoed.

The front door creaked.

He hugged his ridiculous bundle against the bare wall, realizing this was no hiding place should the new visitor tiptoe his way. Yet the minutes stretched. At last, he crept toward the gallery exit and peeked through to find the foyer empty. Exhaling in relief, he took a step toward the main door. Fingers clamped hard around his ankle, yanking him off balance. He slammed to the hardwood floor.

The room spun in a silver-tinted fog. Within that silvery miasma, noise swarmed, the droning of a thousand flies, high-pitched wails of pain, a boy's hoarse tenor begging *Mommy! Mommy!* Out of the haze, a shadow slouched toward him, its long neck capped by a lopsided head akin to a flower with half its petals plucked away.

Joel got his hands beneath his chest and started to push up. An object sharp and solid as a tooth bit into his right knee, directly under the kneecap.

He flipped over with a cry and sat up. No silver haze, no shadow, no hand gripping his ankle — within the doorway between gallery and foyer a single stair rose that he'd failed to notice. "Well, that was not a nice trip," he tittered.

In truth, no drug he'd ever swallowed, snorted, or injected had ever brought on a waking nightmare that fast or that intense.

His knee still stung, though his fretful fingertips found no wound.

But when he stood up, something in his knee felt wrong, looser than it was supposed to be. Nonetheless, he managed to gather up the mannequin bundle and return it to the back of his SUV without further mishap.

TWO

Setting foot inside any Lewisburg restaurant carried a small risk that Joel might be recognized, but he needed to give his still-aching knee a rest. And he badly needed a beer.

He ambled toward Washington Street, downtown

Lewisburg's aorta, homing in on an imposing log manor that bore a green placard bragging of a birthdate circa 1789. Another sign swinging from the eaves depicted tomatoes and cheese wedges, and as Joel drew closer, he discerned the words BY THE SLICE. The northwest half of the pizzeria looked to have been added much more recently, perhaps in the 1970s or later, but Joel had to concede that the owners had taken great care to preserve the original log structure, with whitewashed chinking and everything.

As he crossed Washington Street, he glanced southeast through the city's fashionably retro heart, with chipper, quirky boutiques extending their shingles from the ground floors of buildings erected when the street's namesake was president of thirteen states. He pictured the Battle of Lewisburg raging up and down these postcard-pretty blocks, the backs of Union soldiers as they crouched behind these very structures, charging out to blast musket balls at the stunned Confederate lines — the whites of the Southern soldiers' eyes visible from where he stood as blue-uniformed cavalry thundered toward them. The Johnny Rebs had the numbers and the artillery but learned far too late that the federal forces knew they were coming and had plenty of time to prepare.

The five-score dead sprawled in the dirt were the lucky ones. Those wounded but still living, bound for the depredations of the sawbones — one in particular being the worst of all.

A pickup truck's angry horn snapped Joel's mind back into his body. He'd stopped to lollygag right in the middle of the street like a complete idiot. He dashed to the porch of By the Slice, his knee shrieking in protest. Inside, the anteroom was dominated by a majestic antique fireplace large enough to shelter an entire extended family, or incinerate them. A stringy youth with decidedly non-antique hoops in his ears and nose led Joel downstairs to a table in the recently added wing.

Joel let a sigh escape as he took the weight off his burning knee joint. A further wash of relief arrived as he scanned the menu prices. He could eat well and still afford to eat tomorrow.

A slender swan of a waitress with dyed-black hair gathered in a sensible ponytail approached the table. Her nametag said "Kori." Something about her complexion puzzled him, shadows around her eyes, mouth, and neck that he kept glimpsing in the corners of his vision, though not present when he regarded her directly. After ordering, he more than once experienced a prickling certainty of being observed and turned his head to catch Kori quickly looking away. His gut told him she was studying him, not out of attraction or appreciation, but intense curiosity, and the possibility that she had somehow sussed out his identity worried him a lot.

He didn't want anyone to tip off his cousin to his presence. He doubted Eunice had any friends, doubted anyone in Lewisburg would even smile at her in passing, but money could always persuade the otherwise unwilling.

He made a pretense of visiting the restroom and covertly scanned all the dining spaces. He did not, in truth, know how age might have changed his cousin Eunice through the years since he'd last laid eyes on her. Yet, he could picture her vividly enough to have confidence he'd recognize her instantly, her close-cropped hair gone gray, the lines of her scowl etched even more deeply in her brow and around her thin mouth.

He spied no one fitting her profile. When he resumed his seat, Kori chose to make small talk, asking where he hailed from. His lie paid tribute to that victorious Union brigade. "Ohio."

"Wild," she said. "Your accent sounds local."

His heart rate jabbed in a sharp spike. Funny, yours doesn't, he thought. "Are *you* a local?"

She shrugged. "To the mountains, yes, but not *these* mountains."

"What mountains then?"

"The wilds of Pennsyltucky," she smirked, a dash of mischief that brought out an alluring inner light. A destructive impulse within him speculated whether she'd find **@baccer_ spit** appealing, considered asking her, showing her the feed, admitting his authorship.

"Planning to stay a few nights?" Again, her curiosity unnerved.

"No." He sipped his beer. "Just a quick visit."

"Well." Her gaze turned heavenward as if she peered at the darkening sky through the ceiling. "If you're not out before midnight, that storm's gonna make you stay a while, whether you want to or not. Hope you have a contingency plan."

His rusty Ford had navigated many an unsafe road under his ownership. "I'm good."

"Are you sure?"

He produced his best shit-eating grin. "Why do you want to know?"

That smirk returned. "My fiancé and I, sometimes we take in strays."

"Your fiancé? Does he work here too?"

She laughed. "Part-time cook, sometimes. I'd introduce you but he's away right now." Before he could make up his mind whether to inquire further, her demeanor grew solemn. "Are you sure everything's okay?"

"Why are you asking?"

"I just … it seems like *something* is troubling you."

He noticed, with no small puzzlement, that her gaze wasn't directed toward him, but somewhere over his left shoulder. He resisted the urge to turn his head to see what she was staring at. "Thanks, but I'm good."

She flashed a quick smile, left with a small crease knit between her brows. His meal, sufficiently delicious, concluded without further small talk. Outside, the wind bit harder, a few innocuous snowflakes tossed in its freezing currents like leaves in whitewater rapids.

His "contingency plan" was his usual, though it might well have perturbed Kori. He didn't have credit cards to secure an AirBnB or even the cash reserves for a night in a seedy hotel, so he intended to drive up a long-disused fire trail and camp in his SUV — regardless of the weather. He knew firsthand his trusty steed could handle snow. He wasn't worried about getting stuck.

Objectively speaking, even without the foul weather factor, this return to the county where he grew up could only be called unwise. Yet the impulses that guided his art never erred, in his own estimation, and he thrilled at the opportunity to taunt his childhood demons and escape unscathed, even though he'd be the only one to appreciate that aspect of the escapade.

If he *did* have to hunker down for a long while in his own back seat, though, maybe he'd want something new to read, instead of the crumbling copy of *Hidden Cities* he'd already thumbed through countless times. He strolled southeast toward the cozy-cute bookstore and coffee shop on the other side of Washington Street.

An old-fashioned jingly bell announced his arrival, but the moment he placed a foot on the primary-colored carpet, a deep growl rose from behind the combination checkout counter and cafe bar. He saw a golden canine shape spring to its feet, the portly middle-aged woman behind the register lunging to grab its collar. Long teeth flashed as the beast barked with unhinged abandon. "Sorry! Sorry!" The woman called. "He's never done this before, not ever. Stop it! Bad! Bad!"

Joel retreated, not quite at a trot. He hustled back to his SUV, filled with an irrational certainty that something, the source of the dog's distress, clung to him as he fled.

Behind the wheel, he shook his head. "Always with the magical thinking."

From the corner of his eye, the side mirror showed a man with a misshapen head looming by the Ford's rear tire.

A quick glance out the driver's side window confirmed the empty street.

THREE

The blankets, though wrapped tight, couldn't seem to keep the chill out. Joel shuddered in the dark, unable to sleep, alone with his grudges and regrets and the awkward tangle of mannequins stuffed in the back with the rest of his worldly possessions. Snow massed against the windows, mounded on the roof — Joel could sense its weight even though he couldn't see it.

Between the deepening cold and the endless loops of his own disjointed thoughts, he feared the latter far more. Whenever he lingered in the foothills of dream, he lost the power to stay flippant about his long-term unemployment and his longer-term loneliness. Yet facing off with bad weather and bad mental health only added a fraction more to the tally of injuries he'd self-inflicted in pursuit of his photographs. Crawling through abandoned tunnels under college campuses. Breaking into incomplete or abandoned high rises and taking pictures from the highest possible elevations. Once, he'd scaled a fifteen-story elevator shaft with a flash camera secured to his chest and from the ceiling taken a wide angle shot aimed straight down. More than a hundred thousand followers shared that image.

He had taken that photo eleven years ago, in what felt

like a completely different body. His right knee plagued by a piercing ache of no precise location, the space behind his eyelids swarming with unbidden colors and shapes, he muttered to his confessor of one that part of him had hoped to slip and plummet as he snapped that quasi-famous photo. He would have joined his parents, not an unpleasant prospect.

But unlike his father's along that sharp mountain curve, Joel's heart stayed strong even when his head betrayed, granting him the stamina to survive whatever obstacles he threw in his own path.

He hated the fear his mother must have known before death claimed her at the bottom of a sixty-foot drop, seconds after his father's heart attack

Their traffic crash orphaned him during his freshman year, slaying any chance that he would ever complete college, one of many so-called faults his cousin Eunice would attempt to cudgel him with on the still-not-rare-enough occasions when life forced them into communication.

"But it's a fun life," he repeated in yet another version of this often-imagined argument with his cousin. Long luckless in job searches, he lived out of the vehicle that remained after the bank foreclosed on his parents' underwater mortgage. Things he had: a phone, the **@baccer_spit** social media feeds where followers admired his content, an ultra-cheap franchise gym membership that gave him places to shower, and the ability to use his SUV for ride shares when money dwindled too negative. Living on little was the lesson from his parents that had stuck.

"Here's the only thing you and me have in common," he imagined saying to Eunice. "Both our parents are good and dead. But at least *I* didn't kill mine. God did." He smiled, picturing her outrage. "It's you, Eunice. *You* are the Scarborough curse."

When he and Eunice were young and their parents alive, they had occasionally gathered under the same roof — usually Eunice's, as her family possessed the space, the stores of old money, and the need to flaunt their fortune to a captive audience. Joel's own parents, who lived much more humbly, reciprocated from time to time out of guilt. Joel found memories of those visits, the sneers, the passive-aggressive put-downs, nauseating.

Each household represented the last surviving twigs of the Scarborough tree and knew Lewisburg would not mourn them when they died out. The city would exhale, relieved that the curse had reached its conclusion, that no living reminders of that tree's vile ancestor remained.

The deeper Joel's sleepless delirium burrowed, the more details of those torturous gatherings squirmed loose. His memories congealed in the great sitting room of the massive plantation house where Eunice lived with her mother Rosalee and father Roderick. Their mansion boasted a cavernous fireplace, more imposing than the one in By the Slice. Above the mantle hung a painting of a cleft-chinned, dull-eyed man in the blue uniform of a Union officer.

Tall, round-faced, and cleft-chinned like their shunned forebear, Eunice's dark eyes had glowed with a springheel light. "That's Doctor Scarborough. He's the reason for the family curse. He's why my great-grandfather had this house moved plank by plank from the middle of Lewisburg to the top of *Riiiich* Mountain." She drawled the word "rich" with slow imperiousness.

Joel always thought Eunice's home jutted incongruous from the mountain peak like the last remaining tooth in a broken jaw.

"Daddy told me that the doctor graciously offered his home as a hospital and all his surgical knowledge after the big battle. But the wounded men he was trying so hard to help were ungrateful. They didn't give him the respect he deserved. So he started to teach them lessons. Lessons they deserved. And because of that he was *muuuurrderred.*"

Young Joel couldn't help himself. "He was? How?"

"Well." Eunice had licked her lips, relishing what came next. "They say that he started cutting off the wrong arms and legs, the ones that weren't wounded. And he wasn't putting sticks in their mouths for them to bite on or anything, so some of those bad soldiers bit through their own tongues from the pain." She raised a gracefully tapering hand. "The floor in this very room we're standing in was an inch deep in blood. Daddy told me so."

A queasy-making yet magnetic pulse had galvanized young Joel's nerves.

"They say the worst of all the soldiers in that house yelled for the doctor to stop, but the doctor paid him no mind, so even though that soldier also served the Union, he turned traitor and shot Doctor Scarborough in the head. Daddy says they should have hanged that soldier for treason."

Young Jim had marveled at the picture over the mantle, that such an ordinary face could mask a monster. No wonder the city erased the doctor from their histories.

The very night Eunice had shared that story with him, Joel experienced the first of many night terrors: supposedly safe in his bed, he saw the dead-eyed specter of the doctor swirl out from the ceiling light, right hand clenching a gore-smeared saw. Silver-coin eyes fixed on Joel as he lay staring. Frozen with fear, he ended up wetting the bed.

In his half-waking delirium, Eunice's beady eyes and condescending smile floated above him in the cab of the SUV. He gnashed his teeth at her. "Maybe that was what you were hoping for when you told me that story?"

Joel believed Lewisburg to be indifferent to his existence, thus no source for worry, but he absolutely did not want to see Eunice again, especially after what happened to her parents. Horrible as he knew Eunice to be, he could not fathom how someone could keep posting on social media that COVID was all a big hoax while her father and mother were drowning in the sludge the virus made of their lungs.

"Even *I* wouldn't've wished that fate on *them*," he snarled at her phantasmal effigy. "You psycho."

She reached down with fingers stretched to sharpened talons and dug them into his knee, piercing skin and meat.

He sat up with a scream and smacked his head into the SUV's ceiling. He had fallen asleep after all.

His knee throbbed. He pulled up the leg of his ratty sweats but found no injury to correspond with the aching and the burning.

Snow smothered the windows, diffusing the sunlight. Once he forced the door open, he beheld a composition in black and white, barren trees rising from pristine snow mounds all up and down the slope of the hillock. His vehicle wouldn't be going far just yet. He unpacked his gear and dressed heavy for the hike.

A shadow blotted the white landscape as he fully emerged. He peered up to see the silhouette of a stupendously enormous bird — could a condor even be that big? Never before had he seen its like, and yet … something seemed familiar in its banding, a pattern barely visible at this distance. As he squinted, the shape faded into silvery mist.

He stared longer into the gray sky, then shook his head. "Mirage." Off he trudged.

FOUR

For years, Joel obsessed about conducting one of his photo shoots inside the collapsing barn that once belonged to his branch of the Scarborough family. The thought had grown in recent weeks, restless as a tumor.

If the barn still stood, he'd find it slumped on the hillside a little less than a mile from the fire trail where he'd stashed his SUV.

His boots crunched deep into the snow and the fallen leaves trapped underneath, his sweatpants and socks soaked through. The wind groped under his parka and sweatshirt despite a lessening of last night's intensity. The snow scent calmed him, like chewing spearmint, far nicer than the taint of dirt and oil that accompanied snowfall in Philly.

With no well-worn path to follow, thorny underbrush tangled his ankles, and the effort required to tear them free set off his mysterious knee injury.

Trees thinned out into a barren stretch once used for grazing and planting. This farm had been the property of his father's uncle, who outlived his children and died here alone, the farm unsold, left to decay.

Breath misting, Joel spied the misshapen hulk of the barn.

The view from the hayloft Joel remembered from his youth — that was the picture he wanted to capture, but in a way that made the rot part of the composition. He wouldn't know, though, whether the image in his mind was feasible until he broke into the barn and explored. Perhaps the caption accompanying the photo set could make some oblique reference to the family curse.

As he approached, he expected the barn to appear smaller than he remembered, but the opposite proved true, as if it had swollen while it decayed, calling to mind the corpse of some limbless prehistoric mutant.

The downhill tilt that the building had developed wedged the barn doors shut. Wood splintered against his crowbar until he prevailed, gingerly swinging the freed door panel until it rested against the outer wall.

He had no need for a flashlight. Plenty of sunlight speared

through gaps in the roof, and a dusting of snow lightened the muck and detritus that formed the floor. Had he arrived during spring or summer, every available space would have been coated with webbing and crawling with spiders, which could have made for morbidly fascinating photos … He smirked. "Not sorry I missed you, spider-friends."

The ladder to the slanting hayloft remained intact and in place.

An elevator shaft was at least made of solid concrete. He tested his weight on the first step, muttered "fuck it" and clambered up. The hayloft creaked and groaned. He stayed on all fours once he completed the ascent, distributing his weight as widely as possible. The panels covering the hayloft windows hung askew, each clinging by a single hinge. Good, he would leave them like that. The opening still permitted the view out over the valley and the city that Joel remembered so vividly.

He crawled closer to the windows, not minding the wet, matted straw. Below the hillock slope, the streets of Lewisburg wound among a mix of homes ranging from vinyl siding and brick to logs and wood-shingled roofs. Church steeples grasped heavenward — an arrangement of four marked the corners of a square, centered on downtown. Perhaps by coincidence, they reminded Joel of the points of a compass rose.

The storm had shut the streets down. No cars inched along, and he was too far away to see any people shoveling drives or sledding.

The figure manifested in front of him as if rounding the

corner of a hallway that did not exist. Clad dark from toe to neck, it planted booted feet inches from Joel's face.

Joel bleated "Sorry, man!" and backpedaled in a panic, heart ping-ponging in his ribs. The figure squatted — Joel registered that the interloper wore the uniform of a Union officer, buttons polished, fabric stained — seized Joel's parka by the shoulders and lifted him to his feet.

Joel beheld a misshapen head, one eye staring straight into his, the other half of the face a bloom of glistening meat and exposed bone. The thing possessed of this destroyed visage dangled him off the edge of the hayloft as if positioning him just so, then let go.

Joel's scream never made it out of his lungs. The sensation of his right leg folding up underneath him like a collapsible cane erased all coherent thought.

The mottled white pattern that he blearily interpreted as an overhead view of well-trod snow resolved into the moonscape of a stucco ceiling. He turned his head side to side, confirming he lay under a quilt in the lumpy expanse of an antebellum-era king-size bed. He tried to sit up and the pain in his right leg went nova.

Hollering in agony, he instinctively clutched at his leg, which set off another nova. He froze stock still, whimpering.

"Crybaby." Cousin Eunice stood in the bedroom doorway, arms akimbo. "Always have been. What is the big, big problem?"

Her hair had indeed gone completely white as he'd imagined — there had been streaks of gray in her auburn locks even before she turned twenty. Her brow had somehow grown craggier, such that her eyes might as well have been hollow pits. Her cardigan hung loose on her skeletal shoulders. Her thin lips puckered into a mischievous, cat-that-felled-the-robin smile. "You're going to be fine. I'll show you."

Joel's mouth moved but he was too astonished to speak. Eunice advanced, yanked the quilt to one side. Underneath, Joel was completely nude, except for the bandages that clamped two long, wide boards to the outside and inside of his right leg.

"Doctor Scarborough led me to you. He showed me what to do," Eunice said. "He still knows his stuff. That leg could take a licking now and heal up perfectly straight."

To demonstrate, she put both hands on his right leg, one above his knee, one below, and shoved downward into the mattress with all her might. A black abyss consumed him.

FIVE

He dreamed, or so he believed, of an enormous bird circling in a silver-hazed abyss. A voice that he couldn't quite place whispered a question: *Are you okay? Are you okay?* To either side, shuddering forms gagged, their wet coughs barked right into his ears.

"Good afternoon, sleepyhead," cousin Eunice said, causing him to start and his leg to shriek in response to his body's unexpected twitch. He locked that shriek inside with all of his will.

Some five feet from the bedside, Eunice gripped the handles of an antique wheelchair. "Time for potty."

That sealed-off shriek gained a higher pitch as Joel realized Eunice wasn't alone. A man in a blue Union uniform regarded him from the foot of the bed. This time, Joel recognized the cleft chin and sparkless expression captured in Doctor Scarborough's portrait. The doctor fixed the vacant gaze of his single intact eye on Joel's bandaged and splinted leg. Above that eye and the bushy eyebrow that shaded it, a black blot like a quarter-sized liver spot marred the doctor's forehead. The other side of his head bloomed in a pink and white eruption.

Eunice followed Joel's gaze. "The doctor wants to amputate. I keep telling him you need those legs, because I sure don't want to lug you around like a sack of potatoes." She jiggled the wheelchair. "Come on. Show him you can get around."

Surely, Joel had woken from one nightmare into another and was still sound asleep. Multiple models of the crucified savior hung between family portraits. Multiple photographs of a much younger Eunice smiled craftily from atop a mahogany armoire. Visual evidence to the contrary, he could not possibly be inside Eunice's mansion atop Rich Mountain; there was no way anyone could have physically schlepped him there through the snow. The long-dead doctor could not be present either in this bedroom or the abandoned barn. Joel had fallen, remained on the barn floor with a head injury, out like a light, or maybe still lay sleeping and freezing in his SUV.

"Quit being shy, I've seen your junk and everything else down there." She thumped the wheelchair backrest. As Joel continued to stare, she implored. "Doctor, can you help?"

The doctor pinched the quilt, slowly drew it toward the foot of the bed. The sensations of fabric sliding, cool air kissing skin, felt realer than real. "Stop."

"Come on then." She thumped the wheelchair again.

He tried turning on his side, and his leg twinged sharper. He licked his lips. "That's too far from the bed."

"You can make it. You won't get better playing me for sympathy. No job so no physical therapy for you; this is the best you're going to get."

Even with the doctor's specter watching, the bile of accusations soured the back of his tongue: *Is this how you did your ma and pa? When their own lungs were drowning them?*

What would happen if he dared make mention of Uncle Roderick and Aunt Rosalee? That coughing in his ears — absolute certainty bored through him that he lay in the very bed where they had died.

The doctor leaned forward, single eye glistening with excitement.

Mortified that the specter might touch him, Joel turned his body in tentative stages until his left foot rested on the cold hardwood floor, his right leg protruding ungainly from the edge of the mattress. He pushed up, all his weight momentarily on one leg, arms flailing, groping for the wheelchair's armrest. As he tottered, Eunice gripped his elbow and helped him to hop-turn so he fell rump-first into the wheelchair seat, groaning as the impact jarred the breaks in his bones.

Blinking tears from his eyes, he discovered the doctor had evaporated.

"There, told you, crybaby," Eunice said. "Can you hold it till we reach the toilet?"

By the time they returned to the bedroom, Eunice made it plain she'd had enough. "You can get back in the bed your damn self," she said, parking the wheelchair a couple feet past the door, which she shut behind him.

For several minutes he struggled to simply sit upright in a stable position, using his hands and his good leg to prop up his shattered one. His mind scrambled through a rat's maze while his panic and pain grew. Only gradually did he notice that Eunice had left him within arm's reach of a shelf stocked with wide-eyed porcelain baby dolls and that the backpack he'd been wearing in the barn lay propped against that shelf.

Pain be damned, in seconds he had the pack in his lap, its outer pouch opened, his cell phone in hand. He activated the screen that would allow an emergency call.

EMTs would spirit him away from his deranged cousin's clutches. Police would hear about his horrid treatment, maybe even haul Eunice downtown in handcuffs. The doctor ...

He experienced a moment of sickening clarity, contemplating the tens of thousands of dollars he would owe, for the ambulance, for the ER, for the bone setting, for the hospitalization, a debt he could never, ever pay down. And what could he possibly say about the doctor? How could he explain his presence in Eunice's house, his splinted leg, his SUV hidden along the fire trail?

And these issues would only become problems if the police and the EMTs could even get to this house, huddled at the peak of this completely snowbound mountain.

Agony and confusion clogged his reasoning. He started to hyperventilate, staring at the lone signal bar atop the phone readout. A hand clenched his wrist, its touch like an electrified flash-freeze.

Joel lost his concentration. His right heel banged the floor, and he screamed, the sound twisting high and girlish as the doctor's bullet-blasted head lowered close. The doctor's other hand, the one not clamping Joel's wrist, clutched a gleaming instrument akin to a compact meat cleaver.

When Joel tried to twist his arm free his heel again banged the floor. His mouth stretched in a silent oval of pain and horror.

The doctor's blade sliced into the meat of Joel's forearm. Adding indignity to injury, his phone banged his right ankle as it fell.

The doctor pivoted on a bootheel, raised a foot as if ascending a stair, and was no longer there.

Joel gasped and gasped, straining mightily to lift his leg so his heel wouldn't hammer the floor again. He raised his arm to inspect the horrendous sensation of deep-singed tissue where the doctor had slashed him, and discovered that instead of a bleeding cut, he bore a long linear burn, as if a red hot kebab skewer had been pressed to his skin.

At last he remembered the phone, couldn't find it, and dared finally to move the wheelchair to see if it had bounced underneath.

It had not. Wherever the doctor had gone, the phone had vanished with him.

SIX

Reaching the bed took a nail-biting eon and maneuvering onto the mattress without the use of his shattered leg nearly ended in a tumble to the hardwood. Once he was solidly in the bed, he lay still and panting for long minutes. He had wound up lying on his stomach, a position that grew more uncomfortable by the minute. A new chorus of pain accompanied his cautious movements to right himself, until he lay on his back in the middle of the bed. He didn't try to wrestle the quilt over his nakedness.

He couldn't sleep through the fiery pulsing as bone shards pressed together, that sensation's twin in his forearm, and the deepening chill everywhere else.

Hours trickled past. Eunice stayed away.

Eventually, he slid into a state of waking delirium. On either side, Roderick and Rosalee gurgled in his ears. He floated, a concrete abyss extending below him as if he once again hung by a climbing rope at the top of the elevator shaft where he'd taken his most famous picture.

He wasn't alone. Of all people, the waitress from By the

Slice regarded him from her perch on a horizontal bracket about six feet below, absurdly yet perfectly balanced, with her arms hugging her knees to her chest.

Joel perceived the shadow of a second form occupying the same space she did, an immense bird with dark bands across its chest, neck, and brow — the mirage he kept seeing in the Lewisburg sky.

"Where are you?" Kori asked, her voice sounding as it had when she took his order.

"You're the bird?" he asked dreamily.

She shifted on her perch. So did the bird shadow. "Listen to me. This is not a dream. I'm really talking to you. You're like me and my fiancé, you have a spirit shadow, maybe not as strong as mine, but you can see and feel things in the silver world. And they can see you. Something, I don't know what, has got you, and it's hidden you behind a veil. I'm trying to find you, but you're like an image reversed through a dozen pinholes, so I can't figure out where your light comes from. Can you tell me where you are?"

He could hardly bring himself to take the question seriously, even as a voice somewhere in the swamp of his mind screamed *Tell her you're at your cousin's! The mansion on Rich Mountain!*

Bird and woman cocked their heads. "What was that?"

He opened his mouth, and a hand clamped over it, jolting his lips and tongue with an icy electric current.

He started to shout, then had all his breath crushed out of him. The doctor's arms pinned Joel's own to his sides as the specter lifted him bodily from the mattress. Joel tried to kick free and loosed a muffled shriek as his splinted leg bashed the footboard.

His field of vision spun in three dimensions as the doctor stepped off the bed, clutching Joel to his side like a fleshy, wobbling mannequin, descended *through the floor,* and somehow brought Joel with him.

For a few seconds, he hung upside down in a mausoleum of a sitting room, where a talking head on a huge television blurted that immigrants were the worst scourge this country faces. Swathed in a flower print nightgown, Eunice sprang from the loveseat. "What are you doing? He's not ready yet!"

Another turn, another room altogether, with its cavernous fireplace and the doctor's portrait still mounted above it, both the mantle and the hearth crowded with lit candles that resembled wax-drenched bones. Walls muffled Eunice's shout: "Wait! You made me a promise!"

Another turn, into the fireplace, and a silver tunnel spiraled down into what had to be the core of the mountain, except the substance that formed its walls resembled nothing Joel had ever seen before.

Another turn and Joel raised his head to stare down the length of Washington Street. Or a copy, still recognizable, and yet the copyist had taken liberties. No boutique storefronts snuggled side by side, no electric signs, no wires overhead, no traffic signals, no parked cars. The multitudes of churches and log homes had further proliferated somehow.

Most incongruous of all, a chateau to rival Versailles

dominated the near horizon, its footprint consuming the hill where Carnegie Hall and Greenbrier Center should have stood.

From out of a maddening hum, the droning of a thousand flies, a child's voice shrilled. *Mommy! Mommy! Don't let him cut me up!*

It was Joel's voice, shrieking as the doctor's ghost swirled out of the ceiling light.

Joel could not even begin to wrap his mind around what was happening. He dangled at the doctor's side, dazed and straining for air. His feet settled in a papery powder that resembled snow but was neither cold nor wet. His agony and terror had spiked so far past endurance that the instinct bubbling through him was not to scream but to laugh. Had he been able to breathe, he would have cackled nonstop.

Doctor Scarborough's inhumanly strong ghost advanced toward the palatial estate. Eyes rolling wildly, Joel's mental camera took a snapshot of a familiar building — the log house that contained By the Slice, no longer sporting a modern expansion. The sight triggered an association. The urgent whispers at the back of his brain redoubled their volume. He concentrated on the waitress, on Kori's face, on her question, *Where are you?* He gasped, "I'm on Washington Street, heading toward By the Slice —"

The doctor slammed Joel to the road, sending ash powder billowing. What remained of the doctor's face contorted with rage as he levered a knee on Joel's belly and pressed both hands over Joel's mouth, the cold shock from the doctor's skin like a jackhammer of ice. *Fuck it*, Joel thought and bit at those palms. The jolt reached the Richter scale, but the doctor abruptly sprang away.

No way to understand the cause, but the doctor stared at his shriveled hands, split and torn where Joel had bit them. As the doctor's arms trembled, his eye glowed silver, and his fingers began to *re-inflate*.

Joel questioned neither his new energy, nor his new instincts, or even the dulling of the pain in his splinted leg. He sprang, and a shadow form sprang with him.

Kori's words: *You have a spirit shadow.* Like her banded bird.

But Joel's had claws and fangs.

The doctor's lips formed a surprised O as Joel's gnashing teeth found cheek, ear, and pulpy wound. The taste flowed sweeter than ambrosia across Joel's tongue.

The ghost flung Joel end over end. He landed on his feet. Or his shadow did, and because it did, *he* did. He hollered at the vacant street, "What the fuck is happening?"

A substance like silver smoke rose from the gouges Joel's teeth made in the doctor's head. Joel's ancestor set off at a sprint toward the incongruous palace.

"I still can't see you, but something's changed. The walls are weaker. Are you okay?" Joel couldn't tell where Kori's voice was coming from.

"I've never felt better," he yelled back. It was the truth, the sick, perverse truth. Tasting the flesh of his ancestor's revenant had affected him like the fabled Fountain of Youth.

None of the chemical-induced highs he'd experienced had ever coursed this hot along his nerves.

He laughed. How ridiculous could this situation get? If only Joel knew where the doctor had disposed of his cell phone. Imagine the pictures he could take.

"The ghost of Doctor Scarborough hauled me here, but then I bit him, and now he's running like a chicken with its head bit off."

"Oh lord," she said, reminding him of that crease of worry between her brows. "Please, listen to me. Our kind. We can get our nourishment from ghosts, but it's bad for us, worse than meth. And if a ghost made this nest that you're inside, then it's powerful, the most powerful I've ever heard of. You *must* get out of there! Follow my voice. Find a way out!"

The doctor dashed down Church Street toward the filigreed gate to his personal Versailles.

Watching his enemy run, Joel hungered, craving another taste, and wondered if his ancestor had experienced the same all-consuming euphoria when sawing through a living limb.

"Where do you think *you're* going?" Joel whooped and gave chase. The bandages around his leg tore free as his shadow form gained more density.

"No!" yelled Kori from somewhere in the silver haze of the sky. "Don't go in there!"

The great double doors stood wide open, and Eunice stood in the entrance, still wearing the floral print nightgown, the butt of a long rifle pressed to her shoulder, neck bent as she peered through an expensive scope. She jerked her head up in alarm. "Joel?"

"Cousin." He strode straight at her.

She swore and pulled the trigger. She missed his flesh, but his larger shadow self felt the projectile pass through, a white-hot whoosh gone quick as a chaste kiss.

He sprang. Or rather, his shadow-self did while he enjoyed the ride. He glimpsed the strike of an immense five-stubbed paw, like that of a badger or a wolverine.

Kori's distant cry cut off mid-syllable as he crossed the threshold.

Eunice flopped back onto the marble tiles, blood fanning from her neck, her chest, her belly. Joel drew up short, the sight of that dark fluid, of a *real life* ebbing out, ending so messily, snapping him free of the hunger driving his every move.

He paused, thoughts tumbling. He never liked Eunice, but he had never wished *this*. Should he try to help her? Was this even real?

A flash of silver from the balcony overlooking this great hall. Joel raised his head, but the doctor had retreated from view. He perceived that the hall doubled as a gallery and that the sculptures shuddering and writhing atop the pedestals weren't busts. They were ghosts. Limbs amputated. Eyes, teeth, tongues removed. Dozens of them.

He recognized his uncle. He recognized Roderick and Rosalee. His own mother and father. Many more whose faces meant nothing to him.

The hunger returned, raging, and helped him to end their suffering. The more he ate, the faster, stronger, larger he felt.

When he spied the doctor's ruined face peering down at him from the rafters, he had no trouble leaping to that height, sinking his claws into the lower ledge of a vertical tunnel and pulling himself up. He continued the chase, ascending higher than the top of that elevator shaft that granted his fifteen seconds of fame, higher than any building that would ever exist in Lewisburg. He climbed and climbed; the doctor's shining silver eye always flashed at least a story above, never quite in reach.

Somewhere in a dream, a naked man lay in the snow, real, flesh-freezing snow, laughing as he swept his arms and legs back and forth to make a snow angel. A pale figure in a Union officer's uniform knelt by the man's side, brandishing a saw. As the man's limbs grew numb, the surgeon kindly helped remove them.

MIKE ALLEN is an author, editor and publisher of science fiction, fantasy and horror. He has written, edited, or co-edited thirty-nine books, among them his forthcoming dark fantasy novel *Trail of Shadows,* his sidearms, sorcery, and zombies sequence *The Black Fire Concerto* and *The Ghoulmaker's Aria,* and his newest horror collection, *Slow Burn. Unseaming* and *Aftermath of an Industrial Accident,* his first two volumes of horror tales, were both finalists for the Shirley Jackson Award for Best Story Collection, and his dark fable "The Button Bin" was a nominee for the Nebula Award for Best Short Story. Another collection, *The Spider Tapestries,* contains experiments in weird science fiction and fantasy. As an editor and publisher, Mike has been nominated twice for the World Fantasy Award: first, for his anthology *Clockwork Phoenix 5,* the culmination of the *Clockwork Phoenix* series showcasing tales of beauty and strangeness that defy genre classification; and then, for *Mythic Delirium,* the magazine of poetry and fiction he edited for twenty years. He's a three-time winner of the Rhysling Award for poetry. His six poetry collections include *Strange Wisdoms of the Dead,* a *Philadelphia Inquirer* Editor's Choice selection, and *Hungry Constellations,* a Suzette Haden Elgin Award nominee. With his wife, Anita, he runs Mythic Delirium Books, based in Roanoke, Virginia. Their cat Pandora assists.

HELSINKI

Xan van Rooyen

The snow falls, an antiphonal symphony for wind and revenant choir. A last breath gasped across the freezing Baltic before the city flatlines into dormancy.

It is *Marraskuu*—November—the month named for the dead: Martaat, harbingers of death, souls escaped from the underworld, and ghosts coughed up from Manala to stalk the realm of the living.

I watch the cemeteries teem with mourners. Those who wish to remember the departed, those who stroke crumbling tombstones and whisper 'history,' those clad in dramatic black trailing rose petals across strangers' graves, those carrying candles and lanterns thinking the light will keep the ghouls at bay.

I watch, and I wait.

For the candles to gutter and the lanterns to extinguish. For the cemeteries to return to silence and shadow under the sentinel gaze of the crows, feathers whisking the spectral haze.

The temperature drops; the dead rise.

It is Sunday, November 8, 1942. The snow has yet to fall, but the Martaat sing elegiac, Winter's open palm slow-curling into a fist. Just before noon, children are laughing in The Tivoli as The Three Musketeers entertain on the screen, others crowd the Gloria, and more are down the street at church calling on a god who will not save them.

The Martaat exhale an omen of approaching doom.

The children will not make it to the bomb shelter at Johanneksenkirkko. The crowd gathering at the intersection of Iso Roobertinkatu and Yrjönkatu are turned to shrapnel scatter.

A study in ruined anatomy.

There in the shop window, no longer an infant but a headless rag-doll impaled on broken glass, and–littering the street, caught between crooked tram lines–the twisted abstractions of limb and entrails, burgundy Rorschach smears from which survivors will attempt to divine meaning.

But even the spilled blood of a beloved is simply a stain washed away by tears or rain, to be buried beneath the snow.

She sits in the window, hand pressed to the glass, smudges I've stopped trying to erase. I wish I knew how to give her peace; I wish I knew her name.

Patrons don't like the nearby table. Call it draughty, shiver as they stir sugar into coffee, their cinnamon buns turning stale between bites. They cannot see the diaphanous child, one of the numerous displaced dead roaming the city.

Before the Northern Crusades and Swedish colonization, before Russian imperialism and Soviet bombs, before when it was forest and lake and all things in balance, when this city was just huts at the edge of the sea, the dead were hemmed in by karsikko trees. Now they stalk, attached like parasites to the unsuspecting, feeding, draining.

"What can I get you?" I ask the twenty-something at the counter; baby-faced and oblivious to the wraith barnacled to their shadow.

Love, dignity, acceptance? Wealth, fame, power?

If only they'd look up, I might catch a glimpse of the stars in their eyes and know the truth of their desire.

"Cappuccino," they say, gaze glued to their phone.

I list our kinds of milk–they choose the one with the smallest carbon footprint–then I grind, steam, pour, sprinkle cinnamon, and slip a rectangle of chocolate onto the saucer. The human grunts their thanks; I glare at the wraith, this greedy marta.

It glances at the ghost girl in the window, stretching shadow fingers toward the table. Its human settles, shivering as they stir, destroying foam art they never noticed.

Quickly, the wraith grows tired of the girl. She stares and stares, hand pressed and then taken away, fingerprints and an illegible Morse code. No one is coming for her; she was only ever listed as 'unknown.'

The wraith instead regards its human as it unwraps the chocolate. The wraith snatches it, leaving the human to chew on ashes. This errant marta should be in the cemetery, feasting on corpse meat, picking its teeth with splinters of bone, serenading the crows with hollow songs, but the city has uprooted tangles of green and chopped down the old karsikko trees. The way is open for these ghouls now in this city that is concrete and cobbles, a housing shortage, an infrastructure dilemma, an uptick in crime, a mental health crisis. Citizens escape welfare erosion, find comfort at the bottom of a bottle, or bruise veins with the hope of syringe salvation.

And the ghouls consume.

In a lull, I study my customers tucked into the pocket of warmth my cafe provides. A false respite. They think it's the season making their feet feel leaden, their worries heavier, the shadows stitched to their souls thicker and darker, a density increased by the teetering economy, by seismic political shifts, by the violent tectonics of aging as wrinkles in flesh mirror fissures in hearts forced to give up on the dream of a brighter future while the planet boils.

The lack of light is to blame, they say, cramming vitamin D down their throats or waking to ersatz sunshine—those who can afford it—in attempts to evade SAD-ness. Others simply succumb to the creeping kaamos unraveling a suffocating blanket of perpetual night across the Arctic, the polar gloom a spreading contagion even this far south.

But the sorrow is in their bones, their marrow laced with

frost as ghoulish fingers pluck the stars from their eyes, pearls of optimism cracked between rotting teeth, yet still unable to sate the edacious appetites of the wandering dead.

And we, the few who see, who understand, who know—the last remaining tietäjät—wring impotent hands. Gone are the days of magic and spells, the language lost, the ritual songs a forgotten art swept into the cobwebbed corners of great-grandparent memory, filtered through Christian hymns, or scrawled in splotched ink on crumbling pages, tomes sprouting mold, old knowledge become fungus fodder. We try, but we are stumbling anachronisms without true power.

All I can give now is the comfort of a cozy retreat off wind-bitten streets, the solace of a warm cup, and the opportunity to rekindle the fire in their hearts, perhaps reignite the light in their eyes.

*I*t is December 1710. The frost has finally come and, with it, an end to the plague.

Two-thirds of the population is dead: residents of a town still dreaming of becoming the capital; refugees from starving, sick-stricken surroundings; marooned soldiers as one empire fights another with Finland the battleground between.

The Martaat call to Winter, and the freeze bites deep.

The bodies pile up. The earth bends shovels and breaks tired backs until the remnant of the ice age sitting less than six feet deep unlocks its jaw to welcome the corpses.

The dead are buried beside the old church in what will one day be nicknamed Ruttopuisto—Plague Park—by generations who have forgotten the devastation, who gather in white-capped gaggles to celebrate graduation, who congregate in playful throngs, who short-cut across the oasis of green failing to notice the ghosts snagged on oak boughs or crouched beside the lopsided tombstones.

Some hold their breath now, bury noses in scarves, wishing they still had an N95 in their pocket—another plague chafing at their mind.

But even the recent memory of panic and pandemic is quashed by hand sanitizer and engulfed by more significant concerns like the soaring price of electricity as the snow swirls in threatening eddies.

We meet in the Plague Park at midnight.

The night is clear, the mercury plummeting to double digits below freezing. Our breath steams in clouds before crystallizing on our lashes and the fuzz of woolen scarves or beards.

Moonlight slicks our blades as we gouge and shear, pare and flay the trees. The wraiths watch as we fashion sigils in bark. Once, journalists wrote articles about our botanical vandalism, speculating about the ritual decortication, blaming delinquent youth, the addicts, and the homeless. Never appreciating our work to keep the hungry ghosts confined.

We drift from the park now, humming melodies we think might have once held magic: an adjusted children's rhyme, a passed-down lullaby, a snatch of healing song, or a half-remembered refrain from an old sea shanty. Our voices are inaudible over the electric thrum of the sleeping city.

We meander down the thoroughfares festooned with lights this time of year. Garish and bright, drawing on struggling grids as if strangling the city in strings of LEDs will keep the darkness at bay.

The dead seep through concrete crevices, phantom stalagmites reaching from below, and the forgotten graves turned foundations for the city above: a capital built on skeletons.

The dead will not be placated, and there are too few trees to mark, too many people to protect from the ravenous dead.

We reconvene at the old cemetery home to dead statesmen, famous artists, and other forever cultural heroes. For now, it remains a park, the trees each bearing our marks–only the most tenacious ghosts have been able to escape. Weary and forlorn, we form a circle beneath the light of the gibbous moon.

"What's the point?" Joonas asks. "Soon, this'll be gone too."

The city has promised to preserve the trees, the legacy, this precious patch of foliage beside the sea, a promise they may find impossible to keep once it's sold to private investors.

Every swath of green has been shaped and redesigned. There are no wild spaces left. The modern profane now replaces the sacred ancient.

I notice then how the moonlight fails to sheen his eyes, his pupils dilated black holes; the stars previously flaring in his irises have been swallowed. His shadow is thick as treacle, as black as rye, a congealed distortion at his feet where more than one wraith writhes.

We have lost another to the season of despair.

The breeze riffles the air, carrying with it that scent of musty putrescence peculiar to the ghouls. I sneeze, others pull up their scarves, but Joonas doesn't notice the rot-like mildew already inside.

It never used to be this hard. There used to be more of us, but every generation has been whittled down, and every year, more trees succumb to urban expansion: hallowed spaces turned into parking lots and boulevards, cheaper housing and gentrified neighborhoods needing designer parks, even the sea-filled up with concrete to make room for towering apartment blocks.

"I'm done," Joonas says, pocketing his knife. "None of this will ever make a difference." He hugs himself and staggers away, his shadow dragging at his feet.

We watch him wade back down the path where the old asylum looms. After the last patients were relocated for all the usual bureaucratic reasons, its halls stood empty for years. Later, it became a community center brimming with cheer, serving those in need with art and therapy and not terrible coffee. Now, it awaits once more to be transformed, labeled prime real estate, and threatened with a new purpose. The trees of its surrounds are all that keep the army of ghosts at bay, sigils carved by our cramping hands as we traipse along, inhaling scalpel-edged snowflakes while the rest of the city sleeps.

It is Sunday, January 27, 1918, and Finland is at war with itself. Red versus White, the colors of the conflict, are like blood on snow. In just four months, 12% of the population will be killed, a nation fractured, the collective heart of the recently independent already broken. A deluge of souls turned restless dead, their anger a disease with no easy cure.

It is January now, but no one can spare a thought for those who suffered more than a hundred years ago, not when bullets are still flying, when bombs are still dropping, when violence seems an inevitability of the human condition, and war a never-ending escalation.

Not in this city, not this time, yet our ghosts feel their ranks swell across the ephemeral web of the dead.

But even the outrage at current atrocities is mitigated by daily struggles: flights canceled, trains delayed, car battery dead, and the bus caught in snow-choked traffic. Then— horror of all horrors—when you, weary soldier, finally trudge into the office only to discover the coffee machine is broken.

By the end of January, most holiday lights have been dismantled, and the markets offering cups of hot spice-wine glögi, roasted chestnuts, and rice porridge doused in cinnamon have long since been boarded up. The city hunkers down as the storms blow in, blizzard after blizzard dumping snow while temperatures reach historic lows.

The iron sky keeps us captive, the sun somewhere above unable to pierce the clouds even as we turn our faces toward spring. It is a far-off fancy, mere rumor, a taunt of warmth and thaw none of us can believe.

We sign petitions to save children dying far away—to save the last of the trees in this city stripped bare. We cast our votes, some pray while others burn incense or attempt meditation, we work and work out, we eat, shit, fuck, and I serve coffee to those in need as if shots of espresso might be enough to banish the ones feeding in the shadows.

I sing to the ghost girl, experimental melodies, phrases squeezed from memory, extrapolated from great-grandmother's tale, but still she remains.

The other tietäjät are here, squashed into a corner table, pouring over a treatise liberated from an abandoned collection at the university library. It's in the old tongue, the words familiar but longer and clogged with vowels, the scrawl indecipherable. Yet, even from my place behind the counter serving munkki and mochaccinos to customers storm-crusted and defeated, I feel the power emanating from the tome.

If only we could understand it.

They stay until closing, the table stacked high with cups, hands jittery from coffee, hearts beating staccato at the possibility—perhaps we've found a way: a snatch of song, a snippet of lyrics to get us to spring. My gaze drifts to the ghost girl, her arms up and fingers splayed as if in surrender.

It is Sunday, February 6, 1944, and the sirens are wailing again. People are tired of shrieking and are no longer immediately roused to action. Instead, they wait patiently for the all-clear so they can grumble about a false alarm.

There is no all-clear this time.

Three-hundred and fifty planes drop 3500 bombs across the city.

One hundred souls snuffed into oblivion. 300 more wounded.

Truly a miracle.

The planes return on February 16 and February 26.

Twenty thousand bombs, but the damage is minimal thanks to clever military tactics and upgraded anti-aircraft capabilities. The Finnish spirit remains intact; the 'sisu' or soul mettle for which the nation is known did not shatter before a mightier enemy.

We will not cower now.

It is February, the season shedding darkness in inexorable ecdysis, but the cold holds us in its relentless grip, and the dead thicken like fog. Even as the light returns, the Spring has never felt so far away: 'It gets better' –a promise starting to molder.

May looms on the distant horizon: Toukokuu, the month named for the sowing season–sewing up slashed wrists or self-inflicted bullet wounds perhaps, but no threads can fix a twisted neck eased from a noose or drain poison burning caustic through the blood. There are no sutures for a broken heart, no pins or plates for a shattered spirit. Every year, it's the same, right before they manage to shake free the shackles of winter–just as they might be able to purge the ghoul infestation from their shadows and save a spark yet to be extinguished–too often they succumb, falling victim to the suicide gene written in Finno-Ugric DNA some hypothesize, tired of waiting for better days when nothing seems to change, the result of a failing system.

So we study the book, our tongues left aching and blistered by our aborted attempts at learning old magic. Our gums bleed, teeth loosened at the root as we force ancient syllables across our lips, and still, we fail. Stars gutter and extinguish, eyes turned dim, brimming with nihilism, tears evaporating.

We lose another. Maria didn't make it to May, becoming another statistic while waiting for the help she needed: a number in a too-long queue–dismissed by the system as able to cope. Budget cuts to better balance government speeding, a necessary austerity after financial recklessness, and a welfare system making it too easy for those who lack motivation when survival is simple. Maria knew; she juiced her greens and ran three times a week, she went outside every time the sun oozed through the clouds, she meditated and took supplements, she laughed, she had friends, she limited screen time, she recited a litany of positive affirmations to the face in the mirror, and yet…

The inconvenience of a delayed metro stresses the commuters as they dial bosses and make excuses. Later, they'll learn someone jumped on the tracks. How selfish, how inconsiderate, delaying commuters, interfering with the daily grind, never mind traumatizing the driver, the clean-up crew, the unlucky witnesses.

Maria's family take her ashes north to the town where she was born and give what's left of her to the bitter wind. We sing for her, songs to send her to Manala, to guide her beyond the river, songs to keep her anchored in death, hoping she won't steal back into the living world, hungry and vindictive.

We float adrift in the wake of Maria's passing. We do what we can, but it will never be enough to save them all from the invisible blight siphoning dreams from veins, a thrumming vitality reduced to a trickle. I've studied the tome, sung my throat raw and aching, poured blood and sleepless nights into the hope I've found a way to save at least one hapless soul. Let this be the one thing I can do.

The shop is closed for the night, and the sky is a wound. Layers of pink and red clouds undulate like savaged flesh as the sun retreats between the buildings. The girl stands in the window, her tiny handprints limned in the gold of the dying light. She remains a shade, a density the sunset cannot touch, a cold spot impervious to the inevitability of spring, a mere stutter through chattering teeth.

"I found you somewhere to rest," I say, unsure the child can hear me. Her head bobbles on the untidy seam of severed neck. "I'll take you there. It's the least I can do." I hold out my hand, my shadow extending across the table, phantom fingers grazing the tattered edges of her form.

She turns—eyes empty, face vacant—and steps closer as the

sun slinks lower and the twilight deepens. My shadow grows heavier as she cleaves toward me, sharp nails finding purchase and already I am tired, struggling against the load of this extra weight.

Others are drawn to us, those not yet netted in the shadows of the damned. They follow us to the forest, flit at the periphery of my torchlight as I hike through the cultivated rows of birch and pine toward what I hope will be her final resting place. Not here where trees have a calculated lifespan and market value, not here where war in a neighboring country might cause the death of saplings not yet ripe for slaughter, or where a harsh winter might justify the culling of more trees to heat the homes of those with souls already petrifying.

I slog through snow drifts and skid across patches of ice, all while singing the songs cobbled together from imperfect histories and patchwork memories ornamented by gut feel and good intention. The martaat wail a contrapuntal harmony, and I go deeper, darker–beyond the limits of the logging industry into the preserved and protected pocket of old-growth where the trees are draped in tassels of beard moss, where crows have scratched runic lamentations across the snow, where my blade has carved sigils into pristine bark stained by tears and apologies that it has come to this.

Staggering, I kneel in the narrow glade and feel the ghosts press close. There has been no fresh snowfall, the hole I dug is a welcoming maw ready to swallow my offering. With my tongue bleeding from the flawed magic reduced from song to hum, I slip my blade sharp as moonlight against my skin and pry the shadow free. It's as tacky as a spiderweb between my fingers, but I work it loose and grate the remnants from my palm against the lip of the grave. The shadow ripples where it lies, the girl a dark convulsion but slowly she settles, accepting the offer of rest. I cover her with snow, my fingers numb and heart juddering, entrained to ghost song still filling the glade.

Come spring, flowers will burst from the compost, a carpet of kielo unfurling white blooms: delicate and deadly. Kielo, the national flower of Finland, poisonous and perfect: a name for a dead girl flung through a window, abandoned and forgotten.

"Sleep well," I say through blackened teeth as I curl up in the snow, cradled by the dead.

I'm cold, freezing, but the pain melts into comfort as surely as the earth will thaw. Above me, a leafless thatch of skeletal branches and the sky a stretched canvas pockmarked by star scatter. Their light burns, searing my eyes with a glow that lingers even as I close them, a dozen constellations trapped behind my eyelids. I reach for them, snare them with imaginary fingers that grasp and hold and never let go.

Climber, tattoo collector, and peanut-butter connoisseur, XAN VAN ROOYEN is an autistic, non-binary storyteller from South Africa, currently living in Finland where the heavy metal is soothing and the cold, dark forests inspiring. Xan has a Master's degree in music, and–when not teaching–enjoys conjuring strange worlds and creating quirky characters. You can find Xan's stories in the likes of *Three-Lobed Burning Eye, Daily Science Fiction,* and *Galaxy's Edge* among others. They have also written several novels including YA fantasy *My Name is Magic,* and adult aetherpunk novel *Silver Helix.* Xan is also part of the Sauútiverse, an African writer's collective with their first anthology *Mothersound* out now from Android Press. Feel free to say hi on socials @xan_writer. Pronouns: they/them

QUEENS

Sam Rebelein

Why don't you have more friends? You're thirty years old, and you only have *one* good friend? Christ was thirty-three; he had, like, a dozen close friends. But you've pushed all yours away, or they never cared about you in the first place, and they *let* you slip away. Occasionally, you've tested them: *How long can I go without texting Sean before I hear from him? I'm always the one making plans, so what if I leave the ball in his court? How long before* he *texts* me?

Well, forever, apparently. When you fail to reach out, the friendships always dissolve.

Why? Is it your fault, or are *they* all assholes? Do they even miss you, these "friends"? Are they waiting for you to call? Or are they grateful you've vanished from their lives?

Even Eric, your one remaining pal. Even *he* has been pulling away this year. Or maybe you're pulling back. Are *you* the asshole here? Or does he really just prefer his new work friends more?

You can never tell, and there is no one to consult. In the maze of your own mind, you are always alone.

So, in kind of a last-ditch effort, you drag Eric to this party in Queens. Eric did *not* want to go all the way out there (no one who lives in Brooklyn does). Plus, he doesn't even talk to Shannon anymore. But you offered to pay for the full Uber, and he relented. Barely. *Barely,* your only friend left has agreed to spend time with you.

Shit, what if this was a mistake, you wonder as you wait outside in the cold for your driver Bekzod. *What if by pulling him along, I'm pushing him away?*

Eric doesn't say anything to you while you wait. He gets quietly into the Uber. You chat a bit as you ride along, but his responses are short, clipped—and then you say that thing. That one little thing. And that clinches it.

What *was* that thing you said to Eric? You're driving through these snow-slushed streets—passing neon-blinking bodegas, gated liquor stores, dive bars hidden behind throngs of beanie-clad liberal-arts douchebags—all of it flashing by the windows, on the way to Shannon's party. You're talking about…something. You're buzzing already from the little pre-game you guys had (that you *made* Eric have) in your apartment, and you say this thing, and suddenly Eric gets real quiet. He looks out the window at a homeless man with a swollen leg, skin bare and wrapped in toilet paper, and Eric says, "Yeah… I don't know." And he doesn't look at you for the rest of the ride. Just watches the miles of concrete, broken glass, and steaming dogshit surrounding Bekzod's sedan.

Holy shit, you really offended him or hurt his feelings or *something*. You *are* an asshole.

What did you *say*?

You get all hot and itchy, and the cloying vanilla air freshener is suddenly too gagging sweet, you can't breathe, you're choking, roll down the window, gulp in the fifteen-degree air.

What did you say to him? Are you such an asshole you don't even know?

You writhe inside yourself, staring out the window, feeling Eric very solid and silent at your side, radiating heat in the dark.

What did you *say*?

You know, this kind of thing is exactly why you're alone.

Shannon is throwing a housewarming party. She got an apartment out past Astoria, on the far edge of the city. When the Uber drops you off, you realize you've never been here before. You ask Eric if *he's* been to this neighborhood before. He stuffs his hands in the pockets of his leather coat and hunches his shoulders against the cold.

"No," he says. "I hate Queens. *This* is spooky."

Yeah. It is. You're in some neighborhood now. Rows of townhouses jutting up from the earth. The streets are alien, empty, and dark. It's early December; windows here and there are lit up with holiday lights. Blue and white, red and green, blinking, blinking. The streets are silent, slicing cold. The scrape of stray dead leaves sliding over asphalt…

Shannon is in apartment 3C, on the top floor of a brownstone. The stairs up are crooked and creakedy. Narrow. You have to walk sideways, your coat sliding along the walls. Eric creaks up behind you. He says, "Jesus," and you both laugh. Does Shannon do this every day? Multiple times a day? Where's the closest store? You have a bodega on the corner by your apartment, but Shannon's whole street is in shadows. Where will she get snacks? How will she survive?

"The, uh…spookiness has not died down," Eric observes.

"Yyyeah." You laugh again as you emerge onto the third floor. There are other doors here. Televised voices sliding out under the door cracks from within.

But when she opens the door and swings her arms wide, "Heeey!" you see that Shannon's apartment is actually quite warm and cozy. The previous tenants painted the walls dark red, and the living room has many wide windows along one wall. They look out over more dark streets, but you can see the familiar twinkle of Brooklyn. The red face of the clocktower, smiling on the horizon. It looks so far away. The liquor store beneath your apartment in Park Slope might as well be in another time zone. The bottle of clementine Svedka you bought there feels like a sacred gift now; it's traveled so far.

"Old tiiimeees," you sing-song as you offer the bottle with both hands.

Shannon hugs it to her breast. "Aww. You guuuys." She gives you and Eric a big hug. She smells like sweat and cotton candy.

The bottle, of course, is a reference to your days drinking

cheap, sugary bullshit back in college, when you three met, and when you were at your tightest as a friend group. Over the last couple of years, you, Eric, and Shannon have gravitated toward different careers, new friend groups, separate boroughs… You wonder just how much of Shannon's life you've missed when she puts your Svedka next to several identical bottles on the kitchen counter. How many generations of friends know about Shannon's love for clementine vodka?

Shannon has always had lots of friends. Drama kids, sports bros, band nerds, guys who wear flannel and do stand-up—some of these friends you don't even know about, and you wonder just how deep and gnarled the labyrinth is. That internal underworld filled with people's other selves, whom we can never meet.

You look around. You don't know most of the people here. They laugh in alternating shadow, light, darkness, swirling colored lights. Their teeth shine bright in the misty party light.

"Drink?" Shannon asks, enunciating with her own teeth so that she can be heard over the music, music thumping from the speaker on the floor. Rainbows churning on the walls. You and Eric are fashionably late; the party is already humid.

"I'd *love* a drink," says Eric.

Why does he say it like that? Like he *needs* a drink? Is he mad at you?

Shannon makes you both her signature cocktail. "The Shannonater" is comprised mostly of grenadine. She offers you a bump of coke, too, which is nice. She has some connection through work that always gets clean shit, no fentanyl. Or does she still have that source? Is this new stuff, should you not take that bump, did Eric take a bump? Is he having fun?

Calm down. You're trapped in your head. Take some drugs.

"I'm trying to break in the new key," she shouts over Cher. She offers you the small white lump on the shaft end of her key. You suck it in, inhaling the very building into your blood.

Then she leaves you, spinning with a laugh toward someone else. She dances, moving her hips in a way that makes you stare, awkwardly holding your cup.

Some other old friends from college appear, and soon, you and Eric are chatting with two different circles of people, standing at tangential angles.

It's nice to see old faces, and you mellow into the party vibe for what must be an hour or so. Someone lights a joint, passes it around. You pour yourself another drink from the cache of clementine vodka in the kitchen. Then Eric is there, sighing deeply, the way you do when you have finally reconnected with your anchor person after socializing successfully on your own.

"Hey," you say, pouring vodka. Your voice is strained. "How you doin?"

"Good." Eric shrugs. "Makin two?"

"Sure," you say. You pour him a cup and say, "Cheers." And clap your plastic cup against his.

"Skol," he says.

You drink. You want to ask him, *Hey, what did I say?* But you stifle it. You don't want to be clingy. Or is it good to ask people how they are? Fuck, you're so stuck in your head, you're just standing here awkwardly while Eric checks his phone.

One of your old college friends swings into the kitchen. Gabby. Gabby has a loud personality: "Hey, what the fuck, did you meet *Maya*? Did you know she went to NYU, *too*? Like, what the fuck, what a fucking small *world*?"

And suddenly, you're meeting Maya, who doesn't seem interested in you at all, and Eric is away again on his own party adventure.

The vibe is nice enough. But you can't shake the feeling that something is off between you and Eric. You can't shake that awkward clench when he looks at you.

"Landslide" starts playing. Everyone is making lots of eye contact. You're laughing, fading in and out of the conversation, having more drinks. You dance a little, mostly with your elbows.

Overall, it's a chill night. And that's a relief because there *are* parties that go bad. Not parties that end with cops or parties where fights break out. Not parties where something really dangerous happens, like a fire or a collapsed floor. Even *those* parties can party on without being particularly soured. They're improved, sometimes, even.

But there *are* parties that…turn. You can always tell when that begins to happen.

Certain parties are doomed from the beginning.

You find yourself talking to this guy who doesn't know where he is. You ask him how he knows Shannon, and he gives you this vague answer. Then, finally, he confesses, "I'm sorry, I think I lost my anchor here. I was…supposed to meet someone and they're not here, so. I don't really…know anyone at this party. I think I…might just bounce. I'm sorry to be so awkward. Um." He starts to sweat, starts looking around a lot.

"That's okay," you say. "No worries." Because what else do you say? It's not *your* party.

"Okay, I'm gonna bounce," he says quickly. "Peace." He beelines for the front door.

That's cool of him to admit he was lost, rather than try to continue lurking at this party, staring at everyone. Some people do that. They stand around and lurk in rooms that are not theirs. Staring. Souring the vibe.

Is that you right now? Are you acting normal? Or are you lurking, too?

Someone staggers toward you. You stiffen, figuring you must be creeping them out, they're gonna ask you to leave. But when they come closer, you see it's Gabby. She looks gravely ill. Shaking her head. Her other friends are carrying her toward the bathroom. She looks like she's moments away from puking.

Sure enough, when the bathroom door closes, you can hear the retching.

Someone across the living room shatters a glass, and someone else yells, "Ohh shit!"

You look down. Your shoes are very far away. The floor wavers.

Okay. Time to leave.

You don't know why you have this feeling. It's not the first time you've had it. In fact, you had it a *number* of times back in college. It's just this feeling that it would be good to leave the party *now* before things get very weird. You had this feeling at Ava's pre-finals pajama party sophomore year, in her dorm room. You dismissed it then, and less than a minute later, everyone was making out with each other, and suddenly, you and Eric were standing in the middle of a small room, surrounded by the moaning overture to an orgy. They all ignored you, so you just stood there and stared at each other, mouthing, *What the fuck?*

A few months later, at Pranav's birthday party, you had the feeling again. Remember? Pranav lived in that basement apartment? Around one-thirty, you had this sudden feeling that the party had turned sour, that some strange, hungry energy had taken hold of it. People were laughing too loud; the windows fogged up. You couldn't see outside. You were underground. You couldn't even tell what song Pranav had playing in the tiny kitchen, the bass throbbing so bad, throbbing, throbbing. All of a sudden, you just needed to bounce.

Eric was pissed you made him leave early, but *you* thought you were cool. You thought this was a special premonition you were having. Avoiding danger before it happens.

But nothing particularly *bad* happened at those parties. Ava's orgy was all perfectly consensual and unregrettable. At least, that's what they all said in the dining hall the next day, wearing each other's pajamas. And Pranav's birthday party… Well, Pranav was violently hungover the next morning, but that wasn't, like, worth having a premonition about. It wasn't worth the sudden, terrified urge to leave. Maybe you were just feeling claustrophobic all of a sudden. Maybe *you* were having a mild panic attack.

All the other parties you've ever had this feeling at, it's always been the same. It's never like the world is ending or someone is going to get hurt. It's just this sense that the energy has shifted in a noticeably negative direction. Some force has taken hold of everyone at the party and begun to warp them. You can never pinpoint exactly what it is. Is it because Gabby got so drunk she fell asleep on the floor again? Is it the fact that Pranav's ex showed up, and he always brings a weird vibe? Maybe people get too excited, or too sad, or too horny, or too much of all three. The crowd develops an undertow. A desperation. A loneliness.

Or maybe it's just you.

Hard to say. Some parties just *bend* halfway through.

This was one of those parties.

Alright, dude, you say to yourself in the hallway mirror. Some drunk girl is waving her hands around behind you, telling her friends about the sex she had last month on the J train, late at night when no one was around. You've never had sex on the subway. But from the way she tells it, it sounds very adventurous. She waves her arms around so much that she keeps slapping your shoulders with the backs of her hands, saying, "Sorry." But she doesn't stop or slow down, so how sorry can she be? Your reflection in the mirror sways as she whacks you over and over. "Sorry. Sorry. Anyway, we get to Myrtle Ave…"

Someone barks a laugh from the other room, making you jump.

You're all good, you tell your reflection.

I dunno, I'm drunk, your reflection says back.

That's okay. Let's just grab Eric from wherever he is, and we'll bounce. Call an Uber, order some Taco Bell. Be great.

Okey, your reflection slurs. *Sounz good.* Your reflection gives you a thumbs-up.

You wander in a circuit around the living room, craning your neck around for Eric.

"Hey, you seen Eric anywhere?" you ask a few people. But no one has.

You check the kitchen. Someone's sitting on the counter with their legs around someone else. Neither shape seems to be Eric.

Check the bathroom. It is void of vomiting Gabbys.

You peer into Shannon's open bedroom. Blue lights twinkle from the ceiling, but no Eric. You go down the short hall and push open another door. A dark bedroom. Bodies writhing on the bed.

"Uh, hello?" some guy asks, sitting up.

"Sorry, boss," you say, closing the door.

You turn away and open the closet door on a drunken whim. It's just a closet, no Eric.

Hm. You eye the front door.

Maybe he's outside. Maybe he ditched you.

No, he'd text you. He would. He must still be here.

You can find him. You'll find your friend. You brought him here; you'll pull him out before the party turns.

You owe it to him.

You take a breath and look around. You thought this was a one-bedroom, but there are other doors.

Approach a door and knock.

"Hello?" someone calls from within. Two other voices giggle over each other. "Hello, hello?"

"Eric?" you ask.

A pause.

"No," says the voice, pretending to be low. The other voices laugh.

You drift farther down the hall. There aren't any windows back here. It's *filled* with bodies; everywhere is filled with bodies. Talking, laughing, making out, doing shots, slapping each other, cackling and explaining and "Oh dude, you *gotta* watch it. You *gotta* listen to it. You *have* to go." All these insistent voices squeezing you, air hazy with breath.

Wow, this is a long hall, you realize. And Shannon's apartment didn't have this many rooms before, did it? Wasn't it just a one-bedroom with a short hallway? What's this *other* hallway? Wait a minute, are these...stairs? What the fuck, this place has a second floor? Shannon, this is big. This must be pricey, holy shit.

You peer up the stairs. Clogged with people. As you start moving up the steps—slow and careful, picking your way between bottles and legs—you notice that the people on the stairs seem taller than you, which is odd because you're very tall. But maybe you're imagining. Or maybe those drugs weren't safe after all. You weave your way up and come out into a dark hall with red walls.

"You guys seen Eric?" you ask a few people.

They all shake their heads. "Who?" says one girl. She winks at you and everyone else laughs.

You move deeper into the hall.

Perfect. He didn't even want to come, and now he's fucking lost. You're a *great* friend. And *why* are the people in this far-back section of the party all so much taller than you?

Well, Shannon used to play lacrosse in college. She had sports friends, remember? Maybe she invited the old basketball team.

That must be it. You remember them all laughing together in the dining hall. You remember now. But you remember it the way you remember things in dreams, which isn't really "remembering" at all, it's just your brain improvising logic, filling in the gaps between random shapes and colors. Come on now, do you *recognize* any of them, these tall people leaning against the walls, standing in corners? Looming with their shoulders hunched against the ceiling? You try to peer up into their faces as you stumble past, but you can't focus on them. They're wreathed in shadow. All you catch are pieces—a crooked nose, a flash of teeth, brilliant blue eyes. This basketball team is giving you a headache. You have to stop analyzing them. Besides, you're literally squinting into people's faces. Don't be awkward, don't be rude.

The music isn't helping. You thought it was coming out of that speaker downstairs, in the living room, but it's just as loud up here. Making your stomach vibrate like it's full of hornets. The few pictures Shannon's hung are rattling in their frames upon the walls. The lights strobing red, but you don't see any lamps. *What* is throbbing? The walls? Are they breathing? They're so red, rich, and dark…

Wow. Did you take something? What did you take tonight? A joint, a bump, a few drinks. Nothing crazy. Have you only had two drinks? Three? Fuck, you're *trashed*, you're stumbling deeper into this hall-that-should-not-be, arms out to your sides. Try shouting over the music: "Eric?" But the roar of the party snatches his name the moment it leaves your mouth, smothering it completely. "Eric?" His name flattened again, vanishing the very second you say it. You can't tell if you're saying it at all, actually. Can't even feel the vibration in your throat over the music. For all you know, you might be croaking, gasping, "Eric?"

The hallway goes on and on, turning left, then right, and on…

Shivering crimson glow, coming from the throat-walls of the hall, lighting all these basketball players from behind, beneath. Hooting, shoving, chanting "Chug!" Ignoring you completely as you reach a dead end. The hall ends in a T. Each direction is identical: more bodies and more lights, more deep burning red.

Which way, which way…

Your gut says Left. You obey. Laughter cracks through the hall behind you. You turn and see, down at the other end of the T, some guy and girl stumbling, tangled against each other. They rip open a door and start making out hard as they trip into the room. For a moment, their faces melt together, literally, and then they're gone. Another basketball player is standing at the end of that hall, in shadows, watching.

Lots of doors here. Identical dark wood.

"Eric?" you try again. "Eric!"

Doors, doors. Some are open a crack, laughter and moans rolling out into the hall. Someone screams and you freeze—then they laugh, and you keep moving, heart pounding.

"Eric!"

The hall turns and this next hall is darker, louder. The music keeps pumping, pumping. Nauseating. And there are so many *people*. Drunk girls cackling with their red solo cups. Strange men jostling each other *so* hard. Everyone is *so* tall. How big is this goddamn basketball team?

"Eric!"

Someone pushes you from behind, some unseen hand the size of your face. You can't see *any*one clearly, and you panic a little, throw open a door at random—

A dozen men are sitting on the floor around a Monopoly board. All of them have dice in one fist. They're shaking the dice simultaneously. *Shick, shick.* It's everyone's turn.

Eric isn't here.

"Sorry," you say, hands up, backing out.

Shick, shick, they stare at you. Shaking fists in unison. One of them starts to stand. He snarls, his eyes are red, and he reaches for you with long yellow nails—just before the door slams shut.

"Eric!" Voice rising in panic. You bump into some girl who's talking with both arms, not just her hands. You mumble an apology, "Sorry," but she doesn't even notice. The two dudes she's talking to are leaning against shadows. You can't see their faces at all, but you can see how long their arms are, how skinny and stretched-out their legs.

"Eric!"

The hall turns again, and there are more doors. *More* people. So tall, standing so still.

As you squint at them, you realize they aren't quite… Like, you can't be sure, but…does that guy have two elbows in each arm? As he lifts a bottle of beer to his mouth, you see his arm bend once, then twice. As he lifts it, the arm stretches away from him, then bends back in at the second elbow. You look down as you nudge past him (this hallway is getting narrower), and you can see that his legs have two knees. One forward, one back.

Okay. You're definitely on something.

That's okay. You'll laugh about it with Eric tomorrow. You don't remember what you took, but it can't be dangerous.

Can it?

Your stomach roils, your legs wobble. You feel hot, very

hot. Hard to breathe. "Eric!" Bodies press in from either side. The ceiling is lower. The walls are squeezing in. You can barely see where you're going, you're just trying to push past all these laughing, belching, grinding party people. When you finally make it through the clench of the crowd, the hallway spits you out at an intersection. Three other hallways branch off from this one, all of them dark and congested with bodies.

When was the last time you saw a window?

You start to push your way into the hallway to the right. Deeper. Deeper. Bare arms and fingertips brush against your neck, your arms. Skin warm and damp. People tower over you, you must be practically crawling. Everyone's arms are stretching and buckling, they have so many joints. The people in this section of the party all have arms with two elbows, three. Their legs bend like two chicken legs stacked atop one another. Their faces are longer, protruding at the nose and chin, like miniature snouts, like they're half-horse. You watch a man pick up his bottle of beer from a side table. His fingers curl all the way around the bottle, and you pause for a moment, watching him. Each finger seems to have eight different knuckles. They wrap over each other, and he lifts the bottle to his mouth, which opens once, then again, and a third time, other holes widening in his cheeks, his chin, multiple sets of lips curling around the bottle, tongues licking each other, holes sucking at the bottle from all over his face.

You scramble away as fast as possible, and suddenly, *suddenly*—you realize something. The kind of realization that hits people who are on hard drugs. It may be real, or it may just be drugs. But either way, you're positive it's true.

You realize that this party belongs to *them*. These lurkers in the far back. Past the cigarette smokers and "unpopular" kids, the punks and nerds—*they* have orchestrated this entire thing. They love parties. They just don't like being in the center of them.

You have no name for them, these party-people, but you know now they're not human. They don't play basketball. They play beer pong and flip cup, vigorously competitive. They are winter wind and stale-vomit-stench solidified. They are the whisper that makes you spill your drink on the hostess. They're the ones who give you a bad trip, make you break that TV. They invited your ex, your loud friend, and that greasy guy nobody wants to be friends with, but everyone feels bad for. *These* are the ones who sniff out a good party, and make it sour.

It feeds them. The awkwardness, the gossip. The drama. All that dour energy helps them live. And they can change shape! Yes! You've *seen* them shimmer and gloop and deflate, shrinking down to the size of a short girl with a very low-cut shirt and a wide mouth, wavy hair, glossed lips, saying loudly, "I heard she's cheating on Sean, did you know that?" Stirring the pot, poisoning the vibe. You've seen them slip back into the shadows and become a tall gangly boy with patchy chin hair, slipping things into his pockets from around the apartment. Nothing major, just a lighter here, a remote there. Just enough to drive the host insane, peering under couches and lifting the corners of rugs for weeks after the party is over, "Where the fuck did it go?" And their roommate will exhale, hold out the bong, and joke, "Your remote slipped between the cracks of the *world*, bro. The undersiders took it. Ya know, the people who live *under* our reality? They always take one sock." And they will laugh about this, it's funny, and they're stoned. But they will be right. Somehow, this joke-logic informed by years of cartoons and late-night TV will be spot-on. Cartoons always know things we don't.

You remember all of this suddenly, the way you remember things in nightmares. These people have been around forever. They were at Ava's pajama orgy, nudging people's faces together. They hosted Pranav's birthday shindig and many, many more.

As this understanding hits you, it dawns on you as well: These "people" are keeping Eric from you. You'll never find him. You will rot in here, in the stomach of this party. You will spend eternity in these halls with these people and these *things* looming in the corners with their long arms, watching you, watching all of you. You will never see a window again.

"Eric!" you cry. You're actually crying a little now. You really fucked this up, you got him killed, you fuckin dick. They took him, and it's all your fault.

You start ripping open doors at random. No one notices you doing this. Everyone around you keeps laughing, flirting, licking, "Oh dude, you *gotta* start with season one, but the first three episodes are trash."

You whip open a door, and several tall things are standing

in a ring around two women making out in an armchair. Long fingers massage the girls' backs, pushing them together like two Barbie dolls. No one sees you enter the room, which is bare of any other furniture besides the chair. It's like a stage. The tall things stare down upon the women as the women's hands explore each other's pants, lips and tongues moving in concert. They *seem* into it, but they're both crying thick mascara.

You back away, weaving through bodies to another door, and inside *this* room, the tall things stand around a man singing into a microphone. No furniture, no TV, no karaoke machine. But he sings on and on, eyes wild and burnt, tie loose and askew. Blood drips from his nostrils as he grins and sings, voice cracking, "I don't know about you…" The tall things rub his chest, squeezing out the sound. Around them, the red walls flutter.

They are in every room you enter, and every room is the same. No furniture, no windows, red walls. They stand in a ring, shoulders hunched against the ceiling, watching people "enjoying" a party.

You witness various tableaux:

A woman cornered on a couch by some guy mansplaining *Infinite Jest*, "The real story is in the margins."

Two girls at a kitchen counter gagging on tequila shots. Tall things lifting the glasses to their mouths repeatedly, faster than they can lick, swallow, and suck.

Three people holding cigarettes outside. You can tell they think they're outside because you can see their breath, the tall things holding out a lighter for them as a group. Many long fingers like a web of tentacles, teasing a wavering Zippo that the smokers can never quite reach.

A break-up in process: a couple with arms crossed, shoulders shrugged, voices tight, "I just don't know what you want me to *say*."

Crying, singing, shotgunned beers, charades—the tall things watch them all. Palpating bodies, squeezing out the fear, the angst, the lust…

Do these people know that they're in a room? That they're trapped in an endless housewarming maze? Do *you* know that you're stuck in a room on a loop? Do you know this? Do you know that you've actually been trapped by the tall things for a long time? Do you know, that awkward moment that keeps you up at night—it's never actually ended? Do you know that you're stuck there? Do you know you're not in Queens, you're in Hell?

Door after door. Room after room. It never ends. In fact, it gets worse. You start to recognize people.

You open one door, and there's your old buddy Sean by himself on a stool with a pina colada. One of the tall things is massaging his shoulders. Its fingers reach down over Sean's chest, they are so alien long. It rubs his nipples, pressing hard.

Sean laughs. "Wow, man. That feels great."

The tall thing turns its head to you. It has no features. Its face may as well be a blank stretch of skin.

You open another door, and Shannon's on a bed, crying, curled up fetal.

"I don't know why she has to be such a shitty person," she sobs, tearing up a tissue. "I'm just trying to be her *friend*."

Several tall things sit on the edge of her bed. One of them pats her shoulder with its giant hand. Again, they turn and look at you.

You leave her crying in that room for eternity, and move deeper into the hall.

Rooms with strobing floors, people laughing blinded at the ceiling. Rooms with people giving endless toasts, legs faltering, but they can never sit down. Rooms with frat boys screaming "Drink!" at some pledge with a beer bong down his throat. The tube goes much deeper than it should. The freshman's eyes are bloodshot and his stomach swells as they keep pouring, pouring clementine vodka. Glugging entire bottles down the funnel. The tall things have their hands on the tube. They keep shoving it farther down.

In all these rooms, the tall things feed. Every weird accident and social faux-pas and Freudian slip and grazed boob and smashed bottle and unaired grudge—every awkward party thing that has ever happened since the Greeks threw bacchanals—*everything* is in these rooms. Everything is food. You know this now. The tall things are so grateful to have discovered a planet with so much food. They spent many starving generations between planets, and their people almost went extinct. There are no parties in space.

But how do they trap all these people? Are they *all* missing? Like, do people miss them? How can they have vanished into this liminal stomach? Or maybe it's only their souls that are stuck down here in Queens-Hell, getting fed upon, and their bodies are still aging, still wandering free, empty of heart, and bitter, cold.

Are you still out there somewhere, technically speaking? Cynical and self-indulgent? Is the part of you that may have learned something stuck here now? Is that all *you* are? A fragment of a regret? Your shell out there, your youth left here to decay? Is that why *you* feel so alone and unsuccessful? Because that's what's in your soul?

Yes. It is. In fact, your soul is perfect food. They've fed on you for years:

Yum, remember that time you stained Shannon's favorite shirt.

Yum, remember that time you accidentally hit on a fifteen-year-old.

Yum, remember that time you said that thing to Eric in the Uber.

Yum, remember how few friends you have.

You panic. You stumble out of the most recent room (eighteen tall things lifting a bar mitzvah boy on a chair so high his skull keeps cracking on the ceiling, and he grins as the blood drips down between his teeth). You run out into the hall again—and slam into a wall. You press your hands against it. It is solid red. You turn around—and there is a wall. You put your hands against it. It is solid red. The hallway, the doorways, have disappeared.

You turn and turn again, but there is nothing except walls. You are in your own room now. It has no door, no windows, and no one else. You will never see Eric again. You slipped between the cracks of Shannon's party and shimmered out of existence. You're nothing more than one lost sock.

The tall things step out of the shadows in the corners. They stare down at you with their long arms, five elbows each, twisting and bending, this way and that. They walk forward on springy, many-kneed legs, heads twitching with anticipation. They stare down upon you from the sky.

"Where's Eric?" you ask.

They reach for you, fingers unfurling from their fists, eleven knuckles long.

"*Where's* Eric?"

They put their fingers on you. Cold and clammy. They press against your skin. They slide into your nostrils, pressing deeper, deeper, pushing up, up, popping the membrane into your mind, bursting through your eardrums as they press their fingers into your canals, pushing tears out of your ducts, vining around your entire skull and palpating the agony out of you in sweet, throbbing crimson waves.

Where's Eric? you mumble, voice muffled beneath hundreds of fingers, burrowing down into your mouth, past your tongue.

Yum, you taste good. You're such a weird, awkward douchebag, full of food. They soak you up for eons. And as their fingers close around your eyes, all you can see is the backseat of Bekzod's Uber.

No, you have to get out! Have to find Eric and tell him you're sorry, so sorry. You didn't mean it; it was a rude thing to say; you don't even *believe* it; it's just that sometimes in social situations, you put your foot in your mouth. He knows that, right? You didn't mean it, you didn't mean *any* of it. You're an awkward person! Socially anxious. A selfish person, too. Think about all the parties you've made him leave early because of your "premonitions." Yes, you suck. You're weak. He knows that. But he's still your friend, right? You're *his* friend.

But how can you ever tell him that when you've got these feeding fingers in your mouth? When you're nothing more than a skinny little figment, trapped deep in 3C as your body gets grayer and meaner and older by the day? How can you let it all out? How can you keep one friend, just *one*? How can you say everything that needs to be said? How can you break out of this sour moment in this Uber and scream, "I am more than this!" Who will ever hear you over the moist noise of Shannon's party? Who will ever find you, deep in this internal maze?

Well. These are the wrong questions. These questions don't matter at all. It doesn't matter what you *meant* to say, or that you want one more chance to apologize to your good friend Eric.

No, the thing you should be asking instead is: What makes you think you deserved friends in the first place?

Sam Rebelein holds an MFA in Creative Writing from Goddard College, with a focus on Horror and Memoir. His work has appeared in *PseudoPod, Gamut, Bourbon Penn, Press*

Pause Press, Ellen Datlow's *Best Horror of the Year*, and elsewhere. Sam's debut horror novel *Edenville* was nominated for a Bram Stoker Award for First Novel. His follow-up collection of stories set in the same fictional universe, *The Poorly Made and Other Things*, is coming for you in early 2025. For more about Sam's work (and pictures of his stinky old dog), find him on Instagram @rebelsam94.

CLEVELAND

Gwendolyn Kiste

It's the last week of December when the city starts to serenade you.

You barely notice at first. After all, Cleveland has always been an unusual place with its own soundtrack. The whir of railroads on the outskirts of town. The wicked winds whispering off the skin of Lake Erie. The highways and the byways and the back alleys, all thrumming with the rhythm of bald tires and loose mufflers.

So you can't quite fathom it when the city calls out to you for the first time. And you certainly don't think it's speaking just to you.

You bury your head beneath your pillow. "What is that?" you murmur to yourself, half asleep in your bed.

Then you roll over and drift off again because, let's face it: the city isn't singing with ordinary words. This isn't a church choir on Sunday morning or a folk song around a Summer campfire. This is something else, a strange sort of hum that vibrates deep down in your bones. You feel it more than you hear it. But like it or not, you most definitely feel it, living inside you like a poison. Like a dream.

But there are other reasons you don't notice. This time of year, Cleveland isn't the only one who's singing, holiday carols blaring on every radio station and out of the speakers in every department store. Christmas was two days ago, and you're glad to see it fade in the rearview mirror. You spent the holiday the same way you usually do: with the cheapest takeout you could find, holed up in your warehouse apartment, watching classic movies by yourself.

You don't have family. You hardly have friends. You're a forgotten person in a forgotten city, the world passing you by, one day at a time.

To be fair, your lonely tradition isn't all bad. At least it's quiet. And more than anything else, you like the silence. The way this city echoes around you. Sometimes, emptiness can be a comfort.

Sometimes, it can be a curse.

The next morning, you take a drive to the water, wandering alone on the deserted sand. You're bundled up in your thickest coat, leather gloves on your hands, a scarf twisted twice around your throat. It still isn't enough to keep you from shivering.

December. What a wasteland. You've always loathed this time of year, the pomp and circumstance of the festivities, and now you're trapped in the in-between, the long and liminal week between Christmas and New Year's. It's when everything and nothing can happen. Your office is closed until January, which means you've got no plans at all except to haunt your own life.

And this is a perfect locale to haunt, right along the lonely shores of Edgewater Beach. In the sweet bloom of summer, this place will be teeming with swimsuits and sandcastles, couples and families sprawled out on beach towels and beneath striped umbrellas, but you're a long way from July Fourth. You're the only one here today, and that's how you like it.

There's broken glass on the shore, the shards shimmering in the sunshine like diamonds. It's beautiful in its own odd way.

You've spent your whole life in Cleveland, so you know the truth better than most: darkness is baked into the marrow of this place. A river that catches on fire. A steel industry that dissolved overnight. This is the city of Elliot Ness, of the Torso Murders. It's the unrequited destination of the Edmund Fitzgerald.

It's also a city that has its own sea monster. They call her Bessie, not that you've ever seen her. Not that you haven't tried. Back when you were only a kid in pigtails, hope still brimming in your heart, you'd go to the rim of Lake Erie, and you'd call and call to her.

"Can you hear me?" you'd say, sometimes in a whisper and sometimes in a roar. "Please come get me. Please take me away."

But the monsters never came for you. Time claimed you instead. A nine-to-five job with paltry benefits and a water cooler where everyone but you gathers around for daily office gossip.

"Did you see Brenda's new haircut?"

"How about Dana's ugly orange suit?"

"And don't get me started about John and Jill from accounting. I hear his wife knows all about it."

Your jaw set, you always do your best not to roll your eyes. You wouldn't even listen to them if your desk wasn't three feet away, their forked tongues perpetually wagging in your ear.

But at least you don't have to hear them right now. You're free until next week when you all shuffle back to your cubicles that might as well be your coffins. You often think you'll die at that desk and nobody will notice until your next spreadsheet is past the deadline.

"We appreciate your service, Melinda," they tell you, but you wonder if they only remember who you are because there's a dusty name plaque sitting on your desk.

Not that you should honestly expect anything better. Wherever you go, you've always been the weird girl, the one who fell through the cracks of life. Now you're in the throes of middle age, and after everything, you're simply older but not much wiser.

As the sun dips in the sky and the frothy waves lap languidly at your feet, you tell yourself things will get better. You've been telling yourself that for years.

The snow starts falling after midnight, and it doesn't stop. That's how the storms always go in Cleveland, like a dubious soiree that won't end.

You gaze out the window of your warehouse loft, watching the evening drift by. This city is alive in ways you can't comprehend. It's dead and buried in ways you can't comprehend, too. Sometimes, it feels like the world has given up on Cleveland. No more industry, no more hope. A Rust Belt relic, a goodbye town. Nobody stays here anymore because, according to the critics, there's nothing left to stay for.

But you've never believed that. There are plenty of reasons to stick around. And as you stare down at the streets gleaming with ice and promise, you've never felt so at home.

"Can you hear me?" you whisper, a sudden shift inside you, and beyond reason, you're sure that someone out there whispers back.

You press your hands into the cold glass, trying to listen to what comes next. To the quiet truth this town has tucked away like a filthy secret.

But just as a voice seems to rumble through the window frame, you can't help but shudder and turn away. It's been a long day, an even longer year, and maybe you're not brave enough tonight. Maybe you're afraid of what the darkness might tell you.

You climb into bed, your eyes closed, and that's when you hear it again. The melody of the city sweet and strange and unlike any other. This is what you've been searching for ever since you were young and calling out to a monster. You want somewhere to go. Somewhere to accept you exactly as you are.

But when you open your eyes again, only silence awaits you.

You need to be around people. That's why you find yourself at Tower City the next afternoon. The only shopping mall left downtown. Everything's still decked out in tinsel and holly, shoppers with their knit hats and their knit brows pushing through the cheery crowd.

"Would you like to sample our latest perfume?" the girl at the nearest kiosk asks you, but you look away, not saying a word.

You wander through the labyrinthine stores for hours, reminding yourself not to stay out too late. The world gets dark so early in the wintertime. It's as though the sun itself wants to escape the chill of Cleveland. You can't blame it for that.

You buy a blouse on the first floor and a smoothie on the second, and you pretend these are the things you want out of life. You pretend a lot—the one thing that helps you get by.

"Why don't you act normal?" your family used to ask you. That was back when you were young, and they were young too, all of them still living and breathing and not just a pile of ash pushed to the back of your closet, their discount urns the only thing you could afford at the funeral parlor.

"I'll try my best," you would say to them, and that was when you first started your make-believe, a game you never quite won. Even so, you did the things that were expected of you: grew up, got a degree, got a job. This was supposed to make you happy. It was supposed to make you feel something. Now you worry you gave up too early, that you didn't try hard enough for a life that was your own, and now, it's too late.

Cleveland certainly doesn't give up, that's for sure. It keeps reinventing itself the best it can, one revitalization after another.

What is the life cycle of a city? How many times can it die and be reborn? And what is the life cycle of an outsider like you? Do you have the same chances as this place? Could you fancy yourself a Phoenix rising from the ashes, or is this the best you'll ever do?

You shake your head as you start for the door. There's no point in asking questions nobody can possibly understand except you. But the moment you step onto the sidewalk, you hear it. Cleveland is serenading you again. Maybe it wants to tell you its secrets.

And maybe this time, you want to listen.

You stay up all night in your apartment, conversing with the city.

"How do you feel?" you ask. "Are you lonely? Are you restless?"

It never quite answers you, not in the way that anyone else would ever fathom. But somehow, you comprehend every word, every tremble through the earth, every gleam in the sky.

You laugh for hours, and you cry a little, too, though you don't know why. To be honest, you don't know why you're doing any of this. It seems like a ludicrous way to spend your time telling yourself that your city is alive and aware and reaching out for you.

"I'm tired now," you whisper when it's nearly dawn, the crackle of the television behind you. Just like on Christmas Day, you've still got a string of classic movies playing in the background of your apartment. *All that Heaven Allows* and *Pillow Talk* and *An Affair to Remember*, Cary Grant and Deborah Kerr finding each other again before the credits roll. You're a sucker for a happy ending.

You wonder if you'll get one.

You're lounging in bed the next morning, the melody of Cleveland still ringing in your blood, when an old friend from college calls you up and invites you to a new bar in the Flats.

"It'll be fun," she says, and because you can't think of an excuse quick enough, you find yourself telling her yes. After she hangs up, you roll over in bed and think of how you shouldn't have answered the phone. You should never answer the phone. It isn't safe. You always end up in crowded places among strangers who are supposed to be your friends.

On Friday night, you're the last to arrive, arrayed in your sleekest black dress and your beat-up Doc Martens. Everyone else is already three drinks in, and you don't know if you should try to catch up with them or just give up altogether. You play it safe and opt for a ginger beer with grenadine.

"So, where have you been hiding yourself lately?" your college friend asks, and you only shrug.

"Same place as always," you say, because it's true. Nothing ever changes for you.

But there's something changing in the city.

"Do you feel that?" you ask the others as you gaze out the nearest smudged window, the evening clouds settling on the inky skyline.

"Feel what?" your friend asks, and you exhale a ragged breath because it's already clear she doesn't sense it. Nobody can feel it but you.

Your hands shaking, you take another sip of your drink. "Never mind," you whisper, and your friend loops her arm through yours.

"You seem out of it these days," she says. "What happened to you, Melinda?"

You don't answer. You're not even sure that you can. In a way, all that happened to you was life. It's that simple and that cruel. This world isn't made for the outsiders, the weirdos, the ones who get left behind. Your friend doesn't understand that.

But she doesn't seem to mind either. She just keeps chattering on about her new boyfriend and her new job, everything in her existence shiny and perfect. You sometimes think she's only kept you around all these years because you're the ideal foil. She's a woman who's got everything, and you're a woman who's only got an echo where a life should be.

"It's always great to see you, Melinda," she tells you because that's what a friend is supposed to say. Everyone else is so good at doing the right things at the right moments. Where do people learn how to cobble together their days so seamlessly? It seems like a skill someone ought to have taught you. Meanwhile, here you are, no more than an understudy in your own life.

After everyone else says their goodbyes, you stick around the Flats, creeping up to the edge of Lake Erie.

"What are you waiting for?" you call out to the water, and you wonder who exactly it is you're hoping will answer you. Maybe the ghost of Elliot Ness or Bessie the sea monster or even the Torso Killer come back from the grave to reclaim one final victim.

Or maybe it's all of those things. Maybe you're speaking to the heart of the city, this gorgeous and grotesque landscape, the multitudes of metropolis.

"Please," you say, "answer me."

You move closer to the water, right up to the threshold of darkness, part of you convinced that the past is waiting for you in these shadows. The smog of the steel mills. The maw of a monster. The wreckage of the Edmund Fitzgerald. You'll take every bit of it. You'll absorb it into your bones, and you'll make it your own. You and the city are inextricably linked in a strange kind of love affair. You'll be together forever, and you'll become another eternal specter in this town. Another legend they whisper about after midnight.

But then you can't help yourself. You hesitate, just for an instant, just long enough, the same questions turning in your mind.

What if the thing waiting in the darkness doesn't really understand you? What if it's a siren call, desperate to draw you nearer? Desperate to devour you whole?

You close your eyes, and that's when you feel it. All around you, the nighttime has gone quiet, and the city isn't whispering to you anymore. The moment is lost, slipping between your fingers like the dirty sand on the shores of Lake Erie.

Your college friend calls you up the next day. "Come out with us for New Year's Eve tomorrow night," she says. "I promise you'll have fun this time."

Without hesitating, you answer. You tell her yes.

"See you then," she says brightly, and the line goes dead.

You sit alone in your apartment and do your best not to scream.

But you already know what you'll do. You'll try again. You'll try to be normal. To have the sort of life everyone should want. You won't listen for that ethereal humming in the streets of the city. You won't gaze into the shadows, hoping they'll gaze back. You won't be anything but a normal person in a normal world.

It's the last day of the year, another slice of a life vanishing forever.

There are so many promises lingering in the air. A New Year, a new you. But maybe there was nothing wrong with the old you. Maybe you just needed this city to remind you of who you really are, who you've always been.

You're nearly to the party, the apartment building sparkling in the moonlight. Through the closed windows, you can hear the muffled sounds of gin-soaked voices, their laughter high-pitched and eager, music turned up too loud.

But you hear something else too.

The city is serenading you again, even more fervently this time. As though it might never sing to you again. As though this is your last chance.

You breathe deep, and you admit to yourself what you really need. You want to fuse with this city. You want to hear its melody for all time. You want to be something greater than the sum of your past.

"I'm ready," you say because you aren't afraid this time. You won't ever be afraid again.

You take a long step forward, edging toward the shadows that won't stop singing. You won't pretend anymore. You won't lie to yourself either. There might be only darkness waiting for you. There might even be oblivion. The truth is you don't know where this path is leading you, but one thing's for sure: it's where you want to go. After all, Cleveland is a city that's lost its way, the same as you. Perhaps together, you'll find a road out again.

The voices of your so-called friends fade into the night, everything fading, until at last, you and the city are finally alone.

"Thank you," you whisper, a bright smile on your face, and as you waltz into the gloom, the two of you wrapped up together forever, the city sings you the sweetest lullaby you've ever heard.

GWENDOLYN KISTE is the three-time Bram Stoker Award-winning author of *The Rust Maidens*, *Reluctant Immortals*, *Pretty Marys All in a Row*, and *The Haunting of Velkwood*. Her short fiction and nonfiction have appeared in outlets including Lit Hub, Nightmare, CrimeReads, Tor Nightfire, The Lineup, and The Dark. She's a Lambda Literary Award winner, and her fiction has also received the This Is Horror award for Novel of the Year. Originally from Ohio, she now resides on an abandoned horse farm outside of Pittsburgh with her husband, their excitable calico cat, and not nearly enough ghosts. Find her online at gwendolynkiste.com

MANILA

Mars Abian

A hook from a rhino's horn slices the flurry of snow in the air. In response, the gazelle's legs spring back. Uppercut. Jab. Crunch. Duck. There's a rhythmic drumbeat to the fight. A maelstrom of powerful attacks. Uppercut. Jab. Crunch. *Run.* The circle of featureless shadows vociferate their need for blood, the color of money in the ugliest part of Manila.

This has always been my home. I've come to know the city as an overworked yet tireless mother to delinquents, thieves, killers, and fighters. Children here are born with knives in hand, thrown into a cold life of rifling through landfills and danger – each breath is a fight for survival.

I bite my lip for Isaak; he's grafted with gazelle legs and nimble, but not enough. Another pummel of attacks from a behemoth opponent catches Isaak in the gut and sends him flying. The apathetic winter storm carries the fighter in the air, a ghostly conductor ending the performance with a coda of bones cracking as Isaak's body hits the ground. He lays motionless, fodder for the cold.

"Bato! Bato!" the crowd waves, winning wagers like palm fronds, welcoming their hero's victory.

Tiny, warm hands wrap around mine, and my son beams up at me, beautiful obsidian eyes sparkling. I could stare into these eyes forever – bottomless pits of innocence and admiration. His love for the fight comes from me.

His love for his grandfather, somewhere else.

Pitoy rushes over the patched-up rails and clambers toward the ring, where Bato scoops him up with a fist of steel and carries him on boulder-like shoulders. Bato punches his other fist, a rhino's horn, in the air that gleams from the spotlight.

My son copies, raising his arms, a fighter in the making.

I look away, rage boiling inside me battling the winter until I'm awash with cold and tightening the doctor's smock at my hips. Emaciated boys carting Isaak's limp body to the basement catch my eye and bring more bitterness.

I won't trust the other surgeons to patch him up this time.

There is a peculiar hedonism in my profession as a psychic surgeon. The special kind where my hands feel the delicate yet powerful rapture when reaching out into the fourth dimension, the human soul within my grasp and command. One pinch and I can change bodies and lives, yet it still repulses me, the work of a "proper woman."

But the pit viper around my arm constricts the addiction. The price of indulgence will greatly feed it and, in turn, burst my limb open.

"Lacerated liver," I pronounce, cupping both hands over Isaak's stomach. The defeated fighter lies unconscious on my operating table where I can freely fix flesh, bones, and organs without needing to slice an inch of skin.

My assistant, Grace, holds the surgical tools in a metal tray: bottles of oil and a frozen frog. Underneath the tributaries of tattoos, her expression is unreadable.

Spots of blue blossom beneath Isaak's olive skin and his gazelle legs convulse. I must hurry.

I perform the ancient breathing technique, not just inhaling but fighting the air inside. From this, weak lungs have ruptured, and weak minds have broken.

As I fall through this plane, I feel Pong constricting less and less, the throbbing in my head becoming lighter and lighter.

Until Manila and I are one.

The fourth plane has the smell of lucid dreaming – cotton, fresh, and lavender, a huge contrast to the jarring acridity of reality. The winding streets are veins building organs. The cacophony of sounds and sights morph into Isaak's gushing liver blood, clogging my ears. The bustling restlessness becomes fireworks of neurons. Amid all the noise, I can hear Isaak's body descending into silence that is only broken by the desperate, weak pulse of life.

Nubivagant death dwells overhead.

The soul is miasmic, standing out against the sharp scent of winter. It zig-zags under a labyrinth of bones, hopping on luminescing viscera. It will continue to pick up speed until it's faster than the eye and too far away to catch.

But I have it. This is a smaller battleground where I can grapple with it and drag it back. The soul bleeds from the abdominal cavity, and Pong smells when I cage it. We are of one mind, and when I strike for the liver, Pong strikes with the intent to devour the misfortunes.

I am jolted back to my basement office.

Pong's physical body hovers in the air like a spring branch. But underneath Isaak's skin, something slithers – a phantom duplicate of the pit viper, worming inside Isaak, fixing broken bones and torn flesh.

Grace, a dutiful shadow, picks off ice from the frog and then precisely mixes a concoction of revitalizing oil with gloved hands.

I rub florally sweet ylang-ylang oil between my palms, guiding Pong's phantom to wrap up the surgery, forcing broken parts to close and mend.

Pong curls back to my arm, a job well done, and Grace tosses the frog.

"I'll clean him up. You have visitors." Grace closes the curtains as Isaak flutters his eyes open.

"Nanay, look." Pitoy holds up a painting of himself in clumsy crayons, a red wiggly fighter surrounded by blue confetti snowflakes. I pin it up on the corkboard over my desk, covering an anatomy poster, and step back to admire my delightful collection.

"A smart boy like Pitoy needs a proper mother."

His words echo in my lab as though conquering and reconquering to satisfy impossible standards. Bato tosses me a mauve dress like I'm naked and undignified. "You'll meet your future husband tomorrow. Wear that."

I kneel and guide Pitoy to face me, seeking calm in his wonderful eyes reflecting mine. "I have a fight tomorrow."

Pitoy's face is a universe unfolding, sending me energy, light, and life.

A deafening slam against metal shatters the image.

"*Putang ina*, Nilda! You will marry and stop fighting," Bato booms, a draconian force of nature thundering through, leaving devastation in his wake.

Grace appears from behind the curtain. I caress my son's cheek and withdraw when my talons almost scratch him – my body's response to a potential fight.

"Can I watch your fight tomorrow, Nanay?"

"If you eat your veggies," I tease. Pitoy poses, puffing out his chest and flexing tiny arms.

Grace and Pitoy disappear behind the doors, leaving Isaak and the locker Bato dented. His fists have taken so many lives and sent more under my viper. I grab my fighter clothes from the inside. The boxers and sports bra set are blood red.

"You don't have a fight tomorrow," Isaak says, certain.

"You should train more and spy on me less."

"I'll train double if you give me the minokawa."

"Nobody's stupid enough to try grafting with that again." I flex my fingers, admiring the talons poking through the tips – a safe graft.

The minokawa is a lesson we learned the hard way, and there are still enough blinded fighters and steel graves around to remind us.

"I'll give you my spot for tomorrow's fight. Come on, doc." Isaak smirks, showing me grafted shark teeth with gaps. His surgeon was sloppy.

"It will blind or kill you. It *never* works well."

"You felt my soul yourself. You never felt anyone else's tough as mine, have you?" It's his confidence and egocentric view, but somehow he's right. "I can beat Bato with a bit more help, and if you're not the best surgeon, who is?"

Maybe he will be the one then. Bato is not unbeatable.

Since I have held his soul, undergoing grafting is much simpler.

"Why do you want to risk your life?" I fish out one of the two steel feathers from a jar, careful to hold it at the calamus. The vanes are composed of a million needles eager to taste blood.

"You know already." Isaak smirks.

I position Pong, who wraps herself around Isaak's temple, and then I hover the feather over Isaak's closed eyes. Once again, I summon the breathing technique that transports me to another dimension.

His soul from earlier is no longer a tangle of discordant

energy. It has unraveled to full length, resting and docile, and I guide Pong to nip at it.

Then, I forge the soul and feather in the crucible of the fourth plane. The act is as simple as a horticulturist combining a plant with another, a scion. I whisper commands to reform his body with the minokawa's attributes – steel feathers and mirror eyes. He'll lose his skin and sight in exchange. Grafting always needs sacrifice.

The flickering of the fluorescent light becomes the drum roll to an uncertain fate.

When I pull away, Isaak remains the same. But colder, stiffer. Dead.

Pong slithers back to her terrarium, disinterested in a soulless body.

Manila was left to sag from the weight of an uncaring heaven when the unusual winter came years ago. Snow poured in false hopes of cleansing her decaying body, most of it filled with crystals of tragedy.

It drifts over us as we scour the dense streets of Tondo, a morbific district plagued by pests and vermin swimming in leachate, infections, and tetanus growing like weeds. Rats the size of cats are playmates of children on the landfill playground.

We eke out lives in this city that is crowded with glittering pain. Shanty homes made of rough concrete block gape at people passing by with hollow windows and rusty roof panels as doors. A family huddles on a cement slab, seeking warmth under a leaning and buzzing light post. Live wires dangle like tentacles, waiting to catch bicyclists and motorists. Scant produce is carted down by street vendors, barely shielded from the snow by their hole-riddled umbrellas.

Mang'isda beg for money or raise their enhanced nets to the sky, sieving through snowflakes for rare miracles. Other people treat these desperate scavengers like mice, avoiding their contagious hopes. My glare makes me a bird of prey that scatters their weakness.

I guide Pitoy to the side as jeepneys struggle through the slush: mythical beings that once existed, beautiful sirens, and food that can only be eaten in dreams are uniquely painted on the vehicles' body.

"What are we looking for, Nanay?" Pitoy skips over city dregs and debris, kicking up snowy patches reeking of negative energy. A fat, hairy rat scuttles by, scaring Pitoy, then disappears inside a sleeping man's blanket. The makeshift tarpaulin roof is near collapsing from the snow.

"Guava leaves. If you're lucky, a mutya," I say, walking on.

"Will you give Lolo a mutya to protect him from fights?"

His innocence is a pinprick to my heart. I force a smile, "It's for me."

"You don't need an amulet, Nanay. I can protect you." Pitoy jumps from a gravel mound and poses, arms raised. He picks up wet sticks and squeezes them between his fingers, punching the air and kicking. "I'll have fists like Bato."

"Pitoy, *stop.* You're not helping."

Pitoy drops his sticks, happiness draining from his eyes. He turns and walks away, squatting to pluck up chromite stones and pebbles from the rubble of what was once a sari-sari store. After a while, he proudly shows me his gathered treasures, forgiving. His smile is a warm oasis in the cold.

I feel a sharp object poking my side as sulfur-stenched breath whispers in my ear. "Your money and clothes. The boy's, too. Now."

The violence comes to me like an inhalation, a flurry that the thief takes no better than the items he sought. Everything becomes red; all I can see is pain and death. My arms are pillars pounding men like him away.

Maybe it goes for too long, but I'm done now, and my son is safe. Pitoy shouldn't look at me like this.

"You're bleeding," he says, recoiling when I attempt to comfort him with my touch. It's not my blood, but maybe that doesn't matter. Perhaps this isn't what I'm supposed to be.

But later, when Pitoy is asleep, I find myself in the shop under the snake. I'm filled with a psychotic thrill as I graft Pitoy's cherished pebbles and chromite onto my soul, knowing what's to come. It's always like this, I get sucked into this world, and the tunnel-vision takes over.

War runs through my veins and drives me back to the ring.

My opponent is much too slow and angry, much too insulted at fighting a woman. He snaps at every feint and strikes whenever I taunt him. It feels so good, so much better than cooking or sewing or anything I can imagine.

He catches me enjoying the thrill and slices the epidermis of my leg with raptorial mantis claws. It almost sickens me that I laugh and savor the pain. He's wide open, and I finish him off with my grafted talons reinforced with chromite.

The cost is great.

I'm limping on my victory lap thinking of snow and tasting a miracle. The crowd is loud and raw. My blood runs hot. My head is heavy. The lights are so bright.

Bato pulls a chair for me. The view of Santo Niño de Tondo Church doing its best to soothe my temper with its beautiful ice-coated pilasters holding up disproportionate domes, bell towers, and the weeping gray skies.

Andrés looks like a reptile in a suit, a politician with an aim and enough support to be mayor soon.

"I want your hand, and your father agreed," he says, opening his mouth for a servant to insert crispy lechon. He speaks while chewing mouthfuls, "A beauty like you in my arms…at home…mm…bear me children."

A whole roasted pig on the table gapes at the audacity of his demand.

But I'm more interested in the uproar happening outside the church below. Blundering figures leaking muck hammer their ponderous waste through the streets. I already feel the thrill coming, forgetting the urge to catapult Andrés and the pig.

I throw the chair aside. My leg is still sensitive, but it works fine after the surgery.

"Nilda, sit," Bato commands.

But it's too late; the mass of higante made from garbage floods into the restaurant, and I'm already in action. They're not a serious threat, and Bato handles plenty with ease, but so do I. When one breaks the table and corners a cowering Andrés, I saddle the creature and snap its neck off, bathing us both in sewage.

When all is said and done, I'm laughing with ecstasy, shaking off the slime. I'm disgusting and fetid, and Andrés looks so small now.

"Bato, I expected better from your daughter." He stumbles away, coughing and trembling.

"I'm telling you for the last time," says Bato, towering over me, "stay in your place, or I will take your son." His voice commands so much respect that the cleaning crew pauses, but the snow doesn't stop for him.

"I'm telling you…for the first time then," I say. "I challenge you to a fight."

I tell Pitoy to stay in his room again, but he's still following me down to the basement. I reach for my tools, and Grace cleans the office with headphones on. I scream my request at Pitoy one more time.

He's still standing there watching me and quivering, the pit viper in my grasp. I set Pong around my neck and the jar of mythical scion in my hand. The now empty operating table haunts me with Isaak's memory. Grace finally notices and discards her headphones.

"I'm fighting him tomorrow."

They're both watching me now, helpless bystanders, unable to stop me from my self-made path. I can fight Bato without this, but I need to win.

I'll give up anything to win against my father.

Pong approaches my face, a ravenous mouth revealing a glistening, deadly maw. Her focused eyes are as cold and indifferent as our world. My rapid heartbeat echoes the thrill of weaving my future; the minokawa feather becomes a double-edged sword in my hand.

Pitoy throws himself on me, curling around my arms like another pit viper, constricting my thirst for blood.

"I will do it, Nanay," he cries. "I will fight him for you."

Grace slumps on her feet, too. The gravity of my decisions are dragging her and my son down.

She's been with me all these years and knows what happens once Pong latches on to me. She carries Pitoy away without my command; his cries are sharp and necrotic as frostbite; the weight doesn't leave my heart. Neither does the furious desire to win.

I sit on the operating table like it's my ring, making me a spectator in my own fight. The surgical lamp spotlights me, a glow harsh against my thoughts.

Across the room, Pitoy's paintings burst out in color against the otherwise mundane Manila. Beautiful chaos of pigments. My son's world.

I stroke the minokawa's vanes, inciting blood as I trace the lines of Pitoy's paintings with my eyes, drinking in the vibrant innocence.

Pong coils tight around my neck, but the decision chokes me harder.

I float over Manila, seeing it like I've never seen before. The ugliness becomes raw beauty underneath the snow. Graffiti prayers taunt misery. Haphazard architecture of Manila sticks out like icy, jagged teeth, biting, never backing down. It all comes together to create a captivating chaos that I cannot look away from.

I must hold it in my hand.

I let go and fall headfirst into my mother's arms.

The taste of adrenaline is sweet and sharp on my tongue. Colors and intense lights explode in my head. The crunch of snow beneath my feet and graceful ballet of falling snowflakes become a performance, a symphony of winter in concert with the drumming of my heartbeat.

I dance to the music of war, of the fight.

I listen to the thunderous feet sidestepping, moving with strength and brutality, punctuated by the sharp staccato of grafted fists meeting my now crystallized and barbed arms, hands, and talons.

Each blow received and given is a kaleidoscope, painting the air with swirls of pain that I can taste and touch.

Time seems to slow, every second stretching into an eternity of synesthesia. The snow covering the ring morphs into a canvas of violence.

Fighter against fighter.

Father against daughter.

In the deadly grasp of winter, I find warmth and strength.

The heat of the battle, the fire of wanting to take hold of my path, fuels punches, dodges, kicks.

Until I hear him fall for the last time, an earthquake to my sensitive ears. They'll carry him into the workshop, but no one will perform the surgery. He always wanted to die in the ring. Well, now you rest. Now, I am a free woman.

"You are free now," he says from behind me. His voice is level and calm, with no hint of exertion or energy. Alive and unhurt, yet still beaten.

I kneel from the sound, disbelieving. But I heard him fall, and his last few breaths.

As I reach for his corpse, I'm seized from behind and pulled into a snake's embrace. It's Pitoy first, wet, warm cheeks against mine, then the clean smell of Grace. I want to feel for Bato and call out to his voice, but it's a small selfish desire like another fire.

I can still hear my father saying those words. And I can feel Manila chanting my name.

MARS ABIAN is a Filipino speculative writer and digital artist known as Flairiart. She graduated cum laude with a BA in Literature from the University of Santo Tomas in Manila, Philippines. Her artwork often showcases the mythical and fantastical themes and has been featured on the cover of *Factor Four Magazine's* September 2023 issue. Her work will also appear in the upcoming Dark Matter Presents: *The Off-Season* Anthology.

ZAGREB

Matt Hollingsworth

When I got home from the brewery to the basement dump my wife and I shared, I wanted to sleep but couldn't.

Not with the damned chip in my head.

I cracked open the window for some air. Through the bars, a majestic view of a midwinter night's dream in Zagreb, in the year of our Lord 2033: dog shit bombing the sidewalks, garbage overflowing its cans. A haggard-looking fox crept up and sniffed around. Along came a bald-headed girl wearing gray pajamas and an embroidered blindfold.

Wait. Blindfold?

She sucked her thumb, tiny fingers curled into a fist—a preschooler, no larger than the wild animal that tore through the garbage with its teeth.

Fatherly instincts kicked in. I grabbed a claw hammer from the toolbox, slammed open the door, and rushed up, up, up the stone steps, envisioning myself wailing on the fox in a rain of blood.

I stopped dead in my tracks. Though I couldn't hear the words, the girl was talking to the animal. The fox's mouth moved and it answered her.

I hadn't slept in days, and sleeplessness had transformed my world into a fairy tale. What next? Would the girl say, "My, what big teeth you have"? Nope. Instead, her fingers glowing black, she closed the fox's eyes, and the beast fell and lay there with a serene look on its face as if it no longer needed to sneak and scrounge, as if it could finally rest.

Man, I wished I could sleep like that.

The girl huffed and puffed and blew. She vanished behind the massive plume of her exhalation. By the time the haze cleared, she was gone. The fox, too. I was suffering from exhaustion-invoked delirium, Brothers Grimm style.

I went indoors and set the hammer on the table, where my wife had left a plate of sarma—meat-stuffed cabbage leaves— and a handwritten poem, in English no less. She was sweet, my woman, always adding joyful flourishes to our lives. Her English was improving faster than my feeble attempts at Croatian. Respect. And here I was, the alien living in her country.

She was passed out in front of the TV, her pregnant belly enormous. Buried within that mountain, sheltered from life's harsh reality, was our baby, due any day now.

On the television, a man cowered in a wardrobe and clung to a bouquet of white chrysanthemums while an inferno consumed his home, a Czech art house movie that had worked its soporific spell on my wife, her eyes shut, her breathing slow and steady. It must be nice. No matter how tired I was these days, nothing knocked me out.

I missed California—missed sleeping.

When I arrived in Zagreb, I was required to register at an overcrowded police station. We foreigners lined up, hoping to escape to a brave new world, and one by one, they herded us into a room. *They. The man.* I half expected a dose of soma to pacify me, but they said I had to submit to being chipped, said, "No signature, no chip, no visa, Meester Keene." What could I do, turn around and spend money I didn't have to travel a gazillion miles home? After quitting my job? As soon as I signed, a cold injection gun pressed against the back of my skull, and *ka-chunk*—in went the chip.

People everywhere pay for utilities—gas, water, electricity. On top of those bills, Croatia also charges for sleep, a scheme being beta-tested in the Balkans. If you don't pay, you get nonstop ads in your head every time you close your eyes, plugged into an immersive multi-sensory feed, courtesy of the chip. Everyone's chipped, but those who pay the sleep bill enjoy ad-free slumber. I was skipping payments and squirreling away the money to move us out of this shithole basement, so whenever I dared try to doze, the chip's sleep blockers kicked in, and ads played in my head. Zero sleep for me.

I grabbed our old X-media from the coffee table to read a book, and the cracked screen frag-men-ted the words. After each page, up popped an ad. *Consume, consume, consume.*

My eyelids dropped like a guillotine. Boom! A

commercial: shiny, smiling people consuming content on their shiny smart devices; undoubtedly, the people in these ads were bombarded by ads on their own devices, watching an ad of someone watching an ad of someone else watching ads, mirrors inside mirrors, ad infinitum.

I wolfed down the plate of sarma. Even cold, it was tasty tasty. I lay back on the couch. At least we had a roof over our heads. I was a glass-half-full kind of guy, but my glass often contained piss (see: black mold on the ceiling). God damn. I constantly needed to scrub that shit out. Our living space reeked of bleach and mold, which must be harmful to breathe and be bad for Baby Aidan and his developing brain. We had to get out of this hell. Lord knew our jobs weren't bringing in enough money, but with the little cash I saved from not paying my sleep bill, we'd soon be able to afford a new apartment.

I flipped to the rental listings on the TV. At the top of our favorites was an apartment my wife had taken me to check out. It was heaven: clean, a bedroom, a bathroom. No more crashing on a fold-out couch, no more hauling my ass up the stairs to beg dear wife's cousins—who rented us this pit—to let me crap in their toilet, no more inhaling toxic mold.

A centipede skittered across the floor, and I stomped the bastard. No more creepy crawlies.

"**M**urphy," my wife said. "Are you awake?" Her name's Valerija, but the J in her name isn't like the

J in "Jesus." Croatians pronounce Js like Ys. Her perfume couldn't hide that she stank of cigarettes. Bleach, mold, and cigarettes. I hoped our son wouldn't be born fucked up.

"I'm always awake," I said. I was only half-awake, not wholly inhabiting this world but a nether realm, some crack between the planes of reality, a place from which everything sounded hollow and glassy, easily broken.

Valerija put the X-media on her belly, clicked the baby's playlist, and out boomed an interminably long diaper ad until, at last, dance music thrummed from the speaker.

"Is Baby Aidan busting a move?" I said.

"How many times must I tell you?" With that smirk, Valerija looked wicked cute. "Baby is not a boy. And Anika is a better name." She was dressed for work—a button-up blouse and ironed skirt.

"'Murphy Jr.?'"

"You are delirious, sleep-depraved."

Depraved. Using incorrect pronunciation, she'd stumbled upon abject accuracy.

"I'll sleep later on," I said. "Just a bit longer—"

"We should pay your bill. I work, so that you can sleep."

"I wish you'd stay home. The baby's due."

"How will we pay for food if I do not go to my job? How will we pay bank credit for your brewery?"

Burn. Yeah, my brewery.

Poached from my lowly corporate gig in the States producing industrial lager—speaking of glass half-full of piss—I moved to Croatia for an employment opportunity at a craft brewery, lured with an offer to be head brewer and make real beer. That's where I met Valerija, who worked there as a lab tech. Alas, the dream was not to last. The brewery's owner crossed the wrong people. In a whiskey bar one evening, a grenade landed on his lap. Boom! Bye-bye owner. Bye-bye job. But at least my testicles and entrails weren't painting a wall.

After that, Valerija landed a position as a cog in a Heineken-owned machine. I couldn't find work, so I did the only thing I knew and started my nano brewery.

Exclusive contracts with big breweries tied down most cafe bars—thanks for working for the enemy, Valerija—which made it tough to snag clients. No matter how proud I was of my mind-blowingly awesome beer, I hadn't sold a keg in weeks.

"Not sleeping is bad for your health," Valerija said.

"And smoking *isn't* bad?" The concern about health from a pregnant woman smoking cigarettes lit my fuse. Still, Croatians don't always share the American puritanical belief that smoking is dangerous for a baby in the womb.

"It is not big deal."

"I'm killing myself to escape these shitty living conditions, to look out for us, to look out for the baby's health—" A headache hammered my skull. I winced.

"One cigarette a day gives no statistical risk to me or baby. Smoking is only relaxation I have." She chewed her fingernails, cuticles red from abuse.

Maybe it wasn't my place to dictate how she treated

her body. I mean, I'd caved when she refused an abortion. But now that we were committed, what about the baby's needs? Man, I missed the single life—nobody relying on me, no responsibilities, and I could afford to sleep as much as I wanted.

I closed my eyes. There were no ads or any overwhelming sensory clutter, just a whisper. "Say yes to my offer, and I'll gift you deeply-sleepy sleep."

The ads slammed back into my head. I'd only been given respite so I could hallucinate a creepy voice. Great. Sleep-depraved indeed.

Later, I headed to work, downhill on Mesnička Ulica, Butcher's Street. I paused at the entrance to the tunnel that cut through the hill beneath Grič, where we lived. The concrete network had been built during World War II, as a bomb shelter. Lights strung along the ceiling led deep into the earth. Holding hands, a couple brushed past me and walked straight in. The thought of entering the tunnel gave me the chills.

I walked down Ilica, the main drag—slap of tires against cobblestones, winter wind chapping my lips and burning my cheeks.

Church bells tolled noon.

I arrived at the garage, at Glass Hammer, my brewery. Along with the pocked brick, broken windows, and fruity smell of fermentation was my repurposed dairy equipment:

brew works done cheap, though we still went into debt. I threw a switch, and the hot liquor tank creaked as it heated water. Steam billowed up, tugged at webs that hung from the rafters, and exited through the open door, releasing the brewery's warmth into a cold world.

At the moment, the biggest challenge for my brewery was drought. Brewing is water-intensive, and I relied on rain, which I purified with filters. But if the sky didn't soon open up, I wouldn't be able to brew.

A pair of rats perched on the grain mill, chewing. I grabbed a broom and wailed on the fuckers, made mincemeat of one, but the other scurried off, leaving a trail of blood. I gave chase.

From up ahead came a forlorn mewling. When I rounded the corner, the blindfolded girl I'd seen with the fox was standing there, chewing, her lips smeared red. She cradled the rat like a raggedy doll, just a bloody stump where its head should be.

She whispered, the sound of grit and gravel, her voice familiar. "Say yes to my offer, and I'll gift you deeply-sleepy sleep."

Offer? And gnawing on rat heads? Man. Check her out: bald, face and scalp adorned with henna tattoos like a filigree of roots, iodine color on her freakishly pale skin. She stank of roadkill.

My heartbeat slowed, the pain at my temples eased, and a loamy taste filled my mouth. I choked and spat out mouthful after mouthful of dirt.

"Before you know it, I willy-will return," she whispered, "to make my offer."

No way was she real. I touched her cheek. Her skin felt like pumice and was so frigid it chilled my fingertips.

She shrieked and slapped my hand, then huffed and puffed and blew a massive plume, disappearing into the haze.

The tram brakes screeched and jolted me awake. On my way home after an exhausting day. I picked dirt from my teeth. If the girl was a hallucination, what the actual fuck was up with the dirt in my mouth? And her offer? Was she some sort of Croatian genie? My three wishes would be sleep, sleep, sleep.

The suffocatingly hot air in the tram fried my sinuses. Reflected in the window across from me was a white guy in blue overalls and a lambswool jacket, gaunt, unshaven, stringy hair to his shoulders. I hardly recognized my reflection—just another loser with an advertising implant.

The beta testing for this chip was an absolute disaster, but that wouldn't stop tech giants from rolling it out worldwide to strip mine the populace and extract wealth through trickle-*up* economics.

Me, I was one of the bleeders at the bottom, no different from these commuters, droplets in the sea of humanity: an old man gumming a baguette as though his teeth had been kicked in, punk girls hugging skateboards like shields, fare enforcers hassling a dark-skinned woman in a hijab. Was she an immigrant?

Same as many other immigrants, I moved here for a job. I'd never considered myself superior, never referred to myself as an "expat," a patrician word reserved for white folks from Western society who chose to move abroad, who hadn't fled poverty, famine, war. If you're a person of color or foreigner with an unpronounceable name, you're an immigrant. Or worse yet, an illegal refugee, human garbage to block at the border and imprison in camps, garbage to expel. Me? Claiming the term "immigrant" seemed like cultural appropriation, as if I hadn't suffered enough to earn it. Then again, with the US being so wildly expensive that I'd never be able to afford to go home, maybe it was acceptable to refer to myself as an economic refugee.

Some defeated-looking woman said something to me in Croatian. I didn't understand, so I just nodded and smiled.

When the tram stopped on the main square, the doors sighed open, and we—the sea of humanity—flooded out. Overhead, drones hovered, swarms of buzz-saw quad-copters that no doubt recorded my every move. Their blades fanned us with eddies of fog. I took my graffiti marker from my pocket and scribbled a gigantic middle finger on the tram right over an ad. Bite me, drones.

Again came the forlorn mewling, and a mob of young children emerged from a glowing fog bank at the rear of the tram. Blindfold—check. Gray pajamas—check. Bald, white as bone, henna tats—check, check, check. They whistled and made popping sounds. Echolocation? Was that how they navigated despite blindfolds? Bats loosed from the belfry.

Wiped out, barely able to maintain verticality, I sat on a bench and closed my eyes. In my head, an ad: lab-grown meat called Pravo Meso, Real Meat. My stomach growled like Pavlov's bitch.

Firecrackers exploded in a trashcan, and I about jumped out of my skin. I opened my eyes—no blindfolded kids.

Scaffolding surrounded the buildings along the square, all plastered with painfully bright vid ads, even the cathedral and its towering spires. *Consume, consume, consume.*

I meandered past the brown man who roasted chestnuts, past the bustling cafes, people seated outside in the dead of winter, warmed by glowing red lamps. After I dropped into a bakery for burek—a greasy, meat-filled pastry Valerija loved—I headed toward Grič, Upper Town. Home.

Piano music from some eighteenth-century composer echoed off the shabby buildings, crumbling facades peeking out from beneath ads, symbolizing capitalism's failure to sweep away the wreckage of Yugoslavian Communism's collapse forty-odd years ago. A sign warned of falling debris. I passed Krvavi Most, Bloody Bridge, a bridge that had long since been entombed under cobblestone streets, where Upper Town and Lower Town had fought centuries before.

I stopped at Kamenita Vrata, Stone Gate, the medieval gateway to Grič, with a morning star spike atop the building to hook any invading witches who tried to fly over on brooms, a remnant of historical (read: hysterical) superstition. Tonight, the spike hadn't caught a soul. Good thing I'd left my witch's broom at the brewery.

This city's past spoke as loud as its present.

The gateway contained a chapel with a caged Virgin Mary. Prayers covered the walls. Pay the toll, and you, too, can hang a prayer. Turkish kids crowded the wooden pews, thirty or so earthquake *refugees* (there's that word again) being indoctrinated into Catholicism. A shriveled prune wearing a nun's habit led them in chants, and the kids mumbled along, knowing if they mimicked her, she'd feed them. God is great, God is good, especially when he gives you food. The kids slyly passed a cigarette among themselves. While the nun wasn't looking, I whipped out my marker and wrote an atheist-in-a-foxhole prayer on the wall, a plea that I would give anything to sleep. Anything. Help me, Mary, Jesus, God, genie girl, whoever. Amen.

When I arrived home, the stink of the basement assaulted me. I dumped the pastry I'd gotten for Valerija on the table next to the hammer.

She always paid her bill, so she was out like a light, breathing deeply in the realm of dreams, surrounded by pillows.

Prayers were futile. Some god or magical girl would never rescue me. Or. Allow. Such. Bliss. But I could luxuriate in that serenity if I didn't have Valerija and the baby to worry about.

And sleep forever.

I picked up a pillow and jammed it into her face. My

headache throbbed, a rushing tide of blood in my ears. I pushed down. Held firm. Clenched my teeth.

She flailed and grabbed onto my hands—her skin's warmth against mine, her scent, bergamot and gardenia, memories of kisses, and the taste of her waxy lipstick. This was my wife.

I dropped the pillow.

She bolted upright, confused, not awake. Mumble, mumble. She buried herself under blankets, her back to me.

What a piece of crap I'd become. It wasn't her fault I had cornered myself in this desperate situation.

I sought solace by reading on the X-media. Ads distracted me. I gave up and listened to music, but ads disturbed me, so I gave up and watched TV, but ads distressed me, so I gave up and tried to doze, but ads destroyed me, so I gave up and went for a walk, but vid ads were everywhere, brand after brand from Germany, India, China, fluorescent greens and electric blues and strobing pinks that scorched my retinas.

Gouging out my eyeballs and stabbing my eardrums would give sweet relief.

Come morning, when I got to the brewery, my water filters sputter-coughed, the rain tank empty as a dying wish. I turned the tap on the sink. Nothing. I hadn't paid the water bill. Fucking bullshit. I couldn't brew, so I couldn't earn money, and we'd never escape that shithole.

I t was night.

The genie girl would return to make her offer.

Ad: baby onesies and puke bibs.

Slimy black mold burbled and chortled, melting off the ceiling, a blanket that threatened to fall and smother me in poisonous comfort.

Smoldering headache.

Ad: A grinning girl frolicked through a field of wildflowers, chasing a puppy. When she caught up, she petted the puppy, and it morphed into a fox and collapsed, eyes closed. The girl turned to me, and it was the bald, blindfolded girl—the genie—making her offer, a sacrifice, her beating heart in her palm. She drew roots on my cheeks with her blood and said she would grant my wish.

It was morning. I could tell by the lifeless gray that bled through the curtains.

Valerija rolled over and stared at me, camped upright beside her. "Fancy new apartment is not that important." She caressed my cheek. "Without sleep, you will die."

Ad: hospice care and funeral homes.

"Maybe," I said, "tonight I'll sleep."

I held out my mobile for her to read the message: a cafe bar ordering kegs from my brewery. Today was delivery day. Boom! Cash on the barrelhead, a new client.

"Maybe," I said, "it's time we applied for the apartment."

She gave me the widest grin, a grin that swallowed me whole. It was all worth it. Our baby would arrive, and we'd make a proper nest.

Upstairs, Valerija's cousins blasted turbo-folk—Balkan beat, Romani-influenced music that locals bellowed along to while pounding cola mixed with red wine and roasting a pig on a spit.

Valerija launched from the couch and pulled me up. Giddy about the prospect of moving into an actual apartment, we danced to that obnoxious music as if it were the best music ever.

I had lied to Valerija, though. Sleep wasn't in the cards. The money we'd saved was scarcely enough to cover expenses. The future remained a looming threat.

That night, on my way home, the city was silent—all calm, all bright. No drones observed me, no cars to dodge as I crossed the street, a quiet so thick it hummed.

Snow fell. I trudged ahead, and the accumulating powder crunched beneath my boots. Lit by vid ads on the buildings, the plummeting snow looked like a rainbow meteor shower.

My rainwater collectors would fill up. I could brew! Cash from delivering kegs, and now, water. I howled thanks to the universe and opened my mouth wide to catch snowflakes on my tongue. A tram sped past and disrupted this wonderland as if it had shaken the snow globe I'd been inhabiting, a swirl of flurries trailing the last carriage. Inside, the passengers lay sprawled out, spilling off seats, the driver hunched over, seemingly unconscious. What the fuck?

An arctic wind pushed me toward the night market on

Britanski Trg, British Square. There wasn't a soul out and about. At a fast-food stand, rotisserie kebab broiled under a heat lamp. The kebab meister was passed out. At the kiosk next to him, a woman slept, deathly still. The wind blew her scarf across her face and veiled her.

The entire city was asleep. I scanned the headlines on my mobile but saw no news about what was going on.

A blindfolded boy led maybe a dozen bright-eyed children past, a mix of ethnicities, black, white, brown, each of them shoeless and without jackets, hand in hand, a daisy chain gang, singing in some unknown language. They must be freezing.

More singing approached, a lullaby. Another happy gang, this time led by the bald girl, who whistled and made popping sounds. I surfed the wake of their joy and followed. At Butcher's Street, they turned and romped into the bomb shelter tunnel beneath Grič.

I halted at the entrance.

With a hiss, the vid ads cut to static and went black. Streetlights, too, which left only the full moon to illuminate an empty city.

The only people awake in Zagreb were these blindfolded kids pied-pipering the city's children into the hill. In the dark tunnel, the singing echoed a diaphanous melody.

I activated my mobile's flashlight and entered the tunnel. Farther and farther in I went until I reached a wide-open area. I held up the light and turned in a circle. Painted all over the walls, brown like dried blood, were the same roots tattooed on the blindfolded kids.

The singing had faded. Fuzz sizzled inside my skull, and the air vibrated like the earth was attuning to my mind. I sat on the ground. Warm. Musty.

Again came the forlorn mewling.

"Say yes to my offer, and I'll gift you deeply-sleepy sleep." The blindfolded girl. She put her fist to her mouth and sucked her thumb.

"What do you want from me?"

"You are a member of this city's lively-hive," she said, "a hive whose suffering awoke us."

"Am I in the land of nod?" Woozy. As if I'd huffed turpentine fumes.

"You desire to sleep?"

Sleep? God damn right. "Yes."

Fingers aglow, she lowered my eyelids. Darkness. No ads, no sound but the earth's pulsing. She eased me into her lap.

Sleep.

A shock woke me. My slumber had been all-consuming, concentrated like syrup sucked off Mother Coma's teat. But it wasn't enough. A mere hint.

See my mobile uplighting the girl—a henna-webbed angel sculpted of alabaster.

"When the moment comes," she whispered, "I will gift you more of this deeply-sleepy sleep."

Smell her: freshly turned earth, truffles, linden blossoms. All else blurred; only the girl remained in focus. She lifted her blindfold and stared at me, her pearlescent eyes glowing black with savage beauty. Gaze into her depths. This heavenly creature shared with me; now, I needed to share with her.

Listen to her speak. "I'll take from you such an eensy-weensy thing."

"Yes." My voice was far away. The splash of a stone dropped down a well.

She took my hand, her skin silky. "Once our lullaby ends your city's misery and we rescue your children from life's unruly-cruelly mean reality, we'll depart."

Wait. She would rescue *our* baby? Valerija and I should care for our family together. Whatever. After sleep, I'd figure it out. All I knew was that this magical girl *would* grant my wish.

"You'd be an unbearably-terribly bad parent. Neverly-everly wanted to be a daddy. Stop un-wanting, stop worrying, and say yes to deeply-sleepy sleep."

"Yes." No more responsibilities, free to rest.

We rose and exited the tunnel. A rush of cold air. Empty streets. Snow blanketing the city. Purification. Bach's "Air" chimed on my mobile—many missed calls. Valerija. The tunnel must not have a signal. Up popped a message:

My water broke. Hurry home!

"Do not fret." The girl squeezed my hand. I felt a crunch. Heat shot up my arm, and my facial muscles spasmed, my broken knuckles grinding, distant, someone else's body, someone else's life.

We strolled onward, the city dark, electricity mercifully dead. No vid ads. I closed my eyes. Magnificent black—no ads in my noggin either. We neared home. No barking dog or turbo-folk to wreak havoc on my eardrums, nothing but glorious emptiness.

The girl led me down the stairs. We tracked in snow. Candlelight lit the warm basement. The room was flooded with the scent of melted wax and a coppery, sour aroma. Valerija lay on the couch, breastfeeding a plum-colored baby covered in goo.

"Murphy, where have you been? I do all the work myself." She smiled. "We have a little lady, our Baby *Anika.*"

Me? Dumbstruck. I'd missed our daughter's birth. How the hell had Valerija pulled this off on her own? Such strength. My amazing woman. My family. I kissed beautiful Valerija on the brow and kissed beautiful Anika on the cheek. I was a father.

On the table, candles guttered, wax rivering onto the wood and toward the claw hammer—where I had left it.

Tired. Hot in here. I took off my jacket.

Valerija frowned at the girl. "Who is this?"

The girl lunged and tried to steal the baby, but Valerija refused to let go. They fought. A headache cleaved my skull, half yearning to collapse, half instinct to protect. Unable to breathe, paralyzed. Nausea bile.

Fingers aglow, the girl lashed out, raked her nails across my wife's face, and shredded her eyelids. Valerija drained of color and stopped moving. The girl yanked the umbilical cord from Valerija's belly. Cradled the baby. "Such an eensy-weensy thing. She'll be everly-foreverly safe."

No!

I exploded, regained control of my body, and grabbed the hammer. My broken hand burned like a fistful of razors as I hit the girl with the claw. Cracked flesh, a fissure in stone. The hammer lodged in her eye socket and out oozed black teardrops. I jerked the hammer, and a chunk of her face broke away—craggy lava rock. She dropped the baby and raised her arms in defense. I hammered her. Ebony blood spattered. Her shrieks rose to a gale. Sulfur odor. I struck again, again, again, until her head crumbled, and she collapsed in a landslide of dirt and stone.

I howled. Victory? Anguish.

The TV crackled, sparked to life, a journalist reporting the death wave that hit Zagreb—then, flicker, flicker, the ceiling bulb kindled and illuminated the basement horror in gruesome detail. The girl was a rock pile, eyes visible amid the debris, the ebony glow dying. Valerija, splattered with the scarlet and mucus of birth, stared at me through her flayed eyelids. On the couch beside her, our daughter, slick with black, wailing.

I checked Valerija's breathing and pulse. Nothing.

How do you do CPR? Throw the pillows aside and tilt back Valerija's head. Pinch her nose and breathe into her mouth. Memories of kisses, the taste of waxy lipstick. Push chest to revive heart, one, two, three—is this how to resuscitate someone? Broken knuckles grinding, sweaty agony. Drones buzzing outside, dogs barking, city waking, alive. Breathe into her mouth, push chest, one, two, three. Stench of mold.

No pulse—breathe, Valerija! Centipede skittering past, baby wailing. *Push, push, push*, one, two, three—pump, heart! Reporter's voice on TV: *death, death, death.*

Snap.

I broke Valerija's ribs.

The bald girl hadn't been a hallucination. My wife was dead. My fault for not protecting her.

I rocked the baby and sang to her, but she wouldn't stop crying.

I nestled beside Valerija and held Anika to her. Our daughter latched on to her momma's lifeless breast. Went quiet. Buried beneath the city's noise—the sound of her suckling and my hyperventilating sobs.

So tired I could die, I squeezed my eyes shut against the flow of tears. Up popped a BMW ad, the tail lights a smear of tracer fire.

MATT HOLLINGSWORTH is a neurodivergent human and an award-winning color artist for Marvel, DC, and Image Comics. He's collaborated with such fine specimens of humanity as Alan Moore, Grant Morrison, Garth Ennis, and Mike Mignola on titles including *Tom Strong*, *The Filth*, *Preacher*, and *Hellboy*. He's a degenerate American but has tainted Croatia with his presence since 2006. His prose has appeared in *Interzone* and *Tales from the Moonlit Path*, and is forthcoming at *Tales to Terrify*, and *Wyldblood*. Find him online at: matthollingsworth.com

CAMBRIDGE

Bracken MacLeod

It's a trick the mind plays. Lying in bed at night, staring at the pattern the streetlights make on the ceiling, and seeing a man in a wide-brimmed hat or the Virgin Mary in the center of an MRI brain scan when the doctor is trying to point to the tumor killing your mother. So, when he saw the first face in the side of the plowed snow drift, he dismissed it as an illusion of light and a mind that seeks patterns where there are none. And outside, there were plenty of snowdrifts in which to see faces.

Winter had come on late and hard, and the plows shoved it up as best they could on the side of the road until they stood taller than the stop signs. Because of the oil and other chemicals from gasoline exhaust, road salts, and whatever else spilled on the road, they were filthy and toxic. The snow couldn't be dumped into the Charles or the Harbor, and there simply wasn't anywhere in the greater metro area to haul it off to, so the drifts remained, growing higher with each storm until there was nowhere for the kids waiting for the school bus to stand except in the street or blindly behind them.

Cold weather seemed to arrive later every year, but when the nor'easters swept in toward the middle of February, it felt like winter had come all at once. An unrelenting nine feet of snow fell in six weeks, and the piles grew ever taller, darkening with streaked grime until they resembled miniature simulacra of the great peaks in the Himalayas, jagged black rock ridges jutting from snow-swept glaciers. Everest in the Trader Joe's lot, K2 by the Dunkin over near Brattle and Church. They only looked pristine after a fresh snowfall and only briefly at that.

When he saw the first one, he'd been scrambling aside to let a couple and their baby stroller pass in the narrowly plowed sidewalk channel. He climbed onto a low drift and found himself looking into the placid face of a frozen woman. In the early morning light, a shadow fell, so her eyes, nose, lips, and chin seemed so very obvious. He pulled his sculptor's thumb and loop and ribbon tools out of his bag and began tracing around the edges of indent and bulge, stripping off his gloves so he could feel his tools, refining what he thought he saw until it was undeniably there.

She seemed to frown at him less with annoyance than concern, he thought. As if she wanted him to put his gloves back on, climb down off of a filthy snowdrift, and not be late for class. He glanced at his watch.

Shit.

His students would have left by now, and his advisor was going to be pissed about another missed class. The graduate teaching assistantship was the only way he could afford this MFA. If he lost that, he was fucked.

He carefully descended the slope and shrugged deeper into his coat to ward off the chill he only now noticed had slipped inside with him like a cozy lover with icy feet. It occurred to him he ought to take a picture of his work. Something for his socials. He snapped a few shots and stuck his phone back in his pocket. A bus roared up to the stop with a grey belch of exhaust. Its hydraulics shrieked as it "knelt" for disembarking passengers stepping down onto treacherous ground. He boarded and rode to Porter Square, where he went down away from the soiled snowbanks into the grimy puddles and tracks of other underground commuters. Waiting for the T, he reviewed his pictures. The sculpture was good. One of the best he'd done, he thought. Very lifelike.

He scrolled through the comments on his Pixta app, marveling at the compliments he received for a spur-of-the-moment dalliance with a pile of snow. Single word exclamations like, INCREDIBLE! and WOW! weren't what he envied. When someone posted that the face haunted them or that it made them want to know her, whoever she is, he felt at once elated and deflated. His actual work didn't elicit anything like those kinds of comments from his professors. He chased that feeling of creative admiration like a child after a lost balloon. This piece was exactly that. Ephemeral and gone as the audience floated away to the next thing.

Anonymess: Too bad it's going to melt. LOL

Tremor_NOahhh: wish there was a way to save it

Komoda: SO ZEN!

He'd shown his advisor the pictures that afternoon while apologizing for missing his class. Her response had been, "You had time to do that, but not be *on time?*"

"The buses were all running late," he lied. "I did it while waiting."

She skeptically accepted his story, admonishing him to call next time the T was running off schedule. Then, as a final kick in the soul, she critiqued the piece, telling him while it was technically proficient, he should be striving for much more, not playing in snowdrifts. "Can you put it on a stand? Does it fit the theme of," she paused, closing her eyes in that infuriating way she did as she mentally called up the words from his artist statement, "the artificiality of mass-produced experience and the deadening of participatory ritual?" The fact that she was right hurt the worst. If he was going to have his thesis show ready in the spring, he was far behind where he needed to be, and this dalliance did nothing to move him closer toward that goal. But when he saw that woman's face in the snow, nothing seemed to matter as much as her, not grading papers or working in his studio. Nothing had been in his mind except her.

He kept scrolling his post, searching for new interactions. A few commenters accused him of Photoshopping or using A.I. to create the image, but shots at different angles seemed to satisfy most of them that it was real. As he looked, a new comment appeared on the screen like a gut punch. A user named MonikaAtomika wrote,

OMG! she looks like my sister who died last year!

He'd felt a little in love with this woman in the ice, wanting her to be real so he could know that beautiful, sad face would persist longer than a season. A muse of flesh and blood out there, who he might someday meet. He'd dismissed the thought as a fantasy, but she *did* exist. Or used to. He told himself it was probably just wishful thinking from someone who missed her sister and wanted to see a familiar face in his work, the same way he'd seen a vague face-like pattern in snow and brought her likeness out of it. *A likeness; not hers.*

He clicked through to Monika's profile to search for the unnamed sister, to see the resemblance for himself. Her feed was mostly food shots and selfies in different dressing room mirrors—Monika seemed to have a thing for jumpsuits and sticking her tongue out. Then, he found it. A picture of the woman flashing peace fingers outside the Middle East club. A selfie with her at the Pit in Harvard Square. Another of her in a heavy coat with an ice cream cone on the sidewalk in front of Toscanini's, a broad smile on her face, her tongue protruding like her sister's. The similarity *was* strong. Scrolling back to the pic at the Pit, he switched between Pixta and the phone's camera app, comparing faces. Both had the same slender jawline leading gracefully to a pointed chin. High forehead above almond-shaped eyes framed with carefully sculpted arching eyebrows. She had a prominent but elegant nose that ended in a gentle scooped upturn. She and his snow woman could be… sisters.

He scrolled until Monika finally tagged her. Gillian. She didn't have any socials he could find. Just Gillian living in the moment, occasionally captured in an image eating ice cream, going to a show. He tried searching up "Gillian Cambridge death." Too many results. He added "MA" and tried again. Fewer hits, and none that seemed right. Either wrong picture or wrong age. Reluctantly, he gave up. But not before taking a screenshot of a somewhat pensive-looking Gillian staring straight into the camera. Monika's caption: "I miss you."

His hands ached from breaking the newly cast sculpture from its mold. Staring at the thing, he wanted to smash it, but it was long past the time for that. He should've taken a hammer to the mold or wadded up the clay sculpture and started over. Instead, he looked at an extravagantly expensive hunk of stainless steel that would break him long before he made a dent in it. On the floor in front of him, Steamboat Willie hung crucified on a ship's wheel holding a cross-topped orb—a globus cruciger symbolizing his dominion over the world—in one minstrel-gloved hand while in the other, he clutched a child's heart. He knew his advisor was going to hate it. It was too on the nose. It didn't help his case that the Steamboat version of Mickey was in practically *everything* the undergrad art students had made since it entered the public domain. But he was desperate and had a lot left to do before the show. Messiah Mouse would have to do.

He sighed and locked up his studio early. *Go home, get some rest, and start fresh tomorrow.* He had another piece molded and ready to pour that was probably just as uninspired, but better to sleep on it than do shit work because he was off his game and forcing it.

The wind outside bit. He plunged his hands into his pockets, shrugged deeper into his coat, and forged ahead. More snow had fallen while he was working and he should've gone home hours ago. But he'd had the forge time booked.

Fuck you, Mickey!

Turning a corner, some toy dog in a little plaid coat and tiny booties skidded on the ice in front of him, yapping and snarling as it tried to skirt around him. A woman further up the sidewalk rushing toward him shouted, "Grabbim!" He ducked to scoop the dog up, but the vicious little monster snapped at him with its sharp needle teeth before darting between his legs, its trailing leash painfully whipping one of his shins as it snaked past his legs. The woman barreled past, ripping out a "Thanks fah nothin'," as she rushed by. He slipped, trying not to collide with her, and tipped backward into a bush. Fresh snow fell into the back of his collar, sliding down his back like a frigid snake.

"Fuuuck!"

He pushed out of the hedge and brushed himself off. "Crazy bi—" His breath stalled at the sight across the street. The spectral figure froze him in place. He wanted to look away, run away, but he couldn't. He was transfixed by its stare. Another snowdrift with an unmistakable face looking at *him*.

He crossed toward it. A car horn blared, and he scrambled in the slushy salt grit toward the drift, trying not to get mowed down in the street by a bombardier cabbie. The figure faded into the mound, less present as if backing away the closer he came. "No, come back!" he said, dragging his fingers around the snow, finding the face he'd seen. Eyes reemerged from the pile and apprehended him, leaving him feeling both seen and seized. He kept working until it fully emerged. This time, a man's face stared back at him. Square jawed and sharp angled in contrast to the soft girlish features he'd sculpted a couple of days earlier.

Pulling his phone out of his pocket to get pictures, he caught a glimpse of the time. Over an hour had passed without him noticing. He couldn't remember the last time he'd been *that* in the zone. Years, maybe. It was intoxicating.

With shivering hands and numb fingers, he took pictures from every angle, finally ending with a masked selfie next to it for scale. The piece was magnificent. He despaired afresh at the realization he couldn't mold or cast this. It was as fleeting as the breeze that suddenly cut into him again as if it had been held back while he worked and then let loose like a held breath.

More work with nothing to show for it.

Like everything he did.

He forced himself to move on and head home. At least he could put it online. Though pictures didn't do either piece justice.

His phone kept blowing up. Every time he set it down, it chirped immediately with new notifications. Despite having thought a second earlier *I need to get up and make dinner,* he picked it up again and scrolled to the new praise populating his replies.

> *Boden_Says: its earie how lifelike this is like hes my dad lowkey judging me*
>
> *wheezybreezy: what an amazing artist you are! Jealous!*
>
> *BeatHoof: Bruh! This is straight up witchcraft! You summoning demons and shit! LOL!*

A small but persistent voice from deep in that ever-doubting part of him whispered he should drop out of school and ride this wave. "What wave?" he mumbled. Two pieces, neither of which he could display in a gallery, let alone *sell,* were barely a ripple. *And* it was almost March; the snow would be leaving before long, and with it, his muses.

His phone chirped with its direct message tone.

LennyCollinsWBC5 wants to contact you. Accept. Deny.

"The hell?" he whispered as he opened the D.M.

Good afternoon, "Katastropher." I'm a reporter for Channel 5 News, and I'd like to talk to you about your work and inspiration as part of a piece about people dealing with the winter weather. Please DM me so I can get in touch and get a comment for our broadcast later this week.

"Holy shit!" A reporter wanted to talk to him about his work. *And not that Mickey Mouse bullshit; your* real *work,* his doubt whispered. This could be it. This is the break he'd been looking for. If he could convince her to give him a whole segment, who knew what might come his way? This was what he'd been working toward. A chance to break out of group shows and student art gallery exhibits no one but other students visited. What if a gallery owner saw him? What if?

You need more. They're out there. He filled a musette bag with sculpting tools and headed out, barely remembering his coat and gloves. At the door, he lurched back inside, snatching his cell phone off the sofa, the DM still open and unanswered.

"Give me a minute, Lenny!"

He prowled around the city for hours, looking at piles of snow, searching for the patterns his mind would reshape into something recognizable. A ghostly portrait emerging from a frozen limbo. Nothing appeared. The only faces he saw belonged to red-cheeked commuters rushing to get out of the cold before the biting air did more than give them a flush. Despairing, he ducked into a black-walled corner bar called The Plough and Stars. Inside was small and noisy, but warm. He commandeered an empty stool and nodded at the middle-aged woman behind the bar. She came over and asked what he wanted. He ordered a beer. She asked if he wanted food too. His stomach rumbled at the thought of a burger and fries, but he could barely afford bar prices for a drink. Deflated, he shook his head and said, "Just the PBR, please."

"Comin' right up, hon." She turned away and pulled a can out of a cooler below the bar. She popped the tab and set it and a glass in front of him. He lifted the can and took a long drink. His phone vibrated in his pocket. He ignored it. No point in working himself up again. One drink, he promised himself, then he'd go home and get some sleep. Then, tomorrow, go back to the studio and do *real* work instead of chasing ghosts.

After his third, he finally kept his promise to himself, settled up, and stood unsteadily from the barstool. He left the best tip he could manage and stepped back out into the dark. After warming up for an hour or so and thinning his blood, the cold bit harder. He shrugged deeper into his coat and marched off toward the T.

Under a streetlamp, she spied him, catching his eye with a flirty side glance and smile. He stood, staring for a full minute before reaching into his bag for his tools. "There you are," he said, approaching her slowly, careful not to send the wrong signal. "I've been looking everywhere for you."

Lenny Collins's voice had a touch of vocal fry from years of reporting. She told him on the phone that she didn't do an art beat and had reached out just for the winter blues piece, "But your work is something else. That last one especially. I want to do the segment. I think we can easily fill three minutes on 'Snow Banksy." He couldn't help grinning like a fool on the other end of the line. That single comment on Pixta that had sent him soaring making the doubting voice speak louder and more insistently: *this is your shot!* So, he'd DM'd her with the new pictures and username as a pitch. She bit. The only problem was she insisted he hide his actual identity to really lean into the pun title of the segment. It'll sell. Without an agent, he wasn't sure how he could parlay this into bigger and better, but he'd figure it out. First steps first. In any case, it was a better brand than "Katastropher."

He left his apartment in his best mysterious artist cosplay, including a spray paint respirator mask, despite not being a stencil street artist. He arrived at the sculpt ready to fine-tune it if needed—sharpen anything that might've melted or pack in some new snow and rebuild. It was as fresh as the night he'd carved it. The woman in the drift looked at him as he slid up behind her. Like his first, something about her made him wish he could meet the real person.

His phone vibrated in his pocket. "What's up, Lenny?" he answered. She'd *insisted* he call her Lenny.

"Change of plans. I want to do the segment over by your other piece. The one of the guy, Michael."

"But this one's better. And newer! This is the one that—"

"Trust me S.B." He felt lightheaded when she called him S.B. "This'll be better. Tell me where you are and I'll send a MyRyde driver."

"Nah, s'cool. It's just a couple of blocks up. I'll be there in a minute." She said, "excellent," and hung up. "Wait! *Michael?*" he asked the dead line.

He walked as fast as he could on the snowpack in his Chuck Taylors without slipping and falling on his ass. Dressed in art drag, he was freezing in a hoodie and camo cargo pants instead of his heavy winter coat. He rounded the corner and his heart beat a little faster at the sight of the news truck in the distance up ahead. He quickened his step and started practicing his act under his breath. As he came closer, his excitement muted as it all started to look wrong.

There were new things around the drift. Items left behind, surrounding it like one of those roadside memorials. A cross with a wreath of plastic flowers had been stuck in the snow along with a few other offerings: a toy bicycle and miniature artificial Christmas tree were stuck in the snow next to a framed picture of a young man. The man he'd sculpted.

Lenny and her cameraman climbed out of the van. She stared right in with, "So I figured we'd get a shot of you next to the piece before pulling back to reveal," she gestured with black-gloved fingers splayed, "all of this! Then I'll ask you what it was that made you want to do memorial pieces."

"What?"

"Memorial pieces for these three people."

"Three!" He turned and looked at the offerings left under his carving.

"Well, yes. Gillian Florez, this man, Michael Landry, and Lorinda Taylor."

He shook his head. "I don't know what you're talking about."

Lenny frowned with an expression that said call me Lenny was about to change to Ms. Collins. She tucked a fallen dreadlock over her ear and subtly nodded to her cameraman that he ought to start rolling. "All three of these people died in the last twelve months. Gillian Florez was found drowned in the Charles River last April, Mike Landry was killed on his bicycle in a hit-and-run in July, and Lorinda Taylor's body was discovered in a Dumpster behind the Plough and Stars six weeks ago. How did you select these people to memorialize? Do you know any of them before they died?"

His hands went numb as he struggled to process what she was saying. Realizing the light on the news camera was on, he fumbled with his respirator mask, trying to fix it into place. "I… I didn't know them. But…" he looked at her, wanting help. By the look in Lenny's eyes, none was forthcoming. "I wanted to make a statement about how life is, uh, ephemeral. I used to work in metal—steel mostly— but it's inauthentic. This will only last a while. Like us," he bluffed. His stomach cramped as he waited to see if she'd buy his bullshit and roll with it. The look in her eye told him she'd come out to do a puff piece, but thought now she might've landed a whale.

"Did you talk to their families ahead of time to let them know you had planned this art project or to even ask permission to use their likenesses?"

Run! Delete your socials and go back to school. Forget all of this. Save yourself. Instead, he said, "No. I, uh, understand it might be hard for them, but winter is a fleeting season—they all are, I guess—but with warmer weather on the way, I don't have the time to ask permission."

"*Don't* have time? You intend to do more of these, I take it. Will you involve those people's families in the process or continue with a guerilla-style approach, Mr. Derderian?"

RUN!

"I uh, I…" He looked at his feet. "Could we stop for a minute?"

The cameraman peeked out from behind his eyepiece, asking a silent question. She nodded and he lowered the camera.

"How do you know my name?"

She cocked her head and, with a smirk, said, "You're not a difficult person to find, Kris."

He snapped awake in bed, sweating, head aching, room spinning. The sunlight piercing through the curtains hurt almost as much as the insistent knocking at his door. He hadn't planned on polishing off an entire bottle of whiskey the night before, but how often does one get to celebrate being exposed on the news as a freak? And now, it sounded like not only had his chickens come home to roost but that they'd forgotten their key and were trying to break down the door.

He rolled onto his side, trying to slide out from under the covers, but they stuck to his flop sweat moistened legs and he dragged them halfway off the bed as he slunk out. The knocking continued. He shouted, "Gimme a minute," and held a shaking hand to his head. Upright, his stomach threatened revolt. That bottle had definitely been a bad idea. But not as bad as the one to trust Lenny Collins. To dream of the future.

It was a struggle to get into a pair of sweatpants, but he managed without falling over. Shrugging into a hoodie, he looked through his peephole at whoever was banging on the door. A pair of men in suits stood on the other side. He called through the closed door, "What do you want?"

"We'd like to speak to you, Mr. Derderian," one of them said, holding a gold police badge in front of the fisheye lens. The urge to vomit swelled and reluctantly subsided.

"You got a warrant?"

"Do we *need* to get one? We only want to talk."

He unlocked the door and slowly pulled it open. He hadn't realized how he must smell, but the face of the second suited man told him all he needed to know about the subject. He stepped back to let them in. They lingered in the doorway, not entering, like vampires. *Why not?* "Please, come in."

They slipped inside with practiced ease, entering the space quickly and positioning themselves to ensure he couldn't "try anything funny," as he imagined them saying. He didn't have it in him to try anything at all, funny or otherwise. "Mind if I sit down?"

The taller one said sure and gestured toward the sofa as if he was not the guest in this apartment. "I'm Detective Braddock. This is Detective Dixon. We're here to talk to you about your art." The way Braddock said "art," he might as well have been naming an actual pile of shit in the middle of the carpet.

Kris fell onto the sofa limply as Braddock took a seat opposite him in the worn Ikea Poang chair acquired off the sidewalk one Allston Christmas. Dixon stood behind him. Or was it the other way around? He had already forgotten which was which. The seated one—Dixon, he guessed since his voice seemed different—said, "Do you go to The Plough and Stars often?"

"No, I… wait. How'd you know I was there?"

The detective smiled. "I could say I didn't. But I did. Since your portrait of Lorinda Taylor was near where her body was found, I figured I'd ask around. The bartender recognized you. You're a bad tipper, Mr. Derderian." The man didn't ask if he could call him Kris.

"I already told Lenn—Ms. Collins, everything I know."

The other detective said, "Tell us too. We came all this way."

He let out a breath, smelled alcohol hovering around his head, and said, "I didn't know any of these people. I was bored and waiting for the bus, and I saw this face in the snow."

"Saw a face?"

"Yeah, like, you know, that face on the moon and shit. Random shit that looks like a person. So, I sculpted around what I saw to make it into an actual face. It was random."

"A coincidence," Braddock declared.

"Yeah."

Dixon added, "Three coincidences. In a row."

"Y'know, When you say it like that."

"What? It sounds as bad as it seems from where we're sitting?"

He nodded. "I guess so."

"Walk us through it. Tell us how you '*found*' each face and where."

"First one—"

"Gillian Florez."

"The first one, was at the bus stop, like I said. Just looked up and saw it."

"Her."

"What?"

Dixon frowned. "She's a her, not an it."

"Whatever. The second face in the snow. It was in a snow pile." He rushed his words, not wanting to let the detective interrupt him again and catch him in some linguistic trap. "The guy's likeness, whatever his name was, I found after some lady shoved me over chasing after her ratdog. I looked up and *it* was just there. So, I made another sculpture. And then, this Lorinda person's face I found after getting a couple of drinks at *The Plough and Stars*. I'd been looking around the city all fucking day trying to find a drift with a face in it. I was kind of drunk and—"

"You're a heavy drinker." It was not a question.

He felt nauseous. "I'm *not*, actually."

"Despite appearances."

"Anyway, I was looking for someone to carve so I could convince that reporter to do a whole piece on just me." He regretted saying "*someone* to carve" as soon as the words fell out his mouth like dead pieces of meat. Too late to take them back. There they were.

Braddock leaned forward in the chair. Those curvy Ikea rocking chairs had a tendency to slide out from underneath the sitter if you leaned forward too far. He didn't warn the detective. Let him figure it out on his own. The man said, "Why?"

"What? Why do you think? I'm an art student with a mountain of debt and nothing to show for it except a bunch of bullshit nobody wants to buy." He looked around at the various pieces he'd created over the years, collecting dust on shelves and leaning against walls. "Why? Because I wanted to be famous, successful artist, and somebody called me 'Snow Banksy' on Pixta and I thought, fuck it! Why not lean into it if it gets me some exposure." He stood to get a glass of water. Braddock rose abruptly along with him, his hands at his sides, a bit forward as if ready to grapple. "Water. I just want to get a glass of water. I'm fuckin' hungover as shit."

Braddock nodded and Dixon went to the kitchen to fill a glass from the tap. Kris figured it was better to sit down than get shot for trying to get a Polar out of the fridge and have it mistaken for a gun or something. The detective returned and handed him the glass. The water was room temp and flat. He gulped it down anyway. The men asked him a few more questions about where he was and who he was with and if he could prove any of it. It all made his head ache, but he showed them a bunch of selfies and emails and texts. Braddock finally declared, "That's all we have for now."

For now.

"We'll be in touch."

"Yeah, sure. Don't be a stranger, okay?" Kris said.

The detective stared at him with a coldness he felt deep in his bones. A revealed contempt kept hidden behind a mask of aloofness until that moment. "Kid, I'm pretty sure you didn't kill any of these people. Good for you. But I think you know more than you're letting on. Let me tell you, going on T.V. like that gets noticed by more than just murder cops. If someone thought you were a rat or maybe you just couldn't keep your fuckin' mouth shut because you wanted to be the hipster Sylvia Brown on Xitter or whatever, they might come looking to ask you some questions too, Krisander Derderian of the very-easy-to-search name."

The men left him standing in his doorway with an entirely new terror rolling around in his poisoned gut. He shut the door behind them and ran to the bathroom to throw up.

He filled the cardboard box with sculpting tools and sketchbooks and a few odd pieces of his that would fit, knowing he'd have to get a friend with a car to come back later and help him with the bigger projects. A university police officer watched him pack from the studio doorway, blocking his exit in case, what, he tried to make a run for it with someone else's crucible tongs? His advisor had said in her email that his was a "temporary suspension" pending review by the department chair and administration, but it felt final enough. They sent a fuckin' cop to see him out. He finished up and turned toward the exit. The man stepped aside to let him through.

No one talked to him or even made eye contact as he slunk through the hallways of the Ciaramella Building, his humiliation in full effect. That girl, Ania, the one he'd drunkenly made out with at a Halloween party, looked at him like she always knew he was a piece of shit. Maybe he was.

With the heavy box in his arms, the UPD officer led him to the elevator and rode to the ground floor with him. The guy even held the door for him as he stepped out into the white, glaring day. Full service. He blinked in the light, blind. His sunglasses were in his coat pocket, but there was nowhere to set his box down to get them without it getting covered in snow and soaked. He squinted against the daylight as he made his way toward the T. He could make it a couple of blocks to get underground.

He stared at the sidewalk ahead, only glancing up to try to see if it was safe to cross the street, idly wondering if it was even worth raising his eyes. He noticed it in a drift near the corner. A hint of a cheekbone and ear. He looked away and continued up the sidewalk. A few more steps and he had to hustle out of the way to sidestep a trio of people heading somewhere three abreast on the newly plowed sidewalk. It looked at him from a pile in between a trash can and a bicycle rack. A high forehead and big eyes. He gritted his teeth and moved on again.

At the entrance to the T stop, he had to shuffle the box to one side to see the steps ahead. He lost his grip and it tumbled out of his hands, spilling its contents in a splay of creative tools and created work. A final indignity that made him choke with a stifled sob as he chose whether to collect his things or just keep moving on without them. A person stopped to ask if he needed a hand. "Nah, I'm good, thanks," he said to the figure already moving on after "N—."

On his hands and knees, he scrambled all of his things together, putting them back in the banker's box with less care than before. All that mattered was getting home. He'd likely throw everything out once he had a moment to reflect. And there, in front of him, it stared. Straight out from a low pile of grey and gritty snow. Insistent. Unrelenting. He dug his fingers into the oily, rough snow and began clearing away everything that wasn't chin and cheek and nose until it emerged. The face of a child. Terrified and terrifying, he sat back at the look of it.

His phone let out a shriek, followed a half second later by a similar sound from dozens of other cell phones around him carried by people passing by without looking down at the man kneeling in the grime. People pulled their devices from pockets and purses, if not already staring at them. He glanced at his own cell.

AMBER Alert

An Amber Alert has been issued for 7 year old Sadie Clarke taken this morning at 11:00 a.m. on Beacon Street in Cambridge, MA. She is 4 feet, 80 pounds, blond hair, brown eyes, last seen wearing a pink winter overcoat, Paw Patrol tee shirt, and pink pajama pants. Suspect is a white male, age 40-50, 5'10" 180 pounds with dark hair and glasses driving a white Kia Rio.

A photo followed.

"No," slipped from his mouth like thick saliva, slow and hanging. "Why?" He closed the alert and jammed his phone into his pocket before tearing at the face with raw, aching fingers until there was nothing recognizable of it left before anyone else could see what he'd done.

He lay in bed, shivering, knees pulled up to his chest. That girl's face lingered in his eyes like the afterimage of a bright flash. Hovering in the middle of his vision, she haunted him. They all did. He wanted to forget their names, but they were all there, like the face of the child seared in his retinas. He didn't dare search her name to see if there was a follow-up for the phone alert. He knew she was dead. *All* of them were.

It's not your fault, he kept telling himself. All of them were gone *before* he pulled them out of the snow. The last one—Sadie—she had to have been missing for hours at least. How long does it take to process and issue one of those alerts? He thought about looking it up but chose to stay curled up under the covers instead. No point. Stay in bed. Sleep forever. Of course, he couldn't stay there forever. They had to be writing the letter dismissing him from the program that very minute if it hadn't been done and sent already. Once they kicked him out of the program and fired him from teaching, his stipend would stop. Even *with* that money, he could barely afford food after paying rent and utilities for a third-floor studio in the city. Eventually a Notice to Quit and an eviction summons would join other letters jammed in his mailbox. He couldn't even stay there until the snow melted. It was barely March, and sometimes it snowed as late as April. Eventually—before next month's rent was due, in fact—he'd run out of ramen and coffee and gummies and all the other things he depended on to get through the day.

And then what?

Go home, he reckoned. What else was there? Move back in with his mom and dad and listen to them lecture him about art school and employability and responsibility and adulthood until he couldn't take it anymore.

And *then* what?

He rolled over. There was no "and then what." This was it. He'd taken his shot and come out of it looking like a creep and a fool, without an MFA, but with so much debt, he knew he'd never be free from under it.

His phone rang. He let it go to voicemail. There was no one he wanted to talk to. And anyone who wanted to talk to him wasn't on his side anyway. Another hard lesson learned. He pulled the covers over his head.

And there…

He shoved the covers away with kicking feet and thrashing arms and yelled "No!" into the empty room, loud enough to draw the neighbors ire from downstairs. The sheets landed in a heap and he tried not to look, but couldn't help himself. Just a pile of white cloth that needed cleaning a month ago or more. That's all.

An eyelid.

A brow.

Nose.

Mouth.

And chin.

He climbed out of bed, gathered up the sheets, threw them in the closet, and slammed the door. "I won't. You can't make me. I don't want to know and you can't fucking make me." He slumped to his knees and sobbed. "Make it stop. Please. If I do one more, will you make it stop?"

No one answered. He pushed up off the floor, gathered his boots, coat and tools, and left his apartment.

Outside, the late day was calm and bright. For once, the wind wasn't howling and the air didn't feel like needles. He walked to the corner toward a drift of fresh snow and held a hand up to it. There. He saw it. His fingers traced the contours of the shadows and shapes and pulled out feature after feature with care, making sure not to add his own interpretation but only to reveal what was already there. Not a what. *Who.*

The work was quick. There was little to actually do; the face practically sculpted itself. Something lodged in his throat. An acorn or an apple or the whole damn planet because he couldn't swallow or breathe or cry out. All he could do was look into his face.

"There you are. I've been looking for you."

He turned. "What did you sa

CAMBRIDGE

BRACKEN MACLEOD is the Bram Stoker and Shirley Jackson Award nominated author of the novels, *Mountain Home, Come to Dust, Stranded,* and *Closing Costs.* He's also published two collections of short fiction, *13 Views of the Suicide Woods* and *White Knight and Other Pawns.* Before devoting himself to full time writing, he worked as a civil and criminal litigator, a university philosophy instructor, and a martial arts teacher. He lives in the MetroWest area with his wife and son, where he is at work on his next novel.

ACKNOWLEDGMENTS

It takes a lot of patience and talented people to breathe life into an anthology such as this. I want to thank my coeditor, Anna Koon, for keeping me focused and on track. The 18 authors who took this concept and turned and twisted their words into a deliciously dark version of reality, the advice and design acumen of Todd Keisling and his wife Erica, and for you, dear reader, who purchased or borrowed this collection to consume the stories within.

And, of course, I want to thank my dear wife Tina, who puts up with my shenanigans on a daily basis and has yet to murder me in my sleep. Love you, babe.

Photo © 2024 by Renee DeKona

Former technologist and world traveler, R. B. WOOD is an MFA graduate from Emerson College and the founder/CEO of Ruadán Books. Along with his editing passion, R. B. is a writer of speculative dark thrillers. Mr. Wood has had numerous titles published and is currently working on his next thriller. His shorter, weird stories have appeared in multiple anthologies and online magazines. R.B. and his wife Tina adore animals and are self-professed "crazy cat people." You can find him online via rbwood.com and on most social media platforms.

Photo © 2024 by David A. E. Dixon

Boston-based artist and writer, ANNA KOON, has published articles for a variety of periodicals, one poem, two screenplays and a children's book entitled: *Willamina, Queen of the Worms*. She is the founder and director of an educational series presented to various arts organizations throughout Massachusetts. Additionally, she works as a creative coach and editor. Anna lives at the top of what was once the women's quarters of a Victorian mental institution with her husband and two whippets, Zeta Puppis and Nimble Nimbus. Learn more about her @ www.a2n2.net

Clever and curious reads for
lovers of the strange and mysterious.

Ruadán Books (pronounced ROO-ah-dawn)
derives its name from the Irish god of Mystery
and Espionage.

We have a passion for stories that explore
the darkness within us all in the genres of
horror, fantasy, science fiction, and crime.

Scan the QR code to head over to our website and
submissions center!

Coming April 2025

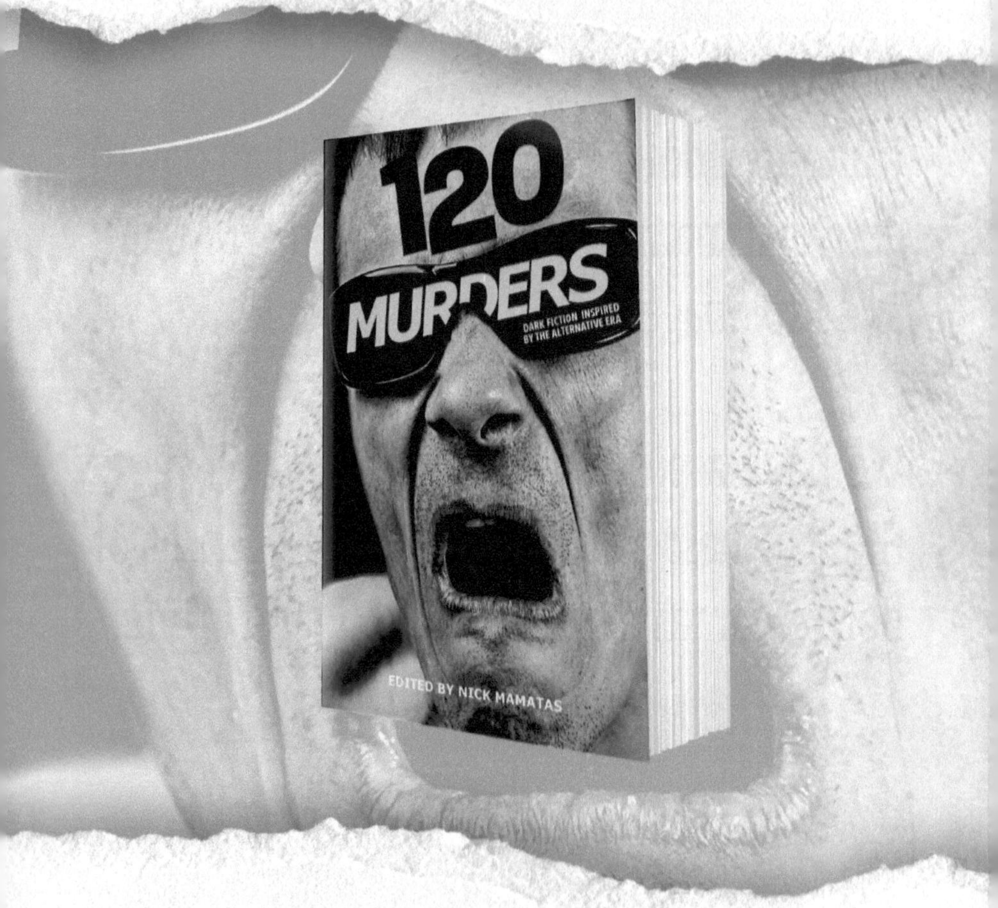

New noir, horror, and gothic stories set to the alternative music of the 80s and 90s!

Available for Pre-Orders Now

www.ruadanbooks.com

RUADÁN
BOOKS

Open for Submissions
1 October, 2024

Coming to Your Bookstore in 2026!